FAST LANE

BOOKS BY C. S. QUILL

The Campus Drivers series
Fast Lane
Crash Course
Test Drive

FAST LANE

TRANSLATED FROM FRENCH BY HANNAH DOYLE

SIMON & SCHUSTER

London · New York · Amsterdam/Antwerp · Sydney/Melbourne · Toronto · New Delhi

Originally published in France in 2020 by Hugo Publishing as *Supermad*

This edition first published in Great Britain by Simon & Schuster UK Ltd, 2026

Copyright © 2020 by New Romance, Département de Hugo Publishing

English language translation copyright © 2026 by Simon & Schuster, LLC

The right of C.S. Quill to be identified as author of this work has been asserted in accordance with the Copyright, Designs and Patents Act, 1988.

1 3 5 7 9 10 8 6 4 2

Simon & Schuster UK Ltd, 1st Floor
222 Gray's Inn Road, London WC1X 8HB

For more than 100 years, Simon & Schuster has championed authors and the stories they create. By respecting the copyright of an author's intellectual property, you enable Simon & Schuster and the author to continue publishing exceptional books for years to come. We thank you for supporting the author's copyright by purchasing an authorised edition of this book.

No amount of this book may be reproduced or stored in any format, nor may it be uploaded to any website, database, language-learning model, or other repository, retrieval, or artificial intelligence system without express permission. All rights reserved. Enquiries may be directed to Simon & Schuster, 222 Gray's Inn Road, London WC1X 8HB or RightsMailbox@simonandschuster.co.uk

Simon & Schuster Australia, Sydney
Simon & Schuster India, New Delhi

www.simonandschuster.co.uk
www.simonandschuster.com.au
www.simonandschuster.co.in

The authorised representative in the EEA is Simon & Schuster Netherlands BV, Herculesplein 96, 3584 AA Utrecht, Netherlands. info@simonandschuster.nl

Simon & Schuster strongly believes in freedom of expression and stands against censorship in all its forms. For more information, visit BooksBelong.com

A CIP catalogue record for this book is available from the British Library

Paperback ISBN: 978-1-3985-6335-3
eBook ISBN: 978-1-3985-6336-0
Audio ISBN: 978-1-3985-6337-7

This book is a work of fiction. Names, characters, places and incidents are either a product of the author's imagination or are used fictitiously. Any resemblance to actual people living or dead, events or locales is entirely coincidental.

Printed and Bound in the UK using 100% Renewable Electricity
at CPI Group (UK) Ltd

FAST LANE

1

LANE

It's past midnight when Carter pulls up outside my apartment building in his crappy old Ford. I honestly have no fucking clue how he can stand getting around in such a wreck. The parking brake screeches like it's being murdered as he yanks it up.

"So?" He turns down the radio and flings an arm over the back of his seat. "What's it like being the passenger princess for once?"

"Doing my best to suffer in silence," I deadpan. "I really shouldn't be friends with a guy whose car is ninety percent rust."

"Hey, now, don't be insulting my ride. She's vintage, man. They literally don't make 'em like this anymore."

"A true blessing to mankind. I thought I was gonna die at least three times tonight. And that was just this one trip. There's absolutely no way you got your license legally."

"How dare you," he says, clutching his chest like I've wounded him. "I'm a great driver!"

"Right. So what was it—bribery? Blackmail? You fucked the driving instructor?"

"I'm a professional, my man."

"Yeah—professional hazard, maybe," I snort.

"Unbelievable! I'm basically like a father to you, Lane, and this is how you treat me?"

"When it comes to father figures, let's just say karma really did me dirty." I shoot him a look, then add, "But seriously—thanks for the rides this week, Cart. Even if my life did flash before my eyes every time we hit a red light."

"Anytime, babe."

He puckers his lips like he's waiting for a thank-you kiss. I duck under his arm, shooting him a look that screams, *Don't push it*.

He laughs and leans back dramatically. "Ruthless! No gratitude, no love—nothing?"

"Thank fuck I'm getting my baby back from the garage in a few hours. An actual decent car. Shiny, reliable, *not* held together by duct tape."

"Just in time for the fall semester—wouldn't want those campus girls dying of thirst for their favorite driver."

I scoff as I unlock my phone and open the app my best friends and I set up a year ago. Campus Drivers: your ride around Sycamore Heights University—one of America's largest campuses—in three simple swipes. Pretty fucking genius idea, if you ask me—easy money, driving always helps clear my head, and, well . . . let's just say the late-night shifts came with nice perks, too. Now that summer's wrapping up, I'm itching to get back in action in more ways than one.

"I'm already booked solid for the next few days," I tease, waving the screen in front of his face.

"School hasn't even started back and they're already all over you. Makes me sick!"

"You could have signed up for college," I remind him with a shrug. "All you had to do was fire up those brain cells and get your act together."

The dean had agreed to our idea but with a few caveats: we could operate on campus and the surrounding area, but we had to pee in a cup every now and then, avoid screwing clients on campus grounds, and be enrolled. Carter can't even stick to one of those rules, let alone three. No pain, no gain, and all that.

"It's not my jam, anyway." He grumbles around a yawn, stretching. "Sitting there listening to some cranky old lecturer drone on about the Spanish Revolution."

He pretends to retch. "I'm better off working on my little indie scripts—that's all the thrill I need."

"Speaking of: You coming over tomorrow evening so we can iron out the last scenes?"

"Sir, yes, sir!"

"Night, Carter," I say, getting out of the car.

"Back atcha, buddy."

I slam his door shut, marveling at the fact it stayed attached, and stroll toward my apartment building. Most of my friends live together on campus, but I like having my own place. It's close enough to college, but just far enough out to get some actual peace and quiet. Plus, it gives me dibs on all the clients who live farther from the dorms.

I punch in the code, shove the door open with my shoulder, and head for the stairs. I usually take the elevator, mostly because I live on the top floor and I'm lazy—but also because I try to avoid bumping into the cougar in 3B. She never leaves her apartment, but her door is right next to the stairwell, and as soon as she hears me pass by her place, she jumps out, ready to pounce. I swear it's like she has this wild sixth sense or something. Problem is, the elevator's been out of order for two days now, which means I'm about to risk it all walking past 3B.

The stairs creak with every footstep, and I wince, picking up the pace past the second floor. The stairwell light's off, and I'm not about to turn it on. Let's just say, I'll need all the darkness I can get to walk by 3B.

Most of the time I'm either at school, in my car, or holed away in my apartment working on screenplays with Carter. It's usually either very early or very late by the time I leave my place. Basically, other than the nympho with the peephole, I don't know any of my neighbors—and I like it that way. *Lane O'Neill, your antisocial Campus Driver. Pleased to meet you.*

I'm about to step foot on the third floor when something moves in the shadows. My heart skips a beat when I realize I'm not alone here. I jump back, a thin layer of pride stopping me from screaming, and I slap the light switch on. The glow is weak but enough to reassure me.

"Jesus—fuck, you scared the hell out of me!" I hiss, dragging a hand down my face.

There's someone crumpled on the floor, back pressed to the wall. Their hood is pulled up tight, legs tucked underneath them, feet ending in scuffed black Vans. I can't tell whether it's a girl or a guy. I wait for them to say something, but they just sit there staring at the floor.

As my heartbeat settles, I catch faint music drifting out. No wonder they didn't notice me. Probably some stoned teenager waiting to come down to earth before heading home to Mom and Dad. They're lucky the super didn't find them first—cops would've been here in no time.

"Have a good evening, then," I toss over my shoulder, heading for the stairs.

Still nothing. Figures.

I make it home in one piece, kick off my boots, and toss my jacket toward the couch. *Fail!* It lands just short, and on the floor is where it'll stay. No girlfriend, no neat-freak roommate. I can mess this place up however I damn please. It's one of the many perks of living alone.

I can't bring myself to shower, so I collapse onto the couch, and knock out in seconds.

I'M WOKEN UP BY THE buzzing of my phone. Feels like I've been out for fifteen minutes, max. I clear my throat before swiping at the screen. It's Carter. *Of course.*

"Yes?"

"Laney! Hope I didn't wake you up."

I hold the phone away from my ear, blink a few times, and check the time.

"Are you fucking for real? It's six a.m. Of course you woke me up, you asshole!"

"Aww, baby boy is all cranky today, huh?" Carter laughs.

"You dropped me home at midnight, Cart. Couldn't wait a couple hours before blowing up my phone? It's Sunday!"

"What can I say? I missed my boo." He laughs again. "Listen, I had this stroke of creative genius for the screenplay. I was getting undressed, and I . . ."

"Is there a short version to this story?"

"We're gonna need actors who aren't afraid to go all in—and a producer who's maybe a little unhinged. Mind if I come by to talk it through?"

"You bet I fucking mind! It's six in the morning, Carter. Ask me again at eleven!"

I hang up before he can respond.

I lie back and close my eyes for five or ten minutes, but the damage is done. There's no way I'm getting back to sleep now. I peel myself off the couch, cursing Carter under my breath, and drag myself to the kitchen island.

Rummaging around in my cupboards, I slowly realize that today is setting up to be a really shitty day: I've searched every nook and cranny, and there's not a single coffee pod, bean, or half-used bag in this entire place. One of my buddies most definitely cleared out my stash. Likely Donovan. *He'll pay for this.*

I jam my feet into my sneakers without bothering to tie my laces, and I slam my front door shut.

As I stab at the button for the elevator, I curse. Out of order. *Fuck me. How could I forget?*

I trip my way down the stairs and practically sprint to dodge the horny ghost of 3B.

But I stop on the third floor.

"Seriously?" I mutter.

The person from last night is still sitting there. Same spot.

No clue why anyone would decide to crash here, but honestly, I've got bigger problems—like needing caffeine ASAP.

It's 6:12 a.m., the streets are dead, and while anyone with any semblance of common sense is still snoozing, I swing by the corner store for coffee. Sami's always open, no idea if the guy ever sleeps. I grab a bag, pay, and head back to the apartment, clutching it to my chest like it's my firstborn.

Back on the third floor, I hesitate. The squatter still hasn't moved. Curiosity wins, and I stand in front of them, but that goddamn hood means I still can't see a thing.

"Hey! Hello?"

Nothing. I try all sorts of noises to get their attention, but still nothing works—no reaction at all.

"You really shouldn't hang around here . . ."

I can't help myself. I step closer, peering at the figure swaddled in all those baggy clothes. I crouch, careful to still keep my distance. I've seen enough horror movies to know how the story goes: weirdos making a sudden lunge for your throat, and all that. No way I'm letting my carotid get chomped.

"Is everything okay?" I poke their shoulder.

That does it. The person jerks up at least six inches off the ground, letting out a hoarse yell packed with a solid string of curse words.

Then a slender hand emerges from the front pocket of her hoodie, and I blink, puzzled, as polished nails disappear under the hood to yank out a pair of earbuds. A second later, the hood slips back, and I'm staring at a wild mess of dark brown hair falling across a tired face. A girl's face.

"What time is it?" she croaks. Her brown eyes are squinting.

"Six thirty."

"Jesus."

I take in her blotchy skin and puffy eyelids.

"Did something happen to you?"

She shoots me a look that seems to waver between dislike and despair, and I shudder despite myself.

"Did somebody hurt you?"

She parts her lips but doesn't answer right away.

She frowns. "Yeah . . ."

I start to straighten up. "Want me to call the cops?"

"For what?" She sneers. "I just got dumped. I doubt they'll give a shit. *Dumped*." She repeats the word as if it's the first time she's ever said it.

I let out a breath I didn't even know I was holding. "Oh my fucking God! I thought it was something way worse."

"Worse?" She spits it out, like nothing in the world could be worse than being dumped.

"Did you spend the night here?"

I immediately regret asking. Obviously, she did.

"Looks that way." She shrugs.

She shifts, wincing, and cracks her neck on both sides.

"You planning on hanging around for much longer?"

"How about you mind your own fucking business, for starters?"

"Whoa, easy!" I hold up my hands. "I couldn't care less about what you do, as a matter of fact. But the super will definitely be calling the cops if she sees you here. She's always roaming the building, looking for wild tenants to take down."

"That bitch Ms. Curtis." The girl wipes her nose on her sleeve.

My mouth falls open. "You know her?"

"Of course I do. I live here. I mean . . . I used to live here . . ."

Out of nowhere, a sob escapes her, and tears start streaming down her face. Her cheeks are already stained black with dried makeup. *Shit. Now what?*

I stare at her. I have no fucking clue what to say. Normally, I'd already be in my apartment by now, but something's holding me back. Maybe it's that her crying is stirring up tough memories—although, to be honest, a heartbreak shouldn't be enough to whip a person into such a state. There's much fucking worse in life. Like losing somebody for good... I bite back on the words, feeling my chest tense. I immediately clench my jaw, taking a deep breath in and letting a deep breath out. Then I look back and forth, from the girl to my prized bag of coffee.

Against my better judgment, I hold it up. "Want coffee?"

She doesn't say a thing, and her sobbing doesn't seem to be slowing down. I've fucking had enough of playing Mr. Nice Guy, so I give up and climb two steps before I stop. I turn back and throw her one last look. I don't know her, but I kind of feel guilty leaving her here like this. *Me and my damn bleeding heart.*

"Last chance," I drawl.

Finally, she lifts her gaze to meet my eyes and glances back down the hallway a couple of times. She's having a hard time making up her mind, I can tell. As if moving now would forever seal her fate.

"I'm not going to chop you up into chunks and stick you in the freezer, you know."

"What if you suffocate me with a plastic bag and dump my body in a moldy basement, though?" She scowls in my direction.

"I don't have a basement, and I only have cheap trash bags. You'd definitely get yourself free."

She bites her lip, as if seriously considering I might assault her. I'm losing patience.

"Fine, have it your way," I sigh, climbing another four steps.

I've already gone too far and broken my loner code, I reason. Time to leave her to it.

I head toward my front door. I'm honestly surprised I spent so long lingering over her. It's not that I'm a selfish bastard, but I'm pretty much immune to heartache at this point.

Without looking back, I enter my apartment and kick my front door to close it, waiting to hear it slam shut. Except I have to turn around because no sound comes. There, in the doorway, one small hand against the worn wood, is the girl from the stairs, gazing at me warily. Her sweater hangs to her knees, almost competing with the length of her hair.

"Oh, so you changed your mind?"

"Yeah." She breathes out, a sob catching in her throat.

"You managed to overcome your fear of being murdered by the resident psycho?"

She shrugs. "Maybe I just don't care if I am . . ."

Right. I raise an eyebrow and watch as she shuts the door behind her, walks to my couch, and slowly sinks into it. I turn back to my coffee machine, glancing over at her from time to time. She stares out the window and, after a while, flings back her head, clamping her hands over her forehead and eyes.

Why the hell did I even ask her up here? I could have spent another two solid hours chilling before Carter got back on my case, but no: Here I am dealing with a sobbing neighbor.

Once the coffee is ready, I fill up a mug and take it over. When I look down at her, she's stretched out across the couch, sleeping like a baby. I reach out to touch her arm but stop a few inches short, changing my mind.

"You look pretty relaxed for such a scaredy-cat," I whisper.

I leave the steaming-hot coffee on the table and look at her for a few seconds. She has pulled her hood back down, and a pair of Ray-Bans have materialized on her face out of thin air. Her breath is still ragged. *What a sight.*

"Well . . ."

I don't know whether I should leave her here or call one of my friends to come get her.

I head to the kitchen, slouching against the counter and gulp down my coffee. In the end, I decide to leave her be. It's not like I have anything worth stealing here. *There's no harm in letting her stay for a short stint*, I tell myself.

I head to my room having no clue I've just hit the gas on a full-blown mess.

2

LOIS

*B*AM!

The fall knocks the breath out of me. My head is spinning. I'm lying face down against wooden floorboards in a pitch-black room, and I don't have the slightest idea where I am.

"What the . . ." My mouth is dry and sticky.

I prop myself up on my elbows, but I'm so weak I fall back to the ground almost immediately. I take off my shades with one frail hand and wipe the damp strands of hair stuck to my cheeks and lips.

I take a few minutes to get my head straight, and before long, I'm back to reality. My first instinct is to roll onto my back and fish my phone out of my pocket. I wrestle it free from my tangled headphones and try calling my boyfriend.

"Pick up, Kirk. Please."

Voicemail.

I try calling again. Once, twice, maybe ten times. Voicemail every time.

This is not happening. This is some horrible nightmare, and soon I'll wake up. *Breathe, Lois. It's all okay. You're going to wake up in your bed next to Kirk and you'll kiss, just the way you've been doing every morning since you moved in together. You'll kiss the way you've kissed for the past four years.*

"I don't want this anymore, Lois."

I can still hear his voice. The same voice that whispered sweet nothings just the day before. Those five words ring hollow. They don't mean anything, right? *I don't want this anymore.* He was probably talking about basketball. Yeah, that must be it: He doesn't want to play anymore; he mostly plays to keep his parents happy, anyway. Or maybe he meant smoking. He's been swearing he'll quit for the past two years now. He didn't mean us. No way. We've been together since we were fourteen. There's no way we're over.

You only get dumped if you did something wrong, right? I've racked my brain, and I can't find a single misstep. The opposite, in fact: If anything, I've built my entire life around keeping Kirk happy. I did sense he was acting weird this summer, but I blamed it on the stress of us starting college. Turns out, I wasn't entirely wrong—he was probably already thinking about how much he'd miss out on if he showed up to campus with a girlfriend. The things he said to me . . . Things I would never have imagined I'd hear come out of his mouth.

Once my breathing settles, I heave myself onto the couch I just fell off and survey the living room where I slept, an open kitchen on the other end of the room. The oven clock shows 3:47 a.m. Shit, I've lost track of time. I can't believe my neighbor let me stay at his place this long.

What do I do now? The one thing I'm certain of is that I shouldn't be in a stranger's apartment. This fifth-floor neighbor must have just moved in because I've been living here since June and I've never seen his face before. Sure, my eyelids are super puffy from all the crying, and my cheap-ass mascara is caked in the corners of my eyes, but still—I'd remember him.

Either way, the facts are: I was in a dirty gross stairwell, and now I'm on a couch that smells like hairy man chest. I'm sitting in a stranger's living room. A stranger who could easily chop me up and stuff me in his freezer. Just thriving, really. I need to get out of this place. But where would I even go?

I can't imagine setting foot outside this apartment building. If I do that, it means Kirk and I are definitely done, and I can't accept that. I consider heading back to my parents' and swiftly discard the idea. They're the greatest, and we're super close, but I don't want to discuss this with them. They wouldn't understand, and that would only make me sadder.

The throbbing in my chest is beating at my temples, too. I shut my eyes and press down with my hands, but the pain is too intense. I lie back down. If I close my eyes tight enough, maybe I can chase away the images of loneliness that are taking shape in my mind. I hope so, anyway. I try it out, but it doesn't work.

"God dammit," I groan, jerking upright.

I start pacing around and I take in a few deep breaths. On my third try, the sobbing makes a comeback, and my eyes well up all over again. Any remaining strength I had is swept away, and I fall to my knees, holding back the whimpers that strain at the back of my throat. My bitten fingernails dig into the worn wooden table. I need more sleep. It's the only tried-and-true form of escapism I know. I set an alarm, slip my shades back on to hide my sorry state, pull my hood over my tangled hair, and head back to the couch. Right in the middle of some stranger's apartment. Whatever. As things stand, I have nothing anchoring me anymore. I might as well rest here a little while longer.

Turns out, I don't get much sleep at all. My eyes open before my alarm goes off, and I slide off my sunglasses before glancing at the oven: 7:19 a.m. I sit up. My eyelids feel swollen, and there are about eleven ice picks burrowing into my brain. There's a twelfth twisted in my gut, and a thirteenth right in the heart, this one thicker and sharper than the rest. I hug my knees to my chest. I pinch at my skin, taking in big gulps of air. It hurts to breathe. I dig through the front pocket of my hoodie for my phone. No calls, no messages. Just a stream of Instagram notifications. I tap at the icon and swipe my way over to Kirk's profile. I know I shouldn't be doing this, but I need to see him. I miss him so hard, as if it's been years since I last saw him. The little voice at the back of my mind is telling me to take a day to think things through, but I can't stop myself. I scroll through his photos. Photos of him alone. *Don't tell me he's already . . .*

I clamp a hand over my mouth and continue down the path of self-destruction. I scroll. And scroll. And scroll. I'm not there anymore. He has deleted it all. It's like I've been erased. All traces of us, gone. *Everything* gone.

It's over, Lois.

I stuff my cursed phone back into my hoodie and stare blankly at the kitchen across the room. The silence I've been swaddled in since I woke up is suddenly shattered by the distant sound of running water, and I remember where I am. *Jesus, I need to get out of here!* As kind as he was, I can't deal with the guy living here again.

I jump to my feet, wincing as the headache beats harder against my temples, and make a dash for the front door. I should thank him really—it's the least I could do. But by the time the thought occurs to me, I'm already on the first-floor landing.

I freeze when I reach my front door. Kirk's front door, I mean. His grandmother had died the spring before, and on the day I announced that I planned on moving into her apartment with Kirk, my dad warned me. He told me I should get a dorm, be independent, blah-blah-blah. But I just chalked it up to normal dad worries and didn't give it a second thought. I couldn't wait for us to live together. I moved into Kirk's place without even considering what a breakup would mean for me.

"I'll leave your stuff with Ms. Curtis," he'd said, and shrugged. "I'm sure you can stay with Rebecca until you find something."

Yeah, right, I'm sure Becca and her roommate would *love* having me crammed into their shoebox of a dorm, sharing a twin bed.

I step toward the door and raise a fist. I want to knock. I want to beg him to let me in, but at the same time, I don't think I'm ready for round two. He had sounded so detached.

I hear footsteps on the stairs and slip away, like a thief fleeing the scene of a crime. I don't want to risk public humiliation.

When I reach the super's office, I push open the swinging glass door, and my heart is in my throat.

She pulls a landline handset away from her ear, a phone that seems as ancient as her wrinkled cheek.

"How can I help?" She sounds annoyed.

"Hello, I—"

"Aha! There you are!" she barks the second she recognizes me. "I told Mr. Olson I couldn't keep this stuff here for more than a few hours. I was about to take it all out to the trash!"

Shit. I had planned on asking her to keep it all for me until this evening! I force myself to look over at the three bags piled in the corner: the very same bags I had been so excited to leave at Kirk's barely two months ago now. Rather than head off on vacation, I had set about building us a cozy nest of a home. How did I get to this point? What did I miss?

Ms. Curtis turns back to the phone: a clear signal that I've already wasted too much of her time. I sling a bag over either shoulder, teetering under the weight. I steady myself as best as I can and reach for the last one, before grabbing my backpack, where my laptop is tucked away.

I'm going to need it—today's my first day of college . . .

"Have a good day," I mutter on my way out.

I turn back and watch as she flaps a hand without looking up.

I stagger out to the sidewalk and drop my bags at my feet. I take a deep breath in and sit down. Okay. So now what? I could call Rebecca, it's true. She might let me crash on her dorm floor, just until Kirk changes his mind. But I don't feel strong enough to face my friend—plus the word "friend" is a little generous. We haven't known each other long; we clicked when she showed me around campus last May. She's super nice. We've been messaging pretty much every day, but I'm embarrassed to ask her for a place to crash. And anyway, nobody can know about all this: I'm going to fix it. And I can't stand the idea of leaving this place behind.

"Hey! You're here!"

The voice behind me makes me jump. I twist around, and it takes me a moment to recognize the guy from the fifth floor.

"Hey," I mutter, biting the inside of my cheek.

"For a second there, I thought my couch might have swallowed you whole. I cross-examined it, but hey"—he claps his hands—"innocent until proven guilty, and all that. I should have remembered!"

He's breezy, talking like it's just a normal day. Blue skies and sunshine. And sure, the weather's great. But the rest of it sucks. Absolutely sucks. I almost resent him for shoving his good mood in my face.

"I'm sorry." I force out the words. "I didn't want to be that person who never leaves, so I left."

"You waiting for a cab?" He takes in the scene: me sitting on my few worldly possessions.

"Umm . . ." That's the best I can muster.

We stare at each other in silence. Or near silence: the sole of my shoe is scuffing back and forth over the asphalt.

The words come tumbling out despite myself. "School's starting up."

"I know, yeah." He laughs, shrugging his shoulders. "You go to SHU, too?"

His question takes me by surprise. I wasn't expecting him to be a fellow student, maybe because he's so tall. There's something mature about him. He must be a senior.

"Do you go to SHU?" He repeats the words slowly.

I nod, feeling the knot in the pit of my stomach tighten. Today was supposed to be special: my very first day at Sycamore Heights University. Same college as Kirk, because . . . because I wanted to be with him. *Pathetic.* That's what my brother had said when we got my college application pack, but he's never been in love—he doesn't know what it feels like.

We were supposed to be getting up early, because Kirk likes to start the day at the crack of dawn. Grab a coffee and a bite to eat together. Hop on his scooter and zip to campus, my arms wrapped tight around his waist. What wasn't supposed to happen was splitting up two days before to "get the most out of the college experience."

"... a ride?"

I look up at my one-night host. He's asking me something.

"What?"

"Need a ride?"

"A ride where?"

"Do you have, like, attention issues or something? To campus! Unless you're already planning on skipping class—which I *do not* recommend," he says, his voice suddenly deeper and mock-serious. "The dean does *not* mess around with rebellious freshmen. Trust me—I had to retake most of my freshman-year courses."

"There's no way I'm missing my first classes . . ."

My gaze shifts to my bags. What the hell am I supposed to do with all of this? I can't haul around my entire life all day. My shoulders are already carrying enough—grief, regret, heartbreak. As much as I want to crawl into a hole and never come out, I can't risk losing my meager scholarship and the money my parents have already spent.

"I'm still not planning on kidnapping you and sacrificing you in a satanic ritual in the desert for what it's worth," he teases.

"There's not even a desert within, like, twelve hundred miles."

"I know. But I'm trying to make a statement here."

"If you say so."

"So, what's it going to be, Heartbreak?"

I widen my eyes at him. *He did not just say that.*

A flash of anger, and I suddenly sit upright. "Don't call me that!" I snap.

"Sorry." He shrugs, not sounding sorry at all.

He almost seemed nice earlier, but right now, there's only one word that springs to mind: *"asshole."* I squeeze my eyes shut for a second and bite back on my irritation before looking up at him.

"It's just that . . . I don't know what to do with my stuff."

"What do you mean?"

"Well, you know..." I gesture stiffly around me. "Girl gets dumped, yada yada."

He nods briskly, scratching his chin.

"Your guy threw you out without wondering where you'd crash? What did you do, sleep with his dad or something?"

"I didn't do anything," I murmur. Tears are welling up again.

He lets out a low whistle. "Damn. That's cold. He sounds like a total dick."

"You don't know what you're talking about!" I instinctively rush to Kirk's defense. "He . . . He's . . ."

I'm not sure how this sentence ends.

"What are you, a relationship guru?" I spit instead.

"Fuck no!"

"Yeah, didn't think so."

I take in his vibe. Casual, trendy. From where I'm sitting, he looks huge, his shoulders so broad they almost block out the sun and take up my entire field of vision. His brown hair is still slicked back from his shower. His mischievous green eyes seem to constantly be daring someone to challenge him. Put it all together, and there's no two ways about it: This guy has no idea what being in a relationship means. Definitely no idea what it means to me. Then and there I decide: I do not like him very much at all.

"Anyway," I say, shifting my attention back to our conversation. "I'll go check with the admin office; they might still have a room for me."

"Unlikely. But you can try."

I side-eye him, overcome by the sudden urge to throw one of my bags at his face. But I hold back because, now that I think about it, I really could do with that ride.

"I accept," I say, offering up a tight smile. "I'd love a ride."

"Well, today's your lucky day, Heartbreak. Meet the smoothest member of the Campus Drivers!"

He flexes his pecs, and I try my hardest not to roll my eyes.

"The what now?"

"The Campus Drivers." He says the words slowly, shooting me an offended look.

I rack my brain, but I'm totally blanking. Nada. "As in, drivers on campus? Okay . . ."

"The ones and only! Four knights on their steeds of steel, ready and waiting to serve damsels in distress!"

"A damsels-only service?" I shoot back, frowning.

"Preferably." He snickers, making a move toward the car parked right next to us.

I cross my arms over my chest and shake my head in disbelief. He's got all the cockiness of a guy who gets around way too much for his own good. Classic douchey player energy. My least favorite type.

"So, shall we do business?"

"How much?" I sigh.

"The first ride is always free, baby." He smirks.

"Building loyalty. Great marketing," I say flatly.

"Building addiction, really. Okay, the clock's ticking: Are you getting in?"

I shoot another glance at my bags. There's a bitter taste of sadness flooding the back of my throat.

"Okay." My lips are quivering. *Damn it.*

I hear him pop the trunk. He strides back over and grabs two of my bags, and I follow. Just as he's scooping up the rest of my stuff, my eyes dart to the inside of the car.

"See? No room left to hide a body," he whispers at me with a creepy grin.

"You really know how to charm your customers, huh?"

I walk around to the other side of the car, when he runs ahead, pulling open the door with a theatrical bow.

"After you, m'lady."

"I wouldn't bother," I warn him, getting into the car and fastening my seat belt. "Once I'm living on campus, I'll be walking. And once Kirk sees sense, I'll be back on his scooter."

"In that case..."

He leaves my door open wide, forcing me to stretch so far out to close it I think my shoulder might pop. He heads back around the car, pausing at the front to kiss the hood and gaze at it lovingly, and slips behind the wheel.

"I just picked her back up from the garage," he says, clocking my raised eyebrow. "I missed her."

"Right..."

"A 1969 Camaro SS," he adds. He's practically bursting with pride.

"Am I supposed to be impressed?"

He looks at me as if I just ran over his dog.

"Sorry, I mean... Wow!" I mime fascination. "A Cama-thingy, that's just... Wow!"

"I'm going to pretend I never heard that."

He starts the car, and I swear even the engine sounds like it's offended.

It will take us around twenty minutes to get to campus, so I pull down the visor and check myself in the mirror. I push my shades up on top of my head, brushing my mass of hair back as best as I can with my fingers. I examine my features and sigh. *Jesus, Lois, you're a mess...* I rummage in my bag and pull out a packet of wipes. The last time I showered was Saturday. It's currently Monday morning. *Lord help me...*

I wipe the grime off my face while pointedly ignoring my driver's occasional side glances. Once the last remaining traces of my heartbreak have been erased, I leave my damp skin to air-dry.

"Want to listen to anything in particular?"

I turn my attention to the car radio. Soft music is playing. He gestures to change the station, but I place my hand over his.

"Leave it. I like this song."

I twist the knob, cranking up the volume.

"You know Tool?" He looks at me, astonished.

"Sure. Why? Is that so surprising?"

"Uh . . . Kind of? I've never met a girl who knows them!"

"Well, I've never met a guy who's never met a girl who knows them."

He squints at me.

"Gives me a rough idea of the kind of girl you hang out with . . ." *God. Why the hell did I just say that?* "Anyway . . ."

"I don't need them to have good taste in music." He laughs. "They can even scream off-key, for all I care."

I pretend to puke, and gaze out the window, watching the world race by.

Once the campus swings into view, my insides tighten. I might just puke for real after all. We skirt around the gates before turning onto a side lane. The campus is teeming with students, and I tug my sweater down over my knees.

"Here we are!"

He pulls up next to a huddle of loud guys.

I shuffle in my seat and go to unclip my seat belt, but my fingers are so tense, I keep missing. I silently curse the seat belt and its oppressive ways.

Click.

I look up at my knight in shining armor. He's shaking his head at me, laughing.

"I've got a feeling you'll never forget your first day of college, Heartbreak."

I flip him off, but he's already turning away and stepping out. I follow suit and stretch my heavy legs. I move to the back of the car, taking in long gulps of air as I go to reach for the trunk.

"Step away from the car, ma'am!"

My driver shakes his head gravely, as if I've just committed the ultimate crime. The trunk squeaks as he heaves it open, and he stands there with his arms raised, so close his tight muscles brush against the tip of my nose. I step back and repeatedly clear my throat as he just stares down at my bags.

"What's up?" I'm starting to lose patience.

He glances at me. "I'll make you a deal. How about you leave your stuff in my trunk for today. You can call me once you have a room. Or a tent."

"I'll be fine," I mutter, but my voice wavers.

God, don't be such a wimp, Lois.

"I'm serious, it's no big deal," he insists. "I'm having trouble imagining you carting this around all day. You don't get just how big this place is. Think of it as my last good deed, okay?" His eyes travel down my body, taking in my outfit. "Honestly, you already look like you're living out of your car, so do yourself a favor and leave your stuff with me."

I know it's true. My sweater is flapping around my lower thighs, and there's a hole in the knee of my black leggings. I'm a horror show.

"And how am I supposed to find you again?" I ask sharply.

"Campus Drivers, Heartbreak. Download the app and DM me."

"Dude! Get your ass over here."

I turn to look at the group of guys waiting beside a bright red car. These must be his friends. Fellow car nerds.

"Meet the rest of the team," he whispers by my ear, his voice low. His breath brushes the curve of my neck.

"It's a privilege. A real honor." I mockingly wipe an imaginary tear from my cheek.

He chuckles, and when I glance at him, his eyes are already on me.

"Why are you doing this?" I ask suddenly.

"Doing what?"

"Helping me out. If this is your way of trying to . . ."

"Trying to what?"

"Like, if this is some kind of move. I just . . . I need you to know, I'm not interested."

His faces freezes. And then he breaks into loud, husky laughter. He drops the trunk and continues cackling as he steps closer.

"Don't take this the wrong way, Heartbreak. But flirting hadn't even occurred to me. Flirting with you, anyway."

Of course not. Who would want a loser like me? Just like Kirk said, I . . .

"Just making sure," I mutter. "Okay, I would like to leave my stuff here, then, yes."

He flashes me two thumbs-up and slams the trunk shut. All I can do now is cross my fingers and pray that he isn't a kleptomaniac. Or that he doesn't have a fetish for mismatched underwear.

He starts stepping back toward his friends. "Have a great first day."

"Thank you. And thanks for last night. And . . . Thanks for everything, really."

He places a hand on his chest and dips into a ridiculous bow. Then he turns on his heel, and I watch him walk away.

"Okay, Lois," I whisper, facing the looming campus gates. "You've got this."

I slide my sunglasses back onto my nose and head for the crowd. Safely hidden behind the dark lenses, I scan the sea of students, searching for a glimpse of Kirk.

And sure, I can admit I'm desperate. Just a little.

You know—the kind of little that weighs a ton.

3

LANE

I stuff my hands deep in my pockets and stroll over to my friends. *God, I love college!* I toss a casual "hey" to two skaters and wink suggestively at the girls walking by. They smile at me and shake their phones. *Hell yeah. I really love college.*

"Heyyy!" Lewis offers up a fist that I bump.

"How you doing, blondie?" I tease, jerking my chin at his freshly dyed mop. "Your mom give you highlights, or what?"

"Nope! I let some Cali girl play with my hair while I played with her boobs. That was some vacation, man."

Donovan swipes at one of his bleached curls. "You must have been very hungry."

Lewis shoves him away. "I'm not one for dieting!"

I high-five Don and blow Adam a kiss as he straightens.

"The Campus Drivers are back in town!" Lewis announces, shouting it over to the other students and striking a series of body-builder-style poses. Enthusiastic whistles and jealous male grumblings wash over him.

Sorry, guys, but the world really is our oyster!

"Who's the girl you dropped off?" Donovan points at my car.

I glance over. She's still right where I left her. "A freshman."

"They usually make some kind of effort for the first day," Lewis teases.

I snicker, watching as she finally decides to make a move toward the main entrance.

"Her boyfriend dumped her," I say flatly. "I found her on my stairs."

What I don't say is how she spent a day and night on my couch. I don't want their imaginations running wild—scripts are my job, not theirs.

"What a saint. Come on, admit it: You gave her the first ride for free."

"I felt sorry for her."

"Grow a pair!"

Lewis squints into the sun. "She cute?"

"Meh. The brokenhearted type doesn't give me a hard-on."

"Right, I forgot you're Mr. I Only Date Actresses now! Damn, when do I get a taste of your film industry perks, huh?"

"You wouldn't make the grade, asshole. And you giving them all chlamydia is not a risk I'm willing to take."

"Hey, you swore you wouldn't mention that again!"

I watch as clusters of students drift toward the buildings, listening distractedly as Adam and Lewis tell us about their vacations. Those two are like twin brothers. They're the only ones who are childhood friends, the rest of us have known each other for two years now.

"Ready for your third back-to-school frenzy?" Donovan claps his hands.

"It's my fourth, remember?"

I'm a junior like them, but I'm a year older. I had to retake my freshman-year courses, which is how I met them. Just goes to show there's always a silver lining.

"Why don't we hang out tonight, guys? We need to get moving, get the app synced up with our schedules. How about we meet at your place, Lane?"

That's Adam for you—always the serious one. Thank God for him!

I nod, shoving a piece of gum in my mouth. This is always the biggest headache of this job: fitting our slots around our various classes so we hit up as many customers as possible.

Lewis is already whining. "We're meeting up with our coach after lunch. Hope he's not going to go wild with the training sessions like he did last year! Hey, can't you nudge him in the right direction, Donovan?"

"Dude, how many times do I have to tell you? Sure, Coach is my dad, but when it comes to campus, he doesn't give a shit about what I say, so just let it go." Donovan shakes his head. "You just spent the whole summer with your finger up your ass, time to get back to work. We've got a championship to win!"

"Men and their basketball . . ." Adam says mockingly.

Donovan flips him the finger. "Nothing comes before basketball!"

"Sure thing, Donny!"

The ridiculous nickname has us in hysterics. Donovan is one of the most talented basketball players this college has ever seen and he's captain of the team, which means he has groupies. Lots and lots of groupies. They came up with the adorable pet name Donny all by themselves and refer to themselves as the Donnies. And that asshole laps it up.

"And on that note . . ." Lewis swings his bag over his shoulder. "My future awaits!"

"And what's she called, this 'future' of yours?" I tease as I follow.

He smirks at me. "Jessica. She's got potential, let me tell you."

I smooth my hair back. "Amen to that."

We part ways in the main hall, and I get back to fending off the girls. This first week is usually pretty laid-back; it's mainly geared toward the newcomers, while the other students come and go, getting themselves ready for the classes that start back up next Monday. The morning rolls by, and I even have time to schedule three student rides. *Did I mention I fucking love college?*

Feeling my phone vibrate, I stop in the middle of the hallway.

"Yes, Carter?" I sigh; this is his sixth call of the day. "Dude, you need to stop stalking me, it's exhausting. You know I'll never love you, right?"

Love anyone, come to think of it. Relationships suck the life out of you: I plan on waiting until I'm forty or fifty before getting started.

"Oh, you're breaking my heart, lover." My friend pretends to sob through the phone before switching tone. "Can I swing by tonight?"

"Nope! Tonight us guys have our big meeting."

"Urgh!"

"You're going to have to do without me, sweet cheeks."

"Bro, you already stood me up on Sunday!"

He has a point. I had to cancel my work session with Carter because of a certain Heartbreak curled up on my couch, and how no matter what I tried, there was no waking her up. I left her to go and pick up my car from RJ that afternoon, and almost threw a glass of water in her face when I returned and found her in the exact same position. Luckily for her, I was on a high from getting my wheels back, so I cut her some slack. And that reminds me: Now that I think about it, I haven't heard from her yet.

"Why don't you come over on Wednesday evening?"

"How about tomorrow night?"

"Wednesday, and that's my final offer."

"Fine." He sighs into the phone. "But I'm warning you, we'll be needing the whole night."

"You have a good day now," I say before hanging up and heading back over to my friends in the park next to the medical wing.

"Where's Lewis?" I fall back into the grass.

"Driving," Adam replies, without looking up from his notes.

"We're going to be doing some serious driving this year." Don stretches. "We've started off strong, I'm betting we'll at least triple our sales. Yesterday we had twice as many downloads in a single day than we did at the start of last year, and we haven't even run the onboarding meeting for new students yet." He grins at us. "By the way, some guy came to see me this morning to ask whether we needed a fifth Campus Driver."

"What did you say?" Adam and I ask in unison.

"I said yes."

"Are you for real?"

His grin widens. "I said we need someone to wash our cars."

"You're such an asshole, Donny." I shake my head, laughing.

I lie back and ready myself for a sun-dappled nap.

THE AFTERNOON SLIDES BY UNEVENTFULLY, and I make it back to my place at the same time as Adam and Lewis. A pair of chatterboxes, to say the least.

"Donovan finished his ride," Adam announces. "I don't know how he did it, but he got a twenty-dollar tip. He's on his way over."

I hold out a beer for him and fall back into my armchair, smiling.

"I forgot to call my mom." Adam puts down his bottle. "Give me a second."

"Send her my love!" Lewis calls out.

Adam retreats into my bedroom, and as I hear him shut the door, I'm hit with the sense that I'm forgetting something, too. I can't think what. It sure as hell isn't calling my parents. It's not like they'd be interested in me starting my junior year, or anything that has to do with me really.

"This your new project?" Lewis is eyeing my notebook.

"Yeah. Carter is coming over on Wednesday so we can wrap it up."

"You shouldn't leave it lying around. If Don gets his hands on it, we'll have to sit through his suggestions all night long! Still not interested in turning the second bedroom into an office?"

I wince, subtly enough for him not to notice. In a way, the room doesn't belong to me. Nobody will ever live in it again, but I can't deal with that fact, and so it stays the way it is.

THE MOMENT THE DOOR SWINGS shut behind them all in a chorus of "byes," I help myself to a second beer.

Finally, some peace and quiet. Seriously, I have no idea how the three of them can stand living together. There's no way I'd manage. I love the stillness of my apartment: not having to make an effort when a bad mood strikes. And this place means a lot to me.

I settle into my armchair and feel my eyes glaze over as I stare at the couch. I'm replaying the day in my mind. That was what I had forgotten!

Fuck! Heartbreak was supposed to be picking up her stuff.

I check my phone, but there's no message from her, and considering it's almost midnight, I guess she'll call tomorrow.

I get up and make my way to the shower, when there's a knock at the door. I peer through the peephole to make sure it's not my horny neighbor and breathe out a sigh of relief.

"Heartbreak!"

She jumps and spins around to face me, biting the inside of her cheek.

"What are you doing here so late?"

"I . . . Today was a mess, time just flew by. I was out on the sidewalk and saw your light was on, so I thought it would be okay to come up."

"Why didn't you get in touch on the app?"

"You've still got my charger in your trunk," she murmurs. "I was out of battery."

"You're pretty unlucky, aren't you?"

"Seems that way . . ."

I bite back a grin when I notice how tired she looks. She's still wearing that ugly sweater with the hood pulled up, hopping from foot to foot, glancing over her shoulder every now and then.

"So did you end up finding a room?"

It takes her ages to reply, as if prying out the words is painful.

"I'm here to pick up my bags," she eventually says.

I frown and straighten, folding my arms over my chest.

"Did you find a place to crash?" I ask again, pinning her down with my gaze.

"Not yet," she mutters. "But I'm sure it'll work out. Tomorrow I'm going back to see the secretary, and I plan on asking at the student council office, too." She forces out a smile, digging her hands deeper into her kangaroo pocket. "I saw a motel down the road. That'll do for now. Other than the shared showers and the receptionist who smells like piss, it looks great."

"Want a beer?" The words come spilling out despite myself.

"I already had a few before I got here."

"You drunk?"

"Not drunk enough." She pouts.

"Come on, get in here! At this stage, I think it's safe to say I'm not going to strangle, eviscerate, or cremate you, don't you think?"

I open my door wide, and her uneasiness deepens.

"Grab yourself a beer and a shower, and I'll drop you at your motel. Sound like a plan?"

She sighs and then steps into the apartment. "Just a shower, and I'll hit the road."

I watch as she dumps her shoulder bag on the couch armrest before perching on the edge, hands flat on her thighs as she gazes at the big painting above my sink. She's as stiff as a board, and it's like she's trying to control her breathing so as not to move an inch.

"The bathroom is right at the end of the hall." I yawn.

She scratches the side of her head. "I need something to change into."

"Don't move, I'll go down to the car."

"Just the blue bag will do. Don't bother bringing it all up, it'll only take me five minutes."

I shake my head. By the time I get back, I can hear water running at the far end of the apartment. I dump her stuff outside the door and wait by the window, pressing my forehead against the glass. The street is silent, until a motorbike comes speeding past, setting the windowpane shaking in its frame. I grit my teeth and try to block out the memories that have surfaced with the noise. Pounding the wall next to me with a fist, I bring the half-empty bottle to my lips, desperate to wash away the thick clump I can feel sticking in my throat. I take the gulp too fast, and beer goes spilling down my front.

"Shit!" I jolt back.

My T-shirt is soaked. I slam the bottle down on the coffee table just as Heartbreak appears in front of me, hair piled up in a towering bun on the top of her head. Seeing her like this catches me off guard. Her skin looks less pale, but the shadows under her eyes are as dark as her hair. She's practically sleep-walking—I'm sure I just saw her sway on her feet.

"Thanks for the shower, I needed that." She tugs at her top. "I'm ready."

She's thrown that shapeless sweater back on over a pair of gray leggings that look just like the ones she was wearing earlier. I look down at my beer-drenched T-shirt.

"I need to change. If we run into any cops, they'll throw me straight in the drunk tank, no questions asked."

She runs a hand over the nape of her neck. "Okay."

As I walk past her, she glances at my soaking clothes, wrinkling her nose and pulling a face.

"Let me get washed up and we'll head out."

I pull my T-shirt over my head, and she quickly turns away, walking toward the couch as she clears her throat. I trot down to the bathroom and strip off the rest of my clothes. The scalding water relaxes me, and I don't want to stop. I treat myself to a few extra minutes and then force myself out of the steam, wrapping a towel around my hips before heading into my bedroom, where I change into track pants and a tank.

Back in the living room, I'm feeling like I'm done with this day.

I stride over to the side table and scoop up my keys. "Let's go!"

Opening the front door, I stuff my phone into my pocket and look over my shoulder when I realize I can't hear footsteps. If it weren't for that blue bag still sitting smack-dab in the middle of my living room, I'd have sworn that Heartbreak had pulled her vanishing act again.

"Hello?"

Leaving the door open, I stalk back over to the couch. I notice a pair of zebra-striped socks first, then folded legs. And then a tousled bun, and a few loose strands of hair falling over closed eyes.

"Are you fucking kidding me?" I groan. "Seriously?"

I cross my arms over my chest. She's asleep. Again! On *my* fucking couch! If she wasn't so distant and evasive the rest of the time, I'd swear she was doing it on purpose. All I have to do is give her a gentle shake to wake her up, but I can't muster up the will.

"Okay . . ." I sigh. I turn to shut the front door. "Here we go again. Night two." I raise my eyes to the heavens. "Someone better be keeping count: I've done my good deeds for the next two years."

4

LOIS

I don't need to open my eyes to know where I am. That's progress from yesterday, I guess, but I still feel a crushing shame pinning me down to the couch. The couch I've taken over again, like some kind of parasite. *A damn cockroach, that's what I've been reduced to.*

I jump to my feet, plumping the pillows to erase any sign that I was here, and tiptoe over to the kitchen sink. I don't want to wake him up . . . the guy who lives here. The guy whose name I don't even know.

Today is the day I solve my housing problem. The motel is my plan B, and sure, just the thought of it sends my anxiety through the roof, but at least it's something.

I splash a little water on my face and eye the coffee maker, but I don't want to run into that Campus Driver and have him think I'm making myself at home.

It takes me less than a minute to change into a fresh T-shirt and scrape my hair up into a ponytail. Seeing my bag, I remember my most pressing issue: The rest of my stuff is in his trunk. I don't have a choice, I'll need to see him again at least once so I can collect my things. This bag here is small and light, so I swing it over my shoulder and creep my way to the front door, pulling it shut softly behind me. I take a deep breath in. The elevator has probably been fixed, but I go for the stairs. You never know: I might run into Kirk in the hallway, and that way I can beg him to reconsider—who cares if I look like a desperate loser.

In the end, I make it out to the sidewalk without a glimpse of him. Luck is definitely not on my side: I bump into Ms. Curtis instead, sweeping the first floor, ranting and raving with every fresh inch of tile exposed.

I head over to the bus stop at the corner of the street, and although the public transportation here is terrible, I manage to catch the one bus of the morning.

"Maybe I'm not so unlucky after all," I mutter to myself as I fall back into one of the frayed blue seats.

Talk about tempting fate. The bus breaks down just one measly mile before campus. I follow the annoyed passengers filing out, offering the driver a small "sorry," as if my bad luck was all to blame.

When I finally make it to campus, the strap of my bag is digging into my shoulder and I'm tilting to one side. Yup, this is me: homeless, soaked through with sweat, and halfway to becoming a hunchback. What a catch.

If yesterday was shitty, today looks set to be just as bad. Once orientation wraps up and the department rattles off our lab group assignments, I wander down the college hallways, searching the crowds for Kirk, my heart skipping a beat every time I see a flash of blond hair. I don't know whether he's avoiding me or whether I'm just the worst sleuth ever, but I haven't seen him once, even when I walked around the dentistry department, doing my best to look casual.

I'm still holding out for a glimpse of him this morning, but right now, I'm stepping into the secretary's office for the second time and joining the line. When it's finally my turn, my throat is dry, the skin around my nails is bleeding.

"Morning!"

I look up at the administrator and force myself to smile back. I hate everybody this morning, especially people who look happy. The woman from yesterday looked half asleep and sniffled just as much as me, and I find myself missing her. But if I want a room, I'm going to have to make an effort.

"Good morning, Mrs. . . . ." I check the little name card pinned to the counter. "Singleton."

I mop my forehead with the back of my hand and drop my bag at my feet.

"I need a dorm room," I offer in response to her inquisitive stare.

She raises her powdered eyebrows. "Last name, first name, major, and year."

"Lois Hogan, sports physiotherapy, freshman."

I wince at the words, but the administrator is peering at her screen and doesn't notice. My family members are all sports buffs, and although I love sports just as much, deep down I know I chose this major because of Kirk. He's just joined the college basketball team, and the sports PT students get up close and personal with the athletes. The Cardinals are heroes around these parts, and everyone is expected to wait on them hand and foot.

Singleton pouts. "It says here that you came by yesterday. It's just as my colleague told you: We've been full since March, I've got a waiting list as long as my arm, and some students haven't even arrived yet. We've already got you down right here. You're twenty-seventh on the list."

She gives me a bored smile, and I screw my eyes shut so as not to break down in front of her.

"There's really no point in coming in every morning, Ms. Hogan. If a room becomes available, we'll be sure to let you know."

I gnaw at the inside of my cheek. "What are my chances?"

"Rooms mostly free up in the second semester. Between now and Christmas, I wouldn't get your hopes up."

"Oh God . . ." I drum my fingers on the counter. "Do you know what I can try next? Have you got a list of agencies?"

She shakes her head and glances over my shoulder. I get the message. People are waiting.

She rolls her chair back. "Go and speak to the student council, they might have some ideas."

"I'll do that. Thank you."

I scoop up my bag and fling it over my shoulder too quickly: a guy is standing super close behind me.

"Oh, I'm sorry!"

"No worries."

I squeeze out of the crowded office and make for the coffee cart. My brain freezes when it's time to order: mint tea or double espresso? Kirk hates coffee, and I realize I haven't had a cup since I left Florida.

The girl behind me is losing patience. "Pick something already."

I go for a triple-shot espresso with no sugar, knocking it back in one go and setting off on a mission to sniff out a miracle. The student council office is just as short on ideas for me, and three hours of investigating and one skipped lunch later, I drag myself out to the central plaza. The place is still heaving, and I scan the crowds. My breath catches in my throat as I finally take in the object of my obsessions, but a distant shout ruins everything.

"Hey! Heartbreak!"

Kirk is sitting there surrounded by a few guys. And girls. I can't tear my eyes away. Too many girls. Too close. Too . . .

"Heaaartbreaaak!"

Oh my God, can't he just shut up?

Just as Kirk turns to look at me, I home in on the person doing the shouting. The dumbass is stretched out on the grass beneath a towering statue, and if looks could kill, he'd be dead already. I stride toward him, mouthing "Shut up" as I go, and he frowns. He mutters something to the guys he's with, and they all burst out laughing. For fuck's sake. He just screwed up my one and only chance.

I hate this guy!

I lunge at him, all my pent-up anger propelling me forward, and he crosses his arms over his chest as if bracing himself for the impact when an obstacle appears before me.

"Hey again!"

I bang into a mass so hard my bag goes flying, my forehead connecting with a fleshy heftiness. I step back, taking in the body standing between me and the jerk.

"We met earlier," says the guy who almost literally threw himself at me.

Narrowing my eyes, I try to think, but my brain is splitting in two, half of it focused on Kirk, the other half taken up with . . . the other guy.

"You bumped into me with your bag," he prompts, seeing my clueless expression.

"Oh! Yeah! Right."

That's all I've got, but he seems happy enough. A broad smile spreads over his spotty face.

He puffs out his chest. "I'm Donald, but everyone calls me Donny!"

"I'm Lois, but everyone calls me Lois."

He forces out a laugh and stuffs his hands into his pockets. Or tries to, at least: His jeans are clinging to his thighs.

"Freshman?"

This guy wants to make small talk. All I want is to make a getaway.

"Yeah."

"I'm a sophomore. You like this place?"

"Yeah."

Despite my curt replies, he's not taking the hint.

He drops his voice. "I heard you're stuck for a place to stay."

Now he's got my attention, and he likes that. As he raises his eyebrows, they brush against a strand of hair that's either very wet or very greasy. I don't even want to know.

"My roomie just left me hanging, so I've got a room available," he continues. "It's just around the corner; the rent is peanuts. I was going to put an ad on the board, but I thought you might be interested." He clears his throat. "You seem cool. Solid."

He blurts the words out, his face suddenly flushed and clammy.

My gut is telling me to say "Thanks but no thanks," but this unexpected offer is one I should weigh up.

I'm about to ask for more details when I notice movement behind him. The Campus Driver jerk is walking over to us, his acolytes trailing behind him, and I raise an eyebrow. Donald turns to follow my gaze, and I swear I see him stiffen. He mutters something I can't make out, thrusts a piece of paper into my hand, and evaporates. The page is folded in fours.

I blink a few times. I'm surrounded by four guys, all a foot taller than me.

"How you doing, Heartbreak?"

The nickname snaps me out of my lethargy, at least.

"Stop calling me that!" I hiss through clenched teeth. "I swear, you call me that one more time and I'll punch your balls right off."

As soon as the words come tumbling out, I slam my mouth shut, shocked by my own behavior. I'm a pretty chill person. I can't remember the last time I lost my shit like this, except with my brothers, and that barely counts.

He gapes at me, stunned. And then he and his buddies burst out laughing.

"Wow! Turns out she does more than just sleep and cry," he teases, raking a hand through his hair.

I feel like telling him he has no idea, but first I glance over to where I saw Kirk earlier. I catch him looking at me. *Shit.*

"In my defense, Your Honor, you still haven't told me your name."

I smirk at him. "Life's a bitch, huh?"

"I mean, it's kind of hard to do social niceties with a girl who spends all her time snoozing. You know you can get help for that, right?"

I swallow back the venom I feel like shooting his way. No matter how annoying he might be, this guy let me crash at his place for two nights in a row when he definitely didn't have to. I practice my breathing while his friends watch on in silence, seemingly fascinated by our sparring. Aside from wanting to crush him, all I really want is for this whole thing to be over.

I sigh and hold out a hand. "Lois."

One of his friends snorts, while another nearly chokes midway through taking a swig from a silver can.

"Lane," the guy offers.

Is he messing with me? I've just made a huge effort trying to get us back on an even keel, and this jerk is still teasing me with his childish jokes?

"Oh, I get it!" I slow-clap. "Lois Lane. Very funny. I've never heard that one before."

The tallest of them is laughing openly. "Damn, it doesn't get much better than this!"

Another one of the guys slings an arm over his shoulders. "Shut up, Lewis. Let them finish, I'm begging you. Go on, dude." He nods at the jerk.

"Lane." His green eyes are boring into mine, and once again he says the words slowly, as if I were dumb. "My name is Lane."

"Oh . . ." I nod. "Okay. Right!"

Great job, Lois! The queen of stupid has entered the building. Not that I'm making excuses or anything, but it is an unreal coincidence.

The idiot from earlier pipes up again. "Lois Lane! I can't believe it!"

I roll my eyes and watch as Lane does the same.

"I'm Lewis." He scours my face. "This here is Donovan, and that's Adam."

"The Campus Drivers?" I ask, despite myself.

"Damn straight! Lois Lane . . . God, that's too good."

"Okay, so now we've got the introductions out of the way . . ."

"What did that asshole want?" Donovan asks me, crushing his can with his hand.

Without thinking, I look over at Lane, and spark a fresh bout of laughter among the guys.

"Not Lane! I mean Donald!"

"Oh! He said he had a room for me."

"You're kidding."

"Nope!" I wave the sheet of paper.

"Bad idea. You just arrived, you don't know that guy."

I turn to the speaker. Adam, was it?

"He said I could call him Donny. We're buddies now . . ."

I'm doubling down like a bratty kid, but my words trail off into silence as all eyes turn to Donovan.

He starts scanning the crowds for Donald, suddenly flustered. "I am going to break that bastard's legs!"

"What did I say?"

"There's only one Donny at SHU," Lewis mutters, leaning into me like it's some sort of grand conspiracy. "There might only be one Donny in the whole of the United States, come to think of it."

He points a finger at Donovan, who's fuming as he spins on his heels.

"It's basically trademarked. That guy's crossed a line," Lewis adds with a scowl. "Absolute disgrace, dude."

"Okay . . ."

This whole conversation is going over my head, and I start edging away from the group.

"You can't say yes," the quiet one calls after me.

Who the hell asked him?

"Adam, right?"

"Yeah. Nice to meet you."

I can feel my hardness melting away, and I can't help but smile. I don't know if it's the gentle blue eyes that remind me of my younger brother, or the way he scrunches his nose up when he looks at me, like my dad does, but he oozes kindness.

"I haven't decided yet, but I have to admit, I'm kind of running short on options, here." I wave at Lane to catch his eye. "Can you give me a ride? My stuff is still in your trunk."

"Like I'd forget. Where are we going?"

"To the motel I told you about yesterday."

"Tonight we're going to Bennett's for our first party of the year," Lewis interrupts, slinging an arm over my shoulders. "You coming?"

"No, thanks, I'm exhausted."

I wriggle free from him and turn back to Lane, who seems delighted I turned down the offer. "So?"

"It would be my pleasure! Did you download the Campus Drivers app? Only the first ride is free," he adds snippily.

I fish my phone out of my bag and tap at the screen for a few minutes, but Lane's huffing is distracting me, and at his twelfth sigh, he snatches the phone out of my hands.

"I'm linking your account to your Venmo," he explains.

Just as he's shoving my cell back at me, his own phone starts to beep. I peer down at the username he's chosen for me.

"'HeartBreak04'?"

"Apparently, you're not the first."

"'CaptainLane,'" I read out, and shake my head.

"At your service!"

He jerks his chin toward his car, and before I follow him, I cast one last look in Kirk's direction. He's gone, and there's a weight nestling in my heart again. I had forgotten all about him while chatting away with these four weirdos.

Lane lifts my bag away from me and places it alongside the ones I left behind, and I slide into the passenger seat without a word.

"We're coming with you!" Lewis chants as he settles himself in the back seat with Donovan. "Adam will see us at Bennett's, he's got a ride to take care of."

I blanket myself in silence, my foot tapping on the floor as I scratch at the stitching on the seats.

As the miles fly by, I can feel the panic rising. I've never slept in a motel before. The one small comfort is knowing it's not too far from Kirk's place. It's stupid, but knowing he's nearby makes the surprise breakup feel less real. Deep down inside, I think that's why I let myself crash at Lane's. I sneak a look at him, and he glances back at me, unsmiling, when suddenly he slams down on the brakes, and I focus back on the road in front of us. There's a traffic jam, and that's unusual in this part of town.

The minutes tick by. We're not budging.

One of the guys pipes up behind us. "Bucket seats are the worst, case closed—you can't beat a good bench seat! How do you manage to screw any girls with this setup, Lane?"

I pull a face, priming myself for a reply that thankfully never comes.

Donovan leans over between our two front seats. "Anyway, Lois: what are you studying at SHU?"

"Sports PT."

"Seriously? That's awesome!"

"Why?"

"Me and Lewis are on the basketball team! You'll be rubbing down our bulging muscles."

I grimace and shift around to press my back to the door. "Why are you phrasing it like that? It's disgusting."

"I know." He snickers, pleased with himself. "You better get used to it. The Cardinals aren't exactly known for their manners."

"Kirk isn't like that," I say, too loud.

Lane's eyes drift off the road for a split second, and he glances at me. "Who?"

Now Lewis is leaning in, too.

"Forget it. I can't believe how backed up this street is." My voice sounds screechy. "Can you see anything?"

I hear Lewis pulling himself out the window to try to see what's slowing us down.

"Flashing lights and smoke. Take a right, Lane. Straight ahead is all blocked up."

The car jolts when we hang a sharp right, and as we crawl around the neighborhood, I'm getting a bad feeling about all of this.

By the time we make it to the other side of the road and pull up near the motel, my fears are proving right. The street is still clogged, and a little farther down, police officers are directing the traffic.

"Oh no . . ."

I unfasten my seat belt and step out of the car, racing toward a security barrier where I stand on my tiptoes, although I can already sense just how big a deal this is.

I freeze when a cop spots me and starts waving me away.

"Move along, please!"

I step back, my eyes locked on the thick black smoke spilling out of the building. The motel. *My motel is going up in flames.*

As I keep backing away, I feel something slam into my back. Or someone, more like. I try battling against whatever is preventing me from moving away, my eyes stinging from the smoke, but a strong arm holds me in place.

"¿Qué pasa?" Lewis asks as he appears at my right.

Donovan comes to my left, and it doesn't take a genius to figure out who's blocking the way behind me. Lane towers above me, surveying the disaster.

"Fuck. I've never met anyone this unlucky."

His voice is so low and deep, I can feel his chest thrumming against my head, and I shiver. I sway on my feet, fighting back a sob.

Lewis isn't getting it. "What's burning?"

Oh, just my soul in the flames of hell.

"The Break Inn," I answer.

"Why the sad face, dude?" Lewis says, looking at Lane.

"Because that was my only backup plan," I hear myself answer on Lane's behalf.

5

LANE

Her fucking motel is on fire!

I replay it over in my head—guess I'm a masochist like that.

"This cannot be happening," Lois whimpers.

She's standing in front of me, my chest flat against her back, and when I finally let her go, she sways dangerously on her feet. Donovan has moved over to the security barrier and is talking to the cop. They seem to know each other, but maybe not. Don will chat with anyone.

"Nobody died!" he shouts, trotting back over to us. "Are you okay, Lois? You're all white."

She's still staring into space, her eyelids fluttering.

Jesus, here come the waterworks again.

The crowd is pressing against us, and we need to move. I tug at Heartbreak's elbow, leading her back to the car, where I slouch against the door with my arms folded.

"Now what?" Lewis perches on the edge of the sidewalk.

I glance at Lois. "The Break Inn isn't the only place in town."

"Sure. Of course not," she whispers, fishing out her phone. "Just dump my bags here, I'll find somewhere else online. You guys go on, I've got this."

She plops herself down on the sidewalk and sighs heavily.

"Plus, I've got Donald's number."

"You kept it?" Donovan sits down next to her.

"Yeah." She plucks out the crumpled sheet of paper from her little bag, and he whips it out of her hand. "Hey! Give it back!"

"Hell no!" My friend tosses it at my feet.

She leans over to grab it, and though I'm tempted to let her, I stamp my foot down, just missing her fingers.

She snatches her hand back. "Are you for real?"

Lewis shakes his head. "Like we said: Stay away from the Duckster!"

She throws her head back and takes in a few deep breaths. Call me twisted, but I kind of get a kick out of seeing her all frustrated.

"We're gonna help you out; there's no way we're leaving you to figure this shit out on your own." Donovan swipes at his phone. "Guys, let's do this. Mission Find the Girl a Room!"

The next fifteen minutes are definitely up there on my list of top five most frustrating moments ever. We make call after call, but all the cheap rooms have been snapped up by the ex-motel's guests, plus the first home football game of the season is happening in town. Just our luck. The universe has a sick sense of humor, and, call me a killjoy, but I'm not laughing.

"Sorry, Lois, but it looks like you're in deeper shit than we thought," offers Don.

"You must have screwed up in a past life!" Lewis jeers, slinging an arm over her shoulders. "Like, badly."

I was expecting her to shrug him off, but instead she annoyingly stands there.

"My dad is a Cardinals coach." Don shoots her a sideways glance. "I can't promise you anything, but I can ask if he's got any ideas."

"Thank you. That's sweet of you."

Sweet of him? Please!

"Still want to come and grab a few drinks with us? It'll do you good!"

Donovan catches me looking at him uneasily and winks.

"No, I'm good. I—"

Donovan cuts her off mid-sentence. "So, okay, let's drop her at your place, Lane, and then we'll hit up the party."

I almost give myself whiplash turning to look at him. "What?"

"What do you mean, 'what'? You're just gonna leave her here? Come on!"

And what if I am?

I walk around the car, sharply motioning at Donovan and Lewis to follow me on the side.

"I've already done my time, guys! Knock it off," I whisper-yell, scrunching my hands deeper into my pockets.

"You seem quite pissed, Lane." Donovan tilts his head at me. "Wouldn't you say so, Lewis?"

Lewis grins. "Oh, I'd say so, Donny. Big-time!"

"She's just a girl who needs a place to crash while she figures stuff out," Donovan says.

"I'm not sharing my place," I snap. "No way!"

"Jeez—maybe relax a little?" Donovan lets out an over-the-top sigh, and pouts in my direction.

"Look at her, wasting away on the sidewalk like that."

"You know me, I like my alone time," I respond.

"She's a girl," Lewis says slowly, wriggling his eyebrows.

"And?"

He squeezes my biceps. "And she needs a big, strong man she can rely on for a night or two," he whispers.

I groan and shove him away, rolling my eyes when he starts to cackle.

"You know, I'm not the only one with a couch, guys. You can have her!"

They exchange meaningful looks, and I swear the hairs on the back of my neck stand.

"Sorry, Lane, but Adam's cousin is in town." Don curls a lip. "He's crashing on our couch."

"His cousin? What cousin?"

"Dexter," he says too quickly, just as Lewis blurts out, "Drake."

"Dexter Drake," they chant together.

Bitches!

"Let me guess—long-lost cousin, right?"

"Exactly! He's from LA, and he needed a break from the scene."

"What scene?"

"All of them!"

"Look, here's a photo of him. Check it out!"

Don waves his phone in my face, and I swipe it off him, irritated.

"This is Google Images, you dumbass!"

Don shrugs. "In LA, Dexter Drake is a local celebrity."

"Why are you doing this to me, guys?"

"We're helping you become your best self, Laney."

"Imagine she's your sister! You wouldn't want her crashing with a total rando."

"What if she ends up having to stay at Donald's?" Lewis's eyes are shining.

"And be real. You wouldn't want her hanging around our place, either," Don finishes, all smug.

The two idiots can barely contain their excitement, and I know them way too well: They aren't going to give up. I don't know what they're angling for, but I do know I'm fucked. My folks really did the bare minimum when it came to raising me, but I'm not a complete asshole. Not to the point where I'd leave a girl high and dry like this, anyway.

"Fuck!" I yell, as I start striding toward the sidewalk. "Heartbreak, get in the car!"

She jerks her head up. "Where are we going?"

"I'm taking you back to my place."

"How come?"

"Get. In. The. Car." I point.

Just before I slide into my seat, I turn back to my so-called besties.

"You guys are staying here. I'm not driving you anywhere. Figure it out!"

As revenge plans go, this one is pretty lame: All they have to do is message Adam and they'll have themselves a new driver. But it feels good, and that's all that counts.

"See you later," Lewis coos, waggling his fingers at me. "Have a good evening, Lois!"

I drive without saying a word, the music turned up to the max. She likes Tool, huh? Well, she's getting it.

I screech to a halt in front of my building, get out of the car, and heave her goddamn bags from my trunk.

"Wait, Lane. Let me—"

"Let you what?"

"I mean—"

"Just get inside before I change my mind."

I hit the stairs, taking the steps three at a time, yanking open the front door and throwing her bags into the hallway before stomping to my room to pull on a fresh tee.

Back in the living room, Lois is hovering between the kitchen and the couch.

"I'm out of here," I sigh, slipping two twenties out of a drawer. "Use the alone time to figure out a plan B, because this is your last night here," I say sharply.

Her eyes are filling up, and my shoulders loosen.

"Listen, it's nothing personal," I sigh. "It's just . . . I've lived alone since forever, and—"

"I totally get it." She cuts me off brusquely, sniffing. "I hate this, too, you know, I can't tell you how bad. You've done more than enough already, I don't plan on overstaying my welcome. Tomorrow, I'll be gone."

I flash her a thumbs-up, turn on my heel, and exit, leaving her alone in my apartment for the third time. This party couldn't have come at a better time, because I seriously need a drink.

I NEVER SET AN ALARM. Why would I, when I have my own personal wake-up call—sweetly named Carter—who repeat-dials me at the crack of dawn every day? Threats don't work; I've tried. No matter what I do, he starts blowing up my phone the second a wild idea strikes. What we do is peculiar enough as it is, but Carter is a complete oddball.

I pick up on his fourth attempt, my voice still husky with sleep.

"Carter, have I told you lately that I hate you?" I rub my eyes. "You're coming by tonight, right? So couldn't this wait? I'm still sobering up!"

"Not my problem, buddy!" It's as if I can hear him grinning down the phone. "I bumped into Lewis. He told me you're free today. I'll be there in fifteen!"

"Awesome," I deadpan.

I drag myself into the kitchen, stabbing at the remote to open the blinds. I'm standing there stark naked, and it takes me a few seconds and a weird, animal-like grunting sound to remember there's some girl on my couch. The way she's slumped there with those druggie-diva shades firmly fixed to her face, I have no way of telling whether she can see my dick from where she's lying. I'm no prude, but I'm guessing she'd go into full meltdown mode if she caught me staring at her from the kitchen with a solid case of morning wood. I hit the button on the remote again, and the blinds stop halfway down.

I'm a little surprised, to be honest: I expected her to be gone by now, since that's what she's done every other morning she's ever slept over. Finding her still here when I get up makes the whole thing feel even more annoying. There's a reason I've lived alone for the past three years. I worked hard to build myself a sanctuary, and this chick is ruining it all. Plus, there's the fact that she's fallen apart over some guy, as if a breakup meant the end of the world or something. I may have been wasted last night, but I could hear her crying and tossing and turning, making it into a whole big deal. It got so bad, at one point I thought about taking her back downstairs to stop myself from suffocating her with my pillow, and then (thank fuck!) she finally fell asleep. She can't hit the road soon enough!

I hardly have time to pull on a pair of shorts and knock back a coffee before Carter knocks on the door. Sorry, I mean: Carter starts by trying to break in using the spare key I should never have given him, except mine is already in the lock—call it a safety quirk of mine. I glance over at Lois. She's fast asleep, her fists clenched. When I unlock the door, Carter pushes it open without a beat, stalking right past me and pulling up a barstool at the kitchen counter, setting up his laptop and laying out a few loose sheets of paper in front of him.

"Heavy night, huh?" he says, chuckling behind me. "I can smell the whiskey fumes from here. You're a walking hangover."

"You were supposed to come tonight," I remind him with a shrug. "Deal with it."

I snatch up his favorite mug and fill it to the brim with coffee while he settles in, kicking off his shoes.

"Uh, Lane?"

I keep my eyes focused on the coffee, throwing in two sugars. "'Sup?"

"Anything you'd care to share?"

"About?" I look up at him.

He's turned sideways, gazing toward the back of the living room.

"What's up with the chick on your couch?"

"Oh, that . . ."

"Yeah, that! Don't make me call the cops on your ass, man. I'm picturing a SWAT team, tear gas—"

"Why does your mind always go to the worst scenarios? Maybe she just fell asleep here."

"I mean . . . There's a girl . . . lying on your couch . . . and that's weird. If this was the guys' apartment we were talking about, then sure. But here . . ." He stands up.

"What are you doing?"

"Checking she's breathing."

"Sit down!" I hiss, grabbing him by the arm. "You're being ridiculous, dude! Drink your coffee!"

"So explain yourself, then. You're not the kind to let a girl hang around once you've screwed her. Wasted or not," he adds.

"I haven't even screwed her yet!"

"'Yet'? Okay, now that makes sense! So, you're keeping her on the back burner, huh?"

"No! That's not what I meant. Jeez, you're fucking exhausting, you know that?"

He scours my face, a wry grin playing on his lips, and it takes everything I have not to launch the sugar cubes at his head.

"Don't look at me like that," I warn, wagging a finger at him.

"Okay," he says, but he keeps staring at me.

"Carter..."

"Lane..."

"I mean, seriously, look at her!" I throw up my hands. "She's a hot mess. I scooped her off the stairs on Sunday morning. Her ex threw her out two days before she started at SHU. I felt sorry for her, and now I have no fucking clue how to ditch her. She was supposed to go stay at a motel, but it fucking burned down!"

"She's been here since *Sunday?* Wow, my best friend is suddenly becoming a saint, and I'm the last to hear! So did you, like, comfort her and shit?"

"Oh, give me a break, Cart! She crashed on the couch, that's all."

"So is she looking for an apartment, or what?"

"An apartment, a dorm, a basement... Whatever, man, as soon as she wakes up, I'm dropping her somewhere, and hasta la vista!"

He seems to think for a moment, and when I catch him sneaking glances down my hall, I stiffen.

"Don't even think about it."

"You've got a spare room." He shrugs.

"It's not spare, Carter!"

He opens his mouth to reply when Lois lets out the grossest yawn I've ever heard.

"Great, she's up!" He claps his hands.

Elbows propped on the kitchen island, chin resting on my fists, I tilt my head for a better look at her, and watch as she stretches her legs, tugging at her hoodie and staring up at the ceiling. She mutters something and slips two fingers beneath her sunglasses, rubbing at her eyes. I'm not sure whether she can suddenly sense us looking at her, but I see her freeze before slowly turning to face us.

"Morning!" Carter wiggles his fingers at her. "Sleep well?"

"Uh, yeah. Thanks."

I roll my eyes. She sits up, pulls back her hood, slips off her shades, and rearranges the hair piled on her head. Her eyelids are red and swollen.

"Bad night?" I raise an eyebrow, but all I get in return is a curled lip.

Carter jumps to his feet. "Coffee?"

"Sure."

"Sugar?"

"No, thanks."

"Milk?"

"Nope."

What the fuck is happening to him? We've known each other since forever, and in all that time, I've never known Carter to make a coffee. Ever. He flashes me a knowing grin, and I don't like that one bit. *Not him, too.*

I focus back on Lois as she makes her way toward me.

"Make yourself at home," I mutter, pointing at a stool.

"Really?"

"No."

She shakes her head, doing her best to ignore my glare.

Carter is back with two piping hot cups. "What's your name?"

Lord, give me strength . . .

"Lois."

His eyes widen. "Lois?"

"Yeah."

I'm expecting him to launch into the same joke my friends made yesterday, but all he does is shoot me a quick smile.

"I'm Carter."

"Nice to meet you," she says politely, disappearing behind her mug. "Are you a student, too?"

"Hell no! Never set foot in the place. I mean, I have—but not for class, if you get me. Don't let the lame attempt at a beard fool you. I'm twenty-four."

She smiles, blowing on her coffee.

"So Lane tells me you're homeless?"

The smile vanishes, and she shoots me a dirty look before turning back to my friend.

"Temporarily." She sighs.

"What are your options?"

She takes a quick sip. "Well, all the dorms are gone, so today I plan on widening my search. What with the fire at the motel, every place in town within my budget is full with guests, so—"

"So you're kinda in a bad spot."

"Just a little," I mutter sarcastically.

"It'll be okay," she replies.

"Can your family help out?"

Damn, chatty much? He's asked her more questions in two minutes than I have in a whole four days!

"No," she says too quickly. "They're in Fort Myers, in Florida. They have other stuff going on. I'll figure something out."

She's holding back, I can tell—but who am I to judge?

She puts down her mug on the table, and I watch her for a minute, ignoring Cart's questioning gaze.

"Okay!" She leaps to her feet. "I'm going to go find somewhere with Wi-Fi; I'll leave you guys to it. Can I . . . Can I leave my stuff with you for a few more hours, Lane?"

"What's a few more hours between friends," I drawl.

"Thank you."

"Why can't she just use your Wi-Fi?"

"Carter..."

"Come on, Laney! We can't let her spend ten bucks on a fancy coffee just to get online for an hour!"

"We've got work to do, remember?"

"No shit," he teases, leaning over the table. "Well, how about that... *Now* you're in the mood for work?"

"Honestly, it's f-fine," Lois stutters awkwardly.

"Once we're done, we can help you out," Carter pushes, shooting me a look. "Plus, it's pouring outside!"

The blinds are still half shut, and opening them all the way, I have to admit he has a point. I sigh. They've backed me into a corner. I don't want her here because... Well, because. But a part of me knows I'm being irrational.

"You can have the coffee table," I hear myself conceding. "For now."

Lois doesn't notice, but Carter is pumping a fist in the air.

Payback's coming, you little shit!

She isn't budging, so I try a more encouraging vibe. "Go on, Lois."

"Okay. Thanks."

She slides off the stool and walks over to her bag, pulling out a laptop and settling back onto the goddamn couch, stuffing a pair of earbuds into her ears and vanishing behind her screen.

She plucks out one of the buds. "Can I get the Wi-Fi password?" she asks meekly.

"'JuicyBalls,'" Carter answers for me.

"What?"

"'JuicyBalls.'" He keeps his face straight. "Capital 'J,' capital 'B.'"

"Right. Got it."

She stabs at her keypad, frowns, and looks back over at us. Carter is struggling to hold back his laughter. And so am I.

She clears her throat. "All one word?"

"You got it."

She chews her lip, like it's taking everything she has to bite her tongue. Over the top of her screen, her eyes are flashing back and forth between us. I wait for her to take a swipe, but it never comes.

That all you got, Lois?

Her mood swings are a lot. Yesterday, she was shamelessly ripping into me, this morning she can hardly get a word out. It makes sense, though: She's in such a shitty situation, she must feel like she has no choice but to hold back. I don't know which I like best. *You don't like any of it, dude! Remember?*

She readjusts her earbuds, and I can hear the bass throbbing from here as Lois seals herself away in her own little world.

"Lane?"

"What?"

"Look any harder and you'll set that couch on fire."

I drag my eyes back to Carter, and before he has a chance to piss me off with any questions, I sift through the notes he brought with him, offering up comments and questions as I read, but it's no use. He doesn't respond to a single one of them. When he twists in his seat to look at Lois, I keep my eyes on the papers.

"It's not bad, I love the tubing idea. Do you think it's doable, technically?"

He doesn't reply, and when he leaves yet another one of my questions hanging in the air, I slam the bundle of notes down on the table.

"Carter! You've been up my ass for three days now, wanting to talk through these ideas. So can we do this, or what?"

"Uh-huh."

I snap my fingers in front of his face.

"Can you please stop staring at her?"

"She's kind of nice," he says slowly, flicking his tongue piercing between his teeth.

"You spoke to her for all of five minutes."

"So?"

"So what?"

"So she's kind of pretty."

"If homeless crybabies are your thing."

He ignores me. "You, on the other hand"—he turns to face me—"you're a dick."

I offer him my broadest smile, but it doesn't land.

"Care to expand on that?"

He holds up a thumb to kick off the list. "For starters, you act like you have a serious personality disorder when you're around her."

"Dude, I was really nice on the first day."

"And instead of helping her out of a shitty situation, you kick her while she's down," he says, adding his index finger to the tally.

"I helped her on the first day," I insist.

"She's all alone, Lane!" He flicks up his middle finger.

"So what? What am I—a charity? I like living by myself, end of discussion."

He's grinding his teeth, ruffling his hair. He gazes out the window, suddenly lost in thought.

"Deep down, you know that's not the issue," he sighs, turning back to me.

"Don't start with that, Cart," I rasp.

"Start with what? You bring him up all the time, and now all of a sudden we shouldn't mention him? Whenever I come over, we somehow always end up talking about Mike. And you know what?" He stares at me. "Since I dropped you off over the weekend, you haven't mentioned him. Not even once."

"We haven't hung out since then."

"So you're not denying it—"

"First of all, my brother has nothing to do with any of this. Second of all, I don't always bring him up."

At least, I don't *think* I do.

"It's been three years, and we still talk about him every day, dude. And I don't mind that, I really don't. I miss Mike, too. We were best friends since we were in diapers, since before you were even born, Laney."

"Adorable," I snort.

"I'm just saying that giving her a place to crash could be a good thing—something new to keep your mind busy. I'm not telling you to put her up forever, but why not help her out? The room is—"

"The room is Mike's room!" I slam a fist down on the counter, and Lois's eyes dart over to me. The music blasting from her ears means she can't hear us, but she must have noticed me lash out.

"Okay, okay." Carter holds up his hands. "That part is harder, I get that. But how 'bout the couch? It's a little basic, sure—but it would do, just for a couple of days while she gets back on her feet."

"You're killing me here!"

"Come on, Lane. You know it makes sense. Helping someone in their hour of need . . . It's good for the soul, especially for a guy like you. Maybe it'll get rid of some of that guilt you've been carrying around."

I turn away from him, clutching the edge of the sink. He has pissed me off so bad, I'm this close to heading out for a drive. He came over to work, and instead here he is, hosting the fucking *Dr. Carter Show*.

What did I do to deserve friends like these?

"Remember when you had to retake your freshman year, how mad and hurt you were that fall? Remember how you didn't want any friends, you just wanted to be left alone, and I had to give you a kick up the ass when Lewis and Adam came over to say hi? And then Donovan showed up, and now you four are like brothers?" He pauses, waiting for the words to sink in. "Who knows? Maybe now Lois needs a bit of that herself." He snorts, easing the tension. "Lois Lane, for fuck's sake! If that's not fate, I don't know what is!"

"If you're that concerned, why don't *you* take her back to your place?"

"Hmm, let me think." Carter holds a finger to his chin. "Because I live in a studio and I already sleep on my own couch?"

It's official: I'm doomed.

"What if I can't shake her off?"

"Trust me, buddy: That girl is hating this just as much as you are. Carry on the way you are, and I'd say the worst-case scenario is she stabs you with a potato peeler in your sleep."

Suddenly, Lois slams her laptop shut and rips out her earbuds, swearing like a trucker. I go to tease her, but Carter places a hand on my arm.

"Think 'potato peeler,' dude . . ."

"What's going on, Lois?" I try to pour as much sympathy as I can into my voice, but it rings hollow, and she stares at me, one eyebrow arched.

"This town is insane," she snarls, jumping to her feet. "The only places left are super expensive. I'd need to sell a kidney. Actually, make that two kidneys. And the cheap hotels are so far away from campus, I'd need to sell the damn kidneys just to pay for transport." She lets out a breath, tugging out her hair tie, her thick hair tumbling loose.

Aaaaand she's back. I suppress a smile.

"More coffee?" Carter offers tentatively.

She nods, sliding onto the stool across from me. I suddenly realize I'm staring at her, because she shoots me a dirty look.

"Don't worry, Lane, I won't hang around."

"I didn't say a thing."

"Your eyes are doing the talking for you."

"He usually lets his dick do all the talking," Carter jokes, fresh coffees in hand.

Lois reaches for her mug. "Sounds fascinating."

I watch as she takes a few long gulps, eyes locked on the ceiling.

"Laneyyy . . ." Carter drawls in a singsong.

I close my eyes and grit my teeth.

"Come on, Laney boyyyy . . ."

I let out a growl, tugging on a curl that's sprung loose across my forehead.

"What are you guys doing?" Heartbreak seems confused, and that makes sense. We're being ridiculous.

"Laney..."

"Enough already!" I thunder, loud enough that Lois nearly falls off her stool. "YoucanstayabitlongerLois."

"I'm sorry— What?"

I need to get the words out fast, before I take them back. "YoucanstayabitlongerLois."

"Huh, can you maybe translate, Carter? I'm lost."

"Lane says you can crash on his couch for a while longer." He beams.

Have I mentioned I hate this guy?

"W-what? Why?"

"Because you've got nowhere else to go," he chirps.

"Yeah, I know that. I meant more like: 'Why is he offering to let me stay?' He can't even stand to be in the same room as me!"

"He's a little grumpy, but he's got a big heart—a real sensitive streak. Oh, and a free couch!"

"He's also sitting right here," I interrupt. My patience is wearing thin.

"Okay, I get it. You guys are messing with me." She looks at Carter, as if I were invisible.

"I'm telling you, it's true! He likes helping people out. And a damsel in distress gets him every time."

"You want some knuckles with that coffee, Cart?"

Lois scrapes back her chair, and I circle around the kitchen island to join her.

"We're not messing with you," I say. "I'm giving you a little more time to figure things out."

"See what I mean?" Carter smirks, glancing over at me. "The host with the most!"

She searches my face, trying to decide whether I'm for real.

"A *little* more time," I say, flipping Carter the finger without glancing his way.

She opens her mouth. Closes it. Opens it again. Weighing her options.

"Make up your mind," I hiss.

Shit! So now I'm the one begging her to stay?

She runs her tongue over her teeth. "Okay."

"No shit!"

"I'll give you rent money."

"I own this place, I don't need rent. Just focus on working your shit out." I shrug. "And pick up some groceries from time to time."

"I'll leave early in the morning and work late at the library. It'll be almost like I'm not even here."

"Almost," I mutter, despite myself.

"Potato peeler, Lane," Carter coughs under his breath. Subtle guy.

Lois raises an eyebrow at him before swiveling back to me. "I'm going to try to find somewhere as soon as I can."

"Let's hope you have more luck with dorms than you do with motels . . ."

"Gee, thanks for believing in me."

"Anything for you, sunshine."

We spend another long minute staring each other down, until Carter brings us back to reality with a few taps on the table.

"You guys are so inspiring!"

"We got a deal, Heartbreak?" I hold out a hand.

She's clenching her jaw, I notice. But whatever she wants to say— her desperation keeps her silent.

Slowly, she nods. "Deal."

6

LOIS

Today's Friday. While most students are cheering for the weekend, I've officially hit rock bottom. It's been almost a week since Kirk broke up with me, and exactly six days since he ghosted me. This morning, I sent him my twenty-third text—*yes, I counted*—left unanswered. I mean, that's not strictly true. He *did* respond to the first one.

KIRK: Please give me some space

Along with the messages, I tried calling eleven times, with just as many knocks on his door. He might want space, but I've got too much of it. I hate what I'm becoming, but my pride is in the exact same state as my heart: broken. That's why Lane's nickname hit so hard.

Lane. Jesus, I can't believe I've been on this guy's couch since Sunday. I could never have imagined I'd be in this situation. I don't have many friends back in Florida—Kirk's friends were the only ones I had. So sharing some small corner of an apartment with a student I just met is pure craziness. Plus, he's a *guy*. As a girl with four younger brothers, you'd think I'd be used to sharing my space with the opposite sex. Growing up, let's just say I never had a moment's peace—but this? It's a different beast entirely. Still, when Lane gave in and offered to let me stay, it didn't take me long to figure out I needed to say yes— because Kirk lives three floors below him. That alone sealed the deal.

Now that I'm *temporarily* not homeless, I can focus on what really matters: cornering Kirk on his way out of the building and winning him back. I mean, it's not like four years of feelings just disappear in a week, right?

The only reason I managed to peel myself off the couch this morning (besides the fact that Lane was hanging around) was the feeling that I'd definitely bump into Kirk here in the lecture hall, where I've been waiting for ten minutes now, along with *every other* freshman. I don't give a damn about the orientation meeting itself: an afternoon-long welcome session where some of SHU's student clubs get the chance to harvest as many new sign-ups as they can. Count me out.

"Lois!"

I jump, sending my notebook fluttering to the ground. I kneel and start scooping up the pages before someone can spot that I've doodled "Kirk" everywhere.

"Becca! Hey!"

She draws me in for a quick hug. "What's new?" She juts out her hip, slouching against the wall in the kind of super feminine pose I could never master.

"Hm. Not much! You?"

I gnaw the inside of my cheek. I can't stand the way I can barely string a sentence together.

"My summer was in*sane*." She grins, smoothing her blond ponytail back into place.

"So makeup classes weren't all that bad, after all . . ." I smile.

"It was amazing." She sighs, her eyes twinkling. "I mean I totally screwed up again, and now I'm retaking some freshman year classes, but you should've seen our English professor . . . Let's just say he seriously made up for my dad's meltdown. You should've seen his hips!"

"His hips? That's what you look for in a guy?"

"He wasn't a guy, Lois. He was a *man*! And yeah, a nice pair of hips slapping against my ass . . . Nothing better."

I can feel myself starting to blush.

"How about you? All good with Kirk?"

My heart is racing.

"Yeah." I squeeze out a smile.

"Is he here with you?"

"Yeah. I mean—no! I mean, he's on his way," I mumble.

Luckily, she doesn't seem to pick up on what a mess I am right now, or maybe she just doesn't give a shit. Either works for me.

Luckily, the doors finally creak open, and we pour into the lecture hall. By the time I grab my bag and turn back to the pressing crowd, I've lost sight of Becca. I slip into a seat at the top near the entrance and pretend to look for something on my phone, perfectly positioned to spot Kirk as soon as he arrives.

"What are you doing? Let's go!" Becca grabs my arm, and before I have a chance to shake her off, she's dragging me away. "The front is filling up already."

She skips down the stairs to the third row, elbowing past a gaggle of girls.

"Do we really have to sit this low down?" I whisper, glancing over my shoulder.

"Yeah, we really do." She yanks at my T-shirt. "Sit!"

I groan, casting looks around me as I fold down the wooden seat.

"Your guy will be fine." Becca elbows me in the ribs. "I promise you'll thank me for the front-row tickets, it's gonna be one hell of a show!"

"What show?"

There's a twinkle in her eye as she raises her eyebrows, and I frown. I have no idea how a couple of campus clubs can get her all riled up like this. I scour the room again, and just when I'd given up hope, my eyes land on him, and it's like I've forgotten how to breathe. I watch as Kirk strolls down the steps, exchanging smiles with the guy he's with, falling back into a seat in the middle of the crowd, dropping his bag on the table in front of him, chatting with his neighbor and the girl sitting behind him. My heart tightens in my chest. I was hoping he'd look a little more heartbroken. A little less... normal. A microphone buzzes on behind me, somebody sound-checking it with a few taps. Kirk turns to look at the stage, and our eyes meet. I draw in a sharp breath, and the pain is worse than death. He assesses me for a moment. Behind his eyes, I see nothing. Blank. Unsmiling. The microphone crackles once more, and, just like that, Kirk turns away.

"Ladies and gentlemen, congratulations." A sunny, upbeat voice. "You just survived your first week of college."

As laughter breaks out, I turn back to face the stage, suddenly overcome by the urge to shout at the speaker to shut up. My mood swings are bubbling up to the surface again, and this time, Lane isn't to blame. I keep flip-flopping between tearful meltdowns and bursts of anger, and I've been taking it all out on my infuriating roomie. Just another side of myself I'm slowly discovering the hard way. *God, I hate myself.*

"They always start with the finance club!" Becca crosses her arms over the desk. "Like seriously, who *does* that in their free time?"

The first hour crawls by, and though I haven't said a word, nothing can get in the way of Becca's running commentary.

"Knitting now? What a rush," she sighs, shaking her head.

"It's supposed to be relaxing," I say flatly.

Maybe I should sign up. I could knit myself a nice rope to hang myself with.

"Watch out, the ventriloquist club is up next. Nothing says well-adjusted like talking through a dead-eyed puppet."

"I guess you must know all the groups from last year, right?"

"Yeah, and I'm telling you: Some of them are insane."

"So why even come this time?"

"It's a sacrifice I'm willing to make," she whispers, plucking a pocket mirror out of her bag, checking her makeup, teeth, and breath, before tucking it back in place.

"Meaning?"

"You'll see, Lois."

She's drumming her nails against the worn wooden desk, waiting with mounting impatience.

As the groups segue by, I realize people around us are starting to whisper. And the murmurs are getting louder.

"Why do all the girls look like they're about to pass out?" I ask, as a leggy redhead in front of me starts fanning herself so hard she almost hits me in the face.

"You'll see. Once this guy stops boring us with his unsolved-murders spiel!"

As the student packs away his slides and slinks offstage, the mutterings ramp up a notch, a series of yelps and screeches rippling through the crowd. *What the hell is going on?*

"Becca—"

"Shhh! Here they come!"

The two front rows turn to gaze up at the back of the lecture hall, and slowly but surely, the entire crowd follows suit. I haven't dared turn back to look Kirk's way since earlier. Now's my chance. I swivel in my seat. He's looking down at his bag while his neighbor whispers in his ear, shaking his head, gazing up at the ceiling, and just as I think he's about to glance over at me, the room breaks into applause. Girls scramble to their feet, blocking my view of the entrance.

"Who even are these guys?" the guy next to me sneers.

Becca babbles something at me, but she's so excited, I can't make out a word. I'm just about to get to my feet, when I finally get it. The chanting. I can suddenly make out what it is.

"Campus Drivers! Campus Drivers!"

No . . . Oh no, no, no. Please, anything but this.

As I spot Lewis walking by, I sink deeper into my seat, watching him hop from step to step, high-fiving his way down to the stage. This is insanity. Once he gets to our row, I shrink back to hide behind Becca. Donovan has followed in his wake, Adam right behind him. None of them have spotted me, and I feel myself relax a little. Now it's

Lane's turn to set the lecture hall on fire as he trots down, and I catch myself hoping he'll twist an ankle and bring this shit show to an end.

"Leaving the best ones for last!" a girl behind me yells.

Up onstage, Lewis points and smiles at her. Just as she starts swooning, I quickly take down my bun and scoop my hair in front of my face. I don't know these guys that well, but I've got a feeling that if they spot me, they'll pounce.

"Hey, everybody!" Donovan starts.

The guy next to me has a face like thunder. "Dick."

"Shut up, Tony," snaps Becca, tossing a paper ball in his face.

I listen intently as they take turns bringing us up to speed, explaining how they help students get around campus and downtown.

When Lane starts talking us through the app, I realize he actually seems pretty friendly—just not with me, apparently. He's generous in the way he answers questions, nodding his head, smiling as he explains timings and slots, and I have to admit: He's persuasive. If he didn't make me want to rip my hair out, I could see myself getting on board.

Adam wraps up the presentation, and if there's one thing I know for sure, it's that I like him best of the four. He's got the kind of broad, warm, sincere smile I could see myself being drawn to, if I weren't already crazy in love with Kirk.

"Any more questions?"

I start quietly tidying my things away in my bag, getting ready to steal out the moment this is all over. I've done a good job staying undercover, and my pulse has gone back to normal.

"I have one!" Becca suddenly hollers.

Oh no! Sweet baby Jesus, no!

I dip down to bury my head in my bag, praying it's enough to hide my face.

"Are you guys free in the evenings, too?"

Becca! Girl, seriously?

"Our availability is updated every half hour. You can message with any special requests."

"That's good to know."

"Anything else?" He pauses. "In that case, let's go get ready for our first weekend of partying!"

I can feel my neighbor fidgeting next to me, and I figure she's done. She taps on my shoulder, totally ignoring how I'm full-on glaring at her.

"I didn't get to sleep with a single one of them last year," she whispers, her eyes glued to the stage.

"Oh my God, I'm so sad for you," I drawl.

She pouts. "I almost got with Donovan. I plan on starting with him this year, too."

My eyes wander over to the Campus Drivers, and I lock eyes with Lane.

Fuck.

He recognizes me instantly, and a nasty smirk spreads across his devilish face as he raises a hand, wiggling his fingers at me while elbowing Lewis.

"You know him?" Becca asks, noticing him noticing me.

"Nope."

"Hey, Lois! How's it going, honey?" Lewis calls out through the mike, breaking my cover in the worst possible way imaginable.

"You can take a ride in the back of my Road Runner whenever you like!" Donovan adds, pointing a finger at me that I suddenly want to snap off.

Never mind, this is the worst.

"What?" Becca turns to me. "You *do* know them!"

"It's not what you think," I manage.

My hands are all pins and needles. It's as if the whole room just fell silent, eyes boring into me no matter which way I turn. I zip up my bag and hug it to my chest, plastering a fake smile on my face, my mouth like cotton wool.

Finally, Adam switches off the projector. "Have a great weekend!"

Praise the Lord.

I jump up as if my seat were on fire, shoving my way along my row, desperate to get out of this hellhole before things get even more intense. *Shit, I knew those guys would find a way of messing with me.*

I pick my way up the stairs, slowing as I get caught in a clump of students, girls shooting me side-eyes, guys throwing creepy glances. *Great!*

I slink my way over to the first vending machine I find, fishing in my pocket for coins. My hands are shaking so hard I miss the slot, and the quarter clatters to the ground.

"Seriously?" I throw my arms up and look at the ceiling. "What did I do to deserve this?"

I turn around, scanning the ground for my coin, when I notice Lane a foot away, turning it slowly between his fingers. If there's a god up there, I'm definitely on his shit list.

"Is God talking back?"

"Give me that!" I lunge at him.

Lane flicks the coin up with his thumb, smug as hell, and I'm left snatching at thin air.

"I need a snack," I hiss.

He sidesteps to the right. "How did we do?"

"Gripping. I couldn't look away," I say flatly.

"Mean, Lois!"

He slips the coin into his shorts' pocket, a dumb smirk spread across his face.

"I already take up so much of your precious space, Lane. So why not stay out of my way on campus?"

"Am I pissing you off right now?"

"Yes!"

"Well, there's your answer."

"Urgh!"

I'm being a little too loud, and people are starting to stare. Worse, I see Kirk coming through the lecture hall doors, and he's staring right at us.

"I'm out of here," I mumble, already turning away.

Lane reaches for my arm.

"Let me drive you, Lois."

My eyes widen in horror. I don't dare look at Kirk. He must have heard Lane's offer, he must think something's going on, when it isn't.

"No," I whisper. "It's too early for me to go back. We have a deal, remember?"

"What's with the whispering?" he whispers back, leaning into me. "You don't want people to know we live together?"

"We don't live together!" I hiss. I jab him in the chest—or try to, anyway. Say what you want, the guy's pecs are as thick as his head.

Donovan interrupts us, laughing. "If you guys are gonna make out, don't let me stop you!"

I whip my hand away from Lane and take two paces back. Becca has wandered over, in full sunshine mode.

"Hey!" I say, with all the perkiness I can muster. "How about a girls' night?"

"Sorry, but Donny invited me to their party! He told me you'll be there, too, so we can still hang out."

She's practically bouncing.

"Well, how about that?" Lane claps a hand on my shoulder. "Great news, huh?"

"What party?"

"Every fall, when school starts, we have a party at Lane's for his birthday."

Lane smirks at me. "Want the address?"

I stare him straight in the eye. "In that case, I'll go to the library."

"No can do. It's not open on weekend evenings."

I close my eyes and take a deep breath in.

"Come on, Lois! You and Kirk can come along, it'll be fun." Becca links arms with Donovan.

"Who's Kirk?" Lane asks her.

Oh, kill me now.

"Her guy."

"Really?"

He tilts his head at me, staring me down. He knows I haven't told Becca about the breakup, and he's wondering why.

"See you later!" She waves. "Will you walk me to the quad, Don?"

"Yes, ma'am!"

As the pair of them vanish around the corner, I'm frantically racking my brain for a way out, when Lane kicks my foot.

"Kirk?"

"Shut up," I hiss with a glare.

Speak of the devil. There he is, just a few feet away from me, and though he's looking away, I've got a feeling he was watching us. I can't believe this is happening! I've wanted so badly to see him and he's been nowhere to be found. Now the moment Lane and his idiot friends are around, he's everywhere I turn. It's official: I'm cursed.

"Lane, could you ask your friends to be a little less . . . intense?"

"Meaning?"

I shuffle my feet. "If they could play it like we've never met, that would be great."

"Why don't you tell them yourself?"

"I don't want to hurt their feelings."

"Oh, so this is how it is! But my feelings you don't give a shit about?"

"See! You get it."

"Despite the fact I'm the one giving you a home?" He raises an eyebrow.

He's not wrong. I shouldn't be so direct with him. It *is* rude of me, and he *is* doing me a huge favor. But jeez, he's always trying to get a rise out of me, and not snapping back is hard. I didn't even know I had this fiery side to me.

"I'm sorry." I do my best to smile.

He looks me up and down before nodding, satisfied. "You know that if I *do* tell them, they'll just do the exact opposite, right?"

I groan, scooping my hair up into a bun.

"Come on, let's hit the road," he offers.

"I really don't want to come."

"It's my birthday, and I need help with the groceries. We have a deal, remember?"

I narrow my eyes. "Are you blackmailing me?"

"Car. Now."

I bite my tongue, running through my options. It takes me all of one second—the truth is, I don't have any.

"Okay, but on one condition." I trot behind him. "No mentioning our temporary roomie situation under any circumstance."

"You're on bartender duty, then."

"Asshole."

"Say what?"

"Nothing."

I throw myself into his car, brooding. *If he thinks I'm paying for this ride, he can think again!* I stuff my earbuds in, crank the volume up as far as it goes, and stay that way until we arrive at the grocery store near his apartment. As we browse the aisles, I think back to his talk earlier.

"How did you come up with the idea for Campus Drivers, anyway?" I ask, taking the basket from him. "Were you guys friends before?"

"Lewis and Adam already knew each other before college. Donovan is captain of the basketball team; Lewis plays for the team, too. They both have awesome cars, which helped them bond."

"And how about you? How did you get in with them?" I ask. "Was it a car thing, too?"

"Yeah. They saw my Camaro on campus, and they asked me to marry them."

"Let me guess: it was love at first sight."

"Not exactly. I'm not easy, you know."

I snort. "Wow, I'd never have guessed."

He adds three bottles of soda to my basket, and there's no hiding my struggle. I need two hands to carry this thing.

"Here, give me that," he says, taking it from me.

"Thanks. So what about the app?"

Lane smiles. "Notice how many groupies Don has? They were always asking him for rides. It started as a joke about how we would charge them, and it all started from there. We realized SHU is one of the biggest campuses in America, and that having a cab service would be an amazing idea. We spent months working on it, and Campus Drivers launched last fall."

"Is the money good?"

"Yeah."

"That's cool. It was a good idea."

He seems surprised by the compliment, and I almost tell him not to get used to it.

Once we're done stocking up on booze, we spend an hour getting the apartment ready. Lane shoves the couch back against the far wall and rearranges the living room, while I stack the cups. It takes me a few tries to get it right, and by the time I'm done, I never want to see a cup again.

"Is that what you're wearing, Heartbreak?"

I glance down. "Umm, yes?"

"So you don't plan on making an effort for my birthday?"

"Get over yourself."

Like I said: He's had enough niceness for one day.

I'M SO RELIEVED TO SEE Becca here, short pink dress and all—finally, a familiar face.

"You look incredible."

"You look . . . like you did earlier." She pouts. "You need to come over for a makeover sometime."

I laugh, handing her an empty cup. "Yeah, let's do that! What are you drinking?"

"Vodka?"

"Give me one sec."

The apartment is filling up fast, and it turns out, I don't mind making sure everyone has enough to drink. Keeps me busy.

I chat with Adam, trying my best to dodge Lewis and Carter. Lane is nice and charming to everyone except me. Standard.

"Lois!" he barks. "How about those cups?"

I shoot him a withering smile. He just loves to see me squirm, doesn't he? I head over to the pyramid I stacked earlier, and I already know this is going to be a toughie. Gripping the edges of the tray, I shuffle my way back across the room, congratulating myself on making it this far as I near the coffee table, almost forgetting my recent unlucky streak.

"Carter!" Adam shouts over from the couch. "Your sister's here!"

I turn to glance over at the front door just as Lane is slamming it shut. A couple are making their way into the apartment, and I freeze. A leggy brunette, with a guy I would unfortunately recognize anywhere. Gravity kicks in, the tray tilting to one side, and I watch as my perfect pyramid collapses to the ground. There's a voice that sounds a lot like Lane cussing, but I can't focus on anything other than the horror movie playing out in front of me.

"Happy birthday, Lane." The brunette flashes him a smile. She hasn't so much as glanced my way.

He leans over and kisses her cheek. "Thanks, Ju. Not working tonight?"

"Yeah, shift starts in an hour. We're just stopping by for a quick one."

The guy she's with rests his palm on the small of her back.

"Make yourself at home, dude," Lane says, holding out a hand.

"Hey," the guy says. "I'm Kirk."

That unlucky streak I mentioned? It just keeps on giving.

"Kirk?" Lane glances at me.

Yep. That would be *my* Kirk. The one who wanted space, all the better to squeeze in a new girlfriend.

7

LANE

Heartbreak looks shell-shocked. It doesn't take a genius to figure out who Kirk is. This is the guy who dumped her, and so, by extension, this is the guy who forced me into sharing my space. He's officially my least favorite person on this planet.

When she finally manages to tear her eyes away from him, Lois crumples to the ground with the cups, and once her ex spots her, he quickly looks away. He clearly didn't expect to see her here.

"Let me help you," I sigh, crouching down to join her.

"It's fine," she whimpers.

"Lois, you—"

"I'm dealing with it!"

"Okay."

I scan the room for Juliet and spot her and the dude standing by the window with a guy from the basketball team.

"What's up with Lois?" Adam asks as he watches her flailing around.

"That guy with Cart's sister? He's her ex."

"The one who threw her out?"

"That's the one."

"Is Lois about to puke?" Lewis walks over to join us. "Why's she making that face?"

Adam whispers in his ear, and Lewis whips around to eyeball Kirk.

"That guy? He signed to the basketball team; I know him. He shoots pretty well, but he runs like a rhino."

"What are you guys talking about?" Donovan has joined us. "Need help, Lois?"

She flaps one hand, clutching the cups to her chest with the other as she lunges for the kitchen. She drops the stacks in the sink, holding on to the counter for dear life.

"Now what have you done, Lane?" Don squints at me.

"Nothing to do with me, for once." I raise both my hands.

"Lois's ex rocked up with Juliet."

"So?"

"So it's not a great look." Lewis shakes his head.

"Facts. Not cool, man." He takes on a deep voice. "Do we need to take care of him?"

I watch Lois pour herself a beer, drinking it down in big gulps.

"I'll be right back, guys."

I sidle up beside her, looking straight ahead. "You okay?"

"Never been better," she mutters, her lips still pressed to her cup.

"Please tell me you aren't about to lose your shit."

She sighs and pours herself another drink. "Leave me alone, Lane."

"What? I'm worried, that's all! It can't feel too good."

She side-eyes me, and I smile at her.

"Are you . . . out of your mind?" she says slowly, biting the inside of her cheek.

"Why do you ask?"

"It's just the way you switch from Asshole of the Year to Mr. Nice Guy."

I spin toward the bottles on my left and start shaking up a cocktail in silence. When I turn to her, I whip her drink out of her hand before she has time to react.

"Give it back!" she snarls, clawing at my hand. "I need it!"

"I know. But try this, instead."

She raises an eyebrow and gives the cocktail a tentative sip before nodding.

"Thanks." She takes a few deep breaths. "I knew I should never have come. This is all your fault!" she snaps, suddenly furious.

"Meaning?"

"You forced me to come. And now I know that Carter's sister is the girl he's . . ."

"'He's' . . . ?"

"You know exactly what I mean. Anyway, whatever—this is all your fault!"

I open my mouth to reply, but her friend cuts us off.

"Can I talk to you, Lois?"

The girls drift off to the bathroom. As I watch them disappear around the corner, my curiosity gets the better of me. I follow them down the hall and lean against the wall, straining to hear through the door.

"Want to tell me what he's doing here with her?" Becca starts.

"Just getting some space," Lois says dully.

"Since when?"

"What?"

"When did it end?"

"A week ago."

"So why didn't you say something earlier?"

"I didn't think you'd care—"

"We're friends, of course I care!" Becca snaps. "And a single friend is the best kind, anyway."

I can't hear what Lois says to that.

"So where are you living?"

Muffled sounds.

"Wait. Where?"

I still can't hear.

"No freaking way! You got a horseshoe shoved up your ass, or something?!"

I press my ear closer to the door, but I still can't make out Heartbreak's voice, so I head back over to join my best friends around the coffee table. Unfortunately for Kirk, he's right there in my line of vision.

"So! How long you been screwing Juliet?" I start, falling back onto the couch.

He splutters on his drink, his eyes darting around the room, looking for Heartbreak, I'm sure.

"It's a recent thing." He coughs.

"Where's Lois?" Donovan has lowered his voice, but it's loud enough for Kirk to hear.

"In my room," I lie.

Don's smile widens as he realizes what I'm trying to do. I have no fucking clue why, but I'm getting a kick out of brushing this guy up the wrong way. The sweet taste of revenge—payback for him saddling me with a roommate I never wanted.

"Time to give Laney his surprise!" Lewis whips out a rectangular box. "Here, birthday boy. This is from all of us."

While I'm busy checking out the wrapping paper, the girls wander back over. I glance up. Lois looks awkward at being forced into the same room as Kirk, surrounded by all of us.

"Isn't this the same gift wrap as last year?"

"You know what Lewis is like." Adam laughs. "Of *course* it's the same. Folded up nice and neat in his 'birthday stuff' box."

"I got that one, too," adds Carter.

"Wrapping paper should be ripped and shredded!" Becca calls out, and the guys exchange glances. She doesn't know she's playing with fire.

"If he rips it, I'm slashing his tires," Lewis threatens.

He's deadly serious, and his wrapping paper obsession is serious, too. He keeps it all, no exceptions. And if I mess up peeling off the tape, he'll make me pay. I start unwrapping my gift like it's a bomb about to explode, Lewis watching me like a hawk, the others smirking.

"Wow, a car radio! This is insane, guys." I hold it up. "Thank you!"

"How old is that thing?" Becca leans over. "Is that from seventies?"

"We went for vintage vibes to match Lane's car," Don explains. "Don't be fooled, though, the features are crazy good."

Lewis holds out a hand for his precious paper. I get to my feet and thank my friends, leaving Juliet until last.

"Sorry, I gotta run." She tightens her braid. "Work calls."

"I'll come with you," Kirk says, too fast.

"Catch you later, guys!"

"See you soon, Kirk!" Carter raises his bottle.

"Or not," I snicker under my breath.

I hug Juliet goodbye, and when Kirk holds out an unsure hand, I shake it loosely, staring him square in the eye. I don't know Lois well at all, but I'm struggling to picture them as a couple. It makes me happy to think of how Juliet will chew him up and spit him back out without a second thought. With any luck, he'll be back in a flash to collect his lost property from my apartment, and everyone will get what they want and live happily ever after. The end. I glance behind me, following his gaze to where Lois is standing back in the kitchen, drinking a little too fast while chatting away to Carter and Becca. He frowns, turns back to the door, and leaves. He's been eyeing Lois ever since he caught sight of her here, but she's so hammered she hasn't even noticed.

The evening rolls by nice and chill, and as the booze, pizza, and video games flow, it doesn't take me long to forget all about Heartbreak.

"Looks like you'll be spending the night alone, Don." Lewis points over at Becca.

She's been draped over the kitchen island chatting to Carter for more than an hour now, and considering the way they're looking at each other, I'm willing to bet they won't be hanging around much longer. I realize that Lois, meanwhile, has vanished.

I stretch. "Okay, guys, party's over. Get the hell outta here."

Carter and Becca don't need asking twice, and as soon as they leave, the others follow suit. I walk them down to the sidewalk, hoping to get a little fresh air.

"Happy birthday again," Adam says when we get to his car. "Say good night to Lois for me."

I shrug.

"Try not to be too much of a douche to her, Lane. Put yourself in her shoes for a minute. This is pretty raw. She bumps into her ex with his new girlfriend, I mean—"

"Hey, you want to be her shoulder to cry on?" I force a smirk. "I'll swap her for Dexter Drake."

"Who?"

"Forget it."

"I know how you operate, dude. You've got no tolerance for sadness unless you decide it's justified. But people are allowed to suffer for all sorts of different things. Even a breakup."

I stare at him without flinching, and he knows what I'm telling him without me saying a word. He's smart enough not to push it.

When I get back upstairs, I slam the front door shut behind me.

"Coast is clear!" I yell.

Nothing. I stand there, unmoving. Silence. I scan the room for a sign of Heartbreak.

"Lois?"

She's not in the kitchen, and she's not on the couch, either. I swipe up the last remaining bottle of vodka from the coffee table and take a swig as I move down the hall. When I get to the bathroom, I slide open the door. Bull's-eye!

She's sitting on the tiles hugging her legs, knees tucked up beneath her chin, gently rocking back and forth. Despite the music pumping in from the living room and how she's doing her best to hold them back, I can hear the sobs from here.

I clear my throat, but she doesn't look up. I take another swig and slouch in the doorway. I instinctively want to tease her—not in a mean way, just to take the edge off the situation—but she opens her mouth before I can speak.

"I'm sorry, Lane."

The sincerity in her voice catches me off guard. "For what?"

"I know it's your birthday."

"Yeah, now that you mention it: Where's my gift?"

My joke falls flat.

"And I know she's your best friend's sister," she continues, "but I hate her."

She sounds so sad, I don't know what to say.

"She's beautiful, she's totally snatched, and to make it worse, she's funny, too. Super confident, amazing hair." Lois shakes her head. "I bet she has the softest skin. Bet she's wild in bed."

I'm about to break into laughter when she bursts into tears, covering her face with her hands. The way she was wallowing in self-pity pissed me off earlier, but now I actually feel sorry for her. I think back to what Adam said, and I hate to admit it, but he's right. While she's spent days in full-blown depression mode, her ex was already out banging someone else. I feel myself soften, and I roll my eyes. Since when do I give a shit about girls and their sob stories?

"I can't compete," she mumbles.

That throws me off, and I suddenly decide that though I might regret this, I need to spill some of the secrets Juliet made me swear I would always keep. I've known Carter's sister since we were kids, and she's definitely not leagues ahead of Lois.

"Are we talking about the same girl? She's had a squishy nose ever since a girl in high school headbutted her; I've got a photo of her somewhere with bruises around her eyes and a shapeless potato in the middle of her face. I'll show you some time."

Lois sniffs, meeting my gaze in the mirror. "Really?"

"I even have a photo of her with puke in her hair. It's at the back of a closet somewhere. Would it make you feel better to see it sometime?"

She rubs her eyes. "No, it's okay."

Not sure why, but I'm trying to coax a smile out of her. There's still some way to go. She spends the next minute staring at herself in the mirror with her shoulders shaking, and just when it looks like she's evened out, a fresh wave of tears come streaming down her cheeks. *Shit!*

I sigh and crouch beside her. "Lois."

"Not now, Lane. Please. Save it for tomorrow."

"I wasn't going to tease you!"

"Sure you weren't."

"If it's any comfort, Juliet has more of a one-night-only approach to relationships."

"So what?" She sniffles, clamping her eyes shut. "What hurts is that I can't kid myself anymore. She's everything Kirk ever wanted, everything he said I wasn't . . ."

I frown. "Meaning?"

"He said . . ."

She bites her lip, fiddles with her sleeve, like the words are too painful to say. I don't know what comes over me, but I drop drown to sit behind her, propping my legs on either side of hers.

"Come on, Heartbreak. Spill."

I rest an elbow on my knee and tilt my head for a better view of her in the mirror.

"I know you think I'm so lame right now—"

"Which means you have nothing to lose by carrying on." I give her a gentle nudge. "You can only go up in my estimation."

"He said there was too much new stuff to try at college, and he didn't want to have any regrets. He thought I was too boring, too predictable, not skinny enough, and—"

"Are you for real? 'Not skinny enough'?"

"He didn't say it like that, exactly. But I put on a little weight over the past few months, and according to him, I was letting myself go . . ."

"Kirk is an absolute jerk." I spit the last word out. "See? It even rhymes. Even just his name is enough to make you barf. *Kiiiirk.*" I say it over and over, making it sound like I'm puking, and her eyes widen through the tears. Suddenly, she bursts out giggling, and I practically jump out of my skin. I realize this is the first time I've heard her laugh, and she must be thinking the same, because she stops as soon as she started.

"My brother Jeff said the exact same thing last year. He'll be happy to hear I've been dumped, at least."

It's the first time she's mentioned her family, and though I'm curious to hear more, I don't ask. I don't want her to throw the question back at me. That's off-limits.

"It looks like he's moved on," I try. "That might help you do the same, don't you think? What if *you* made the most of all the new stuff college has to offer, too?"

She lets out a raspy groan, something between a laugh and a growl.

"I miss him. I don't know who I am without Kirk." She stares at the ground. "We grew up together, I built everything I was around us, and now I'm lost. I want my life back."

A veil of shame clouds her eyes, and I realize she's just voiced a truth that's hard to swallow. It takes everything I have not to tell her what I really think—which is that this is the dumbest thing I've ever heard. I'm way out of my comfort zone here. In fact, I'm probably the worst person for this situation.

"You'll be back on your feet in no time. You just started college; you're in your prime!"

Look at you, Mr. Guru!

"No, you're not getting it." She shakes her head furiously. "I want my life with *him* back. That's what I want." Her tone has shifted. "That's what I'm going to do!"

I snort. "Are you saying you plan on molding yourself to fit his totally unrealistic expectations in the hope you'll get him back?"

"Yup."

"That's not how it works, Lois. You can't be what you're not, trust me!"

"What would you know?" She narrows her eyes.

"Easy there, Heartbreak! I might suck at relationship stuff, but you don't need to be a genius to know your idea sucks."

"I need to become the best version of myself."

I can practically hear her brain fizzing. Her hand slips off her leg and reaches for the bottle of vodka in front of us, and with each fresh gulp, she nods her head harder. Whatever plan she is busy hatching, she seems to be in agreement with herself, at least. There's a light shining in her eyes, and it's almost kind of scary. I ease the bottle out of her hand.

"I think you've had enough."

I give what little is left a shake and knock it back in a single shot. Just as I'm about to swallow, I freeze, my arm hovering in midair, the bottle pressed to my lips. Lois has fallen back against my chest, her hair tickling my chin. The scent of her shampoo fills the space between us, and a fluttering makes its way to the pit of my stomach. *That's what I get for having too much to drink.*

I want to get up, but her back is heavy against my chest, and I don't dare move. She's still lost in thought, and I'm guessing she hasn't realized just how close we are now. She's not the type to be coming on to me, and so I wait for her to put some distance between us.

A few minutes later, and I'm getting impatient. When she finally staggers to her feet and slips out of the room in silence, I'm expecting to feel relieved, but as it turns out, I don't. I blink, jumping to my feet way too fast. My head is spinning. I can't seem to catch my breath.

I listen as the fridge opens and shuts, and head back to the living room, where Lois is knocking back a beer on her couch— What am I saying? On *my* couch!

"I'm wondering: Does Kirk have a soft spot for alcoholics, too?"

"Beer helps me think," she replies hoarsely.

That's the problem with booze. What seems like an amazing

fucking idea when you're drunk turns out to be a car crash the next day. I swipe up the remote from the counter and fall back next to her with a sigh, channel surfing for a while until I find a baseball game, and though I try to focus on the play, my eyes keep drifting over to her.

"I know what you're thinking." She glares at me.

I lift an eyebrow. "Really?"

"Yeah." She shifts in her seat. "*I can feel your bad vibes from here, you party pooper!* Happy birthday, by the way."

What? I barely have time to register the subject change when suddenly she's on her knees on the couch, jabbing a finger at me, eyes wild with defiance.

"I'm gonna show him I can be just the kind of girl he wants," she crows. "I'm gonna change. Starting tomorrow. And you know what? Soon, you'll be thanking me!"

"Oh, really?"

"Yes, sir! Once I've changed, you won't have to deal with my fat ass on your couch."

"Come on now, Lois—"

"Nope! Nuh-uh!" She cuts me off, pressing her index finger to my lips with all the gentleness of a girl who's truly wasted.

"Is that really what you want?"

"Yes," she breathes out, settling back into the cushions. "Yes," she repeats, as if she's just seen the light, and the revelation has drained every last drop of energy out of her. "There's no point feeling sorry for myself. I need a goal, and this one's perfect."

I shrug. At the end of the day, she can do what she likes. I couldn't care less. And though I think the whole thing is a load of crap, at least she's managed an entire ten minutes without crying. That's got to be a record. If a wild plan is what it takes to get her back on her feet, then so be it. I'm sick and tired of hearing her sniffling away, and if this idea of hers gets her out of my apartment sooner than planned, then I'm all for it.

She sinks back into silence, and I do the same, absent-mindedly picking at the couch, smiling when I hear soft snores floating up from my right. I have never seen anyone fall asleep that fast. I glance over at her, wondering how the hell I ever agreed to what's turning out to be the weirdest roommate situation ever. I want my apartment to myself again, but I have to admit that having her here takes my mind off things.

I whisk the beer out of her hand and turn back to the TV. I'll wait until the end of the inning, and then head to bed. That's the plan, anyway.

8

LOIS

As soon as I open my eyes, there's a pounding in my head. I regret last night so bad. My shoulder is numb from being squashed between the cushions for so long. I blink a few times to clear my vision, and the first thing I see makes me recoil. A huge toe is practically sticking up my nose, leading down to a hairy leg lying alongside my body. I crane my neck, trying to figure out what I'm looking at here.

"You have got to be kidding me."

Lane is fast asleep on *my* couch, his head at my feet, his skull wedged into the armrest. We're slotted together in the weirdest of positions, one of my legs laced between his, pulling his T-shirt tight against his chest, my other leg slung over his hip. What the hell is he doing here?

"Hello?!"

I try to wriggle under the weight, but he's blocking pretty much every movement I try. The only thing I can move is my left foot. Lane is so much taller than me, and even when I stretch my leg out, my toes barely reach his neck. *Just* a little push, and I kick blindly at his face. He groans, shoving my foot away.

"Lane!"

I try again—this time my heel hits him square on his chin. I mean, I know I owe him, but this is way out of line.

"Okay, that's enough!" I yell as loud as I can. "Get off my couch! Now!"

He stiffens, slowly lifting his head, taking in my painted toenail, trailing along my calf and hip, his gaze finally meeting mine.

I stare at him with a murderous look. "Sleep well?" I ask.

He squints, shaking his head. I watch as he takes in our tangled limbs.

"Yup, that's right." I sweep the air with my hand. "Still here."

"You've got big feet." His voice is husky.

I open my mouth, but I don't even know what to say to him. I mean, I do have one idea, but then I remember that for the next little while my fate is in his hands.

"Move," I snarl.

"You first."

"I would if I weren't kind of trapped right now."

We stare each other down for a moment, and I steel myself for one of his swipes. He flashes me a broad smile.

"I can't wait until you get your guy back."

"Finally, one thing we can agree on."

He stretches, forcing me to shove his foot out of my face, and grabs one of my calves, pushing my leg into a pretty unladylike position. Free, at long last!

While he pours himself a coffee, I stretch out over the full length of the couch, easing my sore muscles. As memories of last night resurface, it doesn't take long for my inner calm to fade. Fresh tears are welling up in my eyes.

"Don't, Lois," I mutter to myself. "Enough of the pity party. It's time to fight back!"

When I get to the end of my pep talk, I give the cushions a sharp punch and straighten.

"Don't mind me," Lane taunts me from the kitchen counter.

I point at him. "You will not ruin this day. You're dead to me. You're not even here."

"Wow. I need some of whatever you're taking."

"Who's that?" I singsong my way to the bathroom. "I can hear distant voices..."

He snorts, and I can't help but smile as I shut the door behind me. Before I jump in the shower, I stand in front of the sink, examining my face in the mirror. I need a change. Something radical. And there's only one person for the job. Once I'm done, I step out of the foggy bathroom and get straight on the phone.

"Becca, I need your help," I say, cutting her groggy "hello" short.

She yawns.

Lane is watching me over his cup of coffee. He hasn't budged an inch. I drift over to the window so as not to trigger any snark.

"I need you to help me be more..." I think for a moment. "Be better, basically."

It takes her a while to get the words out. "What are you wearing?"

"What?"

"Right now. What are you wearing?"

"Umm...leggings?"

"Jesus. Get your ass over here."

She hangs up. I stare at my phone, taking a moment to let it all sink in, before crouching over my bag. It's still full of stuff. Lane hasn't offered to share his closet, but it's not like I have much, anyway. I pull out my sneakers and lace them up in silence.

"Need a driver?"

"I'm good, thanks."

I stuff my earbuds in, connect them to my phone, and wave goodbye to the world's worst roommate.

I could have taken Lane up on his offer, but today is the first day of the rest of my life, with raw greens, lean protein, and lots of working out high up on the intentions list. I stride toward the campus with a determined spring in my step. My old sneakers aren't right for this, and I make a note to stop by the mall as soon as I'm done with Becca.

Pushing open the doors to her dorm, the stairs up to her room are the final nail in the coffin: By the time I arrive, I'm drenched, mopping my forehead with my wrist before knocking at her door three times.

"Come in!"

I hold back a stab of envy as I take in her space. I hate not having my own place.

"Did you walk here?" Becca peers at me. "You look like you're about to puke."

"Just last night's afterglow," I sigh, letting my bag fall to the floor.

I spin around, taking in the small room. I was right that I couldn't crash here—the place is tiny, shared between her and some girl named Carrie, who I can hear snoring from the bed farthest away. Lane's couch is definitely the comfier option.

"Ready for a makeover? Because I'm pretty sure this qualifies as an emergency." She sizes me up. "Want a Coke?"

"Water would be great."

She skips her way to the bathroom, returning with a tumbler.

"So what happened last night? I couldn't find you when I left."

"Sure you were looking properly?" I wink at her. "It must have been kind of hard to see, what with Carter glued to your face and everything."

She wiggles her eyebrows at me. "Trust me, it was more than just his face."

"Eww! I thought you were aiming for Donovan, anyway?"

"Nah. I'm crushing hard on Carter now. And no, I don't get it, either."

"He's nice. I have no idea how he can be friends with Lane."

She shrugs. "I think they've known each other since they were kids."

"That makes sense."

"How are you feeling, anyway?"

"Hard pass." I massage my temples.

"I don't know how you kept your cool last night. I would've been ripping the place up."

"It wouldn't have made a difference."

"True . . . Okay!" She claps her hands. "Ready for your new vibe? What are you thinking?"

She leads me over to the full-length mirror and stands behind me, chin resting on my shoulder. I take in the loser reflected back at me and sigh.

"I feel like getting tattoos, dyeing my hair blue, and having my nose pierced." The words come streaming out of me.

"Right . . . Let's start with a decent haircut, okay?" Becca tussles my hair and then looks over her shoulder.

"Carrie! Get up!" Becca shrieks, and I pull a face.

The hangover is still pounding in my eardrums, the image of Kirk and Juliet still floating before my eyes.

"What?" a voice groans from the bed.

"I need your hairdresser skills for my friend Lois here."

I watch in the mirror as a sheet flutters, and a blond head peeks out from under the covers.

"When was your last cut?" She peers at me, yawning.

"Let's just say it's been a while . . ."

"I'm warning you, I don't do trims. I'm an all-or-nothing kinda girl."

"Be my guest," I say, twirling a lock around my finger.

She heaves herself out of bed and goes into the bathroom, reemerging with a pair of scissors, a comb, and a bowl of water.

"Once she's done, I'll tackle your skin," Becca adds. "It's gross."

"I'd throw in a little brow shaping, too," says Carrie as she leans over my shoulder. "I don't even want to imagine what's going on with your bikini line."

"What's that got to do with anything?"

"One look at the brows, and I know the lawn ain't mowed! If you get me."

"She knows her stuff, she waxes half the vajayjays on campus. You can trust her."

My eyes dart down to my lower belly, and I scrunch up my nose.

"I guessed as much." Carrie laughs, dipping her comb in the water. "Don't worry! One step at a time, okay? Let's start with this haystack you've got going on here."

Nerves shoot through me as I watch her play with the scissors right near my ear. "Have you done this before?"

"Only about a thousand times."

She rolls her desk chair over to me, and gets me to sit down. I might not cross myself, but in my head, I'm rattling off every prayer I know.

When I hear the first snip, I stiffen and do my best to ignore the long strand of hair that has just floated to the ground. I dig my nails into the armrests and let my eyes fall shut for a few minutes.

Before I know it, the chair is spinning around. A wave of nausea rises from the pit of my stomach, though that could just be the hangover. My tummy starts to gurgle.

"Want some?"

I open one eye to find Becca waving a bag of chips in my face.

"No, thanks. My junk food days are behind me." I can feel myself blushing.

"That's a shame. They're really good." Becca shrugs. "Why do you want to lose weight, anyway? Oh, that's right! Because you want your dumbass ex-boyfriend back."

"Seriously?" My stylist seems shocked. "Am I allowed to say that's the lamest thing I've ever heard?"

"I'm doing it for myself, too," I say unconvincingly.

"Juliet isn't all that, you know," Becca tries to reassure me. She shoves a fistful of chips into her mouth. "And anyway, she's Carter's sister. It makes sense she has this aura about her. It's like Lane. There's stuff that's just innate."

"What do you mean?"

"Just the thought of that guy is enough to get me ovulating."

I shake my head. "Ew. Not me."

"Praise the Lord!" Carrie claps. "Finally, someone who isn't obsessed with the Campus Drivers!"

"Ignore her." Becca sighs. "Her only crushes are guys in books." She juts her chin toward the enormous bookshelf taking up half the room, wiping her fingers down on her pajama top. "Anyway, my turn to make you over! I've got a whole closet of clothes I never wear. Lemme put together a few outfits for you."

"You don't have to . . ."

"Shush it! And the new haircut looks incredible by the way."

"Really?"

I still haven't summoned the courage to look. All I can do is trust how eagerly she's smiling at me.

Becca spends the next hour dressing and undressing me a couple of dozen times. Weirdly, the clothes she gives me actually suit me, and she insists on applying a little light makeup, too. When finally I turn back to the full-length mirror, my mouth falls open.

"You like?"

I stare at my hair, or what's left of it. Carrie chopped off a good twelve inches or so. I examine my long bob in silence, turning my head this way and that.

"I'll get used to it."

It sounds more like I'm asking a question, and Carrie bursts out laughing.

"It'll be fine, Lois." She pats me on the shoulder. "You're really pretty, you know."

I take in the rest of my makeover. "I'm not sure about this top."

Becca jabs a finger at my chest. "Your boobs looks amazing in it!"

"Isn't it a little short? I don't like how it shows my stomach."

I tug on the fabric, but it bounces back up to graze my belly button.

"Gosh, Lois. It's a cropped top. Everyone wears them."

It's the kind of logic that doesn't land right when you're talking to a leggings-and-hoodie girl like me.

"I don't know . . ."

"I'm the fashion coach here." My stylist puts her hands on her hips. "You're the student!"

"Want me to check out the situation 'down there'?" Carrie asks.

I stiffen. "I think we've done enough for today."

"You're the boss."

"I'm gonna hit the road; I have some shopping to do."

"That's the spirit!" Becca strikes a warrior pose. "Go forth and be hot!"

I laugh. "Have a great day, girls. And thank you for everything."

On my way to the mall, I can't help but check myself out in every window I pass. It's going to take time to get used to it, but I'm pretty pleased with the result.

I spend sixty bucks on sportswear and another thirty at the grocery store. I'm starving, and the food stuffed into my bags isn't exactly the kind of thing to get a girl's mouth watering, but where there's a will, there's a way—I guess.

I stop to catch my breath at the door to Lane's building, placing my bags down by my feet to rest my sore arms. When I get to Kirk's floor, I take my sweet time, desperately hoping to bump into him, listening closely as I walk past his door. I don't stop.

By the time I reach the fifth floor, I'm dying. And I'm praying that Lane is still home, too, because I've only just remembered something pretty important: I don't have keys to his place. I press my elbow down on the handle and thank my lucky stars when it gives way and the door swings open. I'm so relieved to have made it inside that it takes me a second to notice the five pairs of eyes swiveling to stare at me.

"Hey . . . guys."

Carter and the four Campus Drivers are gathered in the living room. None of them have said a word. They're all sitting there staring like the devil himself just stepped through the door, and it takes Lewis a moment to break the silence.

"Who are you, ma'am?"

That's when it clicks. They've been stunned into silence by my makeover. The blood rushes to my cheeks.

"D-don't mind me," I stammer as I lunge for the fridge. "I'll be right out of your way."

I can hear them whispering, and it makes me want to disappear into the fridge somewhere between the burgers and the beers. I stuff my supplies into the crisper and hover behind the fridge door.

I sneak a glance over at them. They're still watching me.

"Anyone want a beer?" I say, my voice a bit squeaky.

Adam smiles. "Me! Come join us, I'll scoot over."

"No, don't worry, I've got plans." I grab a chilled bottle and hold it out to him, stretching my arm as far as it will go.

"You look really good," he says, bringing the bottle to his lips.

"Oh . . . Thanks."

"I've got a feeling Dexter Drake will be heading back to LA as soon as he can," Donovan says, elbowing Lewis.

I frown and step back, confused.

"You don't do things by halves, Heartbreak."

Lane's telltale deep, snarky voice. I should never have let the booze loosen my lips the way it did last night. I hate that now he knows what he does about me, and I can't decide how to reply. I'm overwhelmed by a desperate urge to get the hell out of here.

I shuffle back to the plastic bag I left in the hall, dart into the bathroom, and lock the door. I need to ditch my old clothes and change into the brand-new sportswear I've just bought myself, and I need to dig deep for the courage to walk back out there past the guys without looking like I'm running away.

You know what? Fuck 'em! I wiggle my toes in my shiny new sneakers, take a deep breath in, and swing the door open, primed to sprint straight past them.

Bam.

I run straight into an unmovable mass.

I don't need to look up to know who it is, I can tell it's Lane just by the amazing smell of his T-shirt. *Oh God, what is wrong with you, Lois?*

He still hasn't moved.

"Can I help you?" I snap. "What are you doing lurking here?"

He doesn't say a word. I get the feeling he's waiting for something, and when I can't take the silence anymore, I give in and look up, finding him staring at me.

"What?" I sigh, tugging on my tank. "Got something you want to share with the class? Warm-up tips, maybe?"

The words come spilling out, and he just stands there, still as a statue.

"No? Nothing? Amazing! If you don't mind, then, I need to get going. My plan is to go for a run *and* look for a place along the way. See what a great multitasker I am?"

I haven't even started running yet, and I'm already out of breath. Great!

I'm about to barge past him, when he steps aside and lets me by, and just as I make to leave, he speaks.

"I like the hair."

I freeze. I turn back to face him.

"What?"

I must have misheard.

"It suits you," he adds.

The conversation is beyond weird. This isn't the Lane I'm used to. This guy is seriously unpredictable. *Ugh, he drives me crazy.*

"Why are you so . . ."

"Sweet?" he finishes for me.

"Exhausting!" I correct, tucking my hair behind my ears.

He shrugs and slouches against the wall. The way he swings between being mean and playing Mr. Nice Guy is giving me whiplash. I honestly have no idea whether he's serious or messing with me.

He's back to staring at me in silence so I turn to leave before things get even weirder.

"Well! On that note, see you later."

Before I reach the living room, I can't help but stop in my tracks.

"Thank you, by the way," I whisper.

I don't turn back.

9

LANE

Ever since Lois got her new haircut and decided she was going to run her way across the entire town, she's in and out of the apartment every day in her bright pink sneakers and even brighter workout tanks. She's committed, I'll give her that. But I know how people usually roll: There's a sudden rush of motivation and two days of fasting before they go crashing off the rails with an entire cheat month. But it's been a week now, and Lois is still sticking to her stupid hardcore diet, even as I'm digging into an extra-large pizza.

"Not even the smallest sliver of a slice?" I try again through a full mouth.

"Not even that," she snaps back. "I haven't put in all this work to screw up over a bit of stringy cheese."

"There's pepperoni, too."

"I know." She takes a deep breath in and closes her eyes, smoothing back her sweat-drenched hair and clenching her jaw. "I'm gonna jump in the shower, and then I'm out of here."

"Where you going?"

"I saw an ad for water aerobics classes at the pool."

"Okay."

Standing there in the middle of the living room, she falls silent. There's the strangest look in her eyes.

"What?" I ask, squinting.

"This..." She waves a finger back and forth between us.

"This what?"

"This feels like an actual conversation." She tilts her head. "It's weird."

As she heads off to the bathroom, I toss my pizza crust back in the box and stretch out on the couch. Lois has a point: Things are weird. It's been two weeks since she moved in, and I sometimes forget she shouldn't even be here. In my defense, she's super quiet and makes an effort to be nice, even when I try my hardest to get a rise out of her. It's a fun little game I've really come to enjoy, and I especially love it when she tries and fails to rein in her snarky replies.

I don't know how far she's gotten in finding an apartment, but I make a point of reminding her every day that our agreement has an expiration date, simply to see if she'll bite. It's just so easy to push her buttons!

"Clock's ticking, Heartbreak!" I shout as she emerges from the bathroom freshly changed.

"How could I forget?"

She crouches down to stuff her phone into her bag, frowning as she straightens.

"What's up? Muscles sore?"

"A little," she concedes, clasping her ankle and pulling it behind her to stretch her thigh. "I forgot I even had any."

"Where did you say you were going?"

"To the pool at the gym—the one next to the mall."

"Same. I can give you a ride."

"You're heading to the pool?" She shifts to her other leg, raising an eyebrow at me.

"The mall."

"So would this ride be free?" She lets her foot drop to the floor.

"Stop overthinking everything, Heartbreak." I drag myself off the couch, slip on my shoes, and grab my keys from the side table. "So?"

"Okay, but drop me off away from the entrance."

"What, like I'm your father dumping you around the corner from school so you don't look lame in front of your friends?" I gasp, pausing for dramatic effect, and clamp a hand over my mouth. "Oh my God! I said the D-word. The *forbidden* word."

"No, *not* like my dad, because *he* was never embarrassing," she fires back, heading for the stairs.

I have no comeback to that, and it pisses me off. She is so unbelievably annoying. First she took my couch, now she's coming for my one-liners. I head for the elevator instead.

When I get outside, she's hovering in front of my car, staring up at the building. I don't need to ask her what she's looking for. Or *who* she's looking for, to be more precise.

I pat my car roof. "Let's hit the road."

She sighs, teasing a lock of hair between her fingers. "Yeah."

"Let me guess: sweetie pie Kirk has yet to meet the new-and-improved Lois?"

"Nope. I get the feeling he's avoiding me." As we settle into our seats, she mutters under her breath. "Do you know whether he's still seeing Juliet?"

"No idea. We can stop off at the bar, if you want."

"Together?" She sounds so surprised, it's borderline insulting.

"Oh, good point." I roll my eyes at her. "We hang out on the couch like friends, we talk like friends, but you're so right: going for beers would definitely be a step too far."

I hit the gas.

"Why are you smiling like that?"

"Like what?" I glance at her out of the corner of my eye.

"I can't put my finger on it. You've got this weird grin going on."

"Just the Heartbreak effect, I guess."

She shakes her head and turns up the radio, and as the car fills with sound, I'm surprised to hear her singing along to the lyrics. If there's one thing I like about this girl, it's her taste in music.

She plays on her phone as I drive, pulling faces, sniffling, so focused on her screen she doesn't notice when I pull into the main parking lot.

I turn the engine off and slip an arm around her backrest for a closer look at what she's doing.

"Stalking your ex is not a good look," I whisper in her ear.

She startles, dropping her phone and cussing at me under her breath as she fishes it off the floor.

She gets out and heads into the gym, shooting me dirty looks as she goes, and the urge to follow her into the building is too strong to resist. I'm in the mood to get under her skin.

"Now who's the stalker?"

"Maybe I'm really interested in synchronized swimming," I drawl.

"I knew I should've walked. Don't you have anything better to do on a Saturday afternoon? Seriously?"

"I want to support you in living your best life, Heartbreak."

"You could start by getting your own life," she snaps. "Just any kind of life would do."

Now we're on a roll!

I take a step closer, bringing my face inches from hers. "And *you* could start by getting your own place."

She meets my gaze head-on. Doesn't flinch. Doesn't blink. It's like she's daring me to look away first. There's a spark in her eyes I can't tear myself away from. Before I can stop myself, I'm leaning even closer.

She tilts her head. "Is it me, or are you slightly cross-eyed?"

A burst of laughter escapes me. And as she turns back to the gym's front desk, I catch the faintest trace of a smile tugging at her lips.

The receptionist straightens as we draw closer.

"I saw an ad for water aerobics classes," Lois starts. "I was hoping to sign up. I figured if I came in today, I could maybe jump into a class right away."

"Sorry, but registration opened at the start of summer. You're too late, the only slots left are for senior citizens. And you'd need to bring a medical certificate, anyway. We can't let anyone in the pool until those are cleared."

"Karma," I murmur.

Lois's brow furrows. "What if I attend the senior classes and give up my spot if you end up needing it?"

The receptionist looks taken aback by Lois's idea, but I'm not. If there's one thing this girl is, it's stubborn.

Lois flashes her an eager smile.

"I'm not sure, we've never been asked before. But the instructor is right there, let me ask him." She calls across the room. "Ethan, can you come over here a second?"

I turn my head and watch as a beaming guy walks across the room to join us. I roll my eyes as I take in his khaki tank and tiny swim shorts. He's openly checking Lois out and reeks of chlorine and testosterone. I get the sudden urge to trip him right out of his dumb slides.

"How can I help?"

"This young lady wants to take your class, but the only slots available are with the senior citizens. She's suggesting she attend anyway, and says she'll free up her spot if needed."

"Is it just you, or will your boyfriend be joining?" He juts his chin at me.

"My what?" Lois swings around to me, her eyes widening as it clicks. "Oh, he's not my boyfriend. I actually have no clue who this guy is." She smirks at me before turning back to the pool dude.

I cross my arms.

"I'd really love to take the class. Please?"

He's a good foot taller than her. In fact, he's exactly my height, which means I have a front-row ticket to how creepily he's staring at her. He's leading a fucking water aerobics class, and he's giving her the once-over like he's holding a girlfriend audition.

"I don't see a problem with that." He scratches his chin. "Fair warning, though—the grandmas definitely won't be letting you into the front row, so as long as you're not worried about going head-to-head with some badass retirees, then welcome!"

"I'll stay at the back; they won't even notice I'm there."

"That's for sure." He laughs, his eyes trailing her from head to toe. "They're pretty into me—no lie," he adds with a sorry-not-sorry pout.

Real smooth...

He claps his hands. "I'll let you get on with the paperwork, then. See you soon!"

"Thank you so much, I can't wait to get started!"

While Lois and the receptionist run through the details, I replay the scene in my head. *That guy was such a douche.* When she turns away from the desk, she slams into me and takes a step back, scowling.

"*'I can't wait to get started!'*" I parrot back to her in a high-pitched voice.

"Oh, give me a break! This is a full-body workout, I'm about to get ripped."

"Doing baby squats in a pool full of seniors three seconds away from breaking a hip?"

She frowns. "You are so..."

"Wise?"

"Definitely not!"

"Incredible?"

"Try again."

She starts walking, and I pick up the pace to match her stride.

"Don't you have somewhere to be, Lane?"

"Sure thing."

"So what are you waiting for?"

I point ahead of us. "It's this way."

"Oh, really? In that case, I'll head the other way. Have a great day!"

She slips out the front doors, aiming straight for the mall, and disappears into the thick Saturday afternoon crowds. I think she's the first girl to ever stand up to me like that. And kind of the first I have this much fun with. When I think back to all her teary meltdowns, I can hardly believe this is the same Lois.

A group of kids jostle me as they pass by, and I suddenly realize I'm in the way, frozen in place and staring at the space she left behind. I drift around the mall, grab a coffee to go, and pick up a couple of T-shirts without even trying them on.

On my way back to the car, my phone buzzes with a new trip request. When I pull up outside the building, the girl who ordered the ride hasn't arrived yet. I get out of my car and lean against the shining hood, watching clusters of students as they walk by, checking out girls as they come and go, and it's at this point I realize I haven't slept with a girl for a while now. Not since Lois forced her way into my place, actually. *Oh man, that absolutely won't do.* I look down. My phone is ringing.

"Carter," I drawl as I pick up. "Been a while."

"Shane Winfield has invited us to a party." He can barely contain his excitement. "You, me. His house, tonight."

It's like my best friend has read my desperate mind.

"Works for me."

"Sweet! Pick me up at nine?"

"Let's do it."

"Dress to impress, dude. All his latest actresses will be there."

Winfield is a huge producer. Massive. He just won an award, and hanging out with him is a fast-track ticket to some amazing opportunities. His parties are always next-level, too: I already know I won't be going home alone tonight.

"My ride is here, Cart. Catch you later."

I slip the phone into my pocket, head back around the car, and open the rear door.

My passenger is a cute redhead, and she's looking at me strangely.

"You're good?"

"Yes!" she squeaks, clambering into her seat.

I laugh to myself as I slink into the front. I glance in the rearview mirror, watching her get tangled in her backpack straps, yanking too hard on the seat belt, making it catch. When she finally gets herself buckled in, she's blushing hard.

"First time?" I quip, turning the key in the ignition.

"Ummm . . . yes."

She can't meet my gaze, and so I turn my attention back to the road without a word. I'm used to Campus Drivers newbies—the ones who unfailingly crush on their driver.

When I pull up outside her dorm, she seems a little disappointed I got her home so fast, babbling something I don't catch on her way out. I wink in response to her wave and screech off into the night.

Pushing open my front door, the apartment is silent and still. I have no idea what time Lois plans on getting home. I hope she remembered to take the spare keys I gave her last week, after she spent two hours locked out in the hall, clenching her jaw when I implied that she must be used to hanging around in stairwells by now. I honestly don't know what's wrong with me, but pushing her buttons is just too fucking satisfying. I tell myself it's payback for letting her crash on my couch, but the truth is I'm not so sure.

I pull on my go-to outfit, the one that works for both impressing big-deal producers *and* picking up actresses. My friends can make fun of me all they want. Deep down, I know they're just jealous of the bombshells I bring home. The kind of girls I can hook up with and forget—and that's exactly what I want.

I HAD A FEW DRINKS at Winfield's, but I'm not drunk. The only reason my head is spinning is April and the breast she's been trying to feed me since we stepped into my building. She spent the whole evening sniffing around me and then planted herself in my lap. Now here we are in my elevator.

"We're going to have fun," she breathes into my ear as I lift her up against the elevator wall.

She wraps her legs around my hips, and I slowly ease my hand to her ass.

"You're not wearing anything..." I moan into her mouth.

"I left a souvenir in your car," she purrs, pressing herself into me.

"Smart move."

I grapple for my keys with my other hand and throw open the door, watching as it batters the hallway wall, kicking it shut with my heel as April carries on, sucking my tongue.

The living room is pitch black. My hands are on her ass, sliding her skirt up over her hips. She's so wet my fly is soaked through. My head is spinning. All I can think about is the sweet moment I finally get to slide into her. I'm not thinking straight, and that's really too bad. Because just as I lay April down on my couch, I forget it's already taken.

10

LOIS

The dream I'm having is amazing. I'm strolling along a golden beach, in front of me is a man running by the water's edge. In my mind, it's Kirk, even though the body and dark hair look more like Lane, which I'm kind of frustrated about. I hear a door slam somewhere in the distance, and a faraway giggle as sand fills the space between my toes. I feel good. I keep my distance from the lapping waves, and that's weird, because I suddenly feel like my feet are wet. The landscape retreats farther into the distance, the sun is fading, I can feel something pressing into me, and . . .

"Ow!" I scream as a weight crushes my ankles.

A whine stirs me from sleep. "There's someone on the couch!"

"Ya think?" I mutter, slowly coming to my senses.

"Shit," Lane breathes out. "I forgot about her . . ."

I blink to clear my vision, and I can see the outline of a girl's face frozen in shock and Lane fumbling with his pants. Suddenly, I'm blinded by light, and as my eyes refocus, I can't believe what I'm seeing: a leggy girl standing by the couch, tugging her skirt down over her ass. My toes are glistening in the half-dark, and as I look from them to her and back again, it all falls into place. My feet are soaked, and it has nothing to do with my seaside dream.

"Oh. My. God!"

I jolt off the couch, nearly slipping, and start hopping in place.

"Come on, Lois. Don't be so dramatic," Lane mutters.

My mouth drops open. *Screw the gratitude.*

"Dramatic? Are you fucking kidding me, Lane?" I screech.

"Is this some kind of sick joke?" his hookup snaps, whipping around to glare at him. "Is she your girlfriend, Lane?"

"Wow, she's not my girlfriend," Lane blurts with his hands raised.

"He's *absolutely* not my boyfriend," I snap.

"Hey!" Lane looks actually offended.

The girl looks between us, then shakes her head. "You guys are messed up." She snatches her bag off the floor. "Enjoy your little domestic disaster!" And with that, she storms out, slamming the door behind her.

As soon as she's gone, I hiss, "Imagine if I were lying the other way around! I could have suffocated!"

Ignoring me, Lane throws himself on the couch with a frustrated groan. "Thanks for ruining my night, by the way."

"You're very welcome! I'm going to go wash my feet now. Actually, you know what?" I correct myself. "I'm going to bleach them. Maybe I'll even cut them off!"

I shuffle carefully to the bathroom so I don't slip, step into the shower, and turn the water on. Who cares if it's still icy cold? I need to scrub that gunk off my toes.

"Unbelievable." I shake my head.

I grab Lane's shower gel and empty it without a second thought. I am usually careful not to use his stuff, but this time, he got what was coming to him.

When I step out a few minutes later, I decide to grab one of his towels. It barely reaches mid-thigh but it'll do. No *way* I'm using one of the only two towels I own for this.

"I can't find the bleach, but how about these?" I hear him drawl from behind me. "Make sure you get a clean cut around the ankle."

I jerk upright, clutching the towel for dear life. Lane is leaning against the sink, a knife in either hand.

"You better keep those away from me." I glare at him. "You might wake up one morning to find your balls have been chopped off in your sleep."

"I'm shaking."

I close my eyes and try to tap back into how peaceful I felt in my dream. No can do.

"Get out of here," I sigh.

I start to turn toward the sink—very much prepared to ignore him until he leaves—but my foot goes sliding across the damp tiles instead. I flail my arms, expecting the worst.

"No no no!"

I'm falling at a dangerously sharp angle, but Lane rushes to meet me, the knives clattering to the ground as he clasps my shoulders, pulling me into his chest. I grasp his T-shirt for balance, panting hard against his neck. The guy deserves an A for reflex, that's for sure.

"Are you trying to get rid of me?" I grumble, trying to wriggle free of his grip and quickly retightening the towel. *Kill me now.*

"Like it's my fault you can't take a shower unassisted?"

"Well, it's your fault I'm half asleep in the shower in the middle of the night, don't you think?" I press a hand to his annoying-as-hell lips. "Don't answer that!"

I can feel him laughing against my hand, and I fight the urge to jab him in the tonsils.

"I know you can't wait to see me leave." My voice is coming quieter now. "I don't need that kind of showdown to remind me."

He frowns as he pushes my hand away and releases his grip on my shoulders.

"I swear it wasn't intentional," he says slowly. "I forgot you were there, and I still have no idea how, by the way."

I take a deep breath in and ready myself to reply, but the look on his face says he's telling the truth. Still, though . . .

"If that happens again, I swear I'll make damn sure you *never* forget I was here." The words come spilling out of me in one breath.

"Trust me, I won't be forgetting this anytime soon."

"Perfect!"

"Sweet!"

"Great! Now leave."

"Okay, okay. I'm leaving." His eyes drift down, then back up, lingering a second longer, before he steps into the hallway.

LANE SPENDS THE REST OF his Sunday in bed while I study. First round of exams will be starting soon, and I haven't exactly been a grade-A student the past two weeks, so I keep my eyes glued to my books and laptop screen, even when he busies himself in the kitchen and joins me on the couch to watch TV that evening.

We don't speak, and that's fine by me. Whenever we talk, it turns into a verbal boxing match, and I'm finding it harder and harder to bite my tongue. In my study breaks, I browse rental websites, but still come up short. Every now and then, I can feel his eyes on me, checking the screen over my shoulder, and I freeze up, but he's decent enough to keep his comments about me failing to find a new place to stay to himself. In fact, it's been a while since he reminded me that the clock is ticking.

I SLIP INTO THE WATER in my curve-control one-piece, ready for my very first water aerobics class. It's just the right temperature, and I spend a few minutes bobbing around at the end of the pool, far away from the rest of the class. I don't even need to look up to know when Ethan arrives—there's a flurry of excitement, and I swim my way over to the back row, gliding between two silver swim-capped classmates.

"Oh, a newcomer!" the woman to my right says, glancing at me.

I nod, smiling, as I tug my cap into place.

"Oh, a newcomer!" the woman to my left chimes in.

I smile at her, too, before frowning. They look so similar, it's uncanny. I look back and forth between them. Might be the matching caps.

Ethan kicks us off, and by the time we wrap up the last exercise, my legs are Jell-O and my cap is cutting into my forehead. When Ethan finally calls it, I wobble off toward the changing room.

Think positive thoughts.

"Look at that perky little butt."

I hear a voice whispering behind me as I towel down my legs. I glance at the speaker and her identical friend again. They've peeled off their caps, and other than their hair, they're carbon copies of each other.

"And those firm breasts," adds the other. "That was me sixty years ago."

"The good old days!"

I stand there clutching my towel, gaping.

"What's your name, dear?"

"Lois."

"I'm Prudence, and I certainly don't live up to my name," says the gray-haired one.

"I'm Hope, and I certainly do." The second one has an orange perm.

"Are you sisters?"

"Twins!" they cry in unison.

Now I get it. And they're chatterboxes, too!

They disappear in a changing room to get dressed, and I take that as my cue to do the same.

Once I'm out of my swimwear, I check the time and sigh. I need an excuse to stay out a little longer—it's too early for me to go home. I bumped into the Campus Drivers at lunchtime, and Lewis beamed a "See you tonight" at me, so naturally I've been trying to come up with evening plans ever since. But in true keeping-with-my-lucky-streak: The library is closing earlier than usual and Becca is spending the evening with Carter. I also don't have it in me to go to the movies by myself. These moments are the worst—when the loneliness becomes so all-encompassing I can feel the sadness catching in the back of my throat.

I breathe in and stare at the ceiling to hold back the tears that are starting to well in my eyes. I dash out of the changing room before it all comes streaming out of me. Cutting through the mall, I arrive at the main square by the entrance. I sit on a bench, close my eyes, and lean my head against the wall. Goddamn it, I'm starting to think that if I really can't find a place to live, I'll need to bite the bullet and get myself a hotel room.

"What's wrong, my love?"

I blink. Without my even realizing, one of the twins from earlier has joined me. For the life of me, I can't remember whether this is Prudence or Hope sitting next to me, but deep down, I'm wishing it's the second. I could do with a little hope right now.

She leans into me. "You're down in the dumps."

"Maybe a little," I sigh, rubbing at my eyes.

"Prudence, what are you doing?"

So Prudence is sitting next to me, and this must be Hope, then, limping her way over to us.

"You know every time you sit down, it takes you ten minutes to get back up!"

"Our new friend is having a bad day. Do we still have wine?"

"I hid two bottles when that old fart Agustín stopped by yesterday."

"Excellent! Up you get, young lady!"

"I'm sorry?" I babble.

"I need a strong, young thing to get me back on my feet!"

"Oh!"

I jump up and offer her my elbow, and as she slips her arm through mine, I hoist her gently toward me. I hear her hip creaking, and once I'm sure she's safe from a fall, I take a step back. Prudence isn't loosening her grip, though. Before I know it, Hope is clutching my other arm, beaming up into my face.

"We live over there." She points a wrinkled finger to a side street across the road. "Very kind of you to walk two old ladies home."

"Yes, very decent of you indeed," adds the other.

I look back and forth between the two wily women, and the sight of their open, smiling faces softens me. It's not like I have anything better to do, anyway. And maybe a good deed will earn me some karma brownie points.

We cross the road and continue walking for a few minutes, before turning at the corner and heading down a quieter street. We stop outside a worn residence sandwiched between two new builds. The women don't seem to want me to go, and so I let them lead me up to their apartment.

"Welcome to our home, Lois."

"It's lovely," I offer politely, doing a double take on the lewd trinkets littering the surfaces.

"Sit down and we'll have a glass of Shafer."

"That's wine," Hope whispers, noticing my confusion. "Our grandchildren gifted us a whole crateful for our eightieth birthday."

"Thank you for the invitation, but I—"

"Tsk! It's not often we have visitors. Humor us, won't you?"

I fold my arms across my chest. "Are you guilt-tripping me?"

"Can you grab the pretzels from up there?" Hope points at the top cupboard before evaporating into another room.

I snort to myself. Tonight is turning out to be even randomer than I expected. *Whatever. At least it buys me a little time before I head back to Lane's.*

I place the pretzels on the coffee table and settle into the roomy pale pink armchair Prudence shepherds me toward.

"Did you enjoy the class?"

"I'm barely getting started with my fitness journey, so it was pretty intense."

"Ethan is incredibly demanding. If it weren't for the miracles he works on my vaginal dryness, I would have given up a long time ago."

I nearly choke on my pretzel.

"So! Talk us through your heartache," she continues, as Hope settles in next to her.

"Heartache?" Her twin gasps, filling our glasses to the brim. "It's a good thing we have a second bottle!"

"How did you . . ."

"I recognize a bruised heart when I see one." Prudence brings the wine to her lips.

I nibble at another pretzel. It's not on my diet sheet, but I can't be bothered tonight. I shift in my seat, overcome by a sudden urge to jump out of the armchair and run far away. There's no way I feel like going over my breakup, especially not in the company of two grandmas straight out of a sitcom.

I drain my first glass of wine, and I don't need too much convincing to accept a second.

"Come now, my sweet. Hope has been married four times, she's full of good advice."

"You strike me as so very lonely . . ."

I sigh, feeling my throat relax. I could do with some advice, to be honest. I sink back in my chair, resting my hands on the polished armrests, and take a deep breath in.

"My boyfriend broke up with me two weeks ago," I hear myself explain. "We had just moved in together, and though we had been together for four years, he broke up with me like it was the easiest thing in the world. Just two days before we started college. Can you imagine?"

"My poor dear, now I understand why you have that hangdog look about you."

"Did he say why?"

Trick question alert. I'm neither ready nor drunk enough to rattle off the reasons.

"He was just done, I guess. Starting college made him want to feel free . . ."

"Oh, these youngsters, honestly . . ." Hope shakes her head. "Did you get a dorm room?"

"No, it was too late to sign up. I'm staying with a neighbor on the fifth floor. On his couch, to be precise."

"The little bastard turned you out onto the street?" Prudence sounds outraged as she tops up my glass.

"Well, it *is* his place—"

"That's no excuse!"

She isn't the first to point this out, but I can't find it in me to hate Kirk.

"How decent of your friend to take you under his wing. Is he a handsome boy?"

"Lane's no friend!" I say a little too loudly.

The wine works like magic, warming me up and leaving me feeling cozy for the first time in a while. My tongue loosens, and by the time we're down to the last drops, they know every last detail of my forced roomie situation, drinking up the finer points, gesturing excitedly, yapping away without coming up for air.

"So, there you have it." I clap my hands on my knees as I reach the end of the story.

"If we had a spare room, we'd have you stay without a second thought."

"You're so sweet." I glance at the clock, and start. "Oh my God, is it eleven already? I'm going to head home, thank you for such an . . . unexpected evening."

"Oh, Lois. You can't leave us hanging like this," Hope tuts. "You were telling us about the young man who said we'd be breaking a hip working out. We simply *must* know more."

"A driver, you say?" Prudence narrows her eyes.

"That's right."

"Well, it *is* very late." She taps an orange nail against her soft cheek.

"Also true."

"So, why not give him a call? Tell him to come and pick you up!" Hope chimes in.

"I don't think so."

Prudence plants her hands on her hips. "He deserves to be taught a lesson. That whippersnapper is about to see what the Faraday twins are made of."

Their vengeful pouts make me laugh.

"I'm pretty sure he won't come," I say, twirling my phone around in my hand.

"Trust me, I've been married four times," Hope reminds me, and there's a look in her eyes I can't quite read. "He'll come."

11

LANE

"What the hell are you doing, Lane?" Don is sprawled on my couch.

"What?" I keep my eyes latched on the street outside.

"What's the obsession with the window? Someone streaking across the street, or what?"

I hear footsteps running to join me, and a hand shoves me to the side.

"Where?" Lewis presses against the glass.

"Back off!" I shove him back. "Nothing to see here."

He shrugs and slinks back to the others. They came over to spend the evening at my place, their arms weighed down with snacks.

"What's going on, Laney?" Don flips his baseball cap around. "Did Lois break her curfew or something?"

"Shut up, dude."

Adam straightens. "Is that why he's so pissy?"

"Oh, for sure!"

"Fuck off." I shake my head. "I couldn't care less what she's doing with her life."

"She's probably with Becca," Don says, taking a swig of his beer.

"No, Becca is at Carter's," I reply too fast, and I swear I hear them snicker.

"Still, though." Adam checks my watch. "It's pretty late."

I sigh. "Considering the face she made when Lewis said you'd be heading over to our place this evening—"

"'Our place'?" Lewis interrupts me, laughing.

"I didn't say 'our place'!"

"Uh, yeah, you did. Right, guys?"

"Right!" they reply in unison.

Why are they so annoying?

"You know she's avoiding you guys," I say, ignoring their dumb grins.

"More like she's avoiding *you*," Don corrects me, waving his bottle in the air. "Carter told me what happened the other night..."

I am going to kill him...

"What happened?" Adam pipes up.

"Lane brought one of his actresses back and nearly screwed her on the couch, except Lois was on it. Collateral damage. I would've paid good money to see that!"

They all burst out laughing, and I can't help but do the same. That's one memory that's probably going to live rent-free in my mind for eternity. Lois has hardly said a word to me since, though, and I almost miss her comebacks. *Almost*.

"Superwoman must have felt super awkward."

"Super pissed, you mean."

"You guys done?"

"Lois Lane, buddy," Lewis calls over. "It's super funny."

I roll my eyes and move away from my outpost to slump against the kitchen island, unlocking my phone, glancing down at the screen. Every time it flashes off, I repeat the process, and it's so stupid because Lois doesn't even have my number. *Shit, why am I so worried, anyway?* She's been here all of two weeks, and she'll be leaving soon enough. Theoretically at least, because as far as I know, she hasn't come up with a solution yet. I'm struggling to picture dropping her off at a street corner and waving her good luck through my car window. *This is so messed up.*

Just when I'm about to turn to the fridge to top off my drink, the Campus Drivers app beeps.

"Who's that for?" Adam asks.

I tap the icon. "Me."

I lift the bottle to my lips, and pause midair.

> *Ride request: HeartBreak04*
> *Accept—Reject—Send message*

I stand there speechless, staring at Lois's blank profile. She's never contacted me before, and I can't explain it, but anxiety is tugging at me. *Maybe she's in trouble . . .* I approve her request with a tap and slip my shoes on without a word.

"So?" Lewis watches me grab my keys off the hook. "Who is it?"

"Lois."

"Super cool! I'll come with."

"I don't think—"

"Ditto!" Don jumps to his feet.

"Same here!" shouts Adam.

"I can only fit four!"

"Don't give a fuck," they singsong as they strut past me.

"My cute ass can go on Donny's lap," Lewis whispers as he opens the door.

"Come on, guys, seriously. What's your deal?"

None of them reply, and I put up with their racket all the way to the meetup point. Right by the mall. I remember her water aerobics classes were starting tonight, and I wonder what the hell she's still doing here at this hour.

"There! I see her!" Lewis sticks an arm out the back window. "Loooisss!"

I turn the engine off and watch her face turn to a scowl when she catches sight of my crew. She's got company, too, I realize. She's flanked by two prim-and-proper old women who look weirdly alike, tapping their feet on the sidewalk. *Fuck me. What now?*

The guys get to her before I do, and she shoots me the kind of look that could kill.

"Everything okay?" I start tentatively.

"Good Lord, Lois!" the woman with the orange hair shrieks. "You could gobble them all right up."

I widen my eyes and frown. I have no idea what's going on right now.

"Hope!" Heartbreak gives her a gentle, scolding tap on the shoulder.

"Which one is Lane?" the other grandma asks.

"Uh, that would be me."

Two pairs of eyes turn to rest on my face.

"What?"

I hear Lois giggle as her new friends swarm me.

"Look at these arms, Prudence!" the one on my left gushes, squeezing my biceps as the other digs a nail into my pecs.

"Are you for real?" Lois throws her arms up. "Get back here, you bunch of schoolgirls!"

She whispers something to them hurriedly, and I glance back at my buddies, who are lapping up every second of this.

"Sorry, Lois," one of them apologizes. "The truth is I don't care what horrible things come out of that mouth. Just look at those beautiful full lips!" She turns back to me. "Say 'Prudence' for me, will you? I want to hear you say it—"

"Oh, hell no," Lois hisses, wagging a finger at me. "I changed my mind, you can go. I won't be needing your services after all."

"I will," Prudence purrs.

It's starting to make sense now. *Light bulb moment!*

"These your water aerobics girls?" I shove my hands deeper into my pockets.

"Ladies, it's a pleasure meeting Lois's new friends," Donovan says.

"The poor girl needed to get out and meet new people," Lewis adds.

"Care to tell me what the hell you're all doing here, by the way?"

Lois snipes, taking a step toward them. "I ordered a driver, not a convoy."

"Oh, come on!" Donovan throws his hands up. "We're Super Friends!"

"Super close, even," Lewis chimes in with a smirk.

"I don't think so."

"Would you look at those blond locks," Hope croons to Lewis.

Lois slams her cheeks with her hands. She's reaching boiling point, and I'm so glad I accepted this job.

"Go home, you two!" she orders the twins.

"May we avail of your services, too?"

"Hope, that's enough!"

Adam smiles. "We only drive SHU students."

"But friends of Lois's are friends of ours." Donovan flashes them a winning smile. "I should be able to get you some fake student IDs."

"You absolute treasure!"

"This is not happening . . ." Lois scowls.

"See you next Tuesday, kitten?"

"See you next Tuesday," Lois sighs, resigned.

One of the guys lets out a mewling sound.

I wave goodbye to my fan club of two and look around for Lois. I spot her striding ahead of me, halfway down the sidewalk.

"What are you doing, Heartbreak?"

She flips me the finger. "Jet Skiing! What does it look like?"

One by one, my buddies kiss Hope's and Prudence's wrinkled cheeks before tumbling into my back seat. I slide back behind the wheel, laughing to myself as I rev the engine, and it doesn't take us long to catch up with Lois.

I lean across the passenger seat. "Get in."

She carries on walking.

"You're going to have to pay for the ride, you know. Even if you walk. We'll be following you all the way to the apartment, so you might as well quit the sulking."

I'm expecting her to continue on, but she stops in her tracks, and

I slam on the brakes. That was quick. I'm disappointed. One point to me, though.

"Shit, take it easy, Lane," Donovan grumbles, his voice muffled by the weight of Lewis's body.

"You wanted to come along—deal with it!"

I flick the door lock open, and Lois slides into the front seat, shooting the back seat a quick glare, before buckling her seat belt. Seeing Lewis straddling Don and Adam has definitely been worth it.

"So?" I swing back into the road. "How was it?"

"I didn't realize chitchat was part of the service," she snaps back.

Someone in the back seat calls out. "Burn!"

"I'm a five-star driver."

"You don't say." She stares down at her phone before twisting around to flash her screen at me. "The fuck? Twenty-four bucks for a ride? It's four miles, if that!"

"Sure, but it's late—"

"And you've tacked on a *'red flag passenger'* add-on fee? What the hell does that even mean?"

I keep my eyes glued to the road. "I feel unsafe."

"Okay, well, in that case, I might as well make the most of the extra five dollars." She punches me in the shoulder.

"That weak slap is barely worth a dollar, Lois."

I glance in my rearview mirror and find three faces staring back at me.

"We need popcorn," whispers Adam.

"And more space," Don pants.

"Shut up! This is the highlight of my week!" Lewis crows, leaning between the front seats.

Lois glowers at him before hunching up against the door.

"I like your friends," Lewis continues, slinging his arms over our backrests. "Hope and Prudence. So cute."

I glance at her. "Hope and Prudence, huh? Sounds perfect for you. Did you meet anyone else? Sex and Decadence, maybe?"

"I did, actually." She turns back to me. "They gave me their business cards, wait a sec . . ." She rummages in her pocket for a moment. "Here you go!" She thrusts her middle finger in Lewis's face, and he bursts out laughing, falling back onto the other two, ignoring their cussing.

"Can you introduce us?" I turn down my street. "I'm pretty sure they'll love me."

She's scowling, and I don't think I've ever been happier.

"They were supposed to get back at you for being such a cocky little 'whippersnapper' . . ."

"Hey! What did I do to deserve this?"

"You said they were three seconds away from breaking a hip." She glances at me. "Yeah, that's right: I told them everything."

"Oh, come on! So it was a trap, then!"

On that note, I put the car in park and help Lewis clamber out, while Donovan crawls his way onto the sidewalk.

"I'll never walk again! I'm gonna tell Dad to up your training, Lewis. You could do with losing a few pounds—my legs are dead."

"A hundred percent pure muscle, baby."

The four of us are standing on the sidewalk, staring at the empty passenger seat.

"Night, Lois!" Lewis yells.

I turn to the building just in time to see her disappear inside.

"You need to put a ring on it, Lane." Lewis turns back to me. "You could call your kids Lex and Luthor, and get a Lab called Clark!"

Don claps, laughing.

"Remind me why we're friends, again?" I sigh, pushing back a few loose curls.

"You've got to admit, she's funny, man." Adam nudges me with his shoulder.

I bat my lashes. "Hilarious."

Over my dead body will I ever admit that yes, Lois does make me laugh.

I reach the first step of my apartment building. "Okay, guys, show's over."

"Have fun, you two," Lewis teases, before opening his car door.

The elevator squeaks its way up to the fifth floor. My front door is ajar, my roommate slumped on the couch. When I shove her legs to the side and fall back beside her, she glares at me.

"Did you eat? There's still some chicken wings, if you want."

"No, thanks."

I toss a cushion at her. "Okay, enough with the sulking already."

"I can't help the fact you're annoying as hell!"

"You love me, Heartbreak—you just don't know it yet."

"Ignorance is bliss."

I stare straight ahead of me. Lois's feet are propped up on the coffee table alongside mine, and she lets out a snort once she realizes I'm wriggling my toes in time with hers.

"What's new with Kirk?"

She stops fidgeting and lets out a heavy sigh. "Nothing."

"Still in win-him-back mode?"

She nods, tossing her head back against the couch. I'm not sure how long I spend looking at her profile. Truth be told, I don't even realize I'm doing it, until I catch her questioning gaze, and I look away.

"Do you know if Donovan talked to his dad about a dorm room yet?" she asks timidly.

"I'll check with him tomorrow." I hear her swallow, and I'm overcome with a sudden urge to comfort her. "Don't worry. What's a few more days, right?"

She turns to me, a worried expression on her face as she gnaws at the inside of her cheek.

"I'm doing everything I can to make this right..."

"I know you are."

We stare at each other in silence until she stifles a yawn with her hand.

"Want to sleep?" I ask, resting my elbows on my knees.

"Not really . . ."

"Want to watch a movie?"

"Okay."

"Don't make that face!"

"Sorry, it's just your second personality always takes me by surprise."

"Right back at you." I reach for the remote. "Got anything in mind?"

"You choose."

She shifts in her seat, curling up into the corner of the couch, wedging a cushion behind her lower back, placing another over her stomach, getting comfy while I work my way through the movies.

"I wouldn't mind seeing *Lord of the Rings* again," I suggest, twirling the remote around in my fingers.

"Okay."

I flick off the lights and hit play on *The Fellowship of the Ring*. Lois is asleep before we even get to the midpoint, so the next evening, we put it on again, and again the next few nights. She never makes it all the way through—it takes us a full week to finish the trilogy. The same happens with *The Hobbit* trilogy, and that's how a whole other two weeks end up flying by without my even realizing. I never gave her a hard deadline, but Lois should've left my apartment a long time ago now. I should issue her a firm reminder, but I don't mention it, and neither does she. Every time Carter sees her at my place, I know what he's thinking—but he's smart enough to keep it to himself. The weeks go by, September comes and goes, and nothing changes. Nothing except one small detail, maybe. She still fires up whenever I tease her, and I love nothing more than seeing her riled, but there's this weird kind of intimate bond taking root between us. She's my first-ever female friend—and as it turns out, it's actually kind of nice.

I've grown scarily used to seeing her study, sleep, bitch, whine, and eat on my couch, and if I'm being honest, I'm not at all in a rush to see her go anymore.

12

LOIS

I should be over the moon. The clinical practice sessions are finally starting up, which is when sports therapy students get their hands dirty and start learning on actual, real live humans. Today's lesson is all about pool-based conditioning and stretching, and everyone in my class is desperate to get started. A chance to finally roll up our sleeves and dive right in. The Cardinals are our guinea pigs, and I have to admit—there's nothing quite like a basketball player's thigh to practice on.

I watch the guys burst into the sports complex, Kirk leading the charge, pushing open the double doors. I lower my gaze, without really knowing why. Yeah, I should be over the moon. But deep down, I'm terrified.

I look up, and I instantly wish I hadn't. Donovan and Lewis are bringing up the rear.

The professor claps his hands. "I know practicals can be very exciting, but let me remind you that this grade weighs heavily on your final result." He flips open his notebook. "Can the pool group please take up your positions. The rest of you, come over and join me."

I head over to Professor Moretti, silently thanking him for sparing me an hour parading around in my swimsuit. I probably won't be so lucky next week, though.

The coach arrives, and the players fall quiet. Even if I didn't already know, I'd have guessed this was Donovan's dad. They're carbon copies of each other—the same chestnut hair and brown eyes, the same mannerisms.

"Okay, guys. I want half of you in the pool and the other half on dry land. When I blow the whistle, switch."

"Yes, Coach!"

I don't need to scan the crowd for Kirk. I instinctively know where he is. Our eyes meet for a split second, and I freeze. Great. The one time he actually looks at me, and I just stand there looking like a dying fish.

He heads toward the diving board and jumps in, swimming over to a corner, a brunette hot on his trail. I sigh. I know every inch of that body by heart. I miss it all so bad. Over our four years together, I saw him grow up and fill out—I watched him turn into a total knockout. I blink away the rising tears, and turn my attention back to the professor.

"Today, we'll be focusing on the thigh muscles: the adductors, tensor muscles, and quadriceps."

"What about the glutes?" a girl whispers somewhere behind me.

"Don't forget: Grading starts immediately."

I rub my palms together, massaging the pads of my hands as I wait for him to pair us up. *Please, God, anyone but Lewis or Don!* I'd even be willing to take on that super hairy guy over there. Anyone but them.

"I'm feeling generous this morning," he says as he grabs up his pen. "I'll let you choose your own patient."

I jerk my head up, suddenly comforted as I watch some of the girls fighting over the two Campus Drivers.

"Sorry, but I signed an exclusivity clause!" Lewis brushes off the clamoring hands. "Looooisss!"

No. No! I keep my head purposefully turned in the opposite direction, desperately scanning the crowd for another player. He already humiliated me during their stupid welcome meeting—there's no way it's happening again here. I find it hard enough to make friends as it is, the last thing I need is a horde of frustrated college girls on my back.

"Loooisss!"

Jesus, I can't stand when he says my name like that!

Professor Moretti is frowning, and so I do my best to turn back to Lewis, beaming. He waves, and I scowl back.

"Here, kitty-kitty-kitty! Come and sit on Uncle Lewis's lap."

"Conley!" a voice thunders behind me.

"Relax, Coach. Lois is a Super Friend!"

"Do you plan on spending the hour just standing there, Ms. Hogan?" Professor Moretti asks.

"No, but—"

"Then get to work!"

I walk stiffly over to where Lewis is lying on a massage table. Some of my classmates throw me jealous, dirty looks; others sigh with disappointment. They're pathetic. Donovan sits down a little farther along, and blows me a kiss.

Kill me now.

"Be gentle with me," Lewis says. "I'm a sensitive guy."

I ignore him, glancing at the diagrams stuck to the board at the back of the room. I turn back and stand there, staring at Lewis's taut thighs.

"Are you experimenting with telepathic massage?"

I place a hand just above his knee, my index finger braced against his thigh. I take a deep breath in and press down along his quadriceps with all my might.

"Hey!"

When Lewis starts writhing, I tighten my grip on his leg.

"What's going on here?" the professor calls over.

"Just a cramp, sir." I smile.

Lewis rubs his thigh. "That hurt."

"Really? I'm so sorry. I'm just a freshman, you know."

He snickers, crossing his arms behind his head. I decide to tone it down a little. The last thing I need is a bad grade.

"So anyway: What's new in the land of the superheroes?"

I scoop out a little ointment. "Nothing much."

"What about your ex?" he whispers, glancing over at Kirk.

"Let's keep this relationship purely professional, okay?" I say, smoothing my palm up to brush against his shorts.

"You're still crashing on Lane's couch, so I'm guessing nothing's changed there."

My hands tense up.

"I don't mean it that way," he adds. "It's cool you're there—Lane has been way more chill since he started taking his bad moods out on you."

That gets a smile out of me. The truth is my roommate has been much more relaxed for a while now. I don't want to contradict Lewis, but those bad moods he mentioned have all but vanished. Ever since we started our movie nights, things have shifted between me and Lane, and it feels good—though it still stresses me out to think he could put an end to me crashing there at any time. Staying at his was only ever meant to be a stopgap, and I've been on his couch for nearly a month and a half now. I'm carrying on as if it were no big deal, hoping that Lane doesn't randomly lose his shit at some point. I make sure I stock up the fridge every week; I clean the living room; I scour the bathroom. I make sure I never venture down the hallway that leads to his bedroom—the one with the mysterious spare room I've never seen. I asked him about it once and he shut me down so fast I never brought it up again. He's oddly protective about that space, guarding it like it's sacred or something, and I can't help wondering what the hell he's hiding in there.

Lewis's voice snaps me back to reality.

"What?" I ask him.

"I felt something, right there."

I move back to where he's pointing. "Here?"

"Yeah, like an electric current."

I switch positions and move around the table for a little extra space, crouching down and placing a finger on his outer thigh, tracing the length of a large scar I hadn't noticed before. When I press down harder, his leg jerks.

"It's your scar." I stand. "It's normal for it to be a little more sensitive, it looks like the cut was deep. Nerves get more responsive after trauma. How did you do that?"

"My dad builds tree houses, I help out every summer. Six or seven years ago, I hurt myself with one of his saws, a piece of wood landed right there. It was pretty major."

"I can imagine; though it could have been worse."

"True, a little higher up and I would've lost Woody."

"Woody?" It takes me a moment to get it. "You dumbass!"

He pouts, and I burst out laughing, shaking my head. He's a nice guy, when he's not busy teasing me. Professor Moretti wanders over to ask me some questions, watch me work, and take notes, and Lewis makes my job a whole lot easier. When the coach orders us to switch, I thank Lewis. I barely have time to take a step back when he smacks a kiss on my cheek, and I feel myself blush as I watch him head to the pool.

"Next week it's my turn," Donovan crows, nudging me with his shoulder before taking a running leap and dive-bombing into the pool.

I pace in front of the massage table, suddenly on edge as the second group arrives. Kirk is among them. He's dripping wet still, and as I watch him towel himself down, I can't peel my eyes away.

"Come on, guys, get settled in!"

The athletes scatter, and I don't know what I want right now. I'm dying to touch Kirk, but I'm not sure I can handle him blanking me. This would be the perfect time to reconnect, though. My nerves are fluttering. The air is so hot all of a sudden, I'm struggling to breathe. I think I might be chickening out, but ultimately, fate decides for me.

"Hey, Lois."

My tongue has swollen to three times its usual size. I don't say a word as Kirk sits down on the table, stretching out and tugging at his wet swim shorts, his face blank, his eyes turned away. I don't understand how we got to this point, how he can act like we're two total strangers. The worst part is I can't find my anger. All I feel is misery.

"Watch out, I've got a contracture—"

"Right here?" I finish for him, my fingers brushing his inner thigh.

"Yeah."

He breathes out through pinched lips. This is his weak spot. How could I forget? I spent whole hours massaging this exact square inch of skin, and I'm so sad he felt the need to remind me.

My fingers shake as I jam them into the tub of cream, and when I reach for his leg, all my technique has deserted me.

"How are classes?" I hear myself ask.

"Good."

"Great."

I'm breathless, beads of sweat trickling down my back. I wait for him to bat the question back to me, but nothing comes.

"How are your parents doing?"

Did he just sigh?

"Good."

"Do they know?"

As soon as the question leaves my lips, I regret it.

"Of course they do." His voice is horribly flat. "Don't yours?"

"I mean . . . I haven't had the chance just yet."

That's a lie. My parents call me every week, and I always find a way of dodging the question. My mom is all about expanding her store, my dad is obsessed with his matchstick models. So far, they've been busy enough not to pry too hard. Though now I'm terrified they're going to run into Kirk's parents.

The next few minutes are the longest of my life. I struggle not to burst into tears, fighting hard to hold back sniffs, and by the time the coach sounds the whistle, and class is dismissed, my head is spinning.

Most students head straight for the locker room, but out of the corner of my eye, I spot Donovan and Lewis still hanging on the edge of the pool. Kirk drifts off without a word, and I rub my eyes with the backs of my hands.

I stay back for a few minutes, frozen. Then, wiping my fingers down on my track pants, I take a deep breath and drum up the courage to swing around when I hear my name.

"Looois! Over here!" Donovan is calling me over to the pool, where he and Lewis have their elbows propped on the side. Considering the state I'm in, I'd rather drown than chat with these two, but my feet carry me over regardless.

"Were you just crying?" Don frowns.

"No."

Lewis tilts his head. "Your eyes are red."

"It's no big deal—there's menthol in the ointment."

"Sure. So, nothing to do with seeing that asshat Kirk?"

They were watching me more intently than I thought, and though it's weirdly touching, I find myself shutting down.

"Wanna grab lunch with us?" Don is treading water.

"Thanks, but I'm not all that hungry."

"Why do you keep avoiding us?"

"What? I don't. It's just that . . ."

It's just that it's weird. I can't describe the relationship I have with them. They're Lane's friends, and though they're always at his place, and though I often see them around on campus, I wouldn't really call them *my* friends.

"She doesn't like us," Lewis whines.

"It's not that."

If I tell them I've never had guy friends before, they'll make fun of me. I always used to hang out with Kirk's friends, and while some of them were cool, they were never my own—I'm not too sure how to handle the two weirdos in front of me.

"Hey, Lane!" Don cries out.

I blink and turn, following his gaze.

"What the hell are you guys doing? I heard you shout Lois's name."

"We're trying to make friends with Lois, but she's about to crap herself."

"Oh, please!"

Lane laughs and walks over, tugging at a lock of hair. "You okay, Heartbreak?"

I wish so hard he would just drop that goddamn nickname.

"You don't look okay." He grabs hold of my chin and frowns. "What did you guys do to her?"

"It's Kirk, man."

"That piece of—"

"Stop," I grumble, my face still clasped between Lane's hands.

He squints at me. I do my best to avoid eye contact. I hate when they talk about Kirk like that. They don't even know him. They're all chronically single, anyway. What would they know?

"Just drop it already, okay?"

He curls a lip and glances over at his friends. I hear one of them pushing out of the pool behind me, but I'm too busy focusing on the light shifting in Lane's eyes.

"Can I give you a piece of advice, Heartbreak?"

"I'm good, thanks."

"But—"

"I said I'm good!"

"Okay . . ."

He lets go of my face and raises his hands in a shrug as if to warn me I asked for this. Before I know it, arms are snaking around my waist, and my feet are lifted off the ground. I'm doing my best to cling to his chest, and the next thing I know, I'm underwater. I resurface a second later, spluttering.

"F-Fuck!" I can't stop gasping for air. I dog-paddle my way over to the side of the pool, where the guys are laughing. "Are you kidding me?"

As I struggle to heave myself out of the water, a hand catches hold of my ankle and pulls me back. Furious, I whip around to find Lewis laughing, splashing water straight into my face.

I lunge for him. "You're fucking dead."

I have younger brothers just as annoying as this guy, and though I know the only way to deal with it is to pretend they don't exist, I've never actually been able to keep my cool. I grab Lewis's hair with one hand and press down on his head with the other, wrapping my legs around his hips, throwing all my weight into ducking him under.

"What is she *doing*?" Donovan asks from behind me.

"She can't get enough of me!" gushes Lewis.

"Lois?" There's a curious edge to Lane's voice.

"Urgh!"

I take another shot at drowning him, but Lewis is way more ripped than my brothers, so I give up, dashing through the water to the opposite side of the pool, putting as much distance as I can between me and this bunch of jerks. I walk along the poolside with my wet clothes clinging to me, and as if that isn't embarrassing enough, I pass by Kirk, sitting still as a statue on the edge of the bleachers, his blue eyes pinning me to the ground. *Great. He caught every second of that.*

"Here!"

Donovan tosses a towel over my head, and I battle against the folds.

I start towel-drying my hair. "Proud of yourselves?"

They're standing there in a row in front of me, arms folded over chests, sporting wide grins and nodding in time. I peer at them one by one, and despite myself, a smile is spreading over my face. *Traitorous lips!*

"You just made me look bad in front of Kirk," I sigh, toweling down my arms.

I can feel the draft through my dripping clothes, and I shiver.

"Trust me, Lois: Kirk doesn't think you look bad. Not today, anyway," Lewis quips. He looks at me knowingly. "He just didn't like how you had your thighs wrapped around my godlike body. Right, Lane? Tell her he was pissed."

I glance over at Lane. He's standing there in silence, his green eyes boring into me. Actually, they're boring a couple of inches *below* my face.

Lewis grins. "Laney?"

"What are you staring at?" I bristle, knowing all too well what the problem is. I cross my arms over my chest and frown. "Are you kidding me?" I tap my foot. "Are you seriously staring at my boobs?"

He blinks and pulls a face. "No fucking way!"

"He's using his X-ray vision to see under your T-shirt," Lewis says.

"Or maybe he's using his superpowers to dry it," suggests Don.

"That kind of look usually gets them wet though . . ." Lewis waggles his eyebrows seductively.

"Oh fuck off. I wasn't looking at her tits." Lane punches Donovan's arm. "I was thinking."

Lewis laughs, scratching his chin. "Yeah, I spend a lot of time *thinking*, too."

I wrap myself in the towel and watch them volley back and forth until I can't take it anymore.

I turn on my heel. "Whatever, I'm going to get changed."

Lane points at me. "I was *not* checking you out, Lois."

"Fine!" I throw my hands into the air.

"And I'll drive you home. No discussion. Meet me in the parking lot."

"Fine!" I say in exactly the same tone.

I push open the door to the changing rooms and storm out.

13

LANE

I was totally checking her out.

"Are you going to slow down, or is the idea to get us killed?" Lois asks from the passenger seat.

I was checking out those fucking perfect, rock-hard nipples piercing through all that wet fabric.

"Lane!"

"I wasn't looking at your boobs!"

Shit. That's not what I meant to say.

"Jesus Christ, I get the message already. Say it one more time, and I swear: I'm ripping off this T-shirt and shoving your dumb, stupid face between my tits."

As soon as she says it, I start picturing the scene. A surge of electricity ripples straight to my dick, and I wince.

"No need to look so grossed out," she hisses.

I open my mouth to correct her but decide against it. I don't want her getting any ideas. It's just a basic guy reflex. Nothing to do with her personally.

I hit the gas, doing my best to ignore her whining.

"What's the rush?"

"Carter is waiting for me at home. We have work to do."

I park the car and dash into the building without waiting for her, but Lois catches up with me outside the elevator, and we head up to the fifth floor together in silence.

I fling open the front door. "Cart?"

"Honey, I'm home!" He simpers.

I can see his head poking over the back of the couch, and as soon as he spies Lois standing behind me, he waves.

"Sorry, I stole your line." He beams at her.

"I don't think so."

I make a beeline for the sink and pour myself some water, looking at Lois over my glass.

"I'm gonna make a smoothie. Want one?" she asks while opening the fridge.

"Sure, why not?"

"Carter?" she calls out. "Detox smoothie?"

"Beer!"

Lois is bent over shoulder-deep in the crisper, and I avert my eyes immediately. She sticks out an arm to thrust a beer at me. I grab it and stroll over to Carter, who's busy wiggling his eyebrows.

"What?"

"Pretty sweet deal you got going on here," he says, nodding over to the kitchen where Lois's butt is sticking out from behind the fridge door.

Lord save me. Time to change the subject.

I fall back into the couch. "Show me what you've got."

With a snicker, he starts spreading sheets of paper across the coffee table, all covered with notes.

"So I got the green light—we need to wrap up the big scenes as soon as we can. I just wired the first chunk of money over to your account, the second will drop as soon as we're done."

"Amazing."

He starts talking me through the first scene, but we're interrupted by the sound of the blender.

"You nearly done back there, Lois? We're trying to work."

The only reply I get is the sound of the blender roaring into action—once, twice, and then a third time.

"Ta-da!" She pours the green sludge into a tumbler and shakes it in my face. "There you go, buddy."

"Don't smoothies usually involve fruit?" I ask, eyeing it dubiously. "Why is it green?"

She sucks on her straw, ignoring me. "What are you working on?"

"A new movie," Carter explains.

"A movie?"

"Didn't Lane tell you?"

"Tell me what?"

"We're cowriters. We write movies together."

"Seriously?"

"I'm studying screenwriting at SHU, remember?" I say.

She shakes her head. "Are you sure you ever told me?"

Considering how long she's been living here, I'm pretty sure I have . . .

"Now our movie nights make sense." She settles down on a cushion on the ground, and Carter snorts.

"Your 'movie nights,' huh? Sounds cozy."

I roll my eyes at him. "Not that kind of movie."

He bursts out laughing.

"Did I miss something, here?" Lois's eyes dart between us.

"Oh, fuck!" Cart is in hysterics, slapping at his knees. "I can picture the scene. I need to write this one down."

Lois kneels down and reaches for one of the pages. I watch her try to make sense of the scribblings, and as the pieces start falling into place, her eyes widen, a flush creeping over her cheeks.

"You guys are writing porn?" she asks through pinched lips. She puts down the sheet of paper. "Porn." She blinks.

"Yes, ma'am!"

"Got a problem with that, Heartbreak?"

"It's just that . . ." She stares at her smoothie, struggling for the words.

"Spit it out!"

"Do they really use writers for that type of movie?"

Carter gasps. I keep my eyes on her, resting my elbows on my knees.

"How dare you!" He shakes a cushion at her.

"Don't look at me like that, guys! I mean, come on!" She shakes her head. "Porn movies always use the same old story, so excuse me for not realizing it's an actual professional enterprise!"

I do my best to keep my voice level. "Do you watch adult movies, Lois?"

"No!"

I raise an eyebrow.

"I mean, yes," she admits. "This one time. Once . . ."

She's gone a bright shade of tomato, and I'm struggling to keep a straight face.

"And so that one time was enough for you to jump to conclusions?"

She folds her arms over her chest. "Okay, so maybe it was several times. But never all the way through—they're disgusting. *So* male-centric."

Carter seems suddenly interested. "What do you think they're missing?"

"Romance, for a start."

"You can't be serious," I snicker. "That's the dumbest thing I've ever heard you say—and trust me, you say a lot of dumb things. *Romance?* Even the word is a boner killer."

She narrows her eyes. Warrior mode, activated.

"See, Lane? It's because of guys like you that dirty movies don't make girls come."

I don't know whether it's hearing Lois say "come" or "dirty," but something's happened to my brain, and I can't find a single thing to say. All I can do is sit and stare at her pouting. *Don't look at her boobs, dude.*

"Lois!" Carter claps his hands together, cackling. "Nobody has said 'dirty movie' since the nineties!" He shakes his head. "Laney, get her to read through the concept. We need to enlighten her, man."

"Don't you have water aerobics class?"

"No, why? You scared, Laney?" She beams at me.

Two can play this game. "The file is on the desk down the hall. Go get it," I snap at her.

"In your *room*, you mean?"

She's making it sound like I just asked her to head into a haunted house.

"Why? You scared, Heartbreak?"

"Not at all!"

She gets to her feet and disappears into the hall.

"You two are adorable," Carter singsongs as he fiddles with his empty beer bottle.

"Gimme a break."

"Wasn't she only supposed to be crashing here for *a little while*?"

I'm surprised it's taken him this long to call me out on the one small detail I've been trying to downplay.

"This is all your fault, Cart. You dumped her on me. How can I kick her out now?"

"Yeah, that must be it." He nods, but he's still got that shitty little smirk on his face. "So is the plan still to keep her on the couch? Because you could—"

"No way," I snap. "That room is not available."

"Relax, that's not what I was thinking. I was going to tease you about sharing your bed."

"Right. That makes sense." I cock an eyebrow. "*Not*. I'm not interested in Lois, man."

An uncomfortable silence wedges its way between us. I feel stupid that I assumed he meant I should give her Mike's room.

Carter assesses me.

"What?" I hiss.

"Nothing."

"What's taking her so long, anyway?" I turn to the hall, raising my voice. "You get lost down there, Lois?"

"Coming!"

When she closes the hall door behind her, there's a strange expression on her face. She walks over to us, a pensive look playing over her features. *What's up with her? Did something in my room spook her?* I rack my brain, but I still can't make sense of the vibe shift. She looks over at the couch, staring at it for a moment.

Shaking her head, she squeezes in between me and Carter, pulling her legs up to her chest and making a start on our latest script. Cart shoots me a confused look over her head, and I respond with a shrug.

Her lashes flutter as she reads, her eyes darting back and forth from line to line. It feels weirdly stressful, having her see this side of me. I've never been ashamed of what I do, though people are usually surprised when they find out. But seeing her focused on my work like this is the strangest feeling. Or maybe it's the way she's easing herself into my world, smoothie by sludgy smoothie. Delicious smoothies, come to think of it.

She tuts, and I snap back to reality.

"What?" I lean into her. "Too much for your little heart to handle?"

"Cut the crap! Just because I've only ever slept with one guy, doesn't mean I'm a prude or anything."

"Only one . . . You've only ever slept with Kirk?" I gasp and reach for the script. "Avert your eyes, sweet, innocent child."

"Go to hell!" She lifts the pages where I can't get to them.

"As you wish, then, but don't say you haven't been warned!"

Carter interrupts us. "So, what do you think?"

"It's not bad. It's got energy and depth."

"Come again?" I snicker at her choice of words.

She ignores me. "Give me my smoothie."

I hand her the drink, but instead of taking it from me, she mouths for the straw, sucking in a couple of long gulps. I sling an arm over the back of the couch and wait for Her Highness's thirst to be quenched. She comes up for air, and when she tries to grab the straw between her lips again, I tease her by moving it away a couple of inches. Once she realizes what I'm doing, she glares at me, and we keep the stare-down going for a few seconds, until I try and shove the straw up her nose, and she snarls.

"You're so annoying."

"You're so annoying, too."

Carter clears his throat noisily and heads to my bedroom to make a call. When Lois gets to the last page, she skims the sex scene drafts.

"How is this position even physically possible?" She gnaws at a nail and squints, trying to visualize what she's just read.

"Oh, believe me—it's totally doable."

"The girl can't have her legs up there while the guy's mouth is . . . Anyway, whatever. It's impossible, unless this is set in a circus or something."

"I'm telling you it is."

"I'm telling you it isn't."

"Don't take this the wrong way, Heartbreak, but I'm way more experienced."

She rolls her eyes and glances at the hall, where Carter's voice is booming through from my bedroom. She turns back to me and places a hand on my collarbone.

"Lie down."

"Excuse me?"

"Allow me to show you how wrong you are," she says, pressing down more firmly now.

I laugh, letting myself fall back as she shifts in her seat, giving me space to stretch out on the couch. I lace my hands behind my head and stare at her, laughter bubbling up inside me. She's so serious, so focused as she climbs on top of me to straddle my stomach.

"I hope this is squashing you." She grins at me nastily.

Holding on to the edge of the seat, she slips her calves on either side of my head and bites her lip, reading back over the passage before stretching and bending her leg.

"If I put this one here, and then . . ."

I wait patiently for her to finish her demo. I know she's wrong, but this is too funny to stop.

"Hello? Can you work with me, here?"

With a stubborn look on her face, she contracts her abs to try to fold herself deeper. I latch on to her shoulder, lifting my chest to meet hers. Her ass drops a little lower, and I wince.

"See?" she crows. "This position is *literally* a ball-buster!"

"*Realistically*, the actor's penis would be protected by—"

"True," she concedes, cutting me off. "But anyway, by the time I've got this leg here . . . And that one there . . ."

She crinkles her nose and carries on messing up the scene. Once I've let her squirm long enough, I step in and take control. In one sharp motion, I grab her hips and thrust her a few inches lower, before I cup the nape of her neck and pin her knee down with my elbow. I wedge a thigh against her center, at just the right angle, and nudge her a little deeper.

"I win," I beam.

"Yeah . . ." she says reluctantly. "I'm still not convinced how long—"

"This is the part where you start screaming out my name, Lois."

She lets out a fake moan, and just when I think we're done, she throws me off guard.

"No, actually, this is usually where all that weird mouth stuff would start."

She catches her lower lip between her teeth and closes her eyes. She arches her back as far as it will go, pressing against my fly, and moans. My eyes widen. Suddenly, I'm on fire, and I'm springing into the kind of base reaction I'd hoped to avoid. My fingers dig into her skin and she freezes, her eyes slowly working their way back to me. We lie there that way, gazing at each other for three strange seconds, as she takes in what we must look like right now. I pray she can't feel how hard I am.

Time seems to stand still, until she bursts out laughing. Carter walks through the door, and I watch as he taps a finger to his lips. The pressure on my fly evaporates in a flash.

"Interesting." He reaches over to my smoothie on the coffee table. "Let me get a swig of that aphrodisiac."

Lois wriggles away from me. "I still don't think that position makes sense, but hey. What would I know? You're the experts."

She jumps to her feet, places her glass in the sink, and starts yanking clothes out of her bag, like we hadn't just acted out the most sexual thing I've ever seen her do. I blink a few times and focus on watching her get her stuff together, hoping it will distract me from the images forming in my mind. She has never complained about not having anywhere to keep her things, but I feel a pang of sudden guilt. I still don't plan on leaving her so much as a drawer in the hallway, though.

When she leaves for the bathroom, Carter swivels around to face me.

"An assistant like that is just what you need to get writing some hardcore scenes!"

"Like I need her help for that . . ."

Carter snickers, and we finally get down to work. Forty minutes later, Lois reappears, freshly changed.

"Where are you going?" I sound a little too interested, I know.

She's wearing a navy-blue wool dress with matching tights, her hair washed and styled. She's even wearing makeup.

"Got a date?" Carter asks.

She pulls on her boots. "Of course not! Becca is picking me up, we're going to the mall. If I turn up in leggings, she won't let me ride with her. Not after all the hours she spent on my glow-up."

She unplugs her phone, stuffs it in her bag, and tucks her hair into a dark red beanie. As she opens the door and turns back to say goodbye, I cut her off.

"Is it working?"

"Is what working?"

"Your plan to get Kirk back."

She sighs and stares at the door handle. "Not yet. But if you never try, you'll never know."

I hate seeing her bending over backward to try to patch things up with an asshole. She's a smart, funny girl, and I don't get why she wastes her time trying to patch things up with some awful guy. It's none of my business, though.

I slap a smile on my face. "Have fun."

"Thanks. No need to wait for me to eat."

"Got it."

"See ya, Carter!"

"Give Becca a kiss from me. Tell her to come to my place tonight."

She flashes him a thumbs-up and shoots me one last quick smile before slamming the door behind her.

"She's cool," Carter murmurs, staring at the door. "Mike would've loved her."

"I know."

It's true. My brother would have really liked her, and I'm sure she would have liked him much more than she likes me. He had this way of getting people wrapped around his finger, and . . . I push Mike out of mind.

"Come on, let's wrap this up," I sigh.

But no matter how hard I try, somewhere at the back of my mind, there's the distant rumble and roar of a motorbike crashing through space and time.

14

LOIS

I'm sitting to Lane's right, watching the streets of Sycamore Heights rush by. The temperature has plummeted, the locals swaddled in their coats, hurrying down the sidewalks. I can't believe how fast time is flying by. It's been two months since Kirk broke up with me, eight weeks since I decided to whip myself into shape and get my shit together. I've spent sixty nights or so on Lane's couch. It's comfy enough, but ever since I found out the room down the hall is a whole ass empty *bedroom*, the cushions don't feel as soft.

I honestly thought Lane asked me to go and get the script stuff in that room. And when I entered, the spaciousness of it took me by surprise. Despite the closed shutters, I could make out a large bed, a desk, and two dressers. It didn't take me long to realize that the script wasn't there and that Lane never uses the room—no clutter, none of his telltale scent lingering in the air. I stood there rooted to the ground as surprise turned to anger. *I mean, really?* I'd been stuck on that crappy *couch* for *weeks*, while there was a nice plush mattress going spare right down the hall?

When Lane called me back in, I closed the door, ran to the desk in his room to complete my mission, and headed back into the living room, shaken. I was tempted to shoot him down with a quip, but then

I remembered: He's doing me a huge favor, and one that keeps me within striking distance of Kirk. There's no way I can have a meltdown over this.

"What's on your mind, Heartbreak?"

I turn away from the world outside the window to focus on my driver.

"The grocery list I wrote and left in the kitchen." I shrug.

I could ask him about the room, and in fact I've had two weeks to do just that: But something's stopping me. Probably the prospect of being made homeless, all because I disrespected Lane's blurry boundaries.

"Considering that lame-ass diet you're on, you probably don't need a list."

"Uh-huh. Tuning out now."

"Your conversations are fascinating," Lewis calls out from the back seat. "You sound like my fucking parents."

I stick my tongue out at him and glance at Lane again. He's focused on the road, one hand on the wheel, jaw tense. There's something about the way he's driving . . . like he's starring in some moody indie film or something. I hate that I'm even noticing how annoyingly sexy it looks. The relationship we have is a plot twist, to say the least. I'm not sure I can describe it as a friendship, because we've never shared anything too personal, but the fact is, we get on weirdly well. I wonder what will happen to us if Kirk and I ever got back together.

"You're staring at me, Lois. Don't tell me the Campus Drivers effect is finally kicking in."

"Right, that's me busted!" I laugh, maybe a little too hard. "I'm falling in love with you, Laney. The way you buckle your seat belt . . . Your hands on the steering wheel . . ."

"Wait until you see me parallel park." He wiggles his eyebrows.

"Oh, yes! Please." I fan myself with my hand. "Parallel park, parallel park me right this minute!"

"You guys are super weird," Lewis interjects, leaning between our seats.

Lane glances at him as he waits for the lights to change. "Remind me why you're coming grocery shopping with us, again?"

IN THE GROCERY STORE, LEWIS grabs a cart and races ahead like a kid. I swing down the first aisle, on a mission to shake off the boys—I don't need them all up in my business while I buy tampons, that's for sure. I wander past the shelves, filling my arms as I go, and it's only once I get to Lane's cart that I notice what we've done. He's shopped for me. I've shopped for him. I laugh.

"Dude, what is this?" Lewis gestures at the cart with the box of condoms he's holding. "Since when do you eat healthy shit?"

Lane frowns. "It's not for me."

"Where's all the junk food and the good snacks?"

"Here!" I drop my haul into Lane's cart, and Lewis looks back and forth between us while Lane chews on his lip.

"You guys are shopping for each other," he says, jaw hanging.

Lane groans as he watches his friend take a photo of the scene. "What the hell are you doing?"

"I need to show Dexter Drake—the poor guy is still feeling guilty about the whole couch thing."

I don't understand a single world Lewis is saying, and his reaction is making me feel awkward.

"Give me that," snaps Lane.

While he runs after Lewis, I head to the checkout. I can't take my eyes off the cart. I don't know why I picked out Lane's food, or why he did the same for me. I have to admit, it's weird.

When it's my turn to pay, it takes me a few tries to make sense of what the cashier is asking me.

"That your guy?" she repeats.

"What?"

"O'Neill. Are you guys dating?"

"Who?"

She rolls her eyes, pointing at something behind me. "Lane!"

I frown. And then it dawns on me. She's a student at SHU, too. "No. Hell no!"

She narrows her heavily made-up eyes. "I've never seen him in here with a girl."

"He's just a friend."

The words sound off to me, but she seems satisfied.

"Ninety-three dollars and sixty-two cents," she says.

I hand her the money, and she beams at me as she hands back my change. It takes a second for me to get what's going on—the smile wasn't for me at all. I didn't notice Lane coming up behind me.

"How's it going, Zoey?" He grins at her.

She fiddles with her necklace. "Going good."

"Sweet."

"Are you coming to Jonas's party?"

"When's that, again?"

"November twelfth."

I raise an eyebrow at the date, and Lane sighs.

"We'll see," he mumbles. He's done a complete one-eighty.

She leans forward. "Hope I see you there."

He lets out a strangled laugh before grabbing the bags and stalking out to his car.

"You going?" she asks me, dropping her smile.

"No, it's on my birthday."

I'm pretty sure I hear her whisper something under her breath as I turn to leave the store.

Lane is stuffing the grocery bags into his trunk. I feel like his shoulders are tense.

"Are you okay?"

He jumps, hitting his head against the tailgate, and swears.

"Yeah. Get in, I'll drop you off at the gym," he says, before slamming the hatch shut.

"Where's Lewis?"

"He's gone off to play with his condoms."

It's a short ride to the pool, and Lane doesn't say a word on the way there.

"Are you sure you're okay?" I say quietly, unbuckling my seat belt.

"Yeah." His hands tighten on the steering wheel.

"Okay. Well, thanks for the ride. Are you heading back to the apartment?"

"I'm gonna grab a beer at Carter's."

"Okay. See you later."

I swipe up my bag and head for the sports complex, turning back several times as I go.

By the time I push open the glass doors, the car is still there. This guy's mood swings are exhausting.

I get dressed and slip into the water with a shiver. I can't seem to focus on what Ethan is saying, and he calls me out on it throughout class. I don't know if it's because I'm nearer his age, but he picks on me much more than my classmates, which Hope and Prudence love. They keep shooting me knowing glances, while some of the other grandmas look at me like I just stole their cookie. As I'm zipping up my coat after class, Ethan wanders over to me, smiling.

"You're making some serious gains, you know."

"You think? I feel like I move like a drunk whale. I thought I'd be wiping the floor with those little old ladies!" I tug on my beanie.

"What can I say? I've turned them into machines!"

I laugh and sling my bag over my shoulder. "I need to go. See you next week."

"Can I walk you to your car?"

"I'm actually walking home."

"You live far?"

I sidestep the question with a shrug. "Kind of."

"In that case, let me give you a ride."

"Thanks, but it's all good. I'll walk."

"No way. It's dark, it's cold, you just burned off a thousand calories . . ."

I laugh and take a step back. "At least!"

"I'm serious, Lois."

I shift on my feet. I want to turn him down, but the truth is, I'm exhausted. And starving, too.

"Okay. Let's do it."

"I'm parked out front."

We chat about the playlist he made for this evening's class, and I poke fun at some of the lamer songs before stopping in my tracks on the sidewalk.

"Here!" he says, holding out a helmet.

"It's a—"

"Motorbike," he finishes for me. "This your first time? I'll be gentle, I promise."

I pull a face. A second later, there's a helmet pressing against my skull. He clips the strap under my chin and helps me scramble onto the bike.

"Hold on tight to my waist, and follow how I move. I'll take it slow, don't worry. We'll be home before you faint."

He settles in in front of me, and I grip his jacket.

"Ready?"

I part my lips to reply, but there's a voice cutting through the night air so loud that I startle, nearly slipping off Ethan's bike.

"Lois!"

My name is echoing down the street. I turn my head for a glimpse of the person yelling at me, but my helmet is too tight, and all I can see is gray fabric.

"Get off, now."

A raspy, threatening voice. One I'm not sure I recognize. I instinctively clench my thighs tighter around my driver's hips.

"You know him?" I hear Ethan call out to me.

I fumble at the chin strap, and by the time I manage to shrug the helmet off, I see Lane standing in the middle of the road, running toward us. I open my mouth and squint as I try to figure out what's going on with him.

As he nears us, I shrink back, hunching down in my seat. Lane is terrifying. I've never seen him like this before—cussing and cursing as he runs, anger radiating out of every pore. Ethan slips off his helmet and glances at me, confused, but I'm not looking at him. I'm too focused on Lane and the electricity filling the air.

"What the hell are you doing, Lois?"

He sounds furious. He stops two feet away from me, scowling at the bike.

"What's the problem, dude?" Ethan asks.

Lane ignores him. "What the fuck are you doing on this bike?"

"I . . . I was heading home," I say quietly, as if I'd been busted by my parents.

His fists are clenched, his breathing ragged. There's a crazed look in his eyes.

Jesus, what is wrong with this guy?

"What is going on?"

He points at me. "Get in the car."

I raise my eyebrows and burst out laughing. "Are you for real?"

"Who do you think you are, talking to her like that?"

Ethan slips off his bike, puffing out his chest as he steps toward Lane. I slide one foot to the ground, set my helmet down, and barely have time to blink before Lane's hand grabs my arm, moving me to the side. A moment later he's pulled me behind him, still holding me tight, as if to protect me from serious danger.

"Get back on that piece of shit and get the fuck out of here," he growls at Ethan.

His fingers are still digging into my skin, his hands shaking so hard, I can almost feel his pulse.

Ethan steps forward. "Let her go."

"Lane, you're hurting me," I murmur as I try to wriggle free.

He looks down at my arm, and then up to my eyes, and what I see shining back at me knocks the breath from my lungs: pure rage, mixed in with fear. His pupils are dilated, his eyes shimmering with a terror that I don't understand. His breath is coming hard between us, and I can't hold back. I place a hand on his cheek. His eyes are locked on mine. The air between us has never been this charged.

"What's wrong?" I whisper.

"Go and wait for me in the car, Lois—"

"But I—"

"Please."

It's not an order. Not a suggestion. He's begging me. There's a knife twist to my gut.

"Okay."

When he finally releases my arm, I take a step forward. Ethan is blocking my path.

"Lois?"

Lane pushes him back. The air reeks of testosterone.

"Lane, cut it out." I yank on his jacket. "How about *you* get your ass over to the car!"

"You can't—"

"Now!" I stamp my foot.

We stare each other down for a few long seconds, until finally he gives way. Before he leaves, Lane jabs a finger at my water aerobics instructor.

"She's not getting on your bike, ever. I see this happen again, I'll smash your fucking face in."

On that note, Lane strides off, leaving me standing there rubbing my eyes and shaking my head.

"I'm sorry, Ethan."

"Is that your boyfriend?"

"No. Just a friend. I have no idea why he reacted like that."

"Either he likes you, or he has a serious problem with this." He nods at his bike.

I scoff, glancing over my shoulder. "Lane isn't interested in me. I'm really sorry, this is so awkward. I hope you're still okay with me coming to class . . . ?"

"Of course."

"Thank you."

I stiffen as he pulls me in for a hug, the blast of a car horn prompting me to step back.

"Well, see you Tuesday. Have a good evening. And sorry, again."

He glances across the road. "You too."

I stuff my frozen hands into my coat pockets and trot over to Lane's car. Inside, I tug on my seat belt and turn to my driver, arms folded across my chest. Lane stares straight ahead, even when I clear my throat three times. I'm over waiting, so I decide to break the heavy silence.

"What the hell was that?"

My tone spurs him into action but not the way I planned. He turns on the ignition, revs his engine, and pulls out into the road.

"You better open that mouth of yours, or I'm getting out at the next corner."

He breathes in, his gaze landing on mine. He opens his mouth wide. Just when I think he's about to say something, he stops and presses his lips shut tight.

"Oh, I get it!" I slap my knee. "Hilarious."

A traffic jam forces him to stop. Time to teach this guy a lesson and make good on my promise. I unbuckle my belt, yanking on the door handle, struggling to get it open. No matter how hard I try, it won't budge.

"Unlock it!" I snarl.

But he doesn't say a word. I end up giving up, deciding to sulk instead.

When we get to his building, I hop onto the sidewalk and spring up the stairs. *There's no way he's getting away with this!* I toss my bag by the couch and freeze in the middle of the living room waiting for him.

Stepping inside, Lane throws his keys on the table and vanishes down the hall that leads to his bedroom without giving me a second glance.

You have got to be kidding me.

"Is this a fucking joke?" I shout into the silence.

Fine. If he wants to play hardball, I'm game. My heels click as I make my way across the apartment, shoving open his bedroom door, wincing as it bangs against the wall. Lane is sitting in an armchair, elbows resting on his knees, his shoulders heaving like he just ran the whole way home.

"I demand an explanation! You embarrassed the hell out of me back there. If you think I'm going to let you off the hook that easily, think again, buddy."

He keeps his eyes locked on the ground, tapping the floor with his foot. He reaches over to the desk to grab his headphones, shoving them over his ears. Before he can get his phone out and start the music, I whip the headphones off his head and toss them onto his bed.

"Ready when you are." I cross my arms.

He gets up and scoots over to the mattress, reaching over the pillow for his headphones.

"If you think I'm giving up . . ." I huff, throwing myself down on the bed beside him and pinning him down with an elbow to his shoulder blade. He growls and puts his palm against my cheek in an attempt to shove me off, but there's no placating me, and we begin to tussle, him trying to push me off, me hopping forward and half landing on his back before scrambling over his head. I'm this close to winning when Lane rolls over. I grab his shoulder as I feel myself slipping sideways, but my back still slams into the ground—and then a heavy body crashes down on top of me, finishing the job.

"Help!" I choke out, gasping for air. The pressure eases a little, and as I widen my eyes, I see Lane's face hovering right above me.

I try kicking my legs, but his are pinning mine down. With his hands cupping either side of my head, he stares down at me, brows drawn.

"I win," he whispers, not moving an inch.

"No, I win," I counter, scowling back at him.

"I'm on top, you're on bottom. I definitely win."

"I got you to speak, though."

His mouth twists. I lift my hips, trying to shove him off. Correction: I manage a pathetic little wiggle, totally pinned by his weight.

"Get off me!" I gasp, breathless, squirming again.

"Didn't you say you wanted to talk?"

"Not like this!"

He pushes up on his arms, lifting away from me, his smoldering eyes lingering down the length of my body. A shiver ripples through me under the weight of his gaze, but I don't have time to linger on the unease blooming in my chest. Lane jumps to his feet and falls back seated on the edge of his bed, his eyes never leaving mine. He holds out a hand, and I take it, letting him pull me up. I keep hold of his fingers, and his gaze. Whatever it takes, I plan on getting to the truth. And he knows it.

"I didn't know you were planning on picking me up," I start, soft but deliberate, a quiet invitation.

"I didn't know your instructor was the kind of guy to drive a student home."

"I don't see how that's your problem, or any of your business, come to think of it."

I didn't say it aggressively, but Lane looks taken aback. He drops my hand and makes to reply, but changes his mind. Why is he so annoying?

"Why didn't you call me?" he blurts out.

"When you let me stay on your couch, I promised I wouldn't be a pain in the ass."

"Gimme a break—we're past that, and you know it."

"I'm a big girl," I offer, somewhat embarrassed.

"I'm not saying you're not. I'm saying getting on a bike with a guy you barely know is stupidly dangerous."

"Ethan is a nice guy—what's your deal with him?"

"How can you be so fucking unaware?"

I don't get why he's being like this. Okay, so we're not at each other's throats every five minutes anymore, but still: it's not like we're friends or anything. Suddenly, it clicks.

"Wait a minute," I gasp. "Are you actually saying you care about me?"

I'm stunned, and he looks just as shell-shocked.

"We've been living together for two months now," he offers, like that explains it all.

"So?"

"So it makes sense that I'm looking out for you."

"That would be kind of sweet, if it weren't so controlling."

"Controlling?"

"Any other rules involved in you 'looking out for me'?"

He drifts off, lost in thought, and I have to snap my fingers in front of his face to bring him back to the present.

"As long as you live here, no more bikes," he says darkly.

I definitely wasn't expecting that. He sounds so ominous.

"What's with the motorbike thing?" I'm not sure why I'm whispering.

He tenses up, and I watch as he recoils, like a snail shrinking back into his shell. I wait a few moments, but I can tell I won't be getting anything more out of him.

I stand up and stalk out of the room.

"Where are you going?"

I slope into the kitchen without replying and fling open the cupboards, sorting through the food we bought this afternoon, grabbing what I need. I pluck up a knife on my way out and head straight back into the bedroom, climbing onto the mattress and propping myself against the headboard.

"Please tell me you don't plan on eating that in my bed." He stares at the brownie I'm prizing out of the packet.

"You eat on *my* bed literally every day!" I snap back, waving the knife at him. "As do your friends. So, yeah—I plan on eating this right here, right now."

"What happened to all those good intentions?"

"What happened to you answering my questions?" I fire back.

He sighs, grabbing a box of tissues from his desk and tossing two my way as he shuffles over to join me on the bed.

"Eww! Get your jerk-off Kleenex away from me!"

"Excuse me?"

"My brothers have scarred me for life," I explain.

"Anyone ever tell you you're weird?"

"Shhh . . . Let me savor the moment."

I inhale the sweet scent of mass-produced chocolate, and I'm salivating so hard I have to swallow. Then the long-awaited taste hits my tongue and explodes across my taste buds—and I can't help the moan that escapes me. It's the moan of a girl who's just remembered what happiness tastes like.

"Holy hell," I murmur with my eyes closed. "This is the best day of my life."

When I open my eyes again, Lane is staring right at me.

"What?" I ask, mouth full.

"Nothing."

"I cut you a piece, okay? Don't try to act like I was planning to eat the whole tray by myself!" I shove a slice into his hand and grab a fresh slab, raising it up to him in a toast.

I nod at the pages littered across his desk. "How's your script coming along?"

My changing subject throws him off. I can tell he's surprised I'm not beating the point to death. What he doesn't know is that my plan is actually to take the scenic route, and slowly but surely coax him into opening up some more.

"It's not," he replies. "I've been lacking inspiration lately, but Carter's ruthless—he knows how to make sure I pull my weight."

"You guys been friends since you were kids?"

I remember how Becca once told me he and Lane had known each other for ages, but I want him to talk to me about it. Or just talk to me about himself, period. He takes a deep breath in and shoots me a sideways glance. I can't stop looking at his lips.

"Yeah."

What a storyteller. I get the sense he wants to tell me more, but he's shut down again, and though I'm a little disappointed, I don't let it show. If there's one thing living with him has taught me, it's that you have to tread carefully with Lane.

"Want help?" I place the brownies on his bedside table.

"You're offering to help me work on a porn movie?" He cocks an eyebrow.

"Stop looking at me like I'm an old prude! Like I said, I have some pretty horny brothers. Let's just say I know more than I'd like."

"Sounds like there's some kind of ulterior motive here." He grins and shakes his head as he walks over to his desk. "If it were anyone else, Lois, I'd say you were coming on to me."

"Yeah, well, it's just little old me!" I singsong, settling deeper into my seat. "Your phone is buzzing, by the way," I add as it lights up by my knee. "A certain April?"

I swipe up to check the photo on the screen. "Wait, I know her!" I say, outraged. "She's the girl you brought home last month! Give me a heads-up if she's coming over, I'll sleep in your car."

Lane stifles a laugh as he sits back down on the bed.

"She's gorgeous," I say flatly. "Life is so unfair. Aren't you going to answer?"

"No."

He grabs his phone and throws it at our feet, handing me a neatly written stack of notes.

"Read through this and see what we could add. But no girly stuff, Heartbreak—or you're fired."

"'Fired'? Does that mean I'm getting paid?"

He shoots me a warning look, as if to say, *You already live here rent-free, honey*, and I duck behind the page to hide my face. Part of me wonders if this whole porn-writing business has something to do with his spare bedroom. It looked abandoned when I went in—almost staged, actually. Who knows, maybe it's his porn lair. *Ew. Absolute disgrace.*

And that's how, without even realizing it's happening, Lane and I end up spending the night working on his movie. I'm not sure I'm much help with the writing—I burst out laughing way too often—but he doesn't seem to mind, and as the evening stretches on, I can sense him relaxing more and more. While I don't get to the bottom of the whole motorbike thing, I decide to put it on the back burner for now. I'm having way too much fun visualizing these totally unrealistic sex scenes, and the look on Lane's face every time I make a suggestion is hilarious.

The hours fly by, and I don't think of Kirk once—not even when my vision starts to blur and my tired body sinks deeper into the pillows. Right here, right now, the only thing I care about is softening the big, stubborn lump next to me. And I'm more resourceful than he thinks.

15

LANE

I'm scribbling down notes when a hand rips the pages away from me. I watch as Lois tosses them in the air.

"Can I help you?"

She twists, leans forward, and before I know it, she's slipped one leg over mine to straddle me.

"Whoa, whoa, Lois! What the hell?" I immediately tense up with my hands in the air.

"What do you think?" she purrs, trying to push me down.

I fight back, laughing as I grab one of her shoulders, keeping her at arm's length. I'm expecting a dig or a fresh attempt at teasing an explanation out of me, but she giggles, staring me straight in the eye. Just when I think she's about to speak, she slowly, deliberately rolls her hips, writhing as she pulls her T-shirt over her head. My laugh twists into a strangled sound.

"Fuck, what . . ."

I forget how to speak at the sight of the sexiest bra I've ever seen. It's all pearly gray lace, and so sheer that her nipples are poking right through. I swallow hard. *This is Lois, for Christ's sake!*

"That brownie was a bad idea. Sugar high, huh?" I manage, but I can't take my eyes off her breasts.

"Touch me," she orders. Her voice sounds different.

I blink, pushing back on the adrenaline coursing through my veins.

"Come on, Laney. I know you want to."

It's hard to pretend otherwise when she's grinding on my rock-hard dick like that. Her palms drag slowly down my chest, nails grazing just enough to make me shiver. Her hips keep moving with intent, each roll devastating. My hands grasp her hips, instinctively pulling her into me when I had meant to push her away. A moan escapes her as she's biting her lip and tossing her head back. This is insane. *This is seriously insane!* This is Heartbreak, for God's sake. I repeat it like a mantra, but her perfect tits are bouncing inches from my face, and I'm losing my fucking mind. I don't know how long I can hold off. Or if I even want to.

A rush of heat surges through me. "What about Kirk?"

"Who?" She laughs softly and leans over me. "Kiss me."

My lips move to meet hers without an ounce of protest, but Lois shakes her head, grabbing a fistful of my hair and guiding me toward her chest.

"Here. I know you've been fantasizing about it since the pool."

She lets go of my hair, reaching behind her back to unclasp her bra, and my heart starts to pound faster with every inch of fabric that slips off her skin. I don't think I've ever wanted someone this fucking badly. This is probably a massive mistake considering she lives here, but my head is spinning as my mouth hovers a breath away from her nipples. I need to taste her.

Instinctively, I close my lips around one of her breasts. *Fuck, she tastes so good.* She arches into me, and I tighten my grip on her. I'm sucking deeply, pressing her closer. Her skin is hot against my tongue, her nipple stiff as I tease it.

"Oh, Lane," she whimpers, breathless.

"Lane," louder now.

"Lane!" she shouts suddenly, her voice deep and gravelly and *wrong*.

I open my eyes with a jump. My pulse is racing, and it takes me a few breathless seconds to figure out what just happened. My hands grasp at my crumpled sheet.

"Lane! Get up, buddy!"

I stare into my pillow, unscrambling my thoughts. I don't need to flip over. I recognize the sound of Carter barking at me from my bedroom doorway. *It was a fucking dream. Just a dream.*

I don't know whether I'm disappointed or relieved, but there's no time to think. I listen as Carter walks around the bed, his legs swinging into sight.

"Well, would you look at that. Congratulations, brother!"

"It's not what you think. All we did is sleep."

"I could tell. Even when you're sleeping, you guys just can't play nice, huh?" He eyes the mattress. "You were sleeping back-to-back. Right on the edges of the bed. It's so . . ." He sighs and shakes his head. "Platonic."

Right. Tell that to dream-me.

"Got space for one more?"

"Get lost," I growl, aiming a pillow at his head.

As Lois stirs, Carter stifles a laugh. I sit up as quietly as I can, and we look at my bedmate.

"Give me that salami," she mutters sleepily.

I raise an eyebrow and glance at my friend. There are tears shining in his eyes as he bites down on a fist, trying to keep the laughter in. I shush him away.

I slide out of bed and turn back when I get to the doorway, spending just a little too long gazing at Lois as she sleeps. Dream Lois was *wild*. She turns onto her back, like she can feel my eyes on her, and stretches her arms over her head, flashing me a full view of her breasts.

"Fuck," I mutter, slipping out of that godforsaken room.

In the kitchen, Carter sits on a stool, a huge smile plastered over his face.

"I missed the episode where you switched the couch over for the bed," he starts.

"You could have fucking made coffee!"

"I was waiting for you. So you and Lois—"

"Cut it out, man! She was helping me out with the script and fell asleep."

"And you just let her?"

"I was wiped out, I didn't even notice," I snap back, flicking on the coffeepot.

I keep my back to him while I shake my mind free of the last few traces of my dream. I place two mugs between us and sit down across from him, yanking on my boxers, frowning.

"What's the problem, Laney?"

"Nothing."

He tilts his head to meet my lowered gaze and clears his throat with a satisfying sound.

"Just as I guessed." He smiles smugly.

"What?"

"You had a sex dream! I can see it in your eyes—plus, you're sweating like crazy."

"And that's a big deal, because . . . ?" I slam my mug down.

"The fact that you dreamed about *Lois* is kind of a big fucking deal, yeah."

This guy's a fucking mind reader!

"We spent four hours on the script, dude. That's all there is to it."

"Okay," he deadpans.

"I'm serious."

"Okay," he says again with the same tone.

"Fuck off."

"Okay."

He jumps up and starts air-grinding while mouthing the letters "L-O-I-S" like a lunatic.

"Stop that," I whisper-shout, wagging a finger at him.

He carries on miming.

"Is this some big scene you're workshopping?"

Lois's voice echoes across the living room. Carter swivels around to face her.

"Lois! Sleep okay?"

"Meh." She yawns. "I had the weirdest dream."

"Really?" Carter shoots me a look, grinning like the damn Cheshire cat. "What kind of dream?"

"There was food everywhere, and there was this huge—"

"Salami?" He winks at me.

"Cheesecake." *So innocent.* "This diet is grinding me down."

She pads over to the coffeepot, and when she starts tugging her shorts into place, I look away. *Fuck me.* She drains her mug at record speed, checks the calendar pinned on the wall behind her, and sighs as she gazes out the window.

While Carter wanders off to make a call, I decide to make myself useful. "Need a ride to school?"

"No, I'll walk. Work off yesterday's brownie." She pouts.

"What's with the face?"

She shrugs. "No reason."

She bends over the couch and starts rummaging through her bag for clothes, before stalking off to the bathroom without a word. Just before she leaves, she pauses. She turns to face me.

"How would you feel about me cooking us dinner some evening?"

"What's the occasion?"

"No occasion," she says flatly.

"Sure."

"How about next Friday?"

"Uh, sure."

"Cool."

And with that, she steps aside to make way for Carter and vanishes. She's being so weird this morning. Last night's fun and games feel like a distant memory—now something seems to be bothering her, I can tell. I suddenly remember how I lost my shit with Ethan, and the bitter taste of regret floods my mouth. Is that still on her mind? It must be, and I can't say I'm surprised. I fucked up—big-time. Why couldn't I hold it together last night? Why didn't I just explain why seeing her on that bike made me freak out?

"I'm going downtown to see Becca," Carter announces, tucking his phone away.

"Sure thing."

He slips on his jacket. "You're thinking about your brother."

Goddamn mind reader. I take a deep breath in. "Last night when I left your place, I headed over to pick Lois up from class, and when I got there, she was about to catch a ride home with her teacher. On a bike." The words tumble out of me, and I only breathe once they're out.

Carter nods. "What with the anniversary of his death coming up . . . You kind of freaked out?"

"Worse than that," I continue, "I completely lost my shit, dude. I nearly punched the guy in the face."

"So does Lois know?"

I don't answer that. I don't have to.

"I don't understand why you're keeping this to yourself, Lane." Carter shakes his head.

"I don't like talking about myself."

"Yeah, but this is Lois."

"What does that even mean? I barely know her. It took almost a year before I was ready to tell the others."

"What's really going on here?" He takes a step closer, burying his hands deep in his pockets. "Were you jealous, seeing her with that guy?"

"No fucking way!" I shake my head. "And anyway, she's in love with her ex. She'll never hook up with anyone else."

"By which you mean you, or her teacher?"

"Carter. I'm not into Lois, okay? So quit suggesting I am."

"Do you see her as a friend?"

I rub my face, sighing. "Yeah, I think so—in a way."

"Let me tell you something, buddy. I've got friends who are girls, and none of them mess with my head like that. I know relationships aren't your strong suit—or social interactions in general—so let me give you some advice."

"Right. I'm all ears, Dr. Carter," I deadpan.

"Sleep with her."

I bark out a humorless laugh, and he grins at me, pleased with himself.

"Plus, Lois—"

"Yes?" She steps out of the bathroom before he can finish. "What were you saying about me," she adds, suddenly suspicious.

"I was just telling Lane that you should sleep with—"

"Carter," I hiss, shooting him a warning look.

"—a guy. Or a girl, come to think of it. You know, to forget your ex."

She stares at him, eyes wide, then leans forward to grab her laptop off the coffee table.

"I'm not even going to ask for the logic behind that."

She slips on her coat and stomps out of the apartment, shaking her head. She really is in the worst mood ever this morning.

WHEN I GET TO CAMPUS, it doesn't take me long to spot my friends sitting on a bench. I wander over and squeeze myself in next to them.

"What's up, baby girl?" Lewis stretches his arm across the back of the seat.

"I've got a quiz in thirty, and I haven't studied shit," I groan, kicking at a stone.

"You never do, and you're always fine."

Adam pipes up. "It's nearly Thanksgiving. Are we keeping the tradition alive this year?"

"Hell yeah!" Donovan chimes in.

Ever since we met, the four of us have celebrated Thanksgiving with Carter. None of us go home to our families—all of us for different reasons. Lewis's dad builds tree houses every day God gives him; Donovan doesn't get along with his sister, and his dad is going to Poland. Adam's mom is on her annual stint in rehab, and Carter only has Juliet, and she usually comes with us. As for me, my parents will probably be in Cuba, Hawaii, or Bora Bora. Even if they were home, I wouldn't go. Two calls a year are more than enough for us.

"Do you know if Lois has plans?" Adam asks.

"No idea, but she probably won't want to spend it with us."

"Lane doesn't want to share," Lewis pouts.

I flip him the finger. "Not my fault I'm the only one she likes. Will Dexter Drake be gracing us with his presence?"

"No, he's been having major introvert energy."

"What a shame!"

"Well, what do you know! She's right over there. Perfect timing. Let's ask her." Lewis waves. "Loooiis!"

I scan the crowd and laugh when I catch her rolling her eyes. She can't *stand* how Lewis always yells out at her. I notice Kirk standing behind her, but she doesn't. Just as he's about to walk over to talk to her, she starts picking her way toward us. Good. I'm sick of seeing her moon over him.

She tugs her beanie into place. "Do you guys ever actually go to class?"

"We take turns," Don says. "We always need at least one Campus Driver on call. Business, baby."

"Right. Business can't be all that great, huh? Since you're all just sitting here . . ."

"We're in surveillance phase, Lois!" Lewis counters, taking a step toward her.

"Whoa, back up, buddy. I don't want people thinking I like you, or anything."

"Your girlfriend is mean," he whines at me.

He pretends to walk away, but there's a glint in his eye. This doesn't bode well. In a flash, he swivels around, grabs her by the waist, and heaves her onto his shoulder, ignoring her screams as he spins around and around.

"She looooves me!" he yells.

"Now she definitely won't want to join us for Thanksgiving." Adam sighs.

When Lewis finally drops her to her feet, Lois staggers a few steps, blinking hard. I instinctively reach out a hand, and she grabs my wrist to steady herself.

"Thank you." She shoots Lewis a dirty look. "You know, one night I'm going to slip into your room under the cover of darkness—"

"See! She *is* interested!" he crows.

"—and suffocate you in your sleep!"

She's still clasping my wrist. I pull her toward me to sit her down. Adam rests a hand on the back of the bench behind her and pats her gently on the head.

"You heading home for Thanksgiving?"

She glances over at him, and I study her profile. Her cheeks are flushed from the cold and Lewis's antics. Snatches of my dream are resurfacing, and I sigh, forcing them out of mind.

For the briefest of seconds, Lois glances my way, before turning back to Adam.

"I hadn't thought about it, to be honest."

"Us guys are spending the evening together. If you're sticking around Sycamore, you're welcome to join."

Her cheeks have turned red. I like it when she gets all shy like this. We've never invited a girl along before—Juliet doesn't count—because the ones who hang around us are either in it for the attention or a chance of getting laid. And while that's cool with us the rest of the year, this meal here is sacred.

"You've got three weeks to make up your mind." Adam winks at her.

"Okay. Thanks, I guess."

She clears her throat as she stares into the distance. I notice the exact moment she spots her ex—her eyes clouding over, her breath catching in her chest. Kirk is frozen in place, his eyes locked on her, and as I watch him watching her, I try to imagine what they would have been like together. I won't pretend I know everything about Lois, but every time I see this guy, I wonder what it is that makes her try so hard to get him back.

"I should go and talk to him," she whispers.

I stretch my arm out behind her. "I didn't hear him whistle for you, though."

"What?"

"Never mind."

"He's never stared at me like this before. I feel like he's waiting for me to go over there."

She makes to stand, and I drape my arm over her shoulders, pinning her down.

"What are you doing?" she hisses.

"Helping you out."

"Stop it! Kirk will think—"

"That you're not a dog he can make sit whenever he feels like throwing you a bone." I bring my lips to her ear. "I'm a guy, Lois. Trust me on this one."

"And I've known him for years." She jumps to her feet. "So thanks but no thanks."

She spins around to face Kirk and stops in her tracks.

"Great! He's gone." She glares at me. "Great job, Lane. Just great!"

Don and Lewis have wandered back over to join us.

"¿Qué pasa?" Lewis asks.

"I need to get to class before I kill you all, one by one."

As she snatches her bag up and turns to leave, my friends stare at me. I shrug.

"Have a great day, darlin'!" Lewis yells.

She gives me the finger without turning back. "Bite me!"

"You really need to sleep with her," Donovan says wistfully.

"Why the fuck are you all so obsessed with that today?"

"She's perfect for you, man. Rude, with a vicious streak—"

"And completely unhinged," I finish for him.

"Like I said—perfect for you."

I shoot a desperate look at Adam, but he offers no help.

I jump to my feet and stretch, high-fiving my friends before making a beeline for the main building.

I pass the huge calendar by the entrance and do a double take. "November," all in big letters. I stand there for a few seconds and sigh, closing my eyes and pinching my nose shut. I hate this goddamn month. I wish I could snap my fingers and fast-forward straight to December, but I know how the story goes. The weeks will crawl by, day by painful day. The rest of the year, I can handle. But November . . . November is hard. Because in less than two weeks' time, I'll be plunged straight back into the night when everything went wrong. The night my brother died.

16

LOIS

A whole week passes and I still haven't gotten back to Adam about his invitation: I can't decide whether to head home or stay on campus. I haven't seen my family since the summer, but the idea of being in Fort Myers, wandering the streets I used to roam with Kirk, makes me panic. We grew up there. We were friends before we hooked up, and there's an entire memory box of flashbacks I'm too scared to reopen. There's another problem, too. While my parents don't know we broke up or that I'm living with Lane, Kirk's parents do. There's a high chance the whole town is in the loop by now, my parents included, but I'd rather not think about it. There'll be no escaping Christmas, but at least I can buy myself a few extra weeks by skipping Thanksgiving. Mom and Dad have never made a big deal out of that holiday, so I'm sure they'll be fine with me staying in Sycamore. In fact, they'll probably be super proud to hear their little Lois is busy making new friends. I'm torn, though, because I do miss them—and despite myself, I miss my nightmare brothers, too.

I'm so wrapped up in what I should do and what I *could* do, that I miss whole chunks of the class I was just in and walk straight out of the room and smack-dab into a huge, unmovable mass, dropping my bag on the floor and bending to scoop up my things.

"Shit, I'm sorry!"

I straighten, and before I even have time to look up, I hear a voice I know as well as my own.

"Hey."

Kirk and I lock eyes, and the air is sucked from my lungs.

I sling my bag over my shoulder. "Hey there."

"Hey there"? For real? Jesus Christ, Lois.

He's fiddling with his beanie. "What's up?"

"Not much. I'm good."

So smooth. I need to get it together, and fast. I've been waiting for him to come and talk to me for what feels like forever, *and the big moment is finally happening.* He's right here in the flesh, but it's like it's Kirk and not Kirk, all at once. The guy in front of me suddenly feels like a stranger. But I can't stop my heart from racing.

"How about y-you?" I stutter.

"I'm okay."

"I saw you guys won all your scrimmages. That's amazing."

"Yeah, it's cool."

Our conversation isn't exactly scintillating.

He shifts on his feet. "When are you heading back to Fort Myers?"

"Huh?"

"When are you heading home for Thanksgiving?"

Great. Just the subject I was dying for.

"Oh! Yeah, I don't know whether I'm going back yet."

I wince internally. What if he was about to suggest we drive down together?

"Seriously?" He frowns, crossing his arms. "But you always spend it with your family."

"Things change," I say defensively, clutching my bag to my chest. "Friends invited me over."

"Those friends?"

He points behind me, and I whip around to see the Campus Drivers, right there in their usual spot in the cafeteria along with

Becca and Carrie. I can hear them laughing from here. I nod despite myself.

"Since when do you hang out with that kind of crowd?"

Kirk's tone is biting, and I don't like it one bit. I'm about to tell him that they're actually kind of nice, when he cuts me off.

"I know you're screwing the guy you're staying with, but is Lewis getting some action, too?"

His words hit me like a knife to the heart. I step back, shaking my head, replaying the words he just spat my way, double-checking I didn't imagine them. *Did he really just . . .*

"Excuse me? How do you—"

"How do I know you're living with O'Neill? I heard Donovan and Lewis talking about it at training. Now I get why you're always hanging around my building."

I open and close my mouth, unsure what to say next. Electricity is coursing through my body, pulsing in my throat, as if somewhere deep inside me, a floodgate is about to burst open.

"Nothing to say?"

"Since when do you even care?" I spit. "This is the first time you've so much as looked at me in over two months, and this is all you have to say?"

"I don't know who you are anymore," he says icily.

Is this some kind of sick joke?

A fresh wave of rage ripples over me.

"You've been acting like I don't exist since classes started," I start.

"I needed space, Lois." The chill in his voice just deepens the pain. "We spent four years attached at the hip. I needed to shake things up."

How many times have I imagined this conversation? I wanted this moment so bad, but I never dreamed it would pan out this way, and it stings—like reliving the breakup all over again. Except this time, there's no surprise factor to soften the blow.

"It doesn't matter why you did it—it's *how* you did it. You just tossed me out like I meant nothing, Kirk. You dumped my stuff to the super like a selfish asshole and just disappeared," I start. "It was a dick move. You didn't even stop to wonder what I would do or where I would go with just two days until school started. Do you even *realize* how cruel that was? After four years and everything we went through, you just threw me out of your life and apartment like trash, and despite it all, I gave you your precious space. And now you're all up in my face with insults?" My voice rises as I start poking him in the chest. "Now you think it's okay to shit all over the people who helped me up when I was down?" I laugh humorlessly. "I'm embarrassed for you."

As the red mist lifts, I take in his crumpled face and muster up every ounce of coolness I can find inside me.

"I don't even know who *you* are anymore."

I turn on my heel and leave him there, striding over to Lane and his gaggle of friends. For the briefest of seconds, I consider swinging a left and hitting the streets to walk off my anger, but my feet have ideas of their own. I'm drawn toward my roommate, and as soon as Lane sees how overwhelmed I am, he frowns.

I shove my way into the middle of the fold and stare him straight in the eye.

"Hand over the burger, sir."

He freezes mid-bite, his mouth falling open as I hold out my hand. He knows better than to deny me my carbs right now.

"Why, hello to you, too." He waves the bun at me. "You know how many calories are in this thing?"

I watch as he takes a huge bite, and step toward him. "That was an order."

The others are staring, but I don't give a flying fuck about what they're thinking. I need that burger, and I need it now. More than anything, I need to calm down, and this is the only way I know how at the moment. With a sigh, Lane relents, and I rip his lunch out of his hands, shutting my eyes as I dig in, finding my safe space somewhere between the patty and the melted cheese.

"Better?" He laughs, stretching out his legs.

I ignore him, taking another bite and glancing behind me. Kirk is right where I left him, staring at me, his mouth ajar. Anger has whipped the breath out of me. I'm madder than I've ever been.

"I'm in, by the way," I tell the boys with my mouth full.

Donovan cocks an eyebrow. "What did you say?"

"We didn't get a word of that." Lewis laughs.

"I'd love to spend Thanksgiving with you," I say, slower this time.

"Amazing!"

Adam is beaming at me, and it takes everything I have to steady myself and shoot him a smile back. I wasn't too sure about spending the evening with them, but my conversation with Kirk has sealed the deal. *There's no way I'm going home.*

"Lois?"

"What?" I snap at Lane.

"Easy..."

I sigh. "I'm sorry."

He nods over at my ex. "What did he say to you?"

I hadn't realized Lane had been watching us, and that's too bad—that was one time I would have actually liked him to jump in, for a change. I would even have been happy for Lewis to get involved, which is saying something. Though I'd usually try to dodge the question, this time I need to get it all out.

"He knows I'm crashing at your place, and he had the *nerve* to guilt-trip me and give me a moral lecture about it."

"You're kidding?" Lane stiffens.

"He kicked me out." The seriousness of what Kirk did is slowly dawning on me. "He kicked me to the curb like a piece of trash."

"It's happening, guys!" Lane sings to his friends. "Our little Heartbreak is finally getting it."

I kick him in the shin. This really isn't the time to be teasing me.

"We were wondering when you'd wake up and smell the coffee. You've been way too understanding, you know. Kirk is a total loser."

Becca tilts her head. "And he's heading right this way."

I freeze. "Seriously?"

"Heading straight for you. And I don't know what you said to him, but he's pissed."

There's a delusional part of me that almost celebrates. Maybe he's rattled and he's coming to apologize. Maybe I finally got through to him. Or maybe he's just back to throw more crap in my face, and though I stood my ground back there, I don't think I have it in me to go for a second round. I suddenly wish I was curled up in the fetal position on Lane's couch.

"I'm out of here."

"No. Get on my lap, Lois." There's a steely edge to Lane's voice that makes me want to trust him. "Now."

I drop my bag on the grass and clamber onto him. Lane snakes an arm around my waist and rests his chin on my collarbone. That familiar scent of him is suddenly all over me, wrapping around me like a shield.

"Whoa, dude." Donovan widens his eyes. "How do you *do* that? You ask, she obeys." He nods approvingly. "That's impressive."

He glances around, his gaze coming to rest on Carrie.

"On my lap! Now!"

"I'd rather die," Carrie answers, unimpressed.

"I could sit on your lap if you want!" A random girl has materialized out of thin air, but Donovan doesn't even notice her, too immersed in his silent stare-down with Carrie. She's so short, her forehead barely reaches his chin, but she isn't budging an inch. I like the quiet determination she's radiating right now.

"What?" she asks, utterly unbothered.

"I've got the comfiest lap on campus," he argues.

"Do you really?"

Their eyes stay locked until Becca puts an end to the tussle.

"She's just not that into you, Don. Move on."

I can feel Lane shaking with laughter, and I straighten my back, tightening my glutes, suddenly aware of how I'm sitting. *What the hell am I doing? This is just more ammunition for Kirk.*

Just when I'm about to slide off Lane's lap and get to my feet, I feel him tighten his grip, his arm snug around my waist, his breath hot against my skin as he whispers in my ear.

"One more minute."

I twist in my seat for a glimpse of Kirk, but Lane's face fills my entire field of vision. He's so close I can't see past him.

"You tried to play the game your way, and it didn't work. Time to play dirty. Him being pissed is a good sign—it means you're in control." He gives me a soft, knowing smile.

My eyes dart back and forth from his eyes to his lips. The sounds around us are starting to fade, my skin is on fire. All I can feel is the weight of his arm around me, Lane's chest pressing into my back with each breath he takes. I feel like I'm melting away into his body.

A voice breaks the spell.

"Kirk turned around. All clear!"

I shake myself out of my daze and slide off Lane's lap, settling myself between Adam and Becca. As I catch Lane's gaze, I flash him a smile. He did an amazing job helping me troll Kirk.

"Who's going to Jonas's party?" Donovan's eyes are locked on his phone.

Lewis and Adam both cheer. This party rings a bell, but I can't remember why.

"Lane?" Don presses.

"Not sure. I should head out; I've got a ride." He gets to his feet. "Got your keys, Lois?"

"Yep."

"I'll be home late."

I'm about to ask what his plans are, but I change my mind. It's none of my business—plus his voice has suddenly gone all cool, and I have no idea why.

I listen distractedly as the others chat back and forth.

Becca turns to me. "Want to join me and Carrie for a study session?"

"Not today. I think I'll head back."

It's still early, so I decide to walk home. Maybe the fresh air will help me digest that Kirk drama. It takes me over an hour to get back to the apartment, and I spend a while tidying the living room, cleaning the bathroom. Before I know it, the evening has drawn in. I don't want to hit the gym tonight, so I cozy up under a blanket on the couch and binge on chips and TV instead. Talking to Kirk today ruined my mood. He didn't even mention my new hair, didn't even notice all the effort I've been making. This sucks.

I need to talk, so I stay up waiting for Lane. But he doesn't come home.

THE NEXT FEW DAYS ROLL by in pretty much the same way—when we *do* happen to see each other, we barely talk. A growing sense of loneliness starts easing its way into the cracks, and by the time I get home from class on Thursday, I'm not feeling too good. This really is the worst week ever, and something tells me tomorrow will be the same.

I offered to cook Lane dinner on Friday because it's my birthday. I wanted to stick to tradition and cook myself a special meal, just the way I used to do with Kirk back in the good old days. Sure, Lane isn't Kirk—but at least I would be celebrating. I hope Lane hasn't forgotten, but I know I need to remind him, just in case. I won't tell him it's my birthday, though; I don't want him to know. I'll say it's just a thank-you for giving me a place to crash.

Speaking of which . . . I pry open my laptop and shoot off yet another email to the college dorm office. I feel good at Lane's, but I really need a backup plan. Sooner or later, he'll ask me to leave.

I find him more and more distant lately. Sullen, even. He goes to his room earlier than he used to, and when he does grace me with his presence, he seems distracted. I don't make a big deal out of it. I don't even mention it, but I'm scared my being there is annoying him more and more with each passing day. We got on so well, though, which is insane, when you consider how our friendship started. I don't know.

There's something he isn't telling me, and it's driving me crazy. I'm not even the nosy type, but this boy's got my head spinning with a thousand questions.

I slam a fist down on the coffee table with a groan.

"Okay, enough of that."

I want to cook something good tomorrow night. Who knows? A decent home-cooked meal could even help lighten the mood. I spend the next half hour turning over my options, and once I have the perfect menu mapped out in my mind, I put on my sneakers and head out to stock up on groceries, wandering from aisle to aisle, checking off my list and filling up my cart as I go. I throw in the everyday stuff Lane picks up each week and grab some things for me.

By the time I get to the checkout, I realize I might have gone a little off the rails. There are five bags of groceries bursting at the seams. I stagger down the street for a few steps before collapsing on the first bench I see, whipping out my phone and logging on to the Campus Drivers app. I need a driver. I skip over Lane, since I know he's spending the day with Carter. My gut nudges me toward Adam instead.

My phone buzzes.

Ride accepted.

"HEY, LOIS!" ADAM PULLS UP with a smile. "I had to triple-check when I got your request. Just making sure I wasn't dreaming."

"I need a mule to get my groceries home."

"Does Lane know you're cheating on him?"

"He's got work with Carter today; I don't want to disturb him."

"He would've come anyway, you know. But I'm glad you called me."

"He's been in a bad mood lately," I say. "I don't want to be a pain in the ass or anything."

Adam looks at me thoughtfully, like he's got something important to tell me, but he just nods.

"Sometimes people go through rough patches." He shrugs. "But don't worry. Thanksgiving will be a fun reset."

On the way home, we chat about college and his communications course, and by the time we pull in, I'm almost disappointed the drive is over. I like him a lot, and I'm excited to get to know him better. It's the first time I've ever felt this at ease around a guy. There's no ambiguity between us, no mixed signals, and that feels good. Once we've tidied away the groceries, I offer him a drink.

"That's sweet of you, but I should get going."

"Let me know if you need help with Thanksgiving stuff," I say, hugging him goodbye.

When the door slams shut behind him, I collapse onto the couch. I swear, Adam is magic. I feel so much better, like I've finally managed to shake myself out of my funk.

That night, I sleep like a baby, so sound and deep I have no idea whether Lane even comes home.

17

LANE

I didn't go to class this morning. I couldn't bring myself to pretend like today was just some normal day. Today is the twelfth. Three years ago, my brother died in a motorcycle accident. The rest of the year, I just deal with it, but on this one day, I give myself permission to fall apart.

The front door creaks open, and Lois walks through just as I step into the living room.

"Did you skip class?" she asks quietly.

"Guilty as charged, Officer."

I know my voice is flat, but I can't help it. I pour myself a black coffee with one hand, dialing Carter with the other, watching as my roommate dumps her bag near the couch and joins me by the sink. I bring my phone to my ear and glance at her.

"Still okay for tonight?"

"Uh-huh," I answer, without really listening.

I put down the cup in the sink and stride over to grab my wallet and car keys.

"When will you be b—"

Before she can finish, Carter picks up and I cut her off.

"Hey, it's me. Got everything, or should I pick something up on my way?"

"All good."

"Cool. I'm leaving now."

I toss Lois a "See ya" and slam the door behind me.

I drive with the music blasting, but by the time I get to Carter's, there's a tightness spreading across my chest. I knock back a beer as soon as I step through the door.

"I got a new video game." Carter waves the case at me.

I nod and fall back on his couch. I can feel his concern from here, but he knows I'll snap out of it. Today is when I hit peak darkness, and my friend knows just to ride it out. He's not doing all that great himself, anyway—Mike was his best friend, they were Adam-and-Lewis level. Cart and I go deep, but he was like a brother to Mike, too.

He flicks on the console, and we spend the next few hours playing in silence. I can't focus—Cart is destroying me. After one too many easy wins, he tosses the controller on the couch and thrusts a flyer at me.

"Pizza?"

"Whatever."

"I hate seeing you like this, buddy. Mike would, too."

"Good thing he's dead, then." I pinch my nose.

He shoots me a sideways glance. "Hilarious."

"I'm not like you, Cart." I sigh. "It's been three years, but I can't stop thinking about everything him and I should've done together. All the stuff we'll never get to do."

"Why do you look so guilty when you talk about him? It was an accident, Lane—it wasn't your fault."

"I know that. But part of me feels guilty I get to experience things Mike never will. It's not fucking fair."

"Life isn't fair."

"And death sucks."

I look up at the ceiling, breathing hard. The walls are closing in on me, pressing the air out of my lungs.

"Forget the pizza," I say. "Let's hit up that party. Grab your stuff and let's go."

"For real?"

"Yeah. I need space, girls, and more booze."

He frowns. "Girls?"

"What?"

He watches in silence as I pull on my jacket and shoes.

"You coming, or what?"

"I don't know if that's a good idea, Lane. We've always spent today at my place—"

"If you don't want to come, that's your call."

I stalk over to the door and listen as he grabs his jacket and keys.

"I'm driving," he calls out behind me.

"Nope. I need to drive. You can take over when I'm too drunk to talk."

"Still a terrible idea."

Carter isn't happy, but he perks up after a quick call to make sure Becca meets us there. The streets are packed when I pull up outside the house, and as soon as we step through the front door, my friends lunge for me.

"Laney!" Lewis squeals, faking a high voice. "You made it!"

"We were about to start drinking—you got here just in time!" Donovan shakes my shoulder.

I push my way through the crowd, winking at girls as I go. Any one of them will do, but I need to get a few drinks in me first.

Don fills our hands with cups, and we head off to get settled in a corner of the living room. I barely have time to sit myself down when the blond chick from the grocery store jumps into my lap, giggling.

"I'm so happy you made it!" she screeches in my ear.

I'm desperate for my first gulp, but just as I'm about to bring it to my lips, the girl waves at her friends, knocking my elbow and sending the whole thing tumbling to the floor.

"Whoops, sorry!"

"Get off me," I say, tipping her out of my lap.

"I'll go get you a new one."

"Yeah, you do that."

I take a deep breath in and tap my foot while I wait. Once she gets back and tries to drape herself over me, I flap her away without really knowing why.

"Later," I say firmly when she tries to sit on my lap again.

I finally get a gulp of whiskey—just in time for something worse to show up.

Lewis waves. "Hey, Kirky!"

"Where's Lois?" he slurs.

This asshole sure doesn't waste any time. I swallow hard. If there's one thing guaranteed to ruin my night, it's standing square in front of me.

"What's it to you?" I take a fresh swig.

"She still holed up with you?" Kirk asks.

My jaw clenches. I breathe out through my nose, tightening my grip on my cup. I can feel my friends' eyes on me. Not one of them has mentioned the anniversary of my brother's death. They don't need to—they all know what today means.

"Get lost, Kirk," Donovan calls out. "Trust me, dude, now's not a good time."

Kirk isn't taking the warning shot seriously.

He dead-eyes me. "Where is she? I need to talk to her."

"How would I know? It's a free country." I raise the cup to my lips.

"You're all here except her." He frowns. "How come?"

I hate to admit it, but he has a point. I hadn't planned on being here tonight—it didn't even occur to me to ask Lois to come. I don't want her to see this side of me.

"Where is she?" he asks again, taking a step closer.

He's persistent, I'll give him that.

"You've really got issues, man. You dump her ass, treat her like shit, and now suddenly you're all interested?" I snicker. "Get the fuck outta here."

"It's . . ."

As he struggles to find the words, the guys close in around him.

Lewis steps aside. "This house is huge, man. Go find your friends."

Kirk starts to turn but stops near Becca, who just walked over. "Why isn't Lois here?"

Jesus fucking Christ—what isn't this guy getting?

"She's having dinner with Lane."

Dinner? I frown.

"What are you talking about?" I call out.

I straighten in my seat, and as soon as Becca spots me, her eyes widen.

"I mean, that's what she told me this morning."

I watch as she whips out her phone and tries to call Lois, tapping out a message when it goes unanswered. Lois *did* mention dinner a while back, but I had totally forgotten. Was that tonight? I scratch my head. No way. There's no way I would have agreed to it—not today of all days.

"Shit." I rub at my eyes.

"She's not picking up. Maybe she's asleep," Becca offers.

"She's going to be so pissed with you." Lewis shakes his head. "Standing a girl up . . . Not cool."

"Especially on her birthday."

What? I swing around to face Kirk.

"What did you say?"

"Today's Lois's birthday. Didn't you know?" He smirks. "When you start screwing a girl on the regular, knowing her birthday is a smart move."

I don't even argue back. My head is spinning from what I've just heard. I fumble for my phone and scroll through the Campus Drivers app, desperately looking for Lois's number. All this time, and I still haven't even saved it.

The phone rings and rings, but she's not picking up.

"Go," Carter whispers. "I'll head home with Becca."

I give him my cup and rush out.

On my way, I try calling Lois again, and when I burst into the apartment, I flick on the light and scan the room. The table is laid, a faint smell of cooked onions lingering in the air. But Lois is nowhere to be seen.

"I'm such an ass."

I try a few more times. Still no answer. I pace the living room, racking my brain trying to think of where she could be. Her only friends were at the party, as far as I know. I can't figure out where else she could have gone. I just hope she's not with that goddamn Ethan guy and his bike . . .

"Come on, Lois. Pick up." I try calling again, and it's starting to stress me out.

What if something happened to her? *Fuck!* It's only now I realize that I've been ignoring her for the past few days—not because of anything she's done but because I wanted to get through this shitty month without taking it all out on her. Slow-clap, me. I fucked up the only good thing in my sad little life.

I head back to the car and drive aimlessly through the streets. I must have called a hundred times now, but there's still no answer. I feel so bad—and for once, it has nothing to do with Mike.

"Hello?"

I screech to a halt and swerve to the right, car horns blaring behind me, but I couldn't fucking care less.

"Fuck! Finally, Lois!"

"Watch your mouth, young man."

I hold the phone away from my ear and check the screen. This isn't Lois.

"Prudence speaking."

"Where is she?"

"At our place. She's in the bathroom, so I thought I'd pick up."

I lean my forehead against the steering wheel, all my pent-up tension flooding out of me.

"I'm coming."

"You better come up with a watertight excuse on your way over, kid. Otherwise you'll have my sister and me to answer to."

She hangs up, and I burst into nervous laughter.

When I pull up outside the apartment block, one of the ancient twins is waiting for me out on the sidewalk, and I have no idea whether it's Hope or Prudence. Either way, the woman isn't smiling.

"She doesn't know you're here," she warns. "The only reason I'm going easy on you is the meal. We got to eat what she made for you, and let me tell you something—it was divine."

I follow her inside, a wave of guilt crashing over me.

Stepping into the stuffy living room, the first thing I notice is another stony, wrinkly face glaring up at me.

"She's in the kitchen, doing dishes."

As I start down the hall, three dirty dishes are shoved into my arms.

"Watch out for the knives," one of the twins mutters.

When I get to the kitchen, I find Lois at the sink with her back to me. My heart races.

"I'm nearly done here," she says without turning around.

I lay the dishes down next to her. "Here."

She jumps so hard her hand smashes into the stack of plates, and I instinctively lunge to catch them before they fall.

"What the hell are you doing here, Lane?"

Her face is pale and drawn. I really fucked up.

"The meal tonight, I—"

"It's almost midnight," she says coolly, her voice quivering. "You're too late."

"Lois, I'm so sorry. Why didn't you call me back?"

She places a bowl down in the sink and whips the air between us with a dish towel.

"Are you kidding me? I asked whether we were still good this afternoon."

"You did?"

I dig deep, sifting back through the day's memories, but I don't remember her ever asking me. She tosses the towel to the side and glares.

"You said 'uh-huh,' which is more than you've said to me over the past few days combined. I should've guessed it didn't mean anything."

Ouch. That hits hard.

Lois stalks out of the kitchen, huffing at her friends. "I'm really disappointed with you, girls."

"He was worried, kitten."

"Sure he was," she snaps.

"He was white as a sheet! On the brink of a panic attack . . ."

"Bullshit!"

"If I hear one more curse word out of that pretty mouth of yours . . ."

I hear a chair scrape against the floor, a door creaking. I dash out of the kitchen to find Lois standing in the hallway, and by the time I let out a "shit," she's gone.

"Thanks for picking up," I call out to the twins. "I owe you one!"

"This is an Alzheimer's-free zone, sweetie. We'll remember that!"

I race out onto the sidewalk, scanning the street for a sign of Lois, catching a glimpse of her as she turns a corner. I start to sprint.

"Wait!"

Her shoulders tense up, but she doesn't slow down. Cursing, I pick up the pace, finally outrunning her and blocking her way, forcing her to stop. She sighs, trying to skirt around me, but there's no way I'm about to let that happen. Finally, she gives up, folding her arms across her chest, her eyes bright with anger.

"I'm sorry," I try again.

"It's nothing, okay? I'm not mad at you. Everything's fine. I just want to go home."

"Liar."

"Go back to the party, Lane. I'm a big girl, you know—you don't need to tiptoe around me. Anyway, it's not like we were ever really friends."

She's taken a swipe at me, and it stings.

"Of course we're—"

"Lane!" she explodes. "I'm telling you, we're good!"

Before I know it, she's bursting into tears and I'm standing there reeling. I hold out a hand to her.

"Please, don't cry because of me..."

She wipes her cheeks. "I'm just disappointed, that's all. I had a shitty week, and I was looking forward to a good evening. You forgot." She shrugs. "Shit happens."

I want to tell her the whole story, from start to finish. *Just fucking say it! My brother died in a motorbike accident.* It's not some deep dark secret. But no matter how I try, the words won't come.

"I've just been kind of out of it lately."

"I noticed."

"It's just that—"

"You don't owe me anything, okay? I get that, Lane. I'm all up in your space, spreading my shit all over your apartment. I promise things won't be weird between us."

"You don't take up that much space," I mutter, twisting the seam of my jacket.

"There should be some dorms freeing up in January. It's been months now since we first made our deal. You never said I could just crash at your place forever."

I got used to it, though. Even started to kind of like it, maybe.

"I'm heading home," she continues. "I'll see you tomorrow."

She slips around me, but I grapple for her hand, my fingers sliding between hers. She looks down, lips parted.

"Happy birthday," I say.

Her eyes widen. I feel her fingers tightening around mine.

"How did you know?"

"Hope told me," I lie.

I don't want her to know it was Kirk. I don't ever want to hear his name.

"I mean, I..." She bites the inside of her cheek. "Thank you."

"Why didn't you tell me?"

"It's no big deal."

"Of course it's a big deal!"

I'm bummed she didn't tell me—I'd have picked her up a little something to celebrate. Suddenly, my gaze comes to rest on a bush behind her.

"Fair Lady Heartbreak, will thou accept this blossom?"

I pluck a flower off and hold it out to her with a dramatic bow.

"Since it's my birthday, how about you drop the nickname for the night?" She brings the petals to her nose, and pulls a face.

"What's the problem?"

"It smells like piss." She tosses the flower on the ground with a snicker.

"So ungrateful." I mime outrage. "At least it got a smile out of you, though." I tug at her hand. "Come on! Let's go."

"Where? I don't need a ride home, you know. I was planning on calling a cab."

I gasp. "And there I was, thinking you were a loyal customer."

"Go have fun, Lane."

"I'm not interested in fun." I frown, and I can't help tracing a small line across her palm. "We both had a shitty night. We need alcohol. I can sneak you a drink."

"You want a drink? With me?"

"Yes, ma'am. Though we might need more than one drink."

"And who'll drive us back?"

"Don't be such a buzzkill."

She sways from foot to foot, unsure. After what seems like an age, she nods.

"Okay. Let's do it."

I drop her hand and offer her my arm. We hit the street, our shoulders grazing as we drift along to the first bar we see.

We're giggling like two kids over the dumbest stuff. This evening is nothing like I planned. Since Mike died, November 12 usually always goes the exact same way: a black pit of despair and a healthy measure of heavy liquor, followed by me breaking shit and trying to rein in my anger. But tonight, I'm feeling lighthearted, and it's nothing to do with the whiskey or the noise, or anything around us. The light blanking out my darkest memories is Lois and her nineteenth birthday. Lois and her goofy laugh. Lois and the knowing glances we exchange as we watch a bunch of guys shoot their shots and get shut down.

"I totally disagree with what you said earlier," I say, sliding my empty glass across the table.

"Care to narrow it down? We never agree on anything."

"That's because you're always wrong."

"It's my birthday and I'll cry if I want to!"

"Sorry, it's past one in the morning, Heartbreak. The birthday excuse just expired."

She rolls her eyes. "So hit me with it. What do you disagree with this time?"

"We *are* friends."

She parts her lips, my words catching her off guard.

"You're drunk." She laughs, sinking back deeper into the booth.

If only . . . I'm not drunk, though, not in the slightest. In fact, I've never felt so clearheaded in my life.

18

LOIS

Yesterday afternoon, before heading home to spend Thanksgiving with her parents and little sister, Becca dropped by to lend me one of her dresses. I never asked for the help, but she's definitely taking her job as my personal style guru seriously, shoving the bag into my arms and promising to disown me if I dare wear it with leggings—or worse still, if I forget to do my brows. I swore I wouldn't, but I must not have sounded very convincing, because this morning when I checked the mailbox, I found her favorite lip gloss tucked away among the letters. Guilt-ridden, I ran out to buy a nice pair of boots to pull the look together. Just as I'm struggling to put them on, a message pops up on my phone.

MOM: Happy Thanksgiving, honey!

The message is followed by a photo of my dad struggling with a jar of pickles, while my baby brother is bent over laughing in the background. It makes me sad not to be home, and I can't help but wonder whether staying here was a mistake.

My phone beeps again. This time it's Lane. He's been with the others since noon.

LANE: Don's finishing up a ride. He'll come by for you. 15 min.
Hope you're starving, Adam is on fire!

Another photo follows—this time a selfie. Lane laughing into the camera and Adam with his back turned, cooking up a storm, totally unaware that Lewis is right behind him, miming something gross. I start to laugh, and my stress levels drop a notch. Tonight will be fun. I'm pretty sure I'll end up having a bunch of stories to share with my family when I see them over Christmas.

LOIS: Ready when you are.

LANE: He's gonna honk three times when he's outside.

LOIS: Classy.

LANE: Campus Drivers, baby!

I tap out a reply to my mom.

LOIS: I miss you guys, I love you soooo much! Can't wait to see you next month.

MOM: We love you too, sweetie. Have fun with your friends.

No mention of Kirk, thank God.

When I hear the three honks, I race down to meet my driver.

"It's so cold." I shiver as I slide into the car. I'm a Florida girl through and through.

I bury my chin in my coat collar and rub my hands together.

"Need a hug to warm you up?" Donovan wiggles his eyebrows.

"Just drive, Donovan."

"Okay," he sighs, turning up the heat.

We pull over outside his dorm, and I follow him up to their room, gasping as the door swings open.

"Holy crap! And you call this a 'dorm room'?!"

I can't believe what I'm seeing. I knew the college has "superior" rooms as well as the standard ones, but this thing here is an actual apartment.

"How did you guys get the presidential suite?"

"My dad is a Cardinals coach." Donovan grins. "It has its upsides. Plus, Lewis's dad is a VIP, too. Winning combo, right there."

I take in the sweeping living room. "Jeez, I'm actually jealous. And look how nice and tidy it is, too."

"Hey, Loiiiiis!"

Lewis bounds over for a hug, squeezing me way too tight.

"Let her go, you're suffocating her!" Lane shoves him back and grabs the zip on my coat, sliding it down and slipping it off.

Am I imagining things, or do his eyes widen when they land on my dress? He kisses me on the temple like it's the most natural thing in the world before striding away with my jacket under his arm, and I'm officially weirded out. I greet Carter, who shoots me a look I don't quite understand, and head over to where Adam and Lewis are huddled over the stove.

"That smells so good. Need help?" I stand on my tiptoes to peer into the pan.

Don yanks me back. "Forgive her, she knows not what she says!" He wags a finger at me. "Nobody in the kitchen except these two pros. Too many cooks, you know?"

Adam winks at me. "Thanks, Lois, but we're almost done here."

Lane waves me over to the table.

"You look really pretty tonight." He grabs my hand and spins me around, and I feel myself blush. *What the hell is going on?*

"Thank you." I look closer. "And check you out! Is that an actual shirt? Worn denim, sure—but a shirt all the same."

"Lane!" Adam calls out. "Come and carve the turkey."

"Duty calls." Lane salutes me. "I grabbed you a beer—it's on the table."

I collect my bottle and take a sip as I trail Donovan with my eyes. He's walking weirdly.

"Did you hurt yourself or something?"

"Last game was brutal. We played against our biggest rivals—complete assholes." He limps over to the couch and sits with a groan. "Their forward nearly broke my leg."

I perch on the armrest. "Want me to take a look?"

He nods, and it takes him less than a second to whip off his pants, proudly showing off in his boxers. I roll my eyes.

"You're so dumb. Got any balm anywhere?"

"That drawer right there."

I grab the tube and head back over to him, settling down on the edge of the couch and warming the gel in my hands as he points out where it hurts.

"Jeez, that's some bruise. Did you ice it?"

"Yeah."

"If it gets too painful, just holler." I place my hands on his thigh.

"Now you're talking, Mistress Lois! We need a safe word."

"Don't start."

"How about 'kryptonite'?"

"If you want me to help you, Don, you are going to have to pipe down."

Donovan falls quiet, and I focus on the tension I can feel beneath my fingers. It's wild to think how jealous some of my classmates would be if they could see me now . . .

He slides an arm under his head. "You're good at this."

"Thanks. You need a muscle relaxant, though." I smooth a little more ointment over his skin.

"How come you've never been to any of our games? Because of Kirk?"

"Yeah. I've always watched him play, so it hurt when that stopped. But now with everything that's happened . . ."

"I can ask my dad to kick him off the team, if you want."

"No!"

"I'm just kidding, Lois." He smiles. "But it would be cool to see you around sometime. You could get your pom-poms out for me. Shake a little confetti around."

"Not in a million years."

"Donny! Donny!" he squeals.

"Don't you think you have enough fangirls for one ego to handle?"

He pretends to think, before shrugging. "I like you."

I glance up at him, surprised.

"I'm serious," he adds. "You're cool."

"You're pretty cool yourself."

"I'll take that!"

I keep it to myself, but I like that he likes me. I'm starting to build something for myself in the space Kirk left behind, and instead of feeling anxious, my confidence is blooming. Maybe Kirk was right, after all. Maybe I made him too much of a focus.

"Okay, I'm also done."

He stretches his leg. "You're a magician."

"My classes are actually super interesting—I'm really getting into them now."

"You sound surprised."

"Okay, so don't judge me—but I chose my major based on Kirk. It was a way to get to the same college as him. The plan was to study something that would be useful for him one day." I sigh, mortified.

Don eyeballs me. "You really did love him, didn't you?"

"You sound surprised," I say back. "Haven't you ever been in love?"

"I don't think so. I've liked some girls more than others, but now that I think about it, I mainly liked getting it on with them."

"A real Prince Charming."

"I have my whole life to settle down."

Now that I'm done massaging his thigh, he shifts in his seat, gazing over my shoulder. I can't see what he's seeing, but he's suddenly acting suspicious.

"Oh, wow, that feels so so good." He starts moaning.

"What the hell are you doing?"

"Shit, Lois! Yes, baby!"

"Stop it!"

He groans loudly.

I whip my hands back, grimacing, just as Lane appears.

"What's going on?" he asks, voice rough.

Donovan carries on moaning and groaning, until I dig my forefinger right into the spot where I know it hurts most.

"Kryptonite!" he yells, curling up into a ball and tumbling off the couch.

Lewis yells over at us from the table. "Did she do her ninja thing?"

"What the hell was that?" Donovan is still on the floor, whimpering. "I can't feel my leg!"

"What a crybaby." I stand over him, pointing straight down at his knee.

"Consider that a taste of what's to come, Wolinski. Next time, I'll be aiming a little higher."

He widens his eyes, cupping both hands between his legs, ramping up the mock sobs.

"I said I liked you! I thought we were friends . . ."

"Hey! No stealing my super buddy." Lane slings an arm around my shoulders and leads me over to the dining table, where I pull up a chair between him and Carter. Adam is still sweating over the stove with Lewis, the pair of them working in perfect unison, like they've been doing this for years.

"They've known each other a while now, haven't they?" I ask Lane.

"Since they were babies. They grew up together—they're basically inseparable."

"Like brothers."

"Exactly. Actually, they were born the same day, too."

"No way!"

I watch on in silence, my mind drifting back to my own brothers. This is my first Thanksgiving without them, and I miss them so much. Winter break's long enough for a full ten days back home, though, I remind myself.

"I'm hungry!" Don calls out.

Adam walks in with the first dish. I stand up to help bring the rest. By the time the table's overflowing with food, I have no idea where to start—everything looks amazing.

"Hand me your plate?" Lane smiles.

I pass it over, smiling back at him. Ever since my birthday

showdown, he's been back to the Lane I know and have come to love hanging out with. In fact, he's even nicer now—he hasn't called me Heartbreak again. Not once.

"I think Adam set aside some greens for you. They should be somewhere . . ."

Is he kidding me? I quit the diet a while ago now, and though I still walk everywhere and never miss Ethan's class, I never want to see a raw vegetable again.

I sweep the table with my hand. "Load it up, stack it high."

"Looooois!" Lewis shakes his corn bread at me.

"What?"

"As the newest member of the A-team, you get to say grace."

I can see Lane covering his laugh with a napkin, and I shoot him a confused look.

"Umm, I don't know how to—"

"Just thank the Lord for what we're about to receive." Lewis grins. "It's easy, repeat after me: *Thank you, Lord Lewis, for the amazing personality and hotness you bestow on the world.* Now you try!"

The others are laughing. Adam nods at me encouragingly.

"Thank you—"

"Great start! Carry on."

"Th-thank you for inviting me," I stammer, feeling my cheeks flush.

"*Not* what I said."

"Shut up, Lewis!" Carter whacks him with his corncob. "You're making her feel awkward. And anyway, if anyone here is getting thanked, it's Adam, you dumbass."

"Hey! FYI, *I* peeled the apples for the pie."

They keep bickering, which gets me off the hook for my awkward speech.

At long—*long*—last, it's time to tuck in. The conversation ebbs and flows, and soon enough I'm settling into the swing of it all. The food is incredible, and the jokes bouncing back and forth between

Don and Lewis have me in stitches. It turns out Adam is more of an extrovert than I'd guessed.

"So, Lois." Don wipes his mouth. "Who has the best car: me or Lane?"

Considering the look on his face, I'm guessing this question is super important—but sadly for him, I'm clueless when it comes to anything with wheels.

"Pass," I offer.

"Forget it, dude," Lewis mumbles through a mouthful. "Lane's got that big block engine—that's some serious horsepower, I'm telling you. You're not even in the race with your cute little *Plymouth*."

None of what he just said makes sense, though it sounds kind of kinky. Don sighs and pours himself another drink as the others laugh.

I'm having such a good time that when the evening winds down, I'm genuinely bummed. I'm in the most amazing mood, hugging the guys one by one, breathing out a "Thank you" as I go. And I really am so very grateful.

"So? How was your Thanksgiving?" Lane asks, opening the car door for me.

"It was honestly amazing. You're all completely chaotic, but I'm kind of jealous of how great of a team you all are."

"You're pretty wild yourself. Definitely one of us."

One of us. Maybe it's lame of me, but those words fill me with a warm, fuzzy glow.

"We were missing a girl or two, though." I turn to him. "Why do none of you have girlfriends?"

"Because relationships suck."

I snort. "They suck? That's such bullshit. It's like having a really good friend you get to sleep with."

"I prefer having girls I sleep with, and a solid female friend I can tell to take a hike whenever she gets too annoying." He winks at me.

"Wait—do you mean me?"

"You're my only female friend." He shrugs. "So yeah."

"Laney! That means the world to me." I mock-gasp. *"Friends,"* I croak E.T.-style, offering him a finger.

He slaps me away, and I keep teasing him all the way back home—and even once I'm in the shower.

"Hey, Lane! Your friend here is just borrowing some of your body wash!" I yell so he can hear me from the living room. "She forgot to buy some at the store!"

I laugh to myself as I lather up.

"Your friend thinks you seem to be shedding a lot of hair!" I holler louder.

I wrap myself in a towel, plugging in the hair dryer. Before I turn it on, I shout out one last time to Lane.

"Your friend thinks—"

The door swings open, and Lane barges in.

"Can you keep it down? The whole town can hear you!" He narrows his eyes. "If I'd known the 'friend' word was gonna trigger you, I would've kept my mouth shut."

"Get the hell out of here! I could have been naked!" I shriek.

He looks me up and down, a smile creeping over his face.

"What's a little nakedness between friends?" he murmurs, stepping toward me.

"Stop this!"

"Your friend thinks you're being annoying," he says, taking another step closer.

"Freeze, bitch—or I'm going nuclear on your ass." I aim the hair dryer between his legs.

"Ever noticed how you always go for the dick, Lois? What's the story there? Need a little action?"

Instead of trying to fight back, I decide to turn around and start drying my hair without so much as a glance his way. His lips might be moving, but the sound of the hair dryer is drowning him out.

"I can't hear you!" I singsong, tossing my head back and forth, my bob swaying as I move.

I catch his eyes in the mirror—he's laughing.

Just when I think he's finally about to leave, he spins around to the toilet and starts fumbling with his fly, a smug grin on his face.

I shoot him a scandalized look. He glances back with a smug grin.

"I give up." I groan, dropping the hair dryer onto the counter. Shielding my eyes with one hand, I blindly make my way to the door. "I feel sorry for whoever decides it would be a good idea to date you!" I yell out from the corridor.

The toilet flushes in response.

19

LANE

Finals season is in full swing, and my evenings are depressingly monotonous. Beer, study, pizza, study. Rinse and repeat. I fucking hate exam season. In true Lane style, I've waited until the very last minute to start studying—and I'm stressed. That said, this year is pretty different. I've got a rock-solid study buddy who's drilling me like a Marine now. Once she realized how behind and disorganized I was, my roomie put together a military-style schedule. Now I'm stuck with Drill Sergeant Lois, who quizzes me even when I'm in the bathroom. In exchange, I let her practice her physio stuff on me, and trust me: There's nothing enjoyable about it. I get the sense she takes sadistic pleasure in hearing me grunt.

"Quit the whining," she snarls, tugging on my leg.

I'm lying on my bed, Lois sitting at my feet.

"I think you should pick a different major." I wince, trying to shake myself free. "Maybe try something where you only handle corpses."

"I said, don't move!"

"This is literal torture."

"You really are such a crybaby, aren't you?"

She slaps my knee and gets to her feet. While her back's turned, I go for gold, pushing myself up and grabbing her by the waist, pulling her back onto the mattress and watching her squirm once she realizes I'm out for revenge.

"Let me go!" she shrieks as my hands wrap around her lower thigh.

I dodge a foot that comes flying toward my stomach and dig my thumb in above her kneecap, my other hand clasping her wrist.

"Ow!"

"Now who's the crybaby?" I laugh, running my fingers over her skin.

"I'm gonna kill you, Lane!" she yells.

She's thrashing harder now, and I decide to kick things up a notch, hovering over her and launching into a full-blown tickle attack, watching as she wriggles and shrieks. She's wasting her breath—keeping her pinned down is child's play.

"Help! You're squashing me!" she yelps. "Get off me!"

"That's funny, because I think you're super comfy." I pinch her gently on her side, and she falls still, her limbs suddenly loosening. Just when I think she's decided to call it quits, she starts her thrashing again, her knee slamming me right in the balls.

"Fuck!" I groan, collapsing on top of her.

"Oh, I'm sorry." I can feel her breath against my Adam's apple. "Did that hurt?"

I'm too winded to speak. Once the stabbing starts to fade, I lift my head and glare at her.

"I won that round, right?"

Unbelievable. I blink a few times, suddenly aware of how we're sprawled out on the bed, her beneath me. She must have read my mind, because she's blushing.

"So now that we've quit—mind getting the hell off me?" she whispers, before swallowing hard.

"What's a little roughhousing between friends?" I prop myself up on one elbow beside her head.

"No, this is weird. It's like you're about to lick my face, or something."

"Who even does that?"

"Please respect my friendship boundaries, Lane."

"Don't worry." I wince. "I just got my dick smashed in. I'll be out of action for a while now."

"Music to my ears."

I sigh and stretch out on the bed. "In fact, a professional massage would probably do me good."

"So gross."

"Oh, come on. This is just another day at the office for a PT."

"Did you get that from Lewis?"

I nod, just as she shakes her head. She looks me up and down, biting her lip. She's kind of adorable when she does that.

"Okay, let me go grab a rolling pin. I'll be right back."

She flings herself out of the bed and dashes out of the room, and luckily for me, she doesn't come back. I look down. A hard-on has sprung up out of nowhere. *Oh, for fuck's sake. Getting hard for Lois? Really?* I drag the comforter over my lap—just in case—and make a mental note to call April ASAP. It's been way too fucking long since I got laid. All I need is a quick fix to set me straight again.

After my shower, I find her sitting in the living room, deep in conversation with her mom.

"I'll be there late afternoon. Yeah, got it. Me either. I can't wait." She smiles. "Sounds good. Tell Dad I love him. And tell Kesley to get out of my room. If I find his Kleenex in there, I'm shoving them up his ass."

She hangs up and walks over to join me by the fridge.

"When are you leaving, again?"

"Saturday. I'm psyched. Ten whole days back home."

She pours herself a glass of water and gulps it down in one. "Are you getting a tree?"

"Nope. It'll just be me, Carter, a few games, and a microwave meal for two."

"Keeping it rock 'n' roll," she says, pumping the air. "It's sad you aren't seeing your parents, though."

"It's been that way since forever. It's a good thing, trust me."

She frowns, and I tense up. I can feel questions bubbling away under the surface. All I've told her is we aren't close—no more, no less. She didn't press me for details. I'm guessing she can tell it's a touchy subject. She's a good friend like that.

"I'll be back on the thirtieth," she says after a while. "Any New Year's Eve plans?"

"I'm still waiting to hear what we're doing—Lewis is checking whether we can hang out at one of the cabins. Somewhere not too far." I pause. "Would be cool if you came with us, though."

A smile tugs at her lips. "Then I guess you're stuck with me on New Year's."

"Wow. Didn't expect you to say yes so quickly."

She rolls her eyes and ignores me.

"By the way," I continue. "I need to drive Hope and Prudence to a tea dance at seven and bring them home afterward."

"So you're their driver now? That's cute."

"They helped me out that evening on your birthday, and I told them I owed them one. Definitely no problems on the memory front."

She whistles. "You have no idea what you've gotten yourself into!"

"I don't mind. I kind of like them."

"Wow." She smiles widely. "So somewhere under that hard exterior, Lane O'Neill has a gooey marshmallow heart, after all. Or maybe it's the Christmas spirit."

"I'm obviously a saint," I tease. "You should know that by now."

"True. You're so unhinged, I sometimes forget," she says, letting out an exaggerated sigh.

"Need a ride to campus?"

"That'd be great. I'll be a little early, but I can get one last study session in. I can't wait until all this is done."

On our way to our final exams, I'm feeling excited and uneasy, all at once. I can't wait for winter break to finally start, but there's something gnawing away at me, and I can't figure out what.

"LOIS, IF YOU DON'T HURRY the hell up, you're going to miss your flight."

"I'm coming!" she calls out from the bathroom.

I'm pacing the living room, raking a hand through my hair. I'm stressed and I have no idea why. There's no traffic at this time of day: If we leave now, Lois will make her flight, no problem.

"You're finally getting your peace and quiet back," she says, snapping me out of my thoughts.

"It's a Christmas miracle!" I tug on her bag strap, relieving her of the weight. "That all you're taking?"

"My room back home is full of clothes. At the start of the school year, I was planning on taking them to Kirk's over Thanksgiving break, but . . ." She shrugs and takes one last look around her, pulling on her coat, fumbling with the zip. "I can't wait to get to Fort Myers and lose this thing."

"You can lose the hat, too." I yank it down over her nose, so all I can see are her lips pulling back into a smile, the tip of her tongue sticking out.

"Yeah, I won't be missing that, either."

"How about me?" I hear myself ask, barely a whisper.

What the hell? Why did I say that? I drop my hand and step back, suddenly tense. She peels the hat off her face.

"Someone's getting soft." She arches an eyebrow and puts on a sickly-sweet voice. "But don't worry: Yes, I'll miss you, Laney." She pinches my cheeks. "You're such a joy to live with—these ten days without you will be pure hell."

I slap her hands away. "I won't miss you one bit."

"Liar! Your life is going to be one big empty black hole without my positive vibes."

"Oh, really? So all those times you cried—those were tears of joy?"

"Bitch, please!" She glances around the room. "We good to go?"

"I thought you'd never ask!"

"May your Christmas tree be bare."

"No tree—remember?"

She rolls her eyes, swipes up my car keys, and stalks out the apartment, while I hang back, slinging her bag over my shoulder. Now's my chance: the perfect opportunity to tuck a gift into one of the pockets, just a little something for her to find once she gets home.

It takes us thirty minutes to get to the airport. Once I've parked, I shepherd her through the check-in hall toward the departure gates, until I can't go any farther.

"Thanks for driving me," she says, staring at her toes.

"No problem. Message me once you get home, okay?"

"I will. The flight's around four hours. My dad is picking me up, then it'll take another hour or so to get to the house."

I nod, scuffing my feet. I'm not great at goodbyes. I normally just leave people at the drop-off bay, so now I feel stupid as hell, with no idea what to do next.

"Okay. Well . . ."

Lois doesn't let me finish my sentence. She steps closer, slipping her hands around me, lacing her fingers behind my back. When she presses her face to my chest, I almost forget to breathe. My arms are dangling by my sides. I don't know what else to do with them.

"Happy holidays, Lane."

She looks up at me, and the smile I see on her face finally springs me into action. I pull her in for a hug, giving her a clumsy squeeze, and press my lips to her forehead. I can't help but breathe her in.

"You too. I'll be here to pick you up on the thirtieth, okay?"

"Okay," she says into my sweater.

She smells good. It's a scent I know well by now.

"Lane?"

"Yeah?"

"I need to go."

That's when I realize I'm still holding on to her. I let go instantly, stuffing my clammy hands into my pockets.

"Take care of yourself."

She starts walking backward. "Don't worry."

She gives me one last wave, and I watch as she glides through the security checks before strolling past the departure gates' long glass walls.

I LEAN ON THE KITCHEN island, hunched over my phone, tapping the ground with my foot. I messaged Lois to check she got home okay, and I've been waiting for her to reply for ten minutes now. I scroll through socials, looking for news of a plane crash or something. *It's official: I'm fucking losing it.*

LOIS: Made it safe and sound!

Finally, the message lands in my inbox and my chest unclenches.

LOIS: My dad drives like a grandpa. It's definitely gotten worse since summer . . .

LANE: Driving is a skill, you know 😊

LOIS: 🙄

LANE: Did you ditch the coat yet?

LOIS: Not yet, I literally just got in. My mom and brothers are waiting for me in the living room. #ambush

LANE: Good luck with that.

LOIS: If you don't hear from me tomorrow morning . . .

LANE: Kirk's the bad guy, here!

LOIS: I know, but they don't know the whole story yet. Plus I've been living with a stranger the past four months! #RedFlag

LANE: #Triggered

LOIS: #OverAndOut

I hate how my footsteps echo in the empty apartment, though I'm feeling a little better now. I settle down on my bed with a book, but none of the words are sticking. I give it two hours before blasting off another message.

LANE: So?

I can see she's typing, but a minute later, I'm still hanging, when suddenly my phone starts to ring.

"Well, this is a first. I was so shook I almost didn't pick up."

"It's taking too long to write it all out." She laughs.

I don't tell her, but I'm so happy to hear her voice.

"How'd it go?"

She sighs. "So, obviously, they already knew."

"They did? The whole story?"

"Kirk's parents spilled. Guess that makes it easier for me, in a way. But something tells me their golden boy didn't tell them *everything*."

"Why didn't your parents ever ask about it? Weren't they worried about where you were living?"

"I'm the eldest, Lane. They trust me to just figure my shit out. I gotta say, my dad did flinch a little when I told him about you, though."

"That's on you. You should never have told them I'm hot."

She bursts out laughing, and I grin, pleased with myself. On the other end of the line, I hear a door creak open, and I picture her throwing herself down on the bed.

She yawns. "What are you doing?"

"I'm in bed."

"Oh, really? I thought you'd be desperate to hit the couch."

"That's the plan for tomorrow." I prop a pillow behind my head.

We spend a while chatting back and forth, until I hear soft snores over the line.

"You asleep?" I whisper.

Silence. I smile.

"Night," I say to nobody in particular.

I shoot her a message to read tomorrow morning.

LANE: Just a heads-up: your snoring is worse than Lewis and Don combined!

The next night, we have another call. And the night after. And the evening after that. Every night, Lois falls asleep first, and I catch myself hanging on the other end, listening to her breathing. Slowly but surely, our bedtime calls become the one part of the day I actually look forward to.

CARTER: Just passing through—figured I'd swing by!

I'm tempted to say no, but that's all I've been doing this entire break. Days have drifted by, and I've stayed holed up at home, alone on my couch.

The buzzer goes off, and I drag myself across the room to fling open the door. Carter's standing there staring at me like I'm some exotic animal. I run a hand over my beard. It's been a while since I shaved.

"Sorry to bother you, sir. It's just—I could've sworn my best friend used to live here."

"You coming in, or what?" I turn back to the couch.

"Lane?" he yells as he follows, looking from left to right. "Lane? Where are you, buddy?"

"What is *wrong* with you?" I collapse onto the cushions.

"What is wrong with *you*? Dude, have you looked at yourself lately?"

I throw an arm over the backrest and stare at him, one eyebrow raised. "It's not the first time I've leaned into the rugged look, Cart."

He lifts up a pizza box. "Where's the coffee table?" He glances around the room. "Coffee table, come out, come out, wherever you are!"

"Cut it out!"

I toss a dirty sock at his face, and he catches it, holding it at arm's length as he perches on a barstool, lip curled.

"Why don't you tell Dr. Carter what's been going on with you lately?" He reaches for the notepad on the counter.

"I'm not depressed, man. Just on break."

"I see." He scribbles something down, gesturing with his pen for me to continue, deepening his voice into a pseudo-professional baritone. "Tell me about your childhood."

"Can I catch a break, here?"

When my phone starts buzzing on the armrest, I lunge for it.

LOIS: My dad's latest obsession? Waffles.

I'm gonna gain back all the weight I lost . . . #NoHope

My fingers dart frantically across the screen as we fire off messages, and I'm so absorbed in our conversation, I forget Carter is even there.

LOIS: My mom wants help to glue beads onto her fugly lampshade.

#KillMeNow. Talk later 😊

I dispatch two smileys and set my phone aside with a sigh.

"How's our Lois?" Cart smiles knowingly.

"Soaking up the sun." I cross my arms behind my head.

"Must be nice, getting the place back to yourself, huh?"

I can hear the jokiness in his voice, and I think I know where he's going with this.

"Quit looking at me like that." I groan.

"Say it."

"Say what?"

He smiles. "Just say it."

He's pissing me off, and he knows it.

"I know you better than you know yourself, my boy. Now—lemme hear you say it . . ."

He's not going to drop it until I give him what he wants to hear.

"Fine!" My patience is wearing thin. "I kind of miss her, okay?!"

"Amen to that!" He slaps his hands down on his knees.

"She's been up in my business for months now, Cart. Of course I'm gonna miss her a little!"

"Of course you are." He opens his mouth to speak, but his phone rings, cutting him off.

Saved by the bell!

He slips away into my room, and I reach for the remote, absent-mindedly channel surfing as my mind starts wandering back to Lois, picturing her chowing down on waffles with her parents, laughing.

It feels like she's been away forever. *Oh, fuck me. This is getting ridiculous.*

Carter looks pissed when he gets back.

"What's up?"

"Becca," he says, massaging his temples.

"You guys fight?"

"No . . ."

"So what's the problem?" I ask.

"She asked me to spend Christmas with her."

"For real? Wow. Things are getting serious with you guys."

"Yeah. I think I love her—crazy, right?"

"Mike would be proud of you, buddy." I twist open a jar of peanut butter. "He was always the sensitive one."

"Facts."

I dig my spoon into the tub. "So when are you leaving?"

"I'm not."

"How come?"

"There's no way I'm leaving you all alone for Christmas, man."

I roll my eyes. "Don't fuck around, Cart. It's just another day—I'll survive. You don't need to worry about me."

"No way." He shakes his head. "I've always done Christmas with you and Mike, and then just you—"

"And now just Becca. I'm serious, dude. I order you to accept."

"Lane, I—"

"Life's too short," I say, my tongue thick with peanut butter.

"Deep, man."

I shake my spoon at him. "Call Becca back."

He twirls his phone around in his fingers, glancing at me, hesitant. I jump up and snatch it from him, hitting dial on her number. When she picks up, I get straight to the point.

"Becca, it's Lane."

"Bad Lane!" Carter lunges for his phone.

Becca sounds wary. "Everything okay?"

"Yup! Just wanted to let you know that Carter's down for Christmas. I promised to be good while he's away and not open the door to any strangers. I even swore to take a shower every day!"

She thanks me as I hand the phone back to Carter, and though his jaw is clenched, I can tell he's happy.

Once he hangs up, he stares at me in silence for a moment, gnawing on a nail.

"Stop overthinking."

He's about to reply when my phone starts ringing. It's Lois—which is weird for this time of day. My fingers are sticky with peanut butter, so I hit loudspeaker.

"Yup?"

"Are you okay?" Her voice sounds funny.

"Fine, yeah. Why?"

"Just checking. What are you up to?"

"I'm with Carter. Are *you* okay? You sound weird."

"Did you guys get the microwave meals in for tomorrow night?"

"We're going to the store later," I lie, and Carter raises his eyebrows at me.

"Oh, really?"

Carter opens his mouth, but I hush him with a hand. He feels guilty enough as it is—I don't need Lois feeling bad, too.

"Is he sleeping at your place?" she presses.

"Yeah."

"On my couch?"

"Yeah." I frown. I have no idea where this conversation is going.

She sighs heavily. "Okay, then."

Silence settles between us.

"That all?"

"I am going to kick your ass to hell and back, you pathetic little liar!" she yells. "Becca just messaged me—and guess what? She's super excited that Cart's spending Christmas with her. Which means *you'll* be spending it alone!"

"Fucking girls," I sigh.

I glance at Carter, taking in how hard he's grinning right now. I look away.

"So you weren't planning on telling me, then?"

"No."

"Why not?"

"Because who the fuck cares?!"

She's holding the phone away from her mouth, I can tell—I can make out muffled cussing.

"I'll call you back in five," she says.

I stare down at my phone, shell-shocked.

"You just got scolded like a little kid." Carter laughs.

"Yeah—because of *you*!"

My phone is ringing again, but this time, I'm too scared to pick up.

"Answer it before you get a real spanking."

I flip him off, but the bastard grabs the phone off me, sliding it back onto loudspeaker.

"You done yelling?" I grumble.

Lois clears her throat. "Your birthday is August twenty-eighth, right?"

"Why?"

"Just answer," she says coolly.

"Yeah . . ."

I hear her whisper, a man's voice murmuring somewhere behind her.

"You listen to me, you stubborn little shit—" she starts up again.

"You—"

"Zip it! Go to your room, pack a bag, and order yourself a cab for tomorrow morning."

I stare at the phone in disbelief. "Excuse me?"

"Make it an early night. Oh, and insider tip: Set your alarm for six."

"What the hell are you talking about?"

"Your flight leaves at nine forty-five tomorrow," she says. "And I swear, if you miss it—"

"My flight? Lois, I don't get it . . ."

Carter is practically on the floor laughing. I shoot him a dirty look. I'm so lost right now.

"My flight?" I repeat, and that's when it dawns on me. "Wait a minute—are you seriously saying I should come spend Christmas with you?"

"Oh, there's no *should* about it, Lane. My dad bought you a ticket. And it's nonrefundable."

"You've gotta be kidding me. There's no way I'm crashing your parents' place for Christmas!"

"See you tomorrow, Laney!" she singsongs like a maniac.

"No, Lois! I—"

"Oh, and pack a nice shirt. Hard pass on the denim."

"Lois!"

"Safe travels!"

The little bitch hung up on me!

"This . . . this has got to be a joke, right?" I stammer.

Carter is clutching his stomach. "I don't think it gets much more serious than this."

"Fuck! There's no way I'm heading down there!"

My phone beeps. An email from Lois.

"She actually fucking did it." I jump to my feet. "She got me a fucking plane ticket!"

"Don't worry about the cab—I'll drop you on my way to Becca."

"No way. There's no way I'm doing this, Cart."

"Why?"

"I can't go and spend Christmas with a family I don't know."

"But you know Lois."

"So what? It's just too weird. And lame," I add.

"Bullshit. You talked me into spending it with Becca, didn't you?"

"Yeah, but she's your girlfriend."

"And this is Lois."

"Who *isn't* my girlfriend," I snap.

He snickers. I feel like punching him in the face.

"Anyway, it's too late. It would be rude to say no, now that your flight is booked and all. I brought you up to be a nice, polite young man."

"Why does life hate me? This is a conspiracy." I close my eyes. "Let me call her back."

I dial her number, and the phone rings and rings. Just when I think I'm about to hit voicemail, a deep voice greets me.

"Lane, I take it?"

The man sounds friendly.

"Yeah," I start.

"Did you get your ticket?"

"Yes, but—"

"Excellent! Lois will be there when you land. We can't wait to meet her new friend."

"Listen, sir, it's really kind of you, and I appreciate it and all, but I can't accept. Let me pay you back—"

"My daughter doesn't take no for an answer, does she?" he interrupts.

"No, sir."

"And I'm her father." He pauses for effect. "See where I'm going with this?"

"The apple doesn't fall far, huh?"

"You're a fast learner, son. I like that. Your flight leaves at nine forty-five. If you miss it, my daughter will spend the rest of the break sulking—and that's a price I'm not willing to pay. Did she tell you I'm a retired cop?" he adds. "I can arrest you for crimes against Christmas."

I burst out laughing. *He's joking, right?*

"Don't make me get my Grinch on," he shoots back in a gravelly voice.

Fuck! I hold the phone away from my ear and breathe out slowly, trying to rearrange my thoughts. I'm caught between curiosity and an instinctive urge to run for my life.

"We can't wait to welcome you into our home." His voice now is gentle, sincere. "Don't overthink it, kid. I know my daughter hasn't told me everything about her breakup, but one thing I *do* know is that you were there for her. It makes no sense for you to be sitting there, all alone in Ohio. *Ohio*, for Christ's sake!"

I don't know what to say to that.

"And anyway—if you don't come, she'll make you pay." He laughs. "That much is for sure."

"Finally, something we agree on. See you tomorrow?"

I close my eyes and shake my head. Somewhere, somehow, a reply makes its way to the surface.

"See you tomorrow," I say.

20

LOIS

I squint at the arrivals board, checking the line on the screen for the fifth time and pat my brother's head.

"Stop moving, you're making me feel sick!"

I'm perched on his back in the middle of the airport hall. Lane's flight has landed, and I'm scouring the crowds, craning my neck for a glimpse of him. I rest my chin on Jeff's curly hair and wrap my arms around his shoulders.

"Is he here yet?" he groans, shifting on his feet.

"You're the one who nagged me to come—so quit the whining and move me up. I'm slipping!"

He tightens his grip on my knees and jiggles me higher. People are glancing over at us, and I can see why. My brother's well over six five—add me on top, and we're pretty hard to miss.

Suddenly, I spot Lane sloping through the automatic doors. "There he is!"

He's moving slowly, fiddling with his baseball cap, his eyes scanning the space, and my heart races faster with every step he takes. *I missed that idiot!*

"Lane!" I yell, waving. "Over here!"

"Lois, you're destroying my back!"

"Hey, you spend all day downing protein shakes." I tug his ear. "Now it's time to walk the walk."

He tries to bite my finger, and I laugh, slapping a hand over his mouth. I glance up and lock eyes with Lane. He's standing in the middle of the hall, watching me with interest.

I slide down my human footstool and dart my way through the crowds. Before either of us knows it, I leap into Lane's arms, flinging my arms around his neck and locking my legs around his hips. He is nearly knocked over, clearly not expecting it, and drops his bag to wrap his arms around me. He squeezes me tighter, before leaning back for a better look.

"It's gonna take more than a hug to get yourself off the hook," he warns. "You didn't reply to a single one of my messages yesterday, you little brat."

"You should've just called—"

"So I could speak to your dad again?"

"He freak you out?" I grin.

He tries to stay looking pissy, but his green eyes are shining, and I can tell he isn't that annoyed at all.

"Made a new friend?" He glances over my shoulder, and I turn to follow his gaze. My brother is standing where I left him, waving me to hurry. "You know how to pick 'em, don't you?" Lane frowns. "The guy's stacked."

"Wait a minute—are you saying . . . ?"

He arches an eyebrow, and I drop to the ground.

"You think I'm sleeping with him?" I ask, laughter bubbling up inside me.

Jeff wanders over. "Ready to hit the road, guys?"

The combination of my brother's confused face and my roomie's hard stare sets me off.

"What's up with her?" Jeff asks Lane as I double over, tears streaming down my cheeks.

"No idea."

I step to the side to try to catch my breath, then head back over to join them, wiping my eyes dry.

"Jeff, meet Lane."

"No shit." My brother holds out his hand.

"Lane, this is Jeff," I continue, doing my best to hold in a giggle.

"What's so funny, sis?"

"'Sis'?" Lane glances back and forth between us.

I pinch my lips shut and nod, losing it again as realization spreads over my friend's face.

My brother folds his enormous arms over his chest. "You look surprised."

The two guys stare each other down. I'm expecting Lane to act a little sheepish, but instead he doubles down.

"Well, Lois is glow-in-the-dark pale and could probably shop in the kids' section. You, on the other hand . . ."

"Tall, Black, and better-looking than her?" Jeff finishes for him.

"Exactly!"

They bump fists like they've known each other all their lives.

"I'm her adopted brother."

"Now I get it."

"Didn't you tell him *anything* about our family?" Jeff asks me as we head for the exit.

"I thought I had." I bring a finger to my chin.

Lane pretends to start backing away. "You guys are starting to freak me out. I was down for coming, but now . . ."

As we reach the parking lot, I stop in my tracks and grab his cuff, my bottom lip trembling.

"Are you not happy to see me?" I fake-whine.

"Happy and emotionally blackmailed aren't mutually exclusive."

"You two are weird." Jeff dips into the car and settles himself in the back seat, while Lane drops his bag in the trunk. Suddenly, I'm right back to that first morning when I piled my own stuff in his car. Who would've guessed we'd end up like this, four months later? As I go to shut the trunk, I catch his eye, and I'm pretty sure he's thinking the same.

"I'm happy you came."

"Your evil plan paid off." He shrugs off his jacket. "Fucking hell, this heat is insane."

"Told you."

I open the car door, and just before I slide behind the wheel, I jab a finger at him over the roof.

"You better not start liking my little brother more than me."

"'Little'? He's taller than both of us."

"You're such a dumbass! He's seventeen." I roll my eyes. "Come on, they're all waiting for us."

A shadow flits over his face, and he sighs as he climbs into the car.

"Ready to meet the Hogans?" I chirp.

I start the car, and he shoots me a heavy look, so I blow him a kiss.

The first few miles fly by in silence. Lane is tense, I can tell—his breathing shallow. *What a scaredy-cat!* Luckily, Jeff is feeling chatty, and it doesn't take him long to smooth out any edges. As we drive, the guys talk bands. I had already noticed that we liked the same stuff, but Jeff moves in for a deep dive, and as I glance at him in the rearview mirror, I realize he's falling in love with my friend and his taste in music.

"Lois actually brought someone cool home, for once!" he bursts out, and I nearly crash the car.

"Why?" Lane swivels around to face me. "Does she bring guys home often?"

I shoot my brother a dirty look. "Only Kirk!"

"Yeah, but he was lame enough to put us off for life—such a pain in the ass."

"Jeffrey Hogan, I'm warning you." He knows what happens when I use his full name. "Today's a special day," I add in the sweetest voice I can muster. "I plan on living my best life with the people I love, so don't go dragging me down with—"

"That pathetic loser?" Lane cuts in.

Jeff slaps our backrests, laughing. "This guy can *so* have my room!"

"Mom got Grandpa's room ready for him." I beam.

"Oh yeah, I forgot. Sorry, dude—maybe next time."

Lane is glancing from me to Jeff and back again, and I can't wait. I plan on getting sweet, sweet revenge for how he tried to bail on Christmas.

"Home sweet home!"

I pull up outside the house, slam the car door, and stroll over to the porch, turning back only to realize Lane hasn't budged from his seat.

"Come on, Laney!"

He raises a middle finger and holds it up to the window, just as Jeff pushes past me and goes bounding into the living room.

"Guys, we made it!"

I leave my brother to it and head over to the car to coax out my prey.

"Come on, O'Neill. Out."

He unbuckles his seat belt with a groan. "After everything I've done for you."

"Exactly. This is my way of saying thank you."

He freezes and slowly turns to face me. I can tell he's surprised I didn't use my usual teasing tone this time—but it's because I mean it.

"It's going to be great. I promise. My parents are amazing—you'll feel right at home. And tomorrow, we can hit the beach," I add. "The water should be about seventy."

"I didn't bring my swim trunks—"

"My brother can lend you some."

"Seriously? Have you seen the guy? I'm like a matchstick compared to him."

I snicker. "That wasn't the brother I meant."

He looks a bit nauseous then. "There are more?"

I sigh. "Sadly—yes."

"Kids, are you coming?" my mom yells from the house.

Lane pries himself out of his seat, gathers up his stuff, and traipses into the house behind me in silence.

"Just dump your bag and jacket in the hall."

He does as he's told, pulling off his cap and looking at me for a moment. I smile and lead him in by the hand.

"So here he is!" Mom calls out. "The one and only Lane!"

She pirouettes over to him in her hippie apron dress and clasps him in her arms as if he were her long-lost child.

"I'm Mary. Welcome! Smooth trip?" she asks, rubbing his shoulders.

"Uh, yes. Thanks. It was great. Amazing." Lane's gone beet red.

She bursts out laughing, turning to look at me.

"He sounds just like you." She chuckles as she strides over to the dining table. "Honey! Lane is here!"

"Let me just put this gun away and I'll be right with you!" my dad calls out from the landing.

Footsteps echo down the stairs, and I stifle a laugh when he walks through the door, all pursed lips and hard, cold eyes. He's pretty convincing, I'll give him that.

Lane holds out his hand. "Sir."

My dad takes his time looking him up and down. He would've made an amazing actor. Lane clears his throat and shoots me a glance.

"Dad," I sigh.

"Anything I should know about you, young man?" he asks, staring Lane straight in the eye.

"I can give you my parole officer's number, if that helps. He says I'm getting better at my anger management."

A hush falls over the room. And then my father's face breaks into a broad smile.

"Call me Mitch."

He pulls Lane in for a hug, ignoring his outstretched hand, thumping his back. It never gets old: Anytime one of us brings someone home, my dad runs through the same "scary man of the house" spiel. But this is the first time anyone has played along and hit the right note.

"Hey! You're a big guy!" He gives Lane's shoulder a playful punch.

"Careful, Dad, don't break him." I shove Lane out of his way.

"You're a warrior, man," says Jeff. "Kirk nearly shit himself the first time he met Dad. You did an amazing job." He flashes Lane a thumbs-up.

"Kirk was fourteen back then." I narrow my eyes at my brother. "Anyway—where are the others?"

"Kes! Jarrow! Diego!"

As Dad runs through the drill, my mom hands Lane a glass of water. He sips at it, looking at me over the rim.

Jarrow comes flying through the room on his skateboard, and Mom catches him by the ear.

"Not in the house! Say hello to our guest."

"Hello, guest!"

He holds out a fist for Lane to bump.

"And this here is Kesley."

"You got a tattoo?" Kesley stares at Lane.

"Nope."

"Not cool."

"But he saw Anti-Flag," Jeff yells over from the couch. "Live!"

"Very cool!"

I tap Lane's forearm reassuringly.

"How many are there?" he whispers, pressing the empty glass to his lips.

"Just one more to go."

Diego steps into the room, console in hand.

"Lane, meet our resident geek. Geekazoid, meet Lane."

My brother holds out a hand. "You can call me Diego."

The boys throw themselves onto the couches, and I already know what Lane is thinking—Jeff isn't the only one who was adopted. All five of us look completely different. I'm the only biological child, not that it's ever mattered to any of us.

My mom peers at her watch. "Oh Lord, it's past four! Honey, go show your friend to his room, and then come help me in the kitchen while the boys clean the barbecue."

I jerk my head at Lane to follow.

Halfway up the stairs, he grabs my wrist. "Are you adopted, too?"

"No. I was two when we adopted Jeff. Four when we adopted Jarrow, and five for Diego and Kes."

"So you're the eldest?"

"Yeah. Jeff was a baby when he came to us, Jarrow, Diego, and Kes were about one. I thought I told you?"

"I'm starting to realize I don't know much about you at all." Lane is looking at me like we just met.

I turn back to the stairs and lead him across the landing, pointing out the rooms as we go.

"This is my room—that's my bathroom. I recommend you use that one and not my brothers'."

"Got it."

We arrive at the last room along the hallway. "And here's your very own little room. It was my grandpa's. He died last year," I add.

I step aside to let Lane by, watching him take in his home away from home. His face is priceless, and I'm pretty confident that I've aced my attempt at revenge.

"It's . . ." He hesitates before lifting up a thick comforter.

"A hospital bed," I finish for him. "That's right. My mom wants to get rid of it, but my dad likes it too much."

Lane looks appalled, and I snicker.

"She cleaned it all up, I promise. We got all the wet patches out. And look! There's even a chamber pot here in the closet, in case you can't be bothered to use the bathroom."

"When did you say my flight back was?"

"The thirtieth. Same flight as me!"

"Great..."

"Oh, come on! You've won an all-expenses-paid trip to sunny Florida!"

"In a hospital bed that has definitely seen better days," he says, scratching his face.

I lean against the wall and let out a heavy sigh. "Could you at least try to look happy? It's Christmas, after all!"

He rolls his neck and stretches, glancing up at the ceiling before perching on the edge of the mattress. He pats the space next to him, and so I sit on his right, fingering the rip in my jeans, waiting for him to speak.

"Give me a sec to take all this in, okay? It's kind of weird being here, with such an awesome family and everything."

"You said you don't know anything about me—but you don't tell me much about yourself, either," I say carefully.

And it's true. When he's not being moody, Lane can be supersweet. But he does keep mainly to himself. He's almost secretive that way. I'm not the kind of girl who needs to know everything about everyone, but sometimes I'd like Lane to open up a little.

"My parents are nothing like yours. They're cold. Repressed."

I can't take my eyes off his face. There's a hard, stony set to his jaw. It's taking a lot for him to tell me about them, I can see that, and I know I won't get anything more out of him today. It kind of hurts that he doesn't feel he can trust me enough to let me in. And then I remember what my mom once told me: *"Trust isn't something you earn, it has no checks or balances."*

"Mine can be real pains in the ass, you know." I nudge him with my shoulder. "Last year, my dad insisted on coming with me for the campus tour, and he threatened everyone we ran into, telling them he was ex-police and would make life hell for anyone who messed with his baby. It's his favorite lie, by the way—works every time."

"Wait a minute: So your dad isn't really a retired cop?"

"Oh jeez. So he used it on you, too? I told him to keep it in check."

We burst out laughing, the mattress creaking under our weight.

Lane leans forward, plucking up a small box. "What's this?"

"Grandpa's emergency alarm. He would push that big red button and it would start beeping on the other side of the wall."

He raises his eyebrows. "The alarm would go off in your room?"

"Yeah, because I was closest, and my grandpa liked to drive me crazy." A thought suddenly occurs to me. "Give me that—I know what you're like."

I try to grab the alarm off him, but Lane is so much faster and bigger than me.

"This thing is a game changer." He laughs, tucking the box into his pocket.

I roll my eyes. "Okay, I'll let you get settled in, I'm gonna go help my mom. Head out to the yard with the guys when you're done."

He glances out the window. "A Christmas barbecue, huh?"

"What can I say? We're anti-conformists."

"Seems that way."

I race downstairs and into the kitchen, where Mom is taking a break from her pots and pans.

"You didn't mention how good-looking Lane is," she starts, a telltale glint in her eye.

"Okay, cougar lady—relax!"

"Is he single? Please tell me you're dating!"

"Mom, no!" I stare at her. "He's just a friend. It's not like that."

"When we were in the living room, he couldn't take his eyes off you."

"Because he was terrified of meeting the family and needed a little hand-holding," I shoot back.

"You guys have chemistry—"

"Are you reading those weird books again?" I look at her. "He *is* single, by the way. But I'm not. I mean, I am, but you know . . ."

"You know, I think you're better off without Kirk, Lois. You're more yourself."

"What?"

I can't believe what I'm hearing. This is the first time she's ever shared her thoughts on my relationship. She flicks on the oven and mutters something to herself, knotting an apron around her waist, opening a drawer, and turning back to me.

She points a wooden spoon at me. "I want that boy to give me grandchildren."

Say what?

"He reminds me of your father at his age."

I pull a face. "Is that supposed to sell me on it?" I glance over at the stove. "Come on—tell me what I can help with."

Her eyes are shining as she slings an arm over my shoulders and whispers in my ear.

"Well, I've got a cute little dress that would be perfect for—"

"I mean, tell me what I can do to help with the food!" I wriggle free. "Mom, please don't say another word."

She lets it go, and we cook side by side, listening to yelps and laughter drifting in through the kitchen window, Lane's husky voice riding the breeze. I smile to myself. I don't regret making him come—not one bit. I've got a feeling this week is going to bring us even closer together.

21

LANE

"Catch!"

I grab the hot dog Jarrow sends sailing my way and drop it onto my plate, blowing on my fingers. Brat by brat, Lois's family is doing an amazing job of easing my nerves. We've gathered in the yard, the food finally coming off the grill, and my mouth is watering. If it weren't for all the Christmas decorations strung up all over the place, it would feel like the start of a summer vacation.

"Lane, second hot dog incoming!"

"Got it!"

"Nice catch." Mitch is nodding approvingly at me. "Lois told me you're studying film. Play any sport?"

"Nope."

"He does have a side hustle, though." Lois spears her burger with a fork.

I spin around to her, my eyes widening. Don't tell me she's about to . . .

"He writes movies."

"Really? That's incredible!" Her mom is gazing at me.

That was close . . .

"Porn movies." Lois beams at me.

I gape at her. I'm not ashamed of what I do, but is she for real? This isn't exactly family-friendly material.

"I had no idea they used screenwriters for those kinds of things." Mary sounds curious.

"Right? That's exactly what I said, Mom!"

"Of course they do!" Kesley shouts down from the end of the table.

"And how exactly would you know, young man?" Lois's mom eyeballs him.

"Ask Dad."

"Something's burning." Mitch sidesteps neatly, turning back to the grill, while Diego peers at me excitedly.

"So does it pay well?"

"Can't complain."

"Can you hook me up with an actress?" Jeff tries.

"Jeffrey—"

"I'm kidding, Mom!"

His mom might believe him, but I sure as hell don't—not after the secret kick he just sent me under the table.

"Like I said, Lois," her brother says, topping off his glass, "this guy is way cooler than your last one."

It's funny how the simplest of sentences can hit so hard. He just compared me to Kirk as if Lois were my girlfriend, and my eyes slide over to her, a bunch of scenes flying through my mind. It's the kind of movie I would never normally shoot. The Florida sunshine has clearly fried my brain, and now I must be staring at her, because Lois raises an eyebrow.

"Have I got something stuck in my teeth?"

"No, I'm just shocked to see you packing in the calories, for once."

"Since when do you diet, honey?" her mom asks.

Lois is sending me distress signals—I'm picking them up loud and clear. I cock an eyebrow, keeping my eyes locked on her.

"I think my pizza habit kinda put her off for life."

Her mom smiles at me warmly. "I can't thank you enough for taking care of her while she finds a dorm."

"No problem."

"I mean, you weren't exactly down with it at first," Lois adds.

"Maybe not. But I didn't kick you to the curb like Kirk did."

The words come spilling out of me, and when I hear Lois cussing under her breath, I realize what I've just done. Seems like she didn't tell them the full story.

"Thanks, Lane." She narrows her eyes, throwing her knife and fork down on her plate.

"He did what?" the boys and their dad roar as one.

"That's not exactly how it happened."

Lois delivers a swift kick to my shin beneath the table, and I'm pretty sure they all catch it.

"It's his apartment," Lois starts. "So, you know—"

"Don't tell me you're making excuses for him." Mitch bristles.

"That's what she's been doing from the get-go," I say, loud enough for them all to hear.

She's still finding him excuses, and every time she does it, it pisses me off. She'd been making a little progress lately, but I'm starting to realize that she always ends up falling back into the same pattern over and over again.

"He kicked my baby out? After all those years? All those basketball games we went to, cheering him on . . ." Her dad shakes his head. "I'm going to grab my gun—"

"You don't *have* a gun." Lois rolls her eyes.

"Not yet, I don't."

"Dad, please. Don't get involved."

"He's in town, though," Jarrow adds. "I saw him when I was skating yesterday morning. We need revenge. Let's get a crew together and take down that son of a—"

"Jarrow!" his mom hisses. She seems to think for a moment. "The word you're looking for is 'son of a goddamn gun.'"

Jarrow jumps to his feet. "That's the spirit, Mom!"

Lois pushes back her chair. "Look, I can handle this, okay?"

Silence settles over the table, all eyes on her.

"You guys need to calm the hell down and get into the Christmas spirit! I told you everything you need to know, and you promised you'd leave Kirk alone. I'm not a little girl, I can handle my business, and if any one of you starts sticking your nose in, you're dead. Capiche?"

She sits back down, smoothing her napkin over her lap. Her voice softens.

"I was with him for four years. I can't just move on overnight. Plus, none of you know the full story, but trust me—there's no need to worry. Now pass the veggies, Jeff."

I stare at her, shell-shocked. It's wild how she's latching on to this guy, and she might be able to kid her parents, but she isn't fooling me. So they spent four magical years together—so what? She should be madder about this whole situation.

Jesus. Why do I care so much?

I take a bite of meat and do my best to push all the bullshit out of mind. This is Lois's problem, not mine, and yeah, we're friends—but it's her life.

"Shall we exchange gifts?" Mary tries.

I push back from the table just as Lois does the same, and we race inside, sprinting up the stairs. I pull ahead of her to block her way.

"I'm sorry if I ruined the moment."

"Don't worry about it, Lane." She sighs. "By the time we get back down there, they'll have moved on to something else. It'll take more than that to ruin my Christmas." She smiles. "Are you having fun, or do you still hate me for making you come?"

I pull a shocked face. "Weirdly enough, it's actually kinda great."

"I told you my family is cool."

"I got a little something for your parents, but I don't have gifts for your secret brothers."

"I got them some vouchers—let's just say they're from both of us. By the way," she continues, "I found what you rolled up in my panties. Did you have to hide it there, you creep?"

I wiggle my eyebrows at her. I stuffed the small gift into her bag on the day she left without really checking where I was putting it, but I'm not telling her that—I'm getting a kick out of how grossed out she looks.

"Is it something embarrassing?" She looks at me nervously.

"Nope! Relax, you can open it in front of the gang."

"Just checking."

When I step back into the yard, Mary is laying a gift out on each chair, and when she smiles at me, my heart drops. I've never had a Christmas like this—easy, relaxed. With a family. If only Mike could see me now.

"Come on!"

Lois is hopping from foot to foot behind me, and I head back to my seat, my pulse racing.

"I'm so happy we're all here together this evening." Mary gazes at us fondly.

"Thank you for having me," I say, and I mean it.

Lois taps my leg, slipping a little square box into my lap. The wrapping paper is beautiful. Before she snatches her hand away, I give it a small squeeze.

"What a beautiful scarf!" Mary gasps, shaking the fabric loose. "Thank you, Lane. I just love it!"

I smile back at her and open my own gift, thanking her in turn for the leather bracelet.

Mitch holds up the bottle of scotch I picked out for him. "Great choice, buddy! Us men will need to give it a taste before you head back."

"Not cool." Lois pouts.

"I have some French champagne," her mom whispers to her.

Mitch raises his eyebrows. "Where?"

"Some place you'll never find."

"So with the cleaning stuff?" Kesley tosses a ball of crumpled paper at his dad.

"Very good. You definitely got your sense of humor from Aunt Aubrey."

"That's low, man."

I turn my attention back to Lois. She's opening her last gift—my gift.

"No way." She holds up the T-shirt, laughing.

It's blue, with a big "S" in red and yellow right in the middle. I was scared she'd think it was lame, but she looks so happy turning it over in her hands, I think I made the right call. Lewis would be so proud.

"Okay, Lane. You're up next."

I tug at the yellow ribbon and carefully peel back the tape.

"You got a wrapping paper fetish, or something?" Jeff quips. "Rip it off, man!"

"Sorry, dude. My friend Lewis is obsessed with the stuff—he hates it when we tear it. Old habit."

I carry on peeling back the layers, and when I'm done, I fold the paper into fours.

Mary gasps when she sees what her daughter has picked out for me. "Did you two plan this all along?"

"Nope."

"So can we make Superman jokes now?" Diego begs.

"The answer is still no," Lois replies.

"Meanie."

The table bursts out laughing, and I brush my fingers over the fabric. There were a hundred different gifts Lois and I could have picked, and we chose the exact same one.

Mary claps her hands. "We need a photo of this. Come on, you two!"

She whips the Superman T-shirts off us and shepherds us over to the front steps.

"Put them on!"

"Lois, I'm scared," I whisper.

"Whatever you do, don't look her in the eye."

I catch the T-shirt Mary throws my way and strip off before I get my ass whooped.

"Mom, did you just take a photo of Lane with his shirt off?" Lois puts her hands on her hips.

"Just checking the lighting, honey."

"Lord, give me strength."

I slip my arms through the armholes, immediately sensing something isn't right.

Lois starts to laugh. "Shit—you got the wrong one."

I tug down on the fabric, but try as I might, it still doesn't cover my belly button.

"Oh my God." She's bent double. "You're wearing mine."

I close my eyes and shake my head, listening to the peals of laughter all around me.

"That photo will be worth its weight in gold."

Lois leans into me, with my oversize T-shirt on, and I sling an arm over her shoulders, hooking her neck, pretending to strangle her. She dips her head down to my bare stomach and gives it a playful slap.

"Girl, you are giving Florida vibes." She snaps her fingers, burying her head in my chest.

"Say cheese," I mutter between clenched teeth.

She slides a hand along my back, letting it fall to my waist. Mary is laughing so hard it takes her three tries to take our picture.

"Can you send it to me, Mom?"

"If you share it around, I'll cut you up in small pieces," I deadpan.

"I always knew you were a psycho." Lois pinches my side. "Good thing I like to live life dangerously."

"You're lucky I love you," I say without thinking.

"What did you just say?"

"You're lucky I like you," I reply too fast.

What did I just say?

I change back into my clothes, and we spend the rest of the evening wrapped in the same warm, fuzzy glow. By the time we clear off the table, I'm bursting at the sides. I help Mary do the dishes, mainly because I'm a decent guy—but also because I'm hoping for some juicy Lois stories I can use later, too.

"Mom, cut it out!" Lois whines when she joins us in the kitchen. "You have no idea how dangerous Lane will be with this information."

"We're done here." Mary winks at me. "Bedtime, guys!"

She plants a gentle kiss on my cheek, and I fight the urge to squeeze her tight. My own mom was never like this with me, and the rush of feeling is overwhelming.

I race up the stairs and past Lois to make sure I'm first in the shower, playing the day back in my mind while I wash, suddenly wondering how things are going for Carter. I've been so focused on myself, I completely forgot that today must have been weird as hell for him, too.

Lois batters on the door. "You nearly done in there?"

I wrap a towel around my hips, stick a toothbrush in my mouth, and fling open the door. She jumps. I take my time spitting out my toothpaste, drying my hair like I have all the time in the world.

Finally, she can't take it anymore. "Bounce!"

She shoves my dirty clothes into my arms and grins, her smile fading to a frown when I pull my secret weapon out of my jeans pocket.

"Step out of line, and I'll get my revenge," I singsong, waving the alarm in her face.

She glares at me. "I'll be as sweet as pie, don't you worry."

"That's what I like to hear."

I'm lying, of course. I stretch out on the surprisingly comfy bed in her grandpa's old room, and listen to the running water. Once she steps out of the bathroom, I give her a few more minutes. I want to make sure she's tucked up and ready for sleep. I slip the little box out from under my pillow and start counting down in my head—and when the time feels just right, I push the button, muttering the sound of an explosion under my breath. The alarm rings out behind the headboard, the wall nowhere near thick enough, and I can hear her groaning so loud it's obvious her bed is right behind mine.

"Lane, cut it out."

"Who's that there?" I pretend to be terrified.

"Go to sleep!"

"I can hear you so clearly, it's like you're under my bed or something."

"Use that thing once more, and I'll—"

"You mean this thing here?" I laugh, pressing the button again.

A symphony of beeps and curse words explodes on the other side of the wall. Her mattress creaks, and I'm cocking an ear for other tells—when my door flies open, and I jump out of my skin.

"Give me that!"

The room is dark—she lunges for me so fast I don't have time to dodge.

"This is some crazy ninja shit," I splutter as her elbow digs deeper into my chest.

She grabs my gadget and tumbles across the mattress, landing on her feet. I fumble for the bedside lamp and find her standing there in a disheveled mess, prizing out the batteries.

"No more playtime for you!" She shakes them at me, tossing the empty box onto the bed.

I sit up for a better look, jutting my chin at her Superman T-shirt. "It suits you."

She lowers her eyes, swallowing hard when she realizes all she's wearing are panties and my gift. The T-shirt lands just right under her belly button, and she tugs at the hem. She's not wearing a bra—the fabric is clinging to her breasts, I can . . .

She falls to the ground, crouching. "Turn the light off."

"Only if you hand over the batteries."

"Burn in hell."

She drags my comforter off the bed and swaddles herself in it. Cussing as she goes, she catches sight of my Bugs Bunny boxers and arches an eyebrow. "Wow, so—"

A gravelly voice catches us off guard. "What the hell is going on here?"

It's Jeff, watching us from the open door.

"Are you guys fucking in Grandpa's room?"

"What? Oh my God—no." Lois is blushing beet red.

It could look that way, I admit it: I'm practically naked on the bed, while Lois is wrapped in a comforter, her cheeks flushed, her hair a mess.

"What the fuck is going on?" Jarrow has appeared beside his brother.

"Lois and Lane are trying out the hospital bed."

"Naked?" Diego jumps up onto Jeff's shoulders.

"Who's naked?"

I can't see him, but I recognize Kesley's voice.

"This is not happening!" Lois yells. "Go back to bed, all of you!"

I try—and fail—to stifle a snort, which just pisses her off even more. She stomps back into the hallway, shoving past her giggling brothers and slamming her bedroom door shut.

Jeff winks at me. "Nice boxers."

"DROP THE SAND, LADY."

I've got Lois's head trapped in my armpit, and she's struggling to break free. We're on the beach, and though everyone is staring at us like we're crazy, I don't care. I may have *accidentally* tripped her up as we walked along the water's edge, and it was definitely *unfortunate* that she fell on her ass. Now it's payback time, and she's decided her mission in life is to blind me.

"Drop the sand," I repeat.

"Okay."

I can see her hand is still full of the stuff. "You think I'm that stupid, huh?"

One by one, she relaxes her fingers, unfolding them as she waves her hand over her head.

"Take that," she says, flipping me the finger.

"That's a good girl." I pat her on the head.

I still have her clamped under my arm, and when I release her, I take a step back. Her wet hair is stuck to her face—she looks just like the chick from *The Ring*.

"Not my fault you tripped on my foot."

I'm expecting a spicy slap-down, but all she does is shrug and trot toward the water to rinse her hands.

"You know how to lose with style, I'll give you that," I say, creeping up behind her.

She straightens without looking my way or saying a word.

"Are you sulk—"

Splash.

I don't get to finish my question, because the little bitch just threw a clump of wet sand in my face.

"Whoopsie! I don't know what happened there."

I try to open my eyes, but my lashes are weighed down with grit, and rubbing them only makes them worse.

"Here, let me help you."

"No way!"

Too late. She throws water in my face—once, twice, and then with a happy sigh, she empties the whole bottle over my head. I mop myself dry with my T-shirt, gnawing at the inside of my cheek, taking in her smug smile.

She curls a lip. "Truce?"

"Truce," I sigh, holding up my hands.

She's not buying it. She walks backward, eyeing me up.

"Well, this sucks." I nod at the empty water bottle. "I was thirsty."

She points at the water, smiling. "Want me to go fill it up?"

I spot a beach bar farther along the strand and start striding toward it.

"Wait here a second, I'll go buy more."

"Get me a straw!"

I jog over to the hut and wait my turn, plucking up a straw from the glass jar and considering chewing on it, just to gross her out.

Leaning against the counter, I can't help but wink at the girl behind the bar. *Old dog, new tricks . . .*

"What can I get you?"

"Just a water to go, please."

She crouches down to the fridge. "You on vacation?"

"Yeah, I'm here for winter break."

"Thought as much. I would've noticed you around."

She juts a hip out, biting her lip playfully. She hands me the bottle, but when I reach for it, she doesn't seem to want to let go. I would usually enjoy seeing where the conversation leads, but Lois is waiting for me.

I slide a five over the counter. "Keep the change."

"There's a beach party tomorrow night, you know. Everybody goes." She smiles at me. "You could come along."

"I'll think about it."

I head back over to where I left Lois, but there's no sign of her. *If she's planning another ambush, this time she's definitely getting dunked.*

The beach is teeming with people, and I scour the crowds, craning for a glimpse of her, until I spot her chatting with a blonde and redhead by a hut. I can't hear what they're saying, but I don't need to—I can tell from here that Lois is struggling. Something isn't right. Her eyes are narrowing as she nods along with the redhead, and though the sun is blinding, I know her well enough by now.

"Super Lane to the rescue," I mutter to myself.

I sprint across the beach. Lois is panicking, I can see her searching for a way out. Suddenly, she glances up and over at the bar and catches sight of me, relief spreading across her face, followed by a shadow, and though alarm bells should be ringing, I don't have time to stop and think. As soon as I catch up with her, she launches straight into a performance, letting out a yelp, thanking me for the drink in a high-pitched squeal. And before I know what's hit me, she's standing on her tiptoes, kissing me right on the lips.

22

LOIS

I just fucked up. Big, big-time. Lane is looking at me like I'm crazy, and the two brats who've been annoying the shit out of me for the past five minutes look devastated. I acted on pure instinct, and if it weren't for the salt I can taste on my lips right now, I'd swear I'd imagined the whole thing.

Shirley is eyeing Lane. "Introduce us!"

"Meet . . . Shirley and Rona," I stammer.

Lane is still staring at me. He hasn't moved an inch since I kissed him. Slowly, he blinks, and turns back to our audience.

"Lane. Nice to meet you. You guys are Lois's friends?"

"They're Kirk's friends," I say slowly, looking at him meaningfully.

"Same-same!" Rona chirps.

There's a glint in his eye, and I don't like this one bit.

"We were just telling Lois she definitely has to come to the party tomorrow night."

I rearrange my face in a smile. "That's not exactly what you said."

Actually, they said the exact opposite. Just before Lane arrived, dear, sweet Rona had been listing all the reasons why I definitely shouldn't come: according to her, it would be way too much for me to handle—seeing Kirk hand in hand with Rona's cousin, the girl who spent our high school years trying to steal him from me.

Bitch, please!

"I thought you were still getting over the breakup?" She pouts, her voice thick with faux concern.

"She's never been better." Lane smiles, shooting me a quick glance.

Now he gets why I threw myself at him earlier. He moves to stand behind me, slipping his hands under my arms and laying them over my belly, hooking a finger in the waistband of my jean shorts. I tighten my grip on my water bottle, wincing as I hear the plastic crinkling between my fingers.

He keeps his eyes locked on the girls. "You wanna go to the party, babe?" I can feel his breath on my cheek. "I had plans, but . . ."

I try my best to play it cool, but his lips brushing against my neck make it hard, and it's harder still when his finger slips lower, grazing the edge of my panties. There are butterflies going crazy in my stomach, and my senses are buzzing.

"We'll think about it," I manage.

Lane slings an arm around my neck, leaning into me, his cheek pressed to my temple.

"Listen, this has been fun—but Lois has a very, very busy day planned for us." He winks at the girls. "Have a great day!"

"See you tomorrow, then, maybe?" Shirley isn't letting this go.

"Yeah, maybe," he says, saluting her.

In my head, I'm flipping them the finger, but instead I just wave goodbye and let Lane drag me away from the vipers' nest.

Once we're out of sight, I wrestle free, staring straight in front of me, pretending not to notice his sideways glances.

"Don't say a word."

"Oh, don't you worry. My lips are still swollen from that passionate kiss back there."

I shoot him a dirty look.

"I thought you were about to rip my clothes off and start grinding against me. Show your girlfriends what they're missing."

"First of all—they're not my girlfriends. And second—I wasn't trying to prove a point."

"So you just got this uncontrollable urge to suck my tongue off?"

"I didn't do anything to your tongue!" I throw my hands up. "Jesus! I just wanted them to back the hell off."

"What did they say?"

"They spent way too long pretending to give a shit about my feelings."

"Then what?"

"So before you got back—"

"Before you threw yourself at me—"

"Rona was telling me it would be 'super lame' of me to come tomorrow night," I say.

"Because of Kirk?"

"Yeah."

"They know you weren't *just* Kirk's girlfriend, right? They know you're an actual separate person, with an actual separate personality and stuff?"

I look at him. He's just hit the nail square on the head and there's a knot forming in my throat.

"People here have always known me as 'Lois and Kirk.'"

"Until now, that is."

"Yeah," I say. "Thanks for playing along, by the way. I'm sorry I kissed you without asking."

He nudges me with his shoulder, and we spend the rest of the day hanging out.

The afternoon winds down, and we head back to base. As soon as we step through the front door, my brothers are all over me.

"You guys are going to the beach tomorrow night, right?" Kesley starts.

Can't we be done with tomorrow night, already?

"Mom and Dad are cool with us going if you and Lane are there, too!" Jeff bounds over to join us.

"Whoa, relax, guys." I shove them away from me.

Jarrow turns to Lane for a little male support. "It's all about the music and the girls. And the alcohol," he adds quietly.

"I heard that!" I warn.

He clasps his hands in prayer. "Just one drink . . ." He opens his eyes. "And anyway—remember how tanked you were two years ago?"

"Do Mom and Dad know about that?" Diego pipes up.

I roll my eyes and start unlacing my shoes, but Jeff is relentless.

"Lane! You and me—we're brothers now."

"You've known him, what—half a second?"

He ignores me. "You can talk this boring old grandma into it, right?"

"Excuse me?" I toss my sneaker at him, and the boys burst out laughing.

I've officially been overruled.

"Couldn't you guys have adopted girls?" I holler into the living room where my parents are watching TV.

Dad pretends to be horrified. "You want to send me to an early grave?"

"No way. Think of the state of my drains," says my mother, the traitor.

"Lane's our guest," Dad reminds me. "Let him call the shots."

My brothers gather around Lane, begging and pleading and whining for him to give in, until, eventually, he does just that.

"Beach party it is," I grumble, stomping up to my bedroom. "I can't wait to hang out with my *best friends*."

And watch Kirk parading around with his basic bitch.

I WOULD GIVE AN ACTUAL ovary to be anywhere but here right now. I take in the scene, feeling sorry for myself. The beach is teeming with people, and why the hell did I wear a skirt, anyway? It keeps lifting with the breeze, and the temperature has dropped. Actually, scratch that—why the hell did I even come? I could have just left Lane to party alone with his new buddies.

"Stick around!" I call out to my brothers, watching them race ahead of us.

Lane laughs. "Come on, let me buy you a drink."

He pushes me forward, and I obey, dragging my feet and muttering to myself as I go. He clamps his hands on my shoulders and steers me through the crowds.

"If I leave you here while I run to the bar, you're not gonna split, are you?"

"Alcohol. Now."

"I'm on it."

Lane vanishes, and I stand there waiting for him in the same spot, until somebody rams into my back.

"Hey!"

Oh God. I take it back—I'd give two whole ovaries to be anywhere but here.

"Lois? Is that you?"

I stay put. Maybe if I pray hard enough, I'll evaporate in a cloud of smoke. I keep my back turned, until suddenly he's standing right there in front of me.

I slap an Oscar-worthy smile on my face. "Hey, Kirk!"

"You okay?"

"Yep. You?"

He frowns. "What are you doing?"

I just asked you how you were?

Suddenly, there's a nasal drawl whining in my ear.

"Oh, there you are! I was looking for you."

Enter Emily, Rona's skin-crawly cousin. I puff my cheeks out to hide how hard I'm clenching my jaw.

"Oh, you're here, too?" Her tone has shifted.

There's nothing I want more than to walk away and dig a huge hole in the sand—whether for me or her, I can't tell.

"I didn't think you'd be brave enough to come alone."

She blows cigarette smoke in my face.

That settles it—the hole is for her. And Kirk can go in there, too. He hasn't made a single move to put her in her place.

I'm racking my brain for something to say when a cup appears in my hand.

"Your drink, m'lady."

Lane is standing behind me, and I breath out a sigh of relief as he throws an arm over my shoulders, turning to face the other two.

"Hey, Kirk." He keeps his voice steady and smooth. "What's up?"

My ex's eyes dart back and forth, from me to Lane and back again—he's clearly surprised to see him here, a whole world away from Sycamore Heights.

"Nothing much." He scratches the back of his neck.

Lane leans into my cup and casually sucks on my straw. You could cut the air with a knife. I'm getting a real kick out of the look on Kirk's and Emily's faces.

Emily peers at Lane. "And you are?"

Back off.

"Lane," Kirk answers for him. "He's at school with us. The others are back that way," he says darkly, with a nod. "You coming, Em?"

The pair drift off into the night.

Em? Gross.

Lane shoots me a knowing look. "Drink up."

I don't need much encouragement. In fact, I drain my piña colada in one go. *Whoa.* I wince at the hit. I'm not a big drinker, and I make a mental note to keep myself in check—I don't want a repeat of two years ago, when I nearly threw up right in Kirk's lap. Though now that I think about it, I regret not doing it.

Lane peers at me with concern. "You're not gonna cry, are you?"

I shake my head. "Shut up. I'm just pissed, sad, and basically speechless. Oh—and also not drunk enough."

"Did you see his face when I interrupted you guys? I'm pretty sure I wrecked his night."

"You think so?"

I may be stubborn, but I'm not stupid. It's been four months since he dumped me, and he's already on his second rebound. Game over.

"Not sure. But I've got an idea for you."

I sigh, tucking my hair behind my ears. "What kind of idea?"

"This won't be easy, but I think you can handle it."

"Now you've got me worried. If you're thinking skinny-dipping, think again."

"Damn it. Okay, well let's go for option two, then." He pauses. "I'm going to kiss you."

Haha. Good one.

"What's option three?"

He shrugs. "There isn't one."

I peer at him. "Are you wasted already?"

"Nope. I just think Kirk needs to be taught a lesson." He frowns. "It's like he feels he can do whatever he wants, and it's starting to really piss me off."

I'm feeling uneasy about this whole situation. "It's not a big deal, Lane. Okay?"

"Look at you, Lois. You're *this* close to breaking down." He rests his hands on my shoulders. "Take it from a friend."

A friend . . . I lower my eyes and bite my lip.

"Okay—but no tongues." I can't believe I'm actually agreeing to this.

"It'll be more impactful with," he says. "Trust me. I'm a screenwriter."

"On the lips?" I blurt out, without thinking.

He leans back to give me a pointed look.

"I mean, it'll be kind of hard to make out with your cheek, but I'll try anything once."

"Come on, don't make fun of me. It's just that—"

"He's looking straight at us, Lois. It's now or never."

I can hear Kirk's latest rebound giggling over the music. Her screeches are piercing right through me. Nails on a blackboard.

I stare at the ground, then glance at the sea. I watch Lane's Adam's apple as it bobs, and when he parts his lips to talk, I find myself closing my eyes. Lane is a guy—he knows what he's doing. And I have to admit, there's nothing I'm craving more right now than the sweet taste of revenge.

"Do it," I murmur—so softly, I'm not sure he even heard.

A second trails by, then a handful more. I'm just about to open one eye when I feel a soft, warm pressure. His full lips are shy and featherlight against mine, so foreign yet stirring something so sweetly familiar all the same. I'm rooted to the spot. Lane's kiss is slow and smooth, tracing my lips with his without nudging any deeper, maybe because he's scared I might run away screaming. And he's right to hold back—because the truth is I'm terrified. I've only ever kissed one other boy before, and right here, right now, I feel out of my depth. Maybe Kirk broke me. I'm not sure what to do with myself, and so I just stand there, frozen. Maybe this was a bad idea.

"Stop thinking." Lane hushes the words against my lips. "It's just a kiss."

"I'm sorry."

"You want me to stop?"

When I don't reply, he ends this . . . *kiss that means nothing at all*, widening the space between us. He's appraising me in silence, his hands still resting on my shoulders. He brushes my cheeks with his thumbs. I know his eyes by heart now, I know they're green—but in this moment, they somehow look different to me, though I can't pinpoint how.

"Want to head home?" he asks, not letting go.

I can't stop staring into his eyes. This is Lane, right? Kind. Generous. And I know it's strange, but it's like I've only just realized that he's someone I really trust.

"Lois?"

Kirk didn't break me—he just silenced my inner voice by slowly drowning it out. If I'm hoping to move on, I need to take back control.

"Okay, let's go . . ."

He starts to step away, and as he does, all my doubts evaporate. I'm done with the icebreakers. I catch him by the collar and pull him in, my mouth crashing into his as I part his lips with my tongue. I'm about to pull away when his hands rise to cradle my jaw and his mouth opens, tentative and warm. His tongue probes for mine, once, then again, bolder this time. By the third time we're melting into each other. My mind goes weightless, and all that's left is him, and the way we fit.

One of his hands slides to cup my neck and bury itself into my hair. Steadier now, more confident, he tilts his head and kisses me deeper, pressing into me like he can't get close enough. He lets out a groan and I tighten my grip on his T-shirt, holding him near, desperate to keep him here.

I don't know how long we spend kissing, but when we finally break apart and I feel the cool breeze against my wet lips, I am completely dazed. I let go of his T-shirt, flexing my stiff fingers and take a step back, disoriented.

"That was . . . solid work," he says hoarsely. His forehead is creased.

I let out an uncontrollable laugh, and rub my arms to collect myself.

"Kirk looked pissed," he says, nodding over to the campfire.

Wait, he was checking Kirk out while we were kissing? Because personally, I was in no state to be paying attention to anything else.

I feel so awkward all of a sudden. "Right . . . mission accomplished, I guess."

"I'm going to grab another drink. Want anything?"

"Yes!" I'm practically begging. "Whatever you're having."

He disappears into the crowd, and I just stand there, frozen in place, pressing my lips with my fingers, my heart pounding in my chest. It's like the blood in my veins is electric, and though my pulse should be slowing down, it's only picking up. I shift from foot to foot, swaying back and forth. I want to laugh, and I want to . . . *Where's Lane?*

I swing around to check the makeshift bar. The lights and campfire are blinding. I scour the crowds until I lock eyes with Kirk, and I nearly choke on my own spit. Lane was right—judging by the way Kirk is watching me from his seat on that log, he didn't miss a second of what just happened. I'm surprised by how unguilty I feel. I watch as he slowly puts his beer down in the sand and makes to stand. *Is he coming over here?* I see him mouth something. And then he starts walking right toward me. But something makes me look away. It's like my body can sense him. Lane. He's slouching at the bar, a glass in either hand, deep in discussion with a brunette I recognize immediately. *You have got to be kidding me.* In a few quick strides, I close the space between us, so mad I almost spit the words.

"What the hell are you doing?"

Lane jumps.

"Just getting to know each other," Emily purrs.

So now she's trying to steal Lane, too? For real? She got what she wanted with Kirk, and now she's got her eye on my new boyfriend? Shit, fake boyfriend, Lois! I should be stoked that she's moved on from Kirk, but all it does is fuel my anger.

"In that case, let me get that."

I snatch the cup away from Lane and down it in one.

"And you know what? I'll take care of this one, too."

I reach for the second beer, holding it up in an invisible toast. I silently curse Emily as I drain half the beer, putting an end to their cozy little chat. The way Lane is smirking at me is really getting under my skin, and I take a deep breath in to stop myself from yanking his hair.

"Have a great night, *Amelia*," he drawls.

He lunges for me, grabbing me by the waist so suddenly I let out a yelp as he hoists me over his shoulder. My cup slips from my hand and falls to the ground, spattering Lil' Em as it goes. I'm too far now to make out what she snarls at me, but I *am* close enough for her to notice the finger I'm flipping her way.

Lane hauls me through the throng of dancing bodies, and I greet familiar faces with a maniacal smile as we go, watching mouths fall open in our wake.

I pummel Lane's lower back. "What are you doing?!"

"Saving us from a slow and painful death?"

"Seemed like you were enjoying yourself..."

He stops in his tracks and swings me down to my feet, and as I teeter backward, he grabs my T-shirt to steady me. Before he lets me go, he pulls me closer.

"You're full of surprises, you know."

"How so?"

"You do a great job playing the jealous chick." He tugs on a strand of my hair.

"I hate that kind of girl. The ones who flirt with other girls' boyfriends."

He raises an eyebrow, and I thump him in the chest.

"Oh, please—you know what I mean."

He studies me, twirling a lock of my hair around his finger. It feels like he wants to tell me something. My eyes drift down to his lips. *Jesus. Why do I want to kiss him again?* I need to put a stop to this. Immediately.

"Lois?"

"Mm-hmm?"

I blink a few times before shifting my gaze up to his eyebrows. There, that's better. Eyebrows are much safer.

"Come on."

He takes my hand and leads me over to a speaker. The music is pretty good, and Lane is more touchy-feely than he usually is, but I'm guessing he's still in character.

"Now that our mission is complete, can we just enjoy the rest of the night?"

Our mission—right!

"Sure thing! What shall we do?"

"Dance?" He starts moving to the beat.

I laugh, shoving him away. "I don't think so! Keep those hips away from me, or I'm calling the cops!"

"Come on, baby. Shake that a—"

"Eww! Plus, the Lane I know doesn't do dancing."

"Then allow me to introduce you . . ." He clasps my hands in his. "Loosen up, Lois! You complain that I never open up and now you push me away?" he fake-whines. "You do realize that we passed a milestone with that kiss, right?"

Yeah . . . I realize it a little too much, maybe.

"It's just—"

"Come on. Let me lead."

Whoa. Why did that make my heart just skip a beat?

"You were sucking on my tongue ten minutes ago, and now you're acting all shy?" He spins me around.

"Don't say that." It's getting hard to breathe.

"Why? Is it making you want to do it again?" he murmurs, swaying from side to side, a hand on my lower back.

He's joking. Isn't he? I should be saying no—that would make perfect sense, after all. But instead, I'm reliving the feeling of his lips on mine, and I can't think straight.

"You can say it, Lois."

"Say what?" I can't take my eyes off his mouth.

"That I have the lips of an angel, and all you can think about is getting another taste of my honey."

I pull a face. "Is that a line from one of your pornos?"

My eyes drift back up to his.

"Yeah, though in the original, the character isn't talking about saliva."

I mime retching, and he laughs.

"This shit stays between us, okay?" I warn.

"Kind of breaks my heart that you call me giving you the best kiss of your life 'shit.'"

"*I* kissed *you*, remember?"

"Glad you're finally admitting it," he says with a victorious smirk.

"You just pecked at me like a like an awkward teenager."

His mouth falls open, before twisting into an exaggerated scowl. And then he takes my face in his hands, and leans in.

"What are you doing? Stop it!"

Too late. Before I know it, he's licking my cheek, lapping at my face like a dog, and apparently, I'm way too weak to stop him.

"I think I'm gonna puke." I laugh.

Finally, he stops. I try to slip away, but he pulls me in toward him, my back pressed tightly against his chest.

"I'm enjoying this," he singsongs.

"Just think—you could have been back home in Ohio, on a hot date with a pizza box."

"I would've been crazy to miss out on this."

He drapes his arms over mine, takes hold of my wrists, and forces me to dance. We must be getting closer to a speaker, because suddenly the music is deafening, the bass thumping in the pit of my stomach, ringing in my ears. For someone who didn't initially want to dance, I'm doing a good job of letting go, the music guiding my step, leaning into Lane, feeling him move against my back, his breath rushing in my ear as he sings along to the chorus.

A few songs later and Lane's tongue is trailing the length of my neck—and I've forgotten how to breathe.

"Are you done yet?" I giggle, tilting my head to the side.

"What? Isn't that how it's done?"

His eyes are softer than they were earlier. Despite the electro beats pounding through us, we're slowing our sway, and when his lips brush against my skin, leaving feather-like kisses in their wake, I don't push him away. A shiver runs through me, nerves and euphoria shooting through my body.

Slowly but surely, I'm losing control. Lane is getting more assertive, filling the spaces I leave for him to find, his strong fingers still wrapped around my wrists as he tightens his grip, folding my arms over my waist, locking me in place. I drift in and out of the music as he trails his tongue up my neck and captures my earlobe with his mouth, sucking teasingly. A moan slips out of me as I ride the wave of his touch. My knees are weak, and I wonder how we even got here in the first place. Without thinking, I spin around to face him, and slip my arms around his neck. His hands trace the curve of my hips, setting every inch of me on fire. The light shifts in his eyes and his pupils are entirely blown. I hardly recognize him. And for the smallest of seconds, time stands still.

Who moved in first? I have no idea. All I know is my mouth meets his, his tongue parts my lips. Nothing makes sense anymore. Before I know it, I'm pulling on his hair, whimpering against his mouth as he lets out a deep groan. I'm suddenly pressed between a fence and his body, his hot fingers trailing down my lower back to clasp my bare thighs. And I'm definitely not thinking of the revenge mission when I reach down to grab hold of Lane's hand and slide it up beneath my skirt.

Somewhere between his mouth and mine, there's a whimper vibrating as he kneads my ass. Everything else vanishes—my focus is pinned to the ache pulsing low in my belly. My body arches, searching for Lane's, pressing deeper into him, and he meets every roll of my hips with his, our bodies writhing to the same beat, like this is the most natural thing in the world. His hand moves between my legs, and the music is throbbing between us. I want to form words to beg Lane to go further, but the adrenaline only lets out broken, stuttered syllables.

"Lois?"

Somewhere in the distance, I think I recognize one of my brothers' voices, but I'm too far gone to reply. I don't want this moment to end.

"Lane?"

That same voice again.

Lane tears himself away from my lips and looks around as I take a ragged breath in, flooding my brain with oxygen. And that's when I come crashing back down to earth.

"Here they are! You owe me twenty bucks, Jaja," Jeff says calmly.

My eyes widen in horror. Jeff and Jarrow are right there beside us, totally unfazed by the sight of their sister pinned against a wall with her skirt around her waist.

"Shit! You're a pain in the ass, Lois. Couldn't you hold out another two days?"

Jarrow sighs and flips open his wallet, stuffing a twenty into Jeff's hand.

What is going on here? I'm tripping. That must be it. Someone has slipped something in my drink.

I swat Lane's hands away and tug at my skirt. "It's not what you think, we were just—"

"Chill, sis. We like Lane—no judgment here."

"Give me five, bro-in-law!" Jarrow raises a hand.

Lane doesn't respond. Instead, he places his hands on either side of my head, resting against the fence, his chin grazing my forehead, so close I feel him panting against my skin. A full-body shiver runs through me. *Oh God.* What the hell have we done? Everything I felt earlier is being washed away by a riptide of anxiety, and I say the only thing I can think of right now.

"It was just to make Kirk jealous!"

That's a lie—but I can't handle the truth. Lane's breath catches. He pulls back, and the way he's looking at me is unbearably intense. I can't meet his eye, so I decide to focus on my brothers instead. Lane has stopped pressing into me, but I'm suffocating all the same. I feel like a deer in headlights.

He pushes himself off me, freeing me. Without missing a beat, without even stopping to process how weird his reaction was, I start to run, my legs numb and heavy because of the sand. It's got to be the sand.

The music is trailing off into the distance as I press on down the beach, desperate to outrun the shame pooling in my throat, desperate to put distance between myself and the crazy butterflies that fluttered while Lane was kissing me, touching me the way Kirk never did.

The thought alone gets me swaying on my feet. I haven't forgotten how things were with Kirk—I know I haven't. So why does it feel like I've never felt this way before? Shit, I'm so confused. It's my own fault for playing with fire, I remind myself. What the hell was I thinking?

I slow to a walk, breathing hard, gasping for air. I need to get my head straight and try to make sense of what just happened. I was annoyed, plus a little drunk and a whole lot stupid—that's all there is to it. It's not exactly rocket science. Lane helped me out because he's my friend, but he's never been into me like that, not even a little bit. Nothing has changed. We were just messing around. It's not like I have feelings for him. All of this was because of Kirk.

I repeat it over and over, so caught up in my thoughts that I barely even remember making it home.

23

LANE

The sun is spilling in through the blinds, but I'm already wide awake. Lois and I got back yesterday afternoon. Classes start up again in a week, so I should be making the most of this and treating myself to an epic sleep-in—instead, I'm staring at the ceiling, trying to figure out what the hell happened down at the beach back in Florida.

I wish I could forget it ever happened, but I can't stop reliving the moment. This whole situation is driving me completely nuts, and the worst thing is, Lois hasn't even mentioned it. Not once. I thought she'd say something the next morning—but nope. Nada. Sure, I sensed she was a little embarrassed over breakfast, but she just shook it off and went back to acting like normal. When she fell asleep against me on the flight back to Sycamore I nearly jumped out of my seat and activated the damn oxygen masks.

Because yeah, I'm on edge—but seriously, what did I expect? The whole thing was just to piss Kirk off. It didn't mean anything. I have no reason to be mad about it . . . but still. I'm so pissed she just ran away, like what we did was shameful or something. I'm pissed at her dick of an ex and the way he keeps weaseling his way back into her life. And I'm just so pissed at *her*. Her and her damn tongue—soft and warm and wet—that I can still feel in my mouth.

"Fucking stop it!" I chastise myself, springing out of bed and heading straight for the shower.

Once I'm dressed, I make a beeline for the coffeepot. As I'm pouring myself a cup, I look over at Lois. She's out cold on the couch, as if nothing ever happened. *Yeah. Because nothing ever did, you moron!* She stirs in her sleep, burying her head in the pillow, the comforter slipping off onto the ground, offering up a flash of skimpy pajamas. Though they're a faded gray and scattered with a freaking sheep pattern, I'm starting to get hot all of a sudden. In fact, they're making me want to rip them off her and pick up where we left off.

With every sip of coffee, my imagination wanders.

I picture walking over, sliding my hands under her T-shirt, her lips against mine . . .

Enough!

My boxers feel way too tight right now.

I lean my elbows against the kitchen island and exhale loudly. I glance over at the couch. Lois is stirring again, muttering nonsense in her sleep, turning over onto her side.

Great, now her ass is right there in front of me. I slam my cup down on the counter. *Jesus fucking Christ.* There's no way I'm letting things change between us. Yeah, I loved the taste of her tongue, how her ass filled my hands, the warmth spreading between her legs—it's just a human reaction. It'll pass. *This is Lois, for fuck's sake!*

"Come on! Rise and shine!"

I have no reason to wake her up, but I need to snap out of this. I need her to stop making me feel this way.

"But we're on break!" she murmurs.

She rolls onto her back and looks at me, squinting. I squint back. She sticks her tongue out at me, and I return the favor. *That's more like it. That I can handle.*

She pads over to the kitchen, rubbing her eyes and stealing my coffee mug. She drains it before slinking off to the bathroom, yawning. I pour myself a fresh cup and shake my head. What happened in

Fort Myers stays in Fort Myers, and that's for the best—or so I keep telling myself, anyway.

Lois drifts back into the room. "What time you leaving?"

She's talking about the New Year's Eve party tonight. The one she doesn't want to go to. Half the campus will be there, plus plenty of drink and girls, but I just don't feel like it this year.

"Late afternoon. Sure you don't want to come? Becca's going," I add.

"I'm sure. I'm exhausted—maybe I'm coming down with something. I just want to chill."

Why do I get the feeling she's not being straight with me? I step toward her and lay the back of my hand against her forehead. I want to kiss it so bad, but I hold strong.

"Quit playing nurse with me!" She laughs, brushing me off.

I take a step closer. "I think you'd like it."

It was supposed to be a joke, but the air between us feels suddenly charged. Lois bats her lashes and bites her lip, and an image flashes into my mind: me, striding across the floor, pinning her to the wall behind her.

It's official: I'm completely obsessed.

I force myself to meet her eyes. "Why are you staring at my eyebrows?"

"No reason."

She steps to the side and makes for the fridge, leaving me standing there swaying. It's like she is the only thing holding me up.

"I'm gonna head down and pick up some groceries," she says. "Need anything?"

I shake my head. It's only when the door slams shut behind her that I realize I've been holding my breath. Her not coming tonight is a good thing—I could really do with a change of scenery, a reset, with any girl but her. The way I see it, getting laid is the only thing that can fix me.

I'm about to pour myself another coffee when I spot her little yellow coin purse, so I grab it and rush out into the hall, calling after her.

There's no reply, and I figure she must be outside already. I race down the five floors, spilling out onto the sidewalk, where I find her—deep in conversation with her ex. As soon as Kirk spots me, he narrows his eyes.

"What's up, buddy?"

I try to sound friendly, but I'm as cold as ice, and Kirk knows it. Every time I see them together, it hits me straight in the gut. He glares at me as I sidle up to Lois. I slide my hand down her back and leave it to rest on her waist as I pull her into me. I haven't touched her since Florida, and the warmth of her skin sets my heart racing as she wriggles against me.

Kirk turns to Lois. "See you at the party tonight?"

"I—"

"We have plans," I answer for her.

I feel her stomach tighten. She looks up at me, searching my face.

"And groceries to pick up." I wink at her.

I don't even say bye to Kirk. I grab Lois's hand and lead her far away from this guy and his punchable face. I squeeze her fingers and watch as she swings back, waving a quick, awkward goodbye over her shoulder. We get to the corner, and I still haven't let go of her.

She looks down at our hands. "You didn't have to do that, you know. We don't have to do that, I mean. I think he gets the idea—"

"What idea?"

"That you . . . That I . . ." She sighs. "Just forget it."

"Why does that guy live rent-free in your head?"

She stops in her tracks, and my excuse for holding on to her evaporates. I let go.

She stuffs her hands in her pockets and glares at me.

"It's Kirk. I lo—"

She pauses mid-sentence, and we both swallow hard. Or I'm trying, anyway: My throat is as dry as sand.

She scowls. "I don't want to talk about it. You always make fun of me."

"I don't." If I sound surprised, it's because I am.

"You do, Lane. Much less often these days, sure. But . . ."

I sift back through my memories. I don't remember ever making fun of her. Okay, I might have teased her a little at the start—but that was ages ago now.

I tilt my head. "So talk me through it. I won't lecture you, I swear."

"Okay," she starts. "Everything I've ever experienced has been with him. I guess you could say he was my only benchmark," she explains. "In my head, it's like everything leads back to him."

"I don't get it."

And I really don't. This guy dumped her ass months ago, and she's still obsessing over him?

"I know you don't, and that's okay."

Is Lois saying that asshole is the only guy she'll ever want?

"How did it feel when I kissed you?"

The question comes spilling out of me, and it's too late to take it back. *Smooth . . . If I was hoping to act nonchalant, that was a fail right there.*

Lois flushes, standing there in silence staring at me.

"What does that have to do with anything?" She starts chewing on a nail.

I can't take my eyes off her mouth. I step closer, my gaze locked on her lips, watching as she widens her eyes. A car horn blares out somewhere down the street, shattering the moment into a thousand pieces.

"Seriously, Lois," I snap. "You need to get out and live a little. You're being weird about him."

What I really want is to tell her she should sleep with other guys—screw her way to post-Kirk enlightenment. But I can't bring myself to say it out loud.

She flashes me a thumb. "Your advice is always so solid, I'll definitely keep it in mind." She bats her lashes, plastering a smile on her face. "Anyway, why did you come down?"

"You forgot this." I pull her coin purse out of my pocket and wave it at her. "Life hack number two: money is useful for buying stuff."

"Yada yada yada . . . thanks." She snatches it away from me. "Hey—why did you tell Kirk you aren't going to the party?"

Because I wanted to piss him off. But also because deep down inside, I'd rather stay home.

"I changed my mind."

"In the space of three minutes?"

"Yeah."

"I was planning on chilling in front of the TV. So if you want to hang out, I'm the remote boss for tonight."

"Sold." I smile. "What do you say we go find us some microwave meals?"

"Best New Year's Eve ever." She smiles back.

Her cheeks are flushed pink as we head for the grocery store, and I shove down a flicker of disappointment. When I asked about our kiss, I was hoping she'd say she felt the way I did. But what would that change, anyway? It's not like I want to date her, or anything. It's more of an ego thing. Plus the fact that I really could do with getting laid as soon as possible.

Back at the apartment, Lois decides to hit the books, and though I try to squeeze in a little study time myself, I can't focus on anything except what she said about Kirk.

"Okay, Lane." She slams her folder shut, and I jump. "Spit it out."

"What?"

"You keep looking at me like you hate me. What have I done to displease his lordship now?"

"I'm not looking at you like anything."

"You are."

"I'm not."

"Yep!"

"Nope." I shake my head. "I'm thinking, okay? It's just wild to me that you're so obsessed with this one guy."

"Talk about a broken record—"

"It's true, though. There are billions of guys out there, and here you are, clinging to the same old safety blanket."

She brings a finger to her chin. "I think they call it monogamy, you know."

"But you guys aren't even together anymore," I fire back, too harshly.

"Wow, yeah." She frowns. "Thanks for the reminder."

"Sorry. It's just so dumb."

She mutters something and dives back into her books, and I figure I should give her some space for the rest of the day.

Once we've chowed down on our microwave carb feast, I settle into the couch, but I still can't relax. Lois falls back next to me and curls up in the corner.

"You sure you don't want to head out with the others?" she asks quietly. "It's not too late. I don't mind spending the night alone, you know. So if you want to party—"

"You trying to get rid of me?"

"I'm not!"

"I don't give a shit about partying," I say, flinging an arm over the back of the couch.

She nods and turns back to the TV, her legs tucked beneath her, making her look so distant.

"You can stretch your legs out, you know."

She hesitates, and so I reach for her ankles and pull them over my thighs. It takes her a few breaths to relax. There's nothing inherently sexual about this situation, but the heat of her skin against mine is getting to me. I trail my fingers down her calves, and I don't know what the hell I'm doing, but I can't stop. I'm doing my best to play it cool—inside I'm on fire. She shivers, and I can feel her gaze on me like a phantom touch. I keep my eyes fixed on the TV, but as the scenes go flashing by, all I see are images of Lois pushed up against that fence, Lois moaning, Lois coming if only I'd been able to finish what I started. Then she'd see it isn't just Kirk who can get her where she needs to be. The guy has zero experience, but somehow she worships him like he's some kind of sex god. My jaw is clenching. I'm practically panting.

"Lane?" she whispers.

"What?"

"You okay?"

I push her legs off me and jump to my feet. I need water. *I'm losing it!* I pace around the couch, feeling Lois's eyes on my back as I put a little distance between us, laying my hands on the armrest, catching my breath.

"Why are you so antsy? Is it something to do with the New Year?"

I look down at her. "Got any resolutions?"

"Resolutions are just things you didn't manage to do the rest of the year, so—"

"So getting back with Kirk, then?" I can't help myself.

She frowns. "Lovely. How about you?"

"No idea."

That's not exactly true. I do have one idea—and it's getting bigger and harder with every second.

She tilts her head before shifting in her seat, stretching out on one side, an arm folded under her head, her curves gently rising and falling in front of me, sparking a fresh wave of desire.

"Why are you just standing there?"

Because I'm fighting every urge in my body not to throw myself at you. I grip the side of the couch, willing myself not to give in, willing myself not to move. I hold it all back until I can't fight the feeling anymore. It's not a conscious decision—it's a wave that crashes over me and sweeps me under. Adrenaline is surging in me as I leap over the backrest and let myself fall behind her. She gasps as I stretch out spooning her. The seat is wide, but not wide enough for Lois to get away. She's already at the edge and nearly falls off trying to shoot me a confused look. I ignore it and place my hand on her hip to keep her steady. She swallows hard. I can tell her mind is racing behind her furrowed brow.

"Should I scoot over?"

"No, I'm good."

"What are you doing?" she whispers, a quiver in her voice.

I pretend to weigh my options.

"You know what you haven't done these past four years?"

She turns to look at me with a curious air, her body still against mine. Looking her straight in the eye, I run my hand up and down her leg, from her knee to her hip and back again, waiting for her to react. Her hair smells so good. It's making my mouth water. She's staring at me like I'm crazy, when suddenly her gaze clears as she realizes what I'm asking.

"Do you trust me?" I whisper.

The way she's pressed into me like this, I know she can feel how hard I am against her ass. Any minute now, she could jump up and leave and everything could suddenly spiral out of control. But she doesn't move. Either she's too shocked, or she wants this just as much as I do.

Slowly, she nods, and I think I might lose it. There are no more safety buffers here. No Kirk. No mission to complete. Just me and her on the couch, and I tip us past the point of no return, my hand gliding up to her stomach. I feel her muscles tense, and I hold out for few seconds, wanting to make sure we're on the same page. *I need this so bad.* Because I can't get it out of my head. Because I need to see this fantasy through to the end—live out the movie that plays in my mind every fucking time I see her.

My fingers graze tentatively the hem of her shorts—she doesn't stop me. The only thing that changes is her breath, picking up as I start inching my way toward her center.

I watch as she closes her eyes and parts her lips in silence, and I can't take it anymore. My fingers move like they've got a mind of their own, desperate to satisfy this pressure that's been building for days.

There it is—my resolution. The one thing I hadn't done this year. And the only way for us to get back to normal.

I probably should say something, but instead I decide to kiss that damn neck of hers, inhaling her in. She takes a sharp breath in, her back arching in response. She whimpers when her ass grinds against my dick, and things ramp up as I let out a guttural sound I barely recognize. I start sucking at her skin in earnest, nipping at her as I slowly peel back her waistband. She clenches her thighs, and I pause. Her breath is ragged. I watch her writhing on the couch, praying she doesn't stop me. Then one leg falls open, inviting me in. *Thank fuck.*

I find her bare underneath, and I think I might just have died and gone to heaven. Another groan escapes me when I feel how wet she is for me. My fingers part her lips as I slowly slide between her folds, burrowing deeper down. After that, it all goes a little hazy.

I'm used to going hard and fast, but with Lois, I take it slow. Just a single finger and she's already panting. I slide it in and out, my thumb gently circling her clit, savoring the way she squirms beneath me. When I add a second, her whole body starts to tremble. I listen to every sound she makes, how she moans, how she moves, holding her close while covering her neck and mouth with kisses. I reach out with my other arm, lace my fingers through hers, and pin her hand above her head. I feel my pulse quicken as her fingers tighten over mine. Each slow, deliberate thrust between her legs draws a fresh moan from her lips. Then she grabs my wrist with her free hand, steadying herself—and starts to move with me, riding my hand like maybe I'm not the only one who can't get enough. *Fuck. That's it, baby.*

Her scent is everywhere now, something floral cut through with a musky saltiness that makes my mouth water even more—and I'm on fire. What was supposed to feel weird feels so incredibly right, and my cock is aching for more. Sweet torture overwhelms me as my hips buck against her ass, struggling to hold back, every nerve begging to let go. I want to hear her scream my name, and I wasn't expecting to feel this way. I shake off the thought and move faster, nudging Lois to the edge, pushing her toward the moment of release. *Then I'll be able to move on, then I'll be able to . . .*

Her orgasm hits hard, rippling from my fingers to her throat. She tightens around me, shuddering, and my mind goes entirely blank. I'm left completely drained—well, except for the ache between my legs. Lois catches her breath, gulping in the air, and my lightheadedness clears as I come crashing back down to reality. My fingers are still inside her, my lips against her skin. I feel exposed and undone all at once. *Shit.* This was supposed to make things easier, but everything suddenly seems a thousand times more complicated. I'm too scared to move.

I'm still stuck in my head, when someone pounds at the front door. Lois and I jolt upright, and the banging gets harder. I jump to my feet, frowning. Jesus Christ. I've got a raging hard-on—every step hurts like hell.

"Oh, Laaaaney!" Lewis calls through the keyhole.

Lois yelps and makes a dash for the corridor.

"Come on, open up." I recognize Donovan's voice.

What the fuck are they doing here? I open the door a crack to find the entire Campus Drivers crew on the other side, along with Carter and Becca.

"Heading in!" Lewis barges past me and into the apartment. "The party was so lame we left."

Don and Adam follow suit, back-slapping me as they go, Carter peering at me as if he already knows what they've just walked in on. I lock eyes with him. I'm too rattled to look away. I can't decide whether I hate them or I'm grateful they arrived just in time to stop a fallout with Lois. All I know is that I'm an absolute mess. And I need to jerk off immediately.

24

LOIS

I slam my hands against the bathroom door to hold it shut, as if the others might barge in. There's no way they can see me like this. No way. I can't even bring myself to check the mirror. I don't know this version of myself. I've never met her before. *Fuck, I just . . . Fuck!*

I try to regulate my breathing, torn between wanting to laugh and cry. I have no idea how Lane managed to open the door and let those guys in—my legs are like Jell-O, I can hardly stand. *Oh my God! What was he thinking? Like "Happy New Year, Lois! Here, let me stuff my hand in your pants to celebrate!" What kind of fucked-up resolution is that? And why did I roll with it?* Playing the wide-eyed innocent is all well and good—but who am I kidding? I could have said no, and I didn't. Because ever since we kissed on the beach, I can't get that moment out of my head. My plan was to slam my walls up and bury it all deep inside me. I did my best to play it cool. I figured that night was small change to him. I latched on to this idea that Kirk was the only guy in the world for me, but I'm struggling to keep the faith. Lane's whole attitude, everything he said to me before he started . . . My head is spinning.

"Lois?" Becca calls out from the living room. "What are you doing?"

Fighting for my life. And kind of waiting for Lane to come knock on the door and help me get my head straight. But the minutes tick by, and there's still no sign of him. Time to face the music, I guess. It's not like I can hide away in the bathroom forever.

I force myself to stroll back into the living room as casually as I can, slapping a cool, calm, and collected look on my face. I flash the boys a quick smile and wave at my friend before ducking behind the fridge. I kill a little time examining our groceries and consider rearranging them by alphabetic order, desperately dragging my feet.

"What're you doing back there?" Donovan yells.

"Just looking for . . ." I grab the first thing I find. "Pickles!"

I set the jar down on the counter and crack it open, cramming my mouth full. As the sour juices hit the back of my throat and my eyes flood with tears, I remember just how much I hate pickles. Needs must, though—I hold my breath and swallow hard, before reaching for a glass and gulping down some water. *Get it together, girl!*

I wander over to the living room, where Adam looks up from the circle.

"Sorry for rocking up like this. We tried calling, but nobody picked up."

No shit.

"What were you guys doing?" Lewis asks sweetly.

"Nothing," me and Lane answer together.

I glance at him. My cheeks are on fire.

"Wanna sit down?"

Becca pats the couch, and I stare at the cushions, my pulse racing as I play it all back in my mind. The couch. *The* couch I just had the best orgasm of my life on. Nuh-uh. There's no way I'm sitting my ass down there just yet. The floor will do nicely.

"You okay, Lois?" she asks, narrowing her eyes.

I slap my hands down on my thighs. "Sure!"

"You're acting weird."

"What do you feel like drinking, Becca?" Lane asks, too loud.

"Got anything sweet?"

I breathe out a sigh of relief and glance over, meeting his gaze for the briefest of seconds before he looks away. Fuck. I'd hoped to see a glimmer of reassurance from him—but nothing. Not a single sign. Jesus, it was hard enough after what happened in Fort Myers. This is setting up to be way worse.

"So, dude—how was Florida?" Don pops the cap off his beer.

"It was cool," Lane drawls.

"*Cool*"? I'm disappointed that's all he has to say about our week. *Yeah, man. Cool . . .*

As the night unfolds, Lane's behavior just makes me feel worse and worse: He's totally normal, like nothing ever happened. Like it's no big deal. I watch him laughing with his buddies, teasing me, pulling faces at me, just the way he always has, and I know that should make things easier, but instead I feel hollow.

THE FOLLOWING DAYS, IT ONLY gets worse. Classes still haven't started yet, but we spend every waking moment with the Campus Drivers. Lane keeps acting like nothing's changed when we're around them. Unfortunately, that means I keep turning into this uptight, awkward mess whenever he teases me like he's always done. It drives me nuts. I could probably accept that the whole couch thing was just a onetime experiment—if Lane would just *talk* to me about it. I mean, I have zero experience with this kind of thing. Am I overthinking it?

And maybe I *could* move on—if it weren't for the fact he does a complete one-eighty the moment we step into the apartment. Once it's only the two of us, I can feel his eyes lingering on me. When I brush past him, he hardly steps aside. He's a walking, talking contradiction, and it's got me so confused. I've had to stop myself from yelling at him so many times now. I want to scream at him to just *talk* to me, to just *tell* me what exactly is going on—but there's a small part of me that actually enjoys this weird tension we've got going on. This is so messed up. Every time I get a little too close to him, my heart skips a beat. When he falls back onto the couch to watch TV, my breath catches in my throat. And when he drums his fingers a hair's breadth from my thigh, I wish they'd inch a little higher. I'm spending way too much time obsessing over this. I'm even having dreams about it all. I don't know who I am or what I want anymore, and that scares me. I don't recognize *him* anymore, either, and that's ... thrilling.

"Shit."

I stare at myself in the mirror, a toothbrush hanging from my mouth. I've been scrubbing my teeth for a whole five minutes now, playing everything back, going all the way to ... When was it? Christmas—or before?

"I need professional help."

I spit the toothpaste into the sink and dunk my head under the faucet, the water drowning out Lane's footsteps.

"You nearly done?"

I jump, swinging back to face him, wiping my chin dry with my hand.

"I'm in the bathroom!" I clutch my towel tighter around me.

It doesn't cover much, but at least it's something.

"Yeah, you've been in here for like an hour." He folds his arms over his chest, his voice cool. "Your phone rang. Twice. It was Kirk."

My mouth falls open.

"I told him you were just putting your panties back on."

"Please tell me you're kidding."

"Isn't that what you were planning on doing next?" He smiles smugly at me. "Seems like Kirk's having second thoughts about dumping you."

"Shut up."

There's no way. I've been seeing him around way more since we got back from Fort Myers, it's true—but this is the first time he's tried calling. I guess I should be happy, but there's a tightness spreading across my chest.

"I'll call him back tomorrow." Why does it sound like I'm asking a question?

Lane gives me a long, unbearable stare, before sighing.

That's when I remember I'm practically naked, and considering the weird electric tension between us, that's probably not a great idea.

"Let me put my pajamas on," I say, tugging at the towel skimming the tops of my thighs.

I nod toward the door, but Lane doesn't move. He's undressing me with his eyes, and the realization roots me to the ground. *Just leave, already!* Slowly, he uncrosses his arms, looking me up and down, his eyes lingering on my neck, trailing down to my ankles. The air between us is hot and thick, even though the shower steam has evaporated by now, and I'm suddenly not sure I can breathe. By the time Lane steps closer, I'm basically panting.

Suddenly, he's less than a foot away from me. I wish I could tell what he's thinking, but his eyes burning through mine are unreadable. I watch as he clenches his jaw, his muscles rippling, like he's fighting the urge to take another step forward. My throat tightens as I understand he's waiting for me to make the first move and close the distance between us. I don't think I can, though, I'm not feeling very bold. And besides, I need *him* to act—I need some sign that it isn't just me, that I'm not making it all up in my head.

I stand as still as I can, the towel knotted around my chest growing tighter by the second, the only sound the running water. Lane reaches over me to turn off the faucet. The motion closes the distance between us, and my eyes shut instinctively. As his lips brush my temple, I fight to steady my breathing, not wanting him to see how much I love his warm breath against my skin, love imagining how wild he must be feeling right now. I'm scared. I still don't know what exactly flipped his switch, or why the sexual energy is rolling off him in waves, because he hasn't said—he hasn't given me the slightest explanation.

I'm just about to start spiraling down a rabbit hole again when Lane's hand lands softly on my thigh, lingering against my skin for a moment, before sliding up under my towel. The whirlwind in my mind settles in an instant, leaving just one single desire: how badly I want to feel the way I did on New Year's Eve, how much I'm craving everything he did to me.

His left hand rests on my other thigh, inching up and pausing for a moment, giving me a chance to push him back. Once he's sure I want it just as badly as he does, I feel his palms move in to cup my ass, and I think I might be intoxicated. I want him to kiss me so badly, but instead his lips graze the skin behind my ear, unbearably close, with an unrelenting, erotic restraint. I'm fighting hard to stay quiet, but my body betrays me. I tilt my head to the side, giving him better access to cover my throat with kisses, my fingers clinging to the edge of the sink. When his tongue trails up from the nape of my neck, my mouth falls open in a silent "Oh," and I rise on my toes to follow his movement. I lift myself up and then down and then up again, my breasts pressing harder into his chest. I can't see his face, but I can tell he's tuned in to every one of my reactions, his hands reading me.

"How does this feel?" he asks, his voice husky, the words hot against my neck.

He nips me lightly, and I turn his question over in my mind, searching his eyes with mine.

"What?"

"Does it feel good?"

I was desperate for us to talk, but right now his questions just make me feel awkward. I can tell there's more to what he's asking, but this is Lane—the most confusing guy I've ever met.

He slides his hands up to my waist and strokes my sides with his thumbs, staring me straight in the eye. He's waiting for me to reply, but he's being so weird and intense, it's putting a damper on the mood.

"Are you doing this because of Kirk?" I blurt out, the realization hitting me as I say the words aloud.

He doesn't reply. He doesn't have to. His eyes say it all. A part of me is upset, another part can't be bothered to care—the part that's hungry for his mouth. His eyes stay locked on mine.

I tilt my chin up. "It's not bad."

He frowns. I frown back. My skin is cooling, and I shudder. He takes a step back, his gaze trailing down from my lips to my towel to the tops of my thighs, and just as I'm about to ask what's going on, he grabs me by the hand and pulls me into the living room. I drag my heels and yank my arm, but it's no use.

When we get to the couch, Lane spins me around and pushes me backward, sending me tumbling back into the cushions, and as I make to sit up, he's already on top of me, one hand pressing down on my shoulder.

"What is going on?" I prop myself up on my elbows.

The big question. I've been dying to ask it—too *scared* to ask it—since New Year's Eve, and now here I am, practically begging him for an answer.

He flashes me a grin, and my heart skips a beat. Without a word, his hand slips between my legs, his smile turning wicked as he feels how wet I am. He gently traces my lips, and a moan escapes me. My body is thirsty for more, every inch of my skin crying out for his touch, and I'm so sure he's about to push me to the brink again, nudge me over the edge like he did the last time, when he suddenly scoots back to the end of the couch, parts the towel draped over my legs, and vanishes between my thighs. I clamp my legs shut over his head, and he groans in response, pushing my knee aside with one hand.

"Lane, wait."

He can't be doing this, it's too . . .

He lifts his head and looks up at me. "Should I stop?"

He hasn't even started, and I'm already throbbing. I look down at him. Look down at *us*. I don't know what to say. Is this what I want? Kirk's the only guy who's ever touched me like this, and I'm expecting to feel somewhat guilty. I can't just relax and let it all go—that's just not me. And anyway—what if me and Lane aren't on the same page? I need this to mean something, I'm scared of losing myself. I'm scared of . . .

"Lois?"

He's so close, I can feel his breath against the delicate skin between my legs, and my common sense flies out the window. Slowly, I shake my head. I just want to see whether it's as good as I've been imagining, that's all. *No big deal, right?*

I watch as he moves closer, sinking lower between my thighs, and leaving trails of kisses on his way down. His breath ghosts over my slick folds, and the first featherlight kiss he plants there is a slow shock that ripples through me, and I gasp, hips jerking. He looks up at me through roguish eyes and pins my thighs with his hands, thumbs caressing. I swear I can feel his smile against me. And then, with torturous patience, he drags his tongue in one slow stroke from my entrance to my clit, and my vision goes white.

"How does *this* feel?" he asks, circling my clit with his tongue.

That damn question again. My mind is racing—nothing makes sense anymore. Every fiber of my being is on fire, my breath hot and shallow. I never expected to have this with anyone other than Kirk, let alone Lane. He relaxes his grip on my knee, stroking my inner thigh, his eyes still boring into mine, as if he can read the contents of my soul. His cockiness has loosened, giving way to something quieter, more cautious, as if Lane were suddenly as nervous as I am. I've always thought of him as this experienced guy, but now I'm seeing him in a whole new light. This vulnerable side of him is new to me, and I love how it makes me feel. *Careful.*

"What about this?"

He gently sucks on my clit, and my mind starts drifting away from my body, and I shake my head, unable to reply. I don't even know what he's asking me.

"Or this?"

When he slides his tongue inside me, I lose control, arching my back, my elbows giving way beneath me as I fall back into the cushions. My fingers claw at his hair, and he lets out a low sound against me.

"That's it," he murmurs between strokes, "good girl." Then he starts to suck and lick, drinking in every gasp and whimper he pulls from me.

"Tell me how it feels." He runs his tongue flat over just the right spot, again and again. "Tell me. Or do you not want to feel good anymore?"

All I can do is moan in response, the sound raw. Lane's grip tightens as he pushes my legs higher, spreading me wider, and the last of my thoughts shatter. The only thing that exists is the heat building low in my belly, climbing higher with every second of his touch. It's like he knows exactly how to ruin me. His tongue flicks and circles, teasing the edges of my clit, and when he finally slides a finger inside me, curling it deep, I cry out. He pumps it slowly, curling again, while his mouth sucks and laps in a rhythm that has my vision spinning. The pleasure builds, coiling tighter, until it's all I can feel—Lane, and the way he's devouring me like he'll never get enough.

At some point, his hands move up to lace with mine, and I cling to his fingers, strangling them with every wave of ecstasy that crashes through me. I tug him closer—or maybe he pulls me in—I can't tell anymore. It's messy, desperate, and all-consuming.

Once I return to my senses, I roll over and collapse against the couch. Lane is panting hard as he rests his cheek against my pubic bone, wiping his mouth dry on my skin. As my pulse settles, the weight that's pinning me down starts to lift, and I stare up, my eyes wide and wild. My legs are shaking. I gaze up at the ceiling, tears welling in my eyes.

When I feel Lane stir, I clamp my mouth shut, turning away as he retreats down the hallway, listening to the bathroom door open and close. And then nothing. I'm alone here on the couch, struggling to make sense of what just happened. Our friendship just took a sharp turn off the beaten track, and Lane is in the driver's seat. I'm putting my trust in a driver who won't talk to me. And I have no clue where we're headed or how we're getting there. My skin is on fire—so why am I shivering so hard?

25

LANE

I dunk my head under the faucet and let the icy water wash over me. My cheeks are burning, my chest feels tight. I grip the edge of the bathroom counter so I don't wander back into the living room. I don't even know what I want. I'm desperate to get back to the couch to finish what I . . . What I never should have started on New Year's Eve. *Terrible idea, man.* It's safer here, that's why I'm clinging to this sink.

I rub my mouth, trying to erase the traces of Lois's sweet softness, but it's all too new and real right now. The memory won't fade, and it's driving me crazy.

Get back in there. Get your ass back in there and tell her something.

But like what? I don't even know what I was thinking! I was just overcome with this urge, like a craving I couldn't suppress, watching her stand there with her towel and her mouth, talking about Kirk. It was too much. I lost control. She was standing right here where I am now, and no matter how hard I try, I can't forget the sight of her. I fling my head back, sending droplets flying over the walls. *Why is it getting so fucking hard to have her around?*

I open my bedroom door and press my forehead to the window. I need to go in there and talk to her. I can't just ignore her, not after what I just did. Lois doesn't deserve to be given the cold shoulder. She doesn't deserve a repeat of New Year's Eve, either. She didn't ask me a single thing after that night, even when I acted like nothing ever happened. She didn't push it, I guess because for her there's nothing between us. All there is, is me trying to help her forget all about Kirk so she can finally move on. I should just carry on being her friend and let time do the rest. I bury myself under my comforter and swear to myself it won't ever happen again.

"ARE YOU GOING TO BE okay?" I ask.

"Yeah. I didn't sleep well last night." She yawns from the passenger seat, warming her hands on the radiator.

Me either. I barely got any sleep. She glances out the window and sighs when she catches sight of the hordes of students. Technically, classes started three days ago, but this is our first day back on campus. Lois came down with a nasty flu, she's been stuck in bed for a week now, and I've spent my time nursing her, listening to her groan, puke, and sleep. I gave her my bed and watched over her like a worried mom. *Great start to the New Year...*

I'd hoped all the sleepless nights and time to think would help me cool down, especially considering she isn't exactly glowing right now. But nope. It's not that I have a puke fetish or anything, but I can't stop thinking about what we did every time I walk past my couch—or whenever I close my eyes.

I thought making her come would break the spell, but now all I want is a repeat session. I want to do much more than that, to be honest. I've had to take care of myself more times than I'd care to count, and it's... difficult. Luckily for me, I'm pretty good at pretending I'm okay and suppressing that kind of shit.

We get out of the car, the way we've done for weeks now, and make our way up the stairs to the main building.

"I'm gonna grab lunch with the others later. Want to come?"

She stiffens, searching the ground for answers. Since I crossed the line, she's been shakier, somehow, the light in her eyes dimmed, and I can't help but feel a little sad. She's quieter than usual—a shadow of the superconfident Lois I met way back when. Everything I was scared would happen, *has* happened, and despite it all, I still can't bring myself to try and clear the air.

"Yeah," she says after a while. "Sure."

I'm weirdly relieved. She smiles at me and disappears down the left wing without glancing back. I head to my workshop, and three hours later, I'm back in that same spot waiting for her.

I see Kirk bobbing along, but as soon as he notices me, he turns on his heel and vanishes. *Damn, I hate that guy.* Every time I see him, my fists automatically clench. I want him to pay for being such a dick. He's the reason I did what I did, and that only makes me hate him harder: My life was so chill before he came along. I force myself to breathe out, and as I spy Lois coming toward me, my face breaks into a smile.

"I feel like I missed a whole semester in just two days," she says, shaking her head. "This morning was really bad—I'm totally out of it."

"Winter break is tough," I agree, pushing open the glass doors to the dining hall.

We load up our trays, and it doesn't take long to zone in on my friends.

"Lois!" Lewis waves us over. "You survived!"

When he goes to hug her, she freezes.

"Are you still icky?"

"I'm super contagious." She ducks away from his embrace. "You better stay away from me. Like, really far away." She steps back, flapping a hand. "Farther, Lewis."

"Uh-huh."

"Trust me, it's for your own good. I've honestly never been sicker in my whole life. I wouldn't wish it on anyone—not even you." She pats his chest.

"She's so goddamn caring," says Don through a mouthful of chips.

"How about you, Lane? Are you infected, too?" Adam pulls a face at me.

"I'm Teflon, man—nothing sticks. I made direct contact with her puke and lived to tell the tale."

Adam points a trembling finger at me. "A survivor!"

"Oh, give me a break!" Lois is blushing.

Becca waves a spoon at her soup. "Guys! Kinda trying to eat here."

"I genuinely didn't think a human body could contain that much barf. I'm pretty sure the neighbors all heard, including Kirk."

Everybody starts laughing. Everyone, that is, except Lois, who sits there glaring at me.

"Good one, Lane," she snaps. "I should've spat in your coffee and taken you down with me."

"Not sure that it would've changed much," I snipe without thinking.

She widens her eyes at me. Luckily, none of the others seem to catch my slip-up, and the conversation flows on, me playing the good old Lane they know and love, pushing my feelings out of mind. What I said was true, though: considering everything we did on the couch, if whatever she had was contagious, I'd definitely have caught it by now.

Stop thinking about that fucking couch, man.

I dunk a chicken tender into my ketchup and take a bite to distract myself. The table is chatting away happily when suddenly Lois's phone rings and I tune out of the group conversation, my eyes locked on her.

"Uh, sure!" Her face lightens. "Okay, I'll be there. Great. Thank you so much."

She hangs up, and I watch her stare down at her phone in silence. I give her a light kick under the table, and she jerks her head up.

"Who was that?" I ask casually, taking a sip of my fruit juice.

"The dorm office."

The juice goes down the wrong way, and I splutter.

"They've found a room for me. I need to get down there this afternoon."

The breath is snatched out of me. I nod, keeping my gaze lowered to my tray. Silence has fallen around the table, and I should say something, say *anything*. I should tell her—

"That's awesome!"

Becca to the rescue.

"Yeah." Lewis stretches out in his chair. "Awesome. Right, Lane?"

"Totally."

I flash him a smile, and he raises his eyebrows, folding his arms behind his head. Lois stares at her water bottle in silence before leaning down to scoop up her bag, tidying away her stuff, rearranging her tray, scraping her chair back to stand.

"Where you going?"

"I need to jump on a bus. The dorm's pretty far away. I should leave now, give myself plenty of time."

I frown. "But you haven't even—"

"Did she really just say she's going to catch a fucking bus?" Donovan lets his fry fall to his plate.

Becca laughs. "I think she kinda just did."

"Run, Lois! Run for your life!" Adam scowls.

"Absolute disgrace," says Lewis, shaking his head.

Don carries on staring at her, his mouth hanging open.

"You're sitting here at the Campus Drivers' table, and you're telling us you're about to get on a *bus?* Fuck, Lane." He glares at me. "Did you break her?"

"You guys are eating," she says, shrugging on her coat. "And you've got class this afternoon."

"I can fit a ride in," Adam offers.

"Same," Lewis chimes in.

I shove my tray back, steady my voice. "I'm taking her."

All eyes turn to me.

"I can handle myself, don't make this into a big deal." She scowls.

"There is no big deal. I'm taking you."

"You're going to skip class? *Again?*"

"Let's go."

I snatch up her bag and stride toward the exit, ignoring my friends' laughs as I go. Shit. I had totally forgotten about the whole dorm situation, but considering how things seem to be panning out, maybe that's not such a bad thing after all. Every fiber of my being has been wanting to pin her down on that goddamn couch and continue what we started. Maybe it's better she leaves—because I can't deal with this anymore.

"Gosh, Lane, wait up!"

By the time she catches up with me, she's out of breath.

"I don't mind taking the bus, I sw—"

"Oh, but it's my pleasure, ma'am."

You can say that again.

"Well, if you're sure..."

Lois chatters away as we walk, thinking out loud, obsessing over her new room, and I really wish she wouldn't. She's trying to lighten the mood, but I'm not playing ball. All the way there, I stick to a few noncommittal "For sures," with a few grunts thrown in for good measure.

"I was starting to think the whole waiting list thing was bull."

"Yeah."

"This is amazing."

"Yeah."

I can't think what else to say.

Pulling up outside her new building, we sit there in silence, staring up at it for a moment.

"They gave you the one dorm out in the sticks."

"It's no farther from campus than your apartment." She peers out the windshield. "I think it's kind of cute."

While she takes in her surroundings, I watch her biting her lip, batting back flashbacks to the sounds she made when I slipped my tongue into her. *It was just sex.* That's what I try to keep telling myself—but if I'm being honest, she got under my skin, and now I really don't know how to get her back out.

"Okay, let's do it."

I need to get this done and dusted.

A tall guy introduces himself as the resident adviser and leads us from the front desk up to the third floor, opening the door and turning around to face us with a smile.

"It's a triple—you'll be sharing with two other students, so let me just tell you what I already told them: no overnight boyfriends."

He looks at me, as if to say, "Listen, dude, if your sorry ass finds its way up here, I'll know about it." This guy knows his nonverbal communication.

"We're not together," I tell him, shooting him a smile that translates to "But if I want to fuck her here, I'll do what I want, asshole." That was a mistake—fresh visions of me and Lois go flashing through my mind.

He leads us through the room, ticking off the features as we go. "Bed. Shower. Desk."

"It's tiny."

"I don't think so." Lois turns around, taking in the space. "It does the job."

The RA glances at her. "No drilling holes in the wall, by the way."

I stroll over to the window and gaze outside.

"It's so green!" Lois presses her forehead to the glass. "Check out that view!"

I spin around. The guy has gone, leaving the door open in his wake.

I turn back, peering through the glass at the park.

"It feels a little shady to me. Look at that guy, over there—I'm getting bad vibes."

She shifts to get a better view, pressing her arm into mine, her fingers clasping the window a breath away from my hand. I should scoot over, but I'm frozen to the spot.

"The guy sitting on the bench by himself? Eating a salad?"

"Textbook psycho behavior—what kind of dude eats salad on a bench?" I ask. "A pervert, that's who."

"Oh, please! The light here is great—plus, there's a bus stop right there."

I don't know who she's trying to convince, but I'm not buying what she's selling. I hate this place. It's small, it's ugly, and it reeks of cheap perfume. Lois glances over my shoulder, so close I could kiss her without even leaning in.

"And the other girls seem nice." She eyes up their things. "See—one of them has a swimsuit! We could hit the pool together."

Just as I'm about to roll my eyes, she glares at me.

"Quit the attitude. Isn't this what you've been waiting for since August?"

No.

"Yeah."

She carries on staring at me, and I step toward her just as she moves to the side, sitting herself down on the mattress, bouncing up and down, trying it out for size. She flicks on the ugliest bedside lamp I've ever seen and pulls open the closet.

"A bed and a closet," she sighs happily. "Everything I ever dreamed of."

"The toilet is in the shower," I continue. "And I mean that literally."

"What's with the snobby rich-kid attitude? Most students live in dorms, you know." She puts on a fancy accent. "Not everyone has your pedigree."

She shuts the closet, and somehow the RA's back already.

"So," he starts, "you like it?"

"Yes!"

"No."

We reply at exactly the same time, and Lois shoots me a look.

"I like it," she insists. "And anyway, it's not like I have options. So, now what?"

"Come on down to my office and I'll give you the paperwork and checklist. You'll need to sign a housing contract, too—I need everything by tomorrow. Just bring your stuff with you, and we'll get you all moved in on the same day."

"Amazing."

We traipse down to the first floor, and while Lois heads into the office, I wait in the car. I need time to think. So—she could be moving in tomorrow? Fuck. They don't waste time, huh? I thought I'd have the weekend to get used to the idea. I drape my arms over the steering wheel and rest my head against the leather, breathing in the comforting smell and swallowing back on the knot that's tightening in my throat. Lois is leaving, but that doesn't change a thing. Does it? We're friends, we can still hang out on campus—I could even come by and pick her up every morning. Nothing's going to change between us. Plus, it might help me shake off some of the urges I've been having. A fresh start! The only reason I've been weirdly into her lately is the fact that she's in my face every day. And that she's obsessed with her stupid ex. Her moving out could change all that.

A door slams, and I jerk my head up. Lois trots over to the car and slides into her seat.

"Thanks for waiting."

"No problem."

"I don't want you to miss class, you know. Just drop me off at campus and I'll walk home."

"No, I'm gonna head back with you."

"Are you okay?" She frowns. "You look weird."

She stretches out a hand. Changes her mind. Her eyes search mine, like she's hoping I'll say something, and for a fleeting moment, her gaze drifts down to my lips and desire pounds through me. *Seriously, this needs to stop.*

"Yeah, I'm okay. Don't forget your belt."

She clips herself in, and our ride back feels just like the drive over to the dorm, except this time I'm even more stressed. As we stroll from the parking lot to the apartment, her arm brushes against mine with every step. I can hear her sighing, shooting me confused looks as we make our way to the front steps.

"I hate it when you're like this," she bursts out.

We take the elevator up. Slowly, my eyes move to meet hers.

"Like what?"

"Moody. Shut down."

"Winter break is over, Lois. I'm bummed—that's all."

She chews on her nail. As soon as I step into the apartment, I make a beeline for the fridge and grab myself a beer, leaning against the kitchen sink, swigging from the bottle as I stare into space.

"Can I wash some clothes? That way all my stuff will be clean for tomorrow."

I nod, and bring the bottle to my lips. She really can't wait to be out of here, can she?

She sighs again and heads back to the bathroom, returning a few minutes later, standing over her bags, staring down at her things.

"Well, at least we won't need two trips." She smiles at me. "That's a plus!"

She crouches down and starts rifling through her shit. Watching her get ready to leave is putting me in the worst mood ever. There's a knock at the door and she jumps up, racing over to open it up.

"Hey, Carter!"

"I just swung by to pick up Lane's notes. Feeling any better?"

Great. Just what I needed. The one person who can vibe-check me in a second flat. Carter wanders into the living room, watching as Lois turns back to her bags.

"All good, Laney?"

"Never better."

"Are you sick?" He tilts his head, sizing me up.

"Nope."

He purses his lips, grabs a beer from the fridge, and joins me by the sink, jutting his chin at Lois.

"What the hell is she doing? Did you finally make a little space for her stuff?"

I don't answer right away. Watching her crouch on the floor like that, I realize I did her wrong. I should have given her a shelf somewhere. A drawer of her own. And now it's too late.

"She's leaving." My words echo down the bottle neck.

"What?!" His eyes search mine. "But why?"

"She finally got her dorm room."

"Finally?"

"That was the deal," I snap.

I collapse onto the couch and turn on the TV. Carter rushes over to join me.

"Lane, why—"

"Just stop."

I know what he's going to say, and no: the spare room still isn't spare.

He rolls his eyes. "Fine. Just don't come crying to me about it later."

"This isn't a big deal, Cart. Honest. Nothing's going to change."

"Sure. Whatever you say." He drains his beer and scoops up the notes. "I'll swing by at the end of the week."

"Yeah."

"Catch you later, Lois." He glances at me knowingly. "How about we throw you a little party to celebrate the good news?"

She gives him a small smile. "Yeah, sure. Thanks, Carter."

As he leaves, I catch him snickering to himself. He knows that deep down, I'm crushed—and I can hardly believe it myself. This is ridiculous. Living alone has always been my thing, so why is my stomach dropping as I watch her fold away her T-shirts? She could at least *pretend* to be a little sad, couldn't she? I suddenly want to kick her bag over.

"I'm going to my room," I growl.

I can't handle this anymore.

I spend two hours doomscrolling, desperately trying to distract myself—but the stupid videos aren't working. I fall back onto my bed. I wanted her to say that she hates her new room. That she doesn't want to go, that she wants to stay right here. But she hasn't said she's sad to be leaving. Not once. And now I'm stuck wondering whether I was the only one who actually enjoyed living together. And everything that came with it.

26

LOIS

Lane has been holed away in his room for hours, as cold as ever—and it's driving me nuts. I tried my best to seem excited about today's news, digging deep, tapping into my inner actor. I did my best to make it sound like a cramped dorm room was definitely on my bucket list. I finally have a place to call home. I should be psyched—so why does it feel like I'm about to explode?

"Can I come in?" I whisper through the half-open door.

"Sure."

I tiptoe across the room and climb onto the bed, swallowing hard, tapping the hand slung over his face. He's straight-up pretending I don't even exist, so I yank on his wrist for a better look.

"What?!"

"I need pizza." I pout.

"Okay? You know where the leaflets are."

"I mean *homemade* pizza. We've got the stuff to make it . . ."

"You're not going to believe this, Lois—but there are actually people who make pizza for a living. They even deliver."

"Oh, come on! It's our last night." I force myself to smile. "Pretty please?"

"Are you saying we're never hanging out here again?"

"Sure we will! But it won't be the same."

"Yeah." He nods thoughtfully. "I won't wake up to you snoring on my couch the next morning."

"Exactly."

Silence hovers between us. Lane is on edge—I can sense it. Maybe he doesn't actually want me to move out, after all. He jumps to his feet and dashes around the bed, jabbing a finger in my direction.

"You're on dish duty."

I roll onto my back and let out a victory cry.

"And no bitching," he adds.

I nod eagerly, sliding off the mattress.

"And definitely no splashing water all over the place."

"Your life is about to get a whole lot easier!" I laugh, following him out the door.

Somebody get this girl an Oscar.

In the kitchen, I set about getting everything ready, while Lane turns the music up high and washes his hands. I bump into him as I load up on ingredients from the cupboards, rummaging through the drawers.

"What should I do?" he asks.

I give him his instructions, and it doesn't take long for all the awkwardness between us to start falling away. We chat. I sing. We argue back and forth about stuff that doesn't even matter, we fight over pizza toppings, and I let him think he's won before adding whatever the hell I like as soon as his back is turned. It feels great.

We peer in through the oven door at our masterpieces. "It looks weird."

"It's going to taste amazing, though!" I rub my hands together gleefully.

"This place looks like a bombsite—I'm still team delivery."

"You are such a crybaby! You should be proud of yourself. You did a good job, though personally I would've sliced the onions a little thinner."

"Here we go again! Girl, you wanted to add pineapple. Fucking *pineapple*. So leave my onions out of this."

I burst out laughing, watching as his face breaks into a smile. He slides two plates onto the coffee table, while I wipe down the kitchen counters. I pour the drinks as he slices the pizza. I'm finishing up in the kitchen just as Lane settles himself on the couch, and I'm feeling good about life, when I suddenly realize what's happening. We've slipped into a cozy routine, and I'm about to wave it all goodbye.

"This smells amazing!"

I curl up next to him, grabbing a slice, holding a second out for him.

"What do you think, Lane? Aren't you glad you gave into temptation?"

His gaze lingers on me a second, as if what I just said has hit a nerve. And then he bites down on the slice I'm handing out to him.

"Well?" I'm beyond excited right now.

He chews slowly, making me wait for it.

I shift onto my knees for a closer look. "Come on! What do you think?"

"It's good."

"Is that all?"

He takes another bite, chewing even slower this time.

"Lane, cut it out!"

He moves in for a third bite of the pizza I'm still dangling in front of him, but he barely has time to open his mouth when I slap the slice down over his face.

"Fuck!"

He dabs at the tomato sauce in his eye, and I'm bent double.

"For real?"

I glance at him mischievously. His eyes drift down to the rest of the pizza on the coffee table, and by the time I get what's about to happen, it's too late. He grabs me by the shoulders and pushes me back onto the couch, my head resting on his thighs as he suffocates me under a thick blanket of cheese, onion, and pineapple. I don't even fight back. Instead, I just lie there, hiding my sadness under a slice of cheesy goodness.

"Lois?"

He peels back the pizza and laughs when he sees me staring back at him, my cheeks splattered with food, plucking a little stray onion out of my lashes. I want to kiss him so bad right now.

"I hate you," I mutter.

That couldn't be further from the truth—and the truth hurts more than I can say.

When Lane leans over me, my heart leaps into my throat, only to drop when I realize he's just reaching for a tissue. *Silly girl.* I grab it from him and start cleaning myself up. I should get up and scoot over, I know, but I decide to keep my head in his lap a little while longer, as if it's the most natural thing in the world. Because come tomorrow, this will all be gone. He holds me up a peace offering, and as I take the slice from him, he falls back into the cushions.

"You've got to admit, this couch is seriously comfy."

His voice sounds weird. He stares up at the ceiling.

"Yeah," I say. "Nothing beats a real bed, though."

"But with a couch, you've got everything in easy reach," he says, gesturing at the coffee table.

"I hear they have these things called 'bedside tables' now."

"Your roommates might snore."

"I used to sleep next door to my grandpa, remember? I'm good to go."

He nods slowly, fiddling with his lip. This conversation is so weird. It feels like he wants me to say the dorm sucks, but I can't bring myself to do it. I'm too scared to tell him that given the choice, I'd prefer to stay here—with him. I'm scared because that would mean I care about him more than I thought.

I need to get him to open up, and so I start the only way I know how.

"What are you thinking?"

He lowers his gaze to meet mine. I stare at him, but try as I might,

I can't get a read. He's not the same guy I met all those months ago. He's changed—or maybe somewhere along the way, I did. He still hasn't answered my question, I realize. It's ridiculous how much time he can spend lost in thought like this. When I was with Kirk, I guess I never paid much attention to anyone else. Or maybe I just never met anyone worth paying attention to. One thing's for sure: I can't stop watching him think, and I can't stand feeling shut out like this, either. I want him to say it. I need him to say it. *Tell me to stay, Lane. Please. Just say it.*

"I think there's cheese in your nose."

So much for a heartfelt chat.

I hop off the couch and head to the bathroom to clean up. Catching sight of my reflection in the mirror, I peer in for a closer look, my breath rattling in my chest. What is going on with me? What's changed? When exactly did I stop caring for Kirk and start feeling so much for Lane? I can't stop thinking back to how he kissed me, how he touched me, how his fingers . . . The flashbacks are so intense, my head is reeling. What did it all mean to him? I could have asked him straight-up—I had dozens of chances to do just that, but I can't, and he's a closed book, so here we are. He started this whole thing, and then he acts like nothing ever happened. Lane isn't exactly Mr. Sensitive, though. I've seen how he is with other girls—so why would I be any different? If he wanted more, he would have told me. Plus, there's that spare room of his. There were so many times he could have told me to take it, if he really wanted me to move in with him. At least moving out now will help set a few things straight.

I tap the edge of the sink decidedly, and force myself back into the living room. It's my last night at the apartment. I need to make the most of it and quit the overthinking.

I curl back up on the couch. "Want to watch a movie?"

My voice is a little squeaky, but I think I sound convincing. There's no way I'm laying myself bare. I plan on keeping up the act for as long as needed.

"I didn't notice whether there's a TV in my new room," I add.

He looks at me steadily. "There isn't."

"I have my laptop—that'll do just fine." I shoot him a sideways glance.

"Yeah." He plucks up the remote and spends a while channel surfing. I'm pretty sure his eyes aren't even registering.

"Hello?" I wave a hand in front of his face. "You just went through a hundred channels at least."

He tosses me the remote. "You choose."

I don't give a shit what we watch, but I settle on a live concert. We both love the band. I tuck myself into the corner of the couch, my toes grazing the side of his thigh.

"You can stretch out, you know," he says, patting my ankle.

A smile plays on my lips, and I decide to do just that. This is how we spend every TV night together. This is how things first spun out of control. His arms are draped over my calves, and before long, his fingers are brushing against my skin. *I'm going to miss this.*

He nods at the screen. "They really are amazing live."

"Hell yes."

"You know they're coming to town this summer? We should see if we can get tickets."

"Good idea."

He's including me in his plans—that's a good sign. Something for me to cling on to tomorrow morning, when I head over to the other side of town.

"You might be road-tripping with your roomies by then, though . . ."

I look up and wrinkle my nose.

His eyes are still latched on the screen. "Your shiny new BFFs."

"You sound jealous," I counter, giving him a light kick.

He grabs my foot in midair and sets it back down in his lap. I do it again. And finally, he decides to look me in the eye.

"You're doing that moody thing again." I pout. "It's like back when this whole..." I'm stuck on the word. "This whole forced living-together started."

"Was living here really that bad?" he asks.

My breath catches in my throat. I swallow hard and tug down on my T-shirt. He's frowning, as if I just said something mean.

"Not always," I say, keeping my voice neutral. "You were a pain in the ass, though."

"Not always," he repeats.

It feels like he means something else. He turns back to the television in silence, and I force myself to breathe deep, fighting a growing sense of disappointment. I think back to how low I was when Lane found me there on the stairs, and how little by little, I've picked myself up and pieced myself back together without even realizing—all thanks to him. I shift in my seat and swing my knees over to him, placing my hands on my thighs, leaning in to look at him. Slowly, he turns to me.

"What?"

"Thank you."

I lean forward, coiling my arms around his neck, squeezing him as hard as I can, feeling his body tense in shock, and I could let go, but instead I hang on for dear life, breathing in his smell.

Just when I'm thinking it's time to let go, just when I'm biting down on disappointment that he hasn't hugged me back, I feel his hands coming to rest on my sides, and I smile into his neck, before planting a quick kiss on his cheek.

"Thank you for giving me somewhere to call home," I whisper into his ear.

"No problem." His voice is hoarse as he pulls back to look at me.

"Can I come over and make pizza every now and then?"

"You can."

My arms are still slung around his neck, and we stare at each other for a moment without talking. My mom was right. Lane is beautiful. An idea is nudging at the back of my mind, swelling with the ache tightening in my belly. I want to kiss him. He's done way more than that to me, but he hasn't kissed me again—not once—and my lips are aching for his. I feel a jolt of adrenaline shoot from my throat down to my core. Time freezes. Lane's gaze drifts over my face, then lingers on my mouth, his breathing heavier. Something flashes between his eyes and mine—so intense it short-circuits my brain. My fingers take on a life of their own as they search for the collar of his T-shirt, and before I have time to tug at the fabric, his mouth crashes into mine.

Finally. It's the only word echoing in my head as our tongues meet. I hadn't realized just how much I had missed this, but I hear myself moan, and I cling to him tighter. No more questions—I'm done with all that. I'm not going to think about what we're doing, and what it means for the future. Tomorrow I'm leaving, and I want to pack this moment away and take it with me.

He tugs on my bottom lip, before pulling back to look at me. Something in his gaze makes my heart ache, and I try my best to etch it to memory. He gently cups my face with one hand, while the other falls to the arch of my lower back, pulling me closer into him. This feels good—so good, that I hoist myself up until I'm straddling him. I bend my knees, guiding him exactly where I want him. Slowly, I start grinding against him, drawing ragged groans out of him, the sound of which send a rush of warmth straight to my core.

There's hardly any fabric between us, and I can feel every hard inch of him, every twitch of his dick, every pulse of pressure. He grips my hips and answers with urgent thrusts. His mouth is nipping at my jaw, dragging along my throat, leaving hot kisses in his wake. All I wanted was a kiss, but things are spinning out of control. I have absolutely no desire to stop them, though. When my frantic hands yank off his T-shirt, I barely recognize myself. When he pulls mine over my head, I feel myself desperately rising to meet him.

He freezes, eyes dropping to my breasts.

"Fuck, Lois," he rasps. Then he arches me backward, covering them with his mouth. The sensation sends a wave of liquid heat rippling through my body. It's so intense I start to laugh, my giddiness melting into a deep moan. The idea of sleeping with anyone other than Kirk terrified me, but with Lane, all I feel is relief and hunger.

He pulls me up against him, kissing me with wild intensity, then he lowers his lips back to my breasts—sucking hard, tongue sweeping over my skin, teeth grazing until I'm lightheaded. My head is already dizzy when he flips me over and lays me down on the couch. I gasp as his body presses on top of mine. Tongues, mouths, hands—our bodies fuse into one, the whole world blurring into a fevered tangle of limbs.

I'm so swept away in a roller coaster of sensation that I dig my nails into his back, clinging to him like I might fall. I barely register the moment he tugs off my panties and slides on a condom. By the time his lips break away from mine, my heart is hammering in my chest and time skips a beat.

"Are you sure?" His voice is raw, strained. "Tell me this is what you want."

"Please, Lane," I breathe. "Don't stop."

He curses under his breath, jaw tight. "Jesus, Lois . . . You have no idea what you're doing to me."

We lock eyes as he positions himself between my thighs, the tip of him teasing small, maddening circles over the wettest part of me. My body arches toward him, desperate, but he takes his time, giving me one last chance to shut the whole thing down, only winding me tighter in the process. I run my fingers along his cheek, weave them through his hair, and tug him back down into a rough kiss. As his tongue finds my mouth again, my chest swells, and I think I might die with want.

His eyes are searching for mine, and whatever he sees must convince him, because he starts pushing into me, excruciatingly slow, stretching me inch by inch. It feels like every one of my nerve endings are lighting up. A strangled sound rumbles from his chest, mixing with the sharp gasp I can't hold back. He stills, holding there, every muscle tight and vibrating with restraint, checking if I can take it—if I want all of him. I nod desperately, words tumbling out between shallow breaths—a string of pleases, of begging. "I need you." My voice doesn't even sound like mine.

"You're fucking killing me," he mutters, before he pushes into me the rest of the way in one hard, claiming thrust. The force of it knocks whatever air I had left from my lungs, and his own breath tears out in a rough growl. With one hand, he grabs my thigh, pressing it into his hip, and with the other, he laces his fingers through mine, pinning my arm above my head. We're not even kissing anymore—we're too winded, our mouths just pressed together, panting.

I can't believe this is happening. Lane is making me feel things I didn't even know I could. It's like nobody ever existed before him. With every thrust of his hips, tears are springing into my eyes. Emotion rushes at me, my heart so tight I swear it could burst. I want to laugh. I want to cry. There's so much I want to say to him, but all that comes out are ragged gasps. I'm drowning in the sweetest chaos and savoring every second of it. I never want this to end. I want to feel him inside me, again and again.

Lane doesn't say another word. He doesn't need to. His body speaks for him. He looks completely untamed. I give in to his touch, letting him take control. It's like he's unlocking whole new parts of me. At this point, all I know is Lane and the way he fills me. He's so thick and so damn deep. It's making my toes curl and my head spin. Over and over, he drives into me until I forget where I end and he begins.

My legs hold more urgently to his waist, feeling myself rise higher and higher every time our bodies meet, until my heart takes flight. Suddenly, my muscles clamp down, pleasure rippling through me in hot, helpless waves. I cry out, shaking, as my body clenches, release pulsing hard and gripping tight around him. He lets out a string of low and filthy curses. His thrusts turn frantic, and it's like he's unraveling inside me, licking and biting and grabbing wherever he can reach. Then he slams in as deep as he can one last time, shuddering hard before pressing his body to mine, his breath hot and uneven against my skin.

We stay there for a while, our hearts pressed together, pulses beating as one. Then, slowly, Lane edges away, peeling off the condom. He rolls me gently onto my side and lowers himself behind me on the couch, his chest to my back. I lie there, staring into space, half expecting him to leap up and run again. But instead, he slips a hand under my arm and curves it over my stomach, nestling close without a word. Our bare skin touches in a way that feels so very right. He noses at the back of my neck, then gently sweeps my hair off my face and tucks it behind my ear.

What is he thinking? I could guess, but I'm too scared of getting it wrong—and though all I have to do is ask, I can't seem to find the words.

"Do you really like the dorm? Genuinely?" he asks, his voice low and raspy.

I blink, curling my toes. I'm too scared to look around at him.

"It's not bad," I try.

"You could do better."

Yeah. I could have that spare room you never told me about.

"What if you . . ."

I stiffen, desperate for him to finish the question.

He strokes my tummy, tracing my belly button, feeling his way to my foot with his toes.

"There'll be more choice in August. You could . . ."

He freezes mid-sentence, and my pulse is racing. I grip the cushion tighter, holding on for dear life.

"I could what?" I'm practically begging now.

"You could stay."

My heart is hammering so fast I can hardly think, a rush of blood to my head, my cheeks on fire. I squeeze my eyes tight, clamp my lips shut, willing myself to keep it together. I'm stupid-happy right now, and I feel something else, too—something I don't want to examine just yet.

"You want me to stick around?"

I need to double-check—make sure this isn't a dream. He nods. Just the once. I'm so happy I want to throw myself at his feet, but instead I force my muscles still, relishing the words I had stopped hoping he would ever say. I don't want him to realize how touched I am.

"Why?" I ask.

I'm so scared of how he'll answer.

His hand hovers on my rib cage. I can't even hear him breathe anymore. Did sleeping together help unlock something inside him? I need to know what he wants from me. From us. *I think I just realized that what I want is an us. Period.*

"We had a deal, remember? The plan was always that I move out," I offer. "Plus, there's a closet there, there's even a desk . . ."

I don't give a shit about any of that, but I need to hear how far he's prepared to go to stop me leaving, and I want to know whether this whole situation is connected to how weird he's been since Christmas, too. I'm about to bring up the bed, when he cuts me off.

"I should never have waited this long," he starts awkwardly.

Oh my God!

"I'm going to empty the closet," he continues.

"In the bedroom?"

"Yeah. And you can have the desk space—I never use it."

My breath catches in my throat. The secret empty room. All these months, and finally I'm being given the key. If he wants me to stick around, then maybe he does feel the way I do. This is Lane we're dealing with here: the guy who had a zero-guest policy last summer. And now he wants me to stay. In a real bedroom of my own. Sayonara, couch! And sure, he said it's only until next August, only until I find a better dorm—but let's get real: I know that's just an excuse. And no, he hasn't offered up *his* bedroom, but it's a start. This buys me enough time to try and make sense of it all. Kirk has always been the elephant in the room—it makes sense that Lane would be a little wary. As soon as the time is right, I plan on telling him that he's the one I want. I know that now.

I bite my lip. "Are you sure?"

I want him to tell me that yes he's sure, that everything's changed between us, that all he can think about is us and doing it all over again, right now, right here, all the time—

"Yeah," he says. "You?"

I nod slowly.

"Okay. So we have a new deal. I'm spending the whole day with Carter tomorrow—we're meeting a producer to go through a contract. You can put your stuff away, arrange everything the way you want it."

"Sounds good. I'll need to head down to the office to turn down the room. Are you sure you—"

"I'm sure. There's more than enough space here. Beats that overpriced rabbit hutch, that's for sure," he adds.

"I can pay my way—"

"I own this place, Lois. Just keep the groceries coming."

I'm tempted to ask whether there's anything else I should keep on coming, too, but I think we're done here. I don't want to ruin the moment.

The weight of him is warming my back, and I suddenly feel super tired. Just before I drift off to sleep, I start daydreaming about what it would be like if every day was like today.

27

LANE

I'm hovering outside my front door, cussing under my breath. This is my home—so why does it feel like I'm about to break in? Waking up wrapped around Lois sent my head spinning, and this shitty day has stretched on and on ever since. The big meeting I just had was a total shit show. Despite Carter elbowing me under the table, my mind kept wandering off and playing back last night, sifting through a bunch of jumbled feelings. As he drove me back home, Cart tried to get me to open up—but other than telling him to back off, I didn't say a word. What is there to say? I jumped in my car and claimed a few rides to kill time, driving Hope and Prudence to a fabric store, dodging their prying eyes. I nearly asked for their thoughts on the situation but decided against it, and on my next ride, I nearly gave in to a flirty blonde, just as a way of getting Lois off my mind—even that was too much for me to handle. Lois is probably home by now, and I don't fucking know how to deal with her. Up until yesterday, I could just slip into my usual act. But that was before we slept together. Before I asked her to stay. Before I felt her naked body shuddering against mine, and before I fell asleep with her in my arms, waking up to her draped over me. *Did I fuck up? I absolutely did.* But it's too late to turn back now, so I gear myself up and head inside.

I spot her shoes by the entrance, her jacket on the coat hook—but scanning the kitchen and living room, she's nowhere to be seen.

"Lois?"

"Here!" she trills.

I toss my keys down on the side table and freeze. Her voice is echoing down the corridor. Much too far away to be the bathroom. I glance at the space where her bags were earlier. They've vanished. I close my eyes and scratch my jaw. She must be in my room, making a little space for herself, like I suggested yesterday. The knot in my stomach tightens—it's getting hard to breathe. I'm torn. A part of me regrets asking her to stay, because I'm too scared of what that might mean. Why the fuck did I do that? *Because you slept together and it was the best sex of your life . . .* Yeah—it was out of this world. Nothing short of unforgettable, really. But here are the facts: Lois loves Kirk, and I love my life just the way it is, and . . . *Shit*, this girl has been messing with my head since the start, and I'm slowly starting to feel trapped.

Gathering up my courage in both hands, I make my way to the bedroom, breathing in and out, doing my best to look relaxed, but when I push open the door, my face crumples. Slowly, I turn to the far end of the hallway, tension coiling in the pit of my stomach. The door to my brother's bedroom is open, light spilling in to flood the space. I slam my hand down on the wall. *Don't tell me Lois went in there.*

I stride over to the doorway. The first thing I notice is a mountain of clothes piled on the bed. My brother's clothes. I take a step closer, the blood pounding in my veins. Suddenly, I'm back there, all those years ago, when Mike still lived here. The closet door squeaks, and I jump, half-expecting to see his ghost. All I see is sunny, smiling Lois, and a red mist starts to spark at my edges.

"Have a good day?" she chirps, her smile fading when she sees my expression. "What—"

"What are you doing?" Anger is thickening at the back of my throat, and she flinches.

"Well, I—"

"What the fuck are you doing in here?"

My gaze drifts over to her bags, darting back and forth between the bed and the desk. I clench my jaw. You have got to be fucking kidding me. Don't tell me she's—

"I'm tidying my stuff away. You said—"

"Get the hell out of here!"

The words come so harsh, so loud, she takes a step back and stumbles, falling to the ground. Scrambling to her feet, she glances around her, confusion spreading over her face.

"Lane, why—"

"Get out of here!" I yell.

The pain is blinding. I lunge for the desk, raking up the coat hangers, spinning around with my arms full, desperate to make space. I always wondered how it would feel—stepping back into this room. Now I know.

"Move!"

She staggers back, clearing a path for me, and I start hanging my brother's clothes back up. When I'm done, I slam the closet door shut, making her yelp.

I step closer to her. "I told you to get the fuck out of here!"

Finally she leaves, and I can't breathe. My head is spinning around and around. I lean my hands against the closet for balance, pressing the door shut, keeping the memories sealed away. This is all I have left of him, and I can't stand the thought of Lois rifling through it all. *Fuck. What the hell was she doing in here?* This, right here: This was my boundary, and she crossed it.

"Fuck!"

I pound the closet with both fists and leave the room to its silence, slamming the door shut behind me and stalking into the living room. Lois spins around and smacks right into the kitchen island.

I keep my distance, my fists clenched, blinded by rage. I can practically see her heart quivering in her chest. She's breathing hard, her eyes wild and rolling, silently pleading with me to explain. This isn't the girl I thought I knew—when I look at her now, all I see is red.

She grips the counter with both hands. "What's your problem?"

"Who do you think you are, Lois?" I snarl. "What the fuck were you doing in there?"

"Are you kidding me?" She laughs in disbelief. "You're ins—"

"I fucking *told* you not to go in there." My throat feels tight.

"What the hell are you talking about? You told me to put my stuff away!"

"There's no way I ever said that. I told you to put your stuff in *my* closet, I never said to make yourself at home!"

She does a double take. "'At home'? I never . . . Listen, you were the one who asked me to stay!"

"I *never* said you could take over that room!" I roar. "You're a fucking *guest*!"

The anger is spreading through me like wildfire, and I can't even hear myself anymore. Lois can, though—I can tell from her ragged breath that she's upset, but all I can think is how claustrophobic I'm feeling, how badly she misjudged this. My blood is boiling.

"Wait a minute," she says, swallowing hard. "Just to make sure I'm getting this. Are you saying the plan was for me to stay on the couch forever?"

"Yes!" I step toward her.

Truth is I thought she would stay in my room, but it feels easier to lie now.

She slaps a hand over her forehead and shuts her eyes. When she opens them again, I recognize the expression flitting across her features, I've seen it once before. But I'm too pissed to focus right now. She balls her hand into a fist, jabbing a finger in my face.

"This morning, I went down to the office to tell them I was turning down the room I've been waiting months for, because I thought . . ."

She starts to laugh. "You want me to spend the year sleeping on a couch?" she asks flatly.

For a split second, I see her eyes fill with hurt, and it's nearly enough to break me. Nearly.

"That a problem?" I snipe.

"You made me give up a room for that fucking couch?"

"That 'fucking couch' didn't seem too shabby when your ex threw you out like a pile of shit, did it? And it wasn't too bad yesterday, was it?"

I send the words slicing through the air. And they land perfectly. She freezes, her eyes widening. Alarm bells are ringing somewhere at the back of my mind, but all I can focus on right now is my rage.

"What's the big deal with that room, anyway? It's empty—so why can't I have it?"

"It's not . . . You're the big deal! You're the problem here, do you get that?" I shake my head. "I gave you *everything* you wanted—and now that's not enough?"

She frowns, and I watch as something like understanding dawns on her face. She blinks. I can hear her breathing from here.

"So basically—nothing's changed?" she murmurs. "Just so we're clear, Lane: I'm just stupid little Heartbreak, a girl you randomly fuck on the couch whenever you feel like it?" Her voice is louder now, her lip curled with disgust. "Like a kind of sex snack?"

Deep down, I want to tell her she's wrong—but my mouth has other ideas.

"What did you expect?" I narrow my eyes at her. "We slept together, Lois. Get over it. It doesn't mean you get to do whatever the hell you want—that was never part of the deal."

I'm a black belt in the art of self-defense, and I deliver the words like a blow, without so much as a flinch. In a sick way, she's making things easier for me. At least this way I don't have to deal with any complicated feelings.

"Why?" she whispers.

"Why what?"

"New Year's Eve, the week after that, last night—what did it all mean?"

"Nothing!" I yell. "It meant fucking *nothing*!" I've gone too far, but I'm on a roll, and I can't hold back. "Don't go anywhere near that room again. Got it?"

"Got it."

Her eyes darken, and the air between us chills. I can't breathe. I need to get out of here, and fast. Without a word, I turn on my heel and hit the stairs, too out of control to realize what just happened, too caught up in the moment to understand what I've just done.

In the safety of my car, I pummel the steering wheel with my fists. I need to blow off some steam. I hit the gas and go flying down the road, heading nowhere. I decide to call Juliet and let her know I plan on spending the weekend at her place. Juliet is my safe space— never any drama, never too many questions. She's like a sister to me, and between her shifts at the bar and her one-night stands, she's more like me than Carter. I'm guessing she won't even be home, and if she is, she'll be hopping in the shower, having a quick nap, and heading back out, leaving me with the perfect hideaway for a weekend alone.

I spend the next two days knocking back the booze, slumped in a stupor. By the time Monday rolls around I'm back in my car, and it's too late to head to campus. Though I'm not ready to face Lois just yet, I have no choice but to go home, praying that she's fucked off to her dorm by now. This whole situation has been totally over the top. All I want is to get back to my old life: the good old days, before I knew her, before anything she ever made me feel. I turn the idea over and over in my mind like a mantra, and shoot a message off to my friends, asking them to meet me at my apartment. I could crash at their place, but I discard the idea as soon as it lands—I can't keep running away.

I pull up outside my building and sit there in my car waiting for backup like the biggest pussy ever, and by the time Adam rolls up with Don hot on his heels, the sun has firmly set.

"I didn't see you on campus today," Don starts, punching my shoulder. "Don't screw this year up, dude."

I glance over his shoulder. "Lewis not with you?"

"No, I don't know what his deal is. He didn't come to today's practical session. Lois didn't, either," he adds. "Damn, you guys are dropping like flies."

Lois played hooky? That doesn't sound like her . . . *Who cares what she does? Not my problem.* I stare up at the building, taking in the soft glow spilling out of my apartment window. Has she been hanging around waiting for me since Friday? A pang of guilt shoots through me, but I shove it to one side and step toward the entrance.

We tumble into the elevator, my heart racing at the thought of confronting Lois up there—but pushing open the door, I realize the place is empty. I should be glad, but I catch myself scouring the space for her bags, breathing out a sigh of relief when I spot them against the living room wall, back where she first left them all those months ago.

I can't tell whether I'm happy she cleared out the bedroom, or relieved she hasn't left. *Shit, I don't know what I want anymore.*

I rush over to my sound system, hook up to the Bluetooth, and blast the loudest playlist I have.

Don scoops up my controllers and turns on the console. "I demand a rematch."

I do my best to focus on each round, but I can't stop myself from wondering where Lois is.

"Man, you look rough." Adam glances over at me from the corner of the couch. "You sick or something?"

"Anyone got a status update for Lewis?" I ask.

Adam swipes through his phone. "He's flagged as 'off' on the app. He's probably getting laid. You know he's going through a 'hot girls with glasses' phase?"

"Hey, by the way," Don cuts him off, "you didn't tell us what happened with Lois's room."

Saved by the bell: Just as he asks, my phone starts vibrating, the ringtone blaring through the sound system. I glance down at my screen. Juliet. A.k.a. "Not Lois." Fuck. Where the hell is she? I check off the options. Gym class isn't tonight, Becca is with Carter . . . I ignored every one of her calls this past weekend, and now regret is twisting in me like a knife.

My phone starts ringing again, but my hands are busy with the controller. I tap it onto loudspeaker and turn my attention back to the TV as I talk.

"What's up?"

"Hey, Laney."

The noise is deafening. Juliet must be calling from the bar.

"Everything okay?" I take Adam down with a bullet to the head.

"Yup."

"Hey, Juliet!" Don and Adam call out together.

"Oh, you guys are all there? Amazing news!"

"We're just missing Lewis," Adam corrects her.

"Yeah, about that." Juliet clears her throat. "We may have a situation."

Adam frowns at the speaker. "There a problem?"

"A pretty big one, yeah! He showed up at the bar with his girlfriend—both of them tanked. I need you to come pick them up ASAP, or I'm going to have to call the cops."

"Lewis is wasted?" I glance at the oven clock. "But it's not even nine."

"Is his girlfriend cute?" Don wants to know.

"You know her. Short brown hair. She was at your birthday party, Lane."

My thumb misses the joystick and Adam guns me down.

"Lois?" he asks for me.

No fucking way. Juliet must have got her mixed up with someone else. Firstly, Lois doesn't get wasted. And secondly—Lois doesn't get wasted with Lewis. Like, ever.

"I need to get back to work. I'm counting on you guys."

As soon as she hangs up, I dial Lewis.

"Yo!" His voice comes blaring through the speaker, and yeah—he's definitely wasted. "You good, my little chickadee?"

"Dude, what the fuck are you doing?" Don asks.

"Tequila slammers with my Super Friend!"

"Meeee!"

A second voice comes squealing down the line. It's a voice I'd know anywhere.

"For fuck's sake." I pinch my nose in frustration.

Don keeps his eyes latched on the game. "What happened?"

"I'm not too sure. I ran into Lois on campus, she was cr—"

"Why the fuck is Lois wasted?" I cut him off.

You know exactly why, Lane.

"Juliet is kicking our asses out." Lewis starts to laugh. "Hey, Don? Can you come pick us up and take us to the dorms? Me and Lois really wanna fuck."

There's a deafening roar in my ears, my mind swelling with cusswords. When Lewis's voice fills the air again, I squeeze the controller so hard I think it might break.

"She wants me to be her Super Daddy."

"I'm going to kill him," I hiss.

"Minus the cape."

"Definitely not minus the condom, though." Lois giggles, and the sound cuts right through me, the hairs on the back of my neck standing on end.

I look around me. The others are speechless. Don is the first to laugh, followed by Adam, who shoots me an apologetic glance. I bring the phone to my mouth.

"Lewis, I swear to God, if you—"

The worst rendition ever of the Superman theme comes slurring through the speaker.

"If you so much as touch her, I'm going to fuck you up!"

I can feel my friends' eyes boring into me, and I realize the immensity of what I've just said.

"Laney is pissed," Lewis whispers on the other end of the line.

"Oh! You lost, buddy!" Lois singsongs at him. "You owe me fifty bucks."

"Shit!" Lewis sounds saddened. "We were betting on how long it'd take for you to lose your shit. Thought you had more in you, man."

"Game over, Lanus."

She must be leaning into the phone now, because her voice is deafening. Adam is doing his best not to burst out laughing, and it's taking every inch of self-control I've got not to flip this whole coffee table over.

"You fucked up, didn't you?" Donovan points a finger at me. "Now I get why you're in such a pissy mood."

I chew the inside of my cheek, biting back the anger.

Don turns back to the phone, slipping on his jacket. "We're coming to get you, Lewis. Don't you move."

"Thank you, Mommy Donny! Can we borrow your bed? It's much bigger than—"

I hang up before I lose my shit for real. I've got a sudden urge to tear this place apart, and the way Adam is looking at me is really pissing me off. I don't know what he's seeing, and I don't even want to know. All I care about right now is getting Lois away from Lewis's sticky little paws—before he does something we both regret. *This girl has been a pain from the get-go.*

"Let's take your car, Lane. That way I can drive Lewis back in his."

"Yeah. And make sure he's solo." I grab my keys.

"You got it."

On the way down in the elevator, Don can't help shooting me a few knowing glances.

"Wanna talk about it?"

"Nope."

JULIET'S BAR HAS NEVER FELT so far away. I whiz through the streets, Sycamore flying by in a blur, slamming on the brakes when we hit a crossroad.

"Easy, man."

When we finally pull up outside the buzzing neon sign, Juliet is already waiting on the sidewalk, yelling at Lewis, who's crumpled at her feet, bent double. Lois is slumped on the ground, too, laughing with her head resting against my friend's shoulder. *Keep it together, Lane.*

Juliet glances up. "Oh, thank fuck! Get these two out of my sight before I commit double homicide."

She shakes Lewis off her foot, giving me a quick peck on the cheek before heading back inside. I take a deep breath in—and a second when I catch Lois looking up, scowling at me.

"I'd rather go to jail," she slurs.

Clutching her drinking buddy's arm, she lays her cheek against his Cardinals jacket and starts humming to herself.

"Aww, aren't they cute?" Donovan croons.

I clench my fists. "Lois, get in the car."

"Burn in hell!"

I lean down and catch her arm, dragging her off Lewis and throwing her over my shoulder, and though she wriggles hard, and starts hitting me in the back, I hold her tight. When we get to the car, I lower her to the ground and force her inside, gently pushing her head down and settling her onto the back seat, ignoring her whines as I slam the door shut. I lean against the car with my arms stretched for a moment, trying to catch my breath. *Now what?* I feel so pissed right now, but I don't know who I'm mad at—Lois or myself.

There's a finger prodding me in the back, and I spin around to find Lewis swaying on his feet.

I shove him back. "What the fuck were you two doing?"

"I saw her on campus, crying her ass off, you jealous stupid fuck! She told me what you did to her. Absolute disgrace, dude!"

"You don't know what you're talking about," I spit.

"Whatever. All I know is Lois is a super catch, and you're a super dick for not noticing. I told her you were shady as fuck, and I was this close to taking her home . . ." His eyes struggle to focus on the thumb and index he's holding out in front of him. "But don't sweat it—I didn't say anything about your brother."

He mimes zipping his lips.

Don yells at him through the window. "Come on—let's get you home, sloppy joe."

Lewis salutes me as he teeters his way back to the car.

I wait until they vanish down the street and turn to Lois, still slumped in the back. I slide into the driver's seat with a sigh. She doesn't say a word all the way home. Instead, she keeps her forehead pressed to the window, misting up the glass with her breath, drawing circles through the air. I park outside my building and open the back door. Her pale face stares up at me.

"I don't wanna go to your place," she slurs. "Like, ever."

I shut my eyes, dipping into the car and slipping my hands under her arms. I was expecting her to fight back, but instead she whimpers softly, relaxing her body as I lift her up and out.

"Wh . . . Muh . . . Couch," she mumbles.

She smells like fruit and tequila. I scoop her up into my arms and carry her to the elevator, listening to her mutter and groan, checking that she isn't about to puke all over me. Pushing open the door to my apartment, I eye the couch and briefly consider dumping her in my bed. I hate everything I'm feeling right now.

She wriggles in my arms. "Couch!"

I lay her down gently. Her eyes are glazed. Kneeling on the floor, I tug off her shoes and peel off her socks, watching her scrunch up her toes. She's shivering. I wrap her snug in a throw as she rubs her eyes and forehead, pulling a face and rolling over onto her side. I crouch there for a moment like an idiot, looking at her stretched out on the couch.

"Shoulda left me with Lewis."

"No way in hell."

"Things are easy with him." She sighs. "Why do I always end up getting hurt?"

My chest tightens. Did she just compare me to Kirk?

"What am I doing wrong? Why do I always fuck things up?"

Tears are trickling down her cheeks and I can't help but lean into her. This isn't the first time I've seen her cry—but it's the first time I've seen her cry because of me, and it's killing me.

"Lois—"

"We aren't friends," she sobs. "We're nothing. Leave me alone."

Her words cut me to the heart, knocking the breath out of me. I shut my eyes. Anything to stop the wave of dizziness crashing over me. I bite down hard on my cheek. Lois is a hot mess. Now's not the time for anything deep or meaningful. When finally I open my eyes, I realize I was right. Her face is buried in a cushion, her shoulder rising and falling, slow and steady.

I spend too long sitting there watching her sleep, before getting to my feet and padding down to my room. Before I shut the door, I glance over to Mike's room. I like having Lois here. It's just that I can't let her take up space that belongs to Mike. And that will never change. Ever.

28

LOIS

I prize my eyes open and wince. It's the same old room I've called home for four months now. Ceiling, kitchen, coffee table. Check, check, check. My stomach is churning—and not just because I was tanked last night. What happened on Friday was pure hell, especially when I went back to see the administrator on Monday to tell her I changed my mind and that actually I *did* want that room I turned down, after all. She laughed right in my face, waved me away, and before I knew it I was drinks-deep with Lewis—Lewis, of all people!

I've got a blinding headache, and the details are a little fuzzy, but what I do know is that Lane came to the bar to pick me up. The ride back is a haze, but he definitely put me here, on the couch. *The couch, of course. Where else?*

I squeeze my eyes shut. This place suddenly feels cold and claustrophobic—just like Lane's whole vibe. I glance at the oven clock. He's probably sound asleep in his cozy bed.

I should have left on Friday, made a run for it straight after our fight. But instead, I spent all weekend lying here, waiting for . . . something. Him to come back, maybe. Some kind of answer. An apology? The point is: He didn't come home, and he was probably hoping I would leave.

He looked at me like I was trash—like some kind of gross

cockroach he needed to exterminate. Part of me just wants to burst into his room and force him to explain himself, but I know I can't take any more pain. He was pretty clear on Friday, anyway—what else is there to ask? And whatever he says, there's no coming back from this. There's no way we can be friends. *How could I get it so wrong?* He never felt a thing for me—or at least not the way I thought. I get that now. He can just about stomach me—so long as I shut up and just take what I'm given. Which is the couch, basically. I'm his charity case.

How could he sleep with me and then just move on like nothing happened?

I've never felt this ashamed before. Except I have, haven't I? When Kirk dumped me—it was just as painful, just as humiliating. But though it's only been a few months, I actually think Lane hurts even more. I shake my head in disbelief. He never promised me anything. How could I have been so off base? I thought it meant more. If he thinks I'll be the girl who sleeps on his couch and gives him sex whenever he feels like it, he's got another think coming. I know some people would simply roll with it, but I can't. That's just not me—and it hurts to think that's how Lane sees me.

This shitty little couch is suffocating me. I throw off the blanket, jump to my feet, and creep into the bathroom, doing my best not to wake him, scooping up all my remaining things and standing there in front of the mirror, gazing at the total loser staring back at me. One thing's for sure—it's time for me to grow up and stop acting like some lovesick kid. It's time for me to start owning my shit.

Once I've packed away my stuff, I leave the spare key on the table in the hallway along with a hastily scrawled thank-you note, and throw down the fifty Lewis gave me last night when he lost the bet. And then I leave, tears streaming down my face as I race down the stairs, feeling so stupid, feeling so mad, too. Hurt. I toss my bags into the cab that's waiting for me outside, and call Becca as we drive.

"Hey, Lois!" she trills.

I sniff, steadying my voice. "Can I leave my stuff at your dorm?"

I just need to buy myself a little time while I work on finding a hotel room, and though the plan was never to spill my guts, I start to sob. Becca sighs, muttering something pissy under her breath, before clearing her throat.

"No problem. I spend most nights at Carter's, anyway. You can even have my bed, if you want. I'll ask Cart to drop me off—"

"No, I'm serious! Stay where you are!"

I plan on keeping the most painful parts to myself—all these feelings I've conjured out of thin air.

Twenty minutes later, and I'm in her room, bumping into Carrie on her way out to class.

"Becca told me you'd be coming by. Make yourself at home."

"Thanks." I smile, propping my bags against the desk.

"Do I need to call my cousins and get them to go 'round and deal with O'Neill? They're all like six foot three."

"Actually, what I really need right now are M&M's."

"That works," she says, whipping a family-size pack out of the closet. "I gotta run. Catch you later?"

As she shuts the door behind her, I realize she hasn't asked me a single question, and I'm grateful.

I jump in the shower, pull on my ugliest leggings and my oversize hoodie, and curl up in my new bed. Here I am again, leeching off yet another kind soul, and I know I can't keep doing this. I decide to block off the day for a major pity party before I give myself a kick in the ass.

I'VE BEEN CAMPED OUT ON Becca's bed for a whole week now, and I'd love to say the past few days have brought fresh perspective and a new attitude—but I'd be lying. I'm still as lost as ever, and I've got myself stuck in a routine that's making Carrie lose her mind. Luckily, she's way easier to live with than Lane, and I have a real bed all to myself, too. At least, that's what I tell myself whenever I find myself missing him. I just need to ride this out. I'll get over it—I know I will.

"No more overthinking!"

Carrie throws a cushion at my face, and I toss it back at her.

"I never thought I'd end up missing Becca," she says, pulling on her pants. "Cut it out, okay?"

"Sorry..."

"I'm not having another friend lose it over some guy."

"Another friend? What happened?"

"Just... Never mind. Listen, there's more to life than guys, Lois."

Once she's done dressing, she heads to the bathroom, and I sit on Becca's bed, staring at her bookshelf, chewing on my lip. Living here feels so weird, but I'm not complaining. I've been doing a lot of thinking lately, and I'm starting to realize I should have checked out of Lane's place a long time ago. He helped me out when I was at my lowest—I clung to him for reassurance, and while that was exactly what I needed as a stopgap, it didn't help me grow. Carrie is right. I need to take ownership of my life like a big girl.

I force myself out of bed and yank on my clothes. On my way to campus, I consider the facts. I haven't heard a word from Lane, and that tells me everything I need to know. I've done my best to avoid the rest of the Campus Drivers. That leaves Kirk as the only person I keep seeing—wherever I go, he's right there like a shadow. I glance around me. I've been bumping into him pretty much constantly these days, and it's absolutely wild to think that while once that was all I ever wanted, right now it's pissing me off.

"You got a minute, Lois?"

Like I said...

"Kirk. Hey."

He peers at me. "You okay?"

"Never better," I drawl. "How can I help?"

My coolness catches him off guard.

"So you're not living with Lane anymore," he blurts, gawking at me.

Talk about getting straight to the point.

"It took a while, but I got a dorm room in the end."

I decide to leave it there, but his face is brightening, and I wonder how he found out.

"That's awesome!"

I grit my teeth. "Yeah. Really awesome. Thanks for caring, by the way."

"Ouch." He winces, a pained expression on his face. "I deserved that. So—you guys still together?"

"Nope."

We were never together in the first place—but Kirk doesn't need to know that. And I know that Lane's the reason he's back sniffing around me.

"Can I buy you a coffee?"

Coffee? I can't handle this anymore.

"What is wrong with you?" I snap.

He breathes out, stuffing his hands deeper in his pockets. "Listen, I've been thinking. I'd really love if we could talk about what happened."

"You want to talk?"

"Yeah, I've been—"

"Doing a lot of thinking?" I scoff. I'm so tired of this shit. "Yeah, I got that part. Today doesn't work for me, Kirk."

And with that I turn on my heel and walk away. I'm not even the slightest bit curious. Life has a funny way of reshuffling the deck, sometimes. I never get what I want when I want it. I wanted Kirk—and I got Lane. And now Kirk's back on the scene, and all I can think about is Lane. All these guys do is fuck with my head. I'm slipping into my empowered-woman phase, and they can all suck it.

"Leave me the fuck alone!" I cry as I shove open the doors to the building, slamming them right into a student as I go.

"Ow!"

I gasp. "I'm so sorry!"

"No worries, Lois."

I freeze. I recognize that voice.

"I was just looking for you."

Adam is standing right there, beaming at me.

"Hey..."

"How you doing? It's been a while."

I glance over his shoulder, checking whether the others are with him.

"It's just me. I could tell something was up with you and Lane, and that you were avoiding us, too." He smiles. "Lewis is devastated, you know. He told me to tell you it's an absolute disgrace."

I roll my eyes. "That guy seriously needs to expand his vocabulary."

Adam laughs. "We miss you, you know. Don saw you get on the bus earlier this week, and he was so mad."

As I listen to him tell me about the other Campus Drivers, I start to realize I've missed them all more than I thought.

"Anyway—Lewis and I are having a birthday party next month, and we'd love if you could make it."

"Oh, I..."

I don't know what to tell him, and Adam seems low-key offended.

"This year's a leap year, so it's gonna be a big one. It would mean a lot if you were there."

"Why?"

He stares at me incredulously. "Why? Because we want to celebrate with friends. And that means you."

I stare back at him, just as surprised. I hardly know what friendship means, these days.

"Lois, I don't know what exactly happened with you and Lane, but that doesn't change how the rest of us feel about you. And I'm pretty sure things will work themselves out."

That's where he's wrong. The stuff with me and Lane changes everything: there's no way I can spend another evening with them, and there's especially no way I can hang out with Lane—not until I've moved on.

"I'm running late—can we check back in about this?" I ask, hooking my thumbs under my backpack straps.

He folds his arms over his chest, scowling.

"Can I ask a favor, at least?"

"Anything."

"Lewis and Don are busy with basketball, obviously—I could do with some help picking up drinks and decorations next week."

I like Adam. I like him a lot. Right from the start, he always made me feel at ease. I don't have the heart to say no.

"You can count on me."

"Amazing. Thanks, Lois. I'll give you a call and we can figure it out."

He makes to walk by me, and just as I turn, he scoops me up in his arms and hugs me goodbye.

"What's wrong?" he asks.

He can feel me tense up, and with good reason.

Standing there behind him is Lane. It's been days since I last saw him, and it's like a punch to the gut. He's chatting to a girl I don't recognize, and when he turns to glance at me, tears prick behind my eyes. He stares at me for a moment, before blinking and turning away, as if I were a passing shadow. It reminds me of how Kirk acted—except this is ten times more painful.

"See you later," I mumble to Adam.

I make a dash for the classroom, changing my mind on the way, dipping into the restroom instead. I lock myself in a cubicle and fall back onto the toilet seat, dropping my head between my knees as I gasp for air. Somewhere buried deep within all that hurt, a flicker of rage is sparking. I'm still good old Lois who nobody takes seriously—and that needs to stop. Everyone else is busy living their lives, and here I am, shaking on a toilet seat.

That's it. Lean into the anger.

I get up, flush the toilet, and watch the water swirl down the bowl.

Time to woman the fuck up.

29

LANE

I glance at my phone, checking the clock for the hundredth time. I'm waiting for Adam to swing by, and I'm already regretting saying yes to us taking just the one car. I could have been on the road already, instead of pacing around my apartment waiting for my ride. My eyes keep drifting back to the corner where her stuff used to be—I still can't believe the disappearing act Lois pulled.

It's been two weeks since she left. When I woke up and noticed her bags were gone, it just made me even madder at her. She came crashing into my life, turned it all upside down, and then just vanished overnight. Who does that?

My phone beeps—Adam. I grab my jacket and stop in my tracks when I realize the spare key is still right where Lois left it. I take a deep breath in, and hit the stairs.

Adam needs me to help him out, and I've been distant with my friends the past few weeks: today I'm going to make sure I don't project my negative energy onto him. I haven't told the guys what happened with Lois, but they definitely know something's up. I bet they all heard she's staying at Becca's. I know that's where she is, because the moment I realized she was gone, I did the only thing I could think of—I called Carter. When he asked me what had happened, I hung up on him.

I recognize the sound of Adam's engine running, and stride down the sidewalk, slipping in beside him and leaning the passenger seat back a little so I can stretch out.

"Good to see you, man!" He pulls out into the street. "What's up?"

"Nothing much."

"Thanks for helping me out. Don and Lewis have so many practices and games right now, it's a lot."

I don't know how those two have the energy, and I'm pretty jealous they have something so all-consuming to keep themselves distracted.

I brush my hair back. "This is like their Super Bowl."

"Facts."

"So—what's first on the list?"

"Let's swing by the mall and grab the decorations."

"What did Lewis pick for this year's theme?"

"It's my turn to choose, thank fuck. He tried to bully me into a *Mad Max* vibe, so I'm leaning more toward glittery unicorn feels."

I snicker. "I'm team Mad Max."

"Not happening."

It feels good to laugh. We pull up outside the mall and climb out, strolling through the parking lot in comfortable silence, him whistling nonchalantly, sneaking me the occasional look.

"What?"

"Nothing. You look like you're running on empty, that's all."

Makes sense. My sleep has gone to shit, ever since—

"Lois!"

I nearly jump out of my skin at the sound of Adam shrieking. How did he know what I was thinking? I glance at him. He's waving a hand, staring straight ahead. Slowly, I turn to follow his gaze, nearly tripping over my own feet.

"What the fuck is this?" I mutter.

We're so close, I could swear I just saw Lois mouth the exact same thing, and I'm wondering whether this is the weirdest coincidence ever when Adam sets me straight with a single sentence.

"Ready to get your confetti on?"

Something in his tone makes me realize he planned this whole situation.

What is he doing?

I wish I could drag my eyes away from her—but I can't. After the initial shock, a whole wave of confusing, conflicting feelings comes crashing over me. I take in her curves, my eyes drifting up to her face. She's staring at Adam, a horrified expression on her face—she didn't know I would be here, either. She turns to look at me, and when our eyes meet, I suppress a shiver.

"Hey."

I nod in reply. Her voice is polite. Flat. Worlds away from how she sounded with me before. It should suit me just fine—so why am I so triggered?

Adam loops his arm through hers and leads her into the store as I follow, watching Lois whisper in his ear. Those two clicked from the get-go, and seeing them so close and friendly is setting my teeth on edge.

Inside the store, I clutch the cart to keep my hands busy.

"What do you think, Lane?"

I look up. Adam is waving two different piñatas at me.

"A fucking piñata?" I snort. "How old are you guys—five?"

He sighs. "Lois?"

"The green one."

"Lewis hates green," I snap.

Lois glares at me. "Guess he'll do a great job of smashing it up, then." She says it like she's imagining caving in my skull with a baseball bat.

"Green it is!" Adam beams.

"Remind me again—why I am here?"

"My thoughts exactly," Lois mutters, before dipping off to the right.

I sigh. "Gonna be a long fucking day."

I don't know whether I'm imagining things, but it's like my friend is enjoying stretching the shopping expedition out as long as possible. The atmosphere is icy, but he doesn't seem to care. I can't stop rolling my eyes, and it's the same for Lois: when we spot each other doing it, we exchange a quick smile, a split second of softness that evaporates as soon as Lois catches herself and shuts it down again. Before today, I was still so pissed at her. But I've spent the past two weeks without her, and I suddenly feel tired and guilty in equal measures.

"Cups."

Adam points to somewhere behind me, and I stretch out a hand without looking, my fingers closing around something soft and warm. I glance down. I've caught Lois's hand by mistake, and as she tries to shake loose, I can't help but tighten my grip. She blinks a few times, breathing hard. I watch as she frowns, defiance glinting in her eyes, before she drifts over to a stack of cups, my hand still in hers as she reaches out to grab them.

She yanks harder. "Let go."

"You first," I shoot back.

"He asked me to grab them."

"Nope, he asked me."

Neither of us is willing to back down. I'm stronger than her, and though it wouldn't take much for me to overpower her, I don't want to let go.

"Guys, I need two hundred of 'em. You can both grab a few." Adam glances back and forth between us, smiling.

Lois breaks free from me with a sudden jerk, scurrying away with her stash.

At the checkout, my fingers brush hers with every item I lift out of the cart. *What are you doing, Lane?* Just an hour ago, I was raging. Now I can't even remember why I was ever mad in the first place—the same old roller-coaster ride I've been on since we met.

"We need to pick up some booze," Adam says, swinging open his trunk. "We'll get the rest the day before, once we know exactly how many people are coming."

"Lewis always invites people at the last minute," I remind him, holding out a bag.

"Absolute disgrace, dude," Lois mutters.

I bite back a laugh. It's like she's always been part of our family, and the realization cuts me to the core—things wouldn't be the same without her. Shit, I hadn't realized just how much I've missed her. *Don't forget what she did, though.* She made herself at home, taking space that was never hers to take, finding my chinks, cracking them open.

I slam the trunk shut, slip into the passenger seat, and fasten my belt while Adam swings open the door. I listen as Lois clears her throat.

"Sorry, Adam, but I need to head out. I'm meeting up with someone..."

Who?

"And since Lane is here"—she leaves the sentence dangling in the air—"you guys don't really need me."

Why do I want so badly to tell her she's wrong?

"Your call. Can you come help decorate on the twenty-eighth, though?"

She shifts from foot to foot. "Yeah, sure. I said I would."

"And you'll be there for the party?"

I can make out the warmth in Adam's voice but not her reply, and while I should just keep focusing on my feet, I can't help but look up and watch her walk away down the parking lot, wishing so hard she would glance back one last time. *Turn around, Lois.*

When she vanishes behind a pickup, I let out a sigh.

I stare at Adam as he reverses out. "You proud of yourself?"

"Are you?"

"Did she say anything?" I know I shouldn't ask, but I can't help it.

"No, you know what she's like—Lois never spills her guts. You're the only one who really knows what's going on in that head of hers."

There are a million things Adam could've said, but this—this right here is the hardest to hear.

"You should talk to her." He glances at me, concerned.

"It's kind of complicated, man. She did something, and I'm really pissed about it . . ."

At least, I think I am. The weird thing is that now I've seen her again, I don't feel so sure. I'm still mad—but I'm not so sure it's her I'm mad at.

We stock up on booze, and Adam drives me home, leaving me alone with my thoughts in my empty apartment. I spend the next ten minutes staring at my couch, playing back all the times Lois made me feel glad I wasn't alone.

I drag out a stool, settle down behind the kitchen island, and turn on my laptop, pulling up a new document and letting my fingers loose on my keyboard. I need to get these past few months down on paper, starting with the morning Lois fell asleep on my couch. Maybe seeing it all written down in black and white will give me some perspective. Or maybe not.

I SIT ON THE FLOOR against the front door, drafting the lines, deleting them, reworking and rewriting over and over. I've been on this new screenplay for a week, and while I started out strong, I've been stuck on the same scene for days now—the part where Lois stepped into Mike's room and everything went wrong.

The screen strain is making my eyes burn. I can't even bring myself to read back over what I just wrote. It feels like none of it makes sense—like I'm missing something just beyond my reach.

I want to just stand up and throw my laptop out the window, but every time I'm about to give up, something pushes me on.

Suddenly, three loud bangs come pounding above my head. I push the laptop to the side, and open the door to find Carter standing there, frowning at me.

"You going to level with me, or what?"

I take a deep breath in, rubbing at my eyes. I've been pushing back our work sessions, telling him I had too many assignments due, and he looks pissed.

"I'm a student, Cart. I have assignments." I lean against the doorframe.

"That's funny, because I haven't seen you around campus much lately. Don't bullshit a bullshitter. I know you like I know my own dick—you can fool the others, but I'm not buying it." He shoves open the door. "You better start talking. Maybe start with the part where Lois has been staying at Becca's for almost a month now, avoiding everyone—even her friend."

"What do you say we just grab a few beers?" I try.

"Hmm, let me think about that." He pretends to consider. "No. Not when you look as shitty as you do right now."

"Gee, thanks."

"You look like you did when your brother died."

I don't like talking about Mike's death with him—or anyone. I know he feels the loss as sharply as I do, but he's so much more resilient than I am—every time we go there, I end up feeling small.

"You know me—what's the big deal?"

"The big deal is you were solid for a while. Then shit started getting weird again when you met Lois."

The sound of her name makes me wince.

"So that's it!" he crows. "Listen, buddy—you can playact in front of the others, but that shit doesn't work with me."

"What are you even talking about?"

"You guys lived together for a few months. So it makes sense that your rela—"

"Dude, enough," I snap. "There was no relationship. It was supposed to be temporary, remember? Now she's gone, and it's better that way."

"You sure about that?"

"She was all up in my face . . ."

I start churning out the sentences, the same words I spat Lois's way that fateful day. Hearing myself now, the excuses sound alien.

"Lane, come on." He eyes me. "Tell me what *really* happened."

My pulse is racing. And despite everything, the words come spilling out of me. I need Cart to understand why I reacted the way I did.

"Tell me you gave her a chance to explain what she was doing in Mike's room, at least?" he interrupts.

I don't answer.

"Lane?" he warns.

"She had *no* fucking right to be in that room!" I kick the chair between us. "I gave her a place to crash—I didn't have to do that!"

"Is that what you told her? Because if you did, then you're a bigger asshole than I thought. You might not see it this way, but she's your friend."

"I don't give a fuck. She had no right."

"And how is she supposed to know that, you ass? Of *course* she assumed she could move into that room."

No way. I remember exactly what I told her—I mentioned my desk, and my closet.

"In all the time she stayed at my place, I never mentioned that room once. Not *once*."

"I mean it's not like the door was covered with police tape and a big red 'NO ENTRY' sign, right?" Carter snorts. "She spent months here—of course she fucking noticed it. And if you never mentioned it to her, you must have said something that made her think you meant that room."

"No. I know I didn't."

"Did you guys sleep together?"

I stare at him in silence. *What's the point in denying it anymore?*

"Fuck." He stares up at the ceiling. "Laney, you guys need to talk. Enough with the bullshit. It's like you've built it into this crazy-ass secret, and it's fucking stupid. Your brother died, okay? It was a tragedy, and it wasn't fair. But—"

"I lost my shit because she was all up in my space. Everywhere, Cart." I fling my arms in the air. "She was all over my life. First, on the anniversary of Mike's death. Then Christmas, and the final straw was his room. She was fucking *everywhere*."

"Oh, what a heartless bitch!" He throws his hands up. "She was the first person to drag you out of your shitty little life. She was a breath of fresh air when you needed it most—it must have been so, *so* hard for you!" He shakes his head, raking his hands through his hair. "You're such a loser, Lane. And stubborn as fuck, too."

I let it sink in, taken aback. I knew he'd go hard on me, but I wasn't expecting this.

"You know what your problem is?" He glares at me. "Lois is the only girl who ever made you feel good. And you're projecting all the shit you can't handle onto her, so you don't have to deal with your feelings."

"I don't have any feelings—"

"For her? I don't believe that for a fucking second. Look at you! But you know what? Whatever, man." He shrugs. "This is your problem—not mine. Once you get over yourself, maybe you can do a little soul-searching." He takes a step toward me. "But if you were an asshole to her—which I get the feeling you were—my advice is go find her, and tell her you're sorry. She's a nice girl, Lane. And you know I've always got your back. But not this time."

I stare at him.

"And honestly? The whole 'sleeping on the couch' thing? Yeah—that needs to stop. What were you thinking, making her live like that?"

I stand there, frozen in place. He seems to be saying the couch is like a punishment, but I just wanted her to keep on living here, and ...

"Shit ..."

"Yeah," he drawls. "Shit."

He claps a hand on my shoulder.

Once he leaves, I stand there for a second, stunned. Before I know it, I'm pulling on my jacket and heading to my car, racing down the streets and all the way to campus, where I pull up outside the place I've forced Lois to call home now. Carter is right. I need to apologize. I'm not sure I'll be able to say everything I need to say in one go, but I should never have treated her that way. I know that now.

I knock on the door a few times. No answer. If I leave now, I'm scared I won't have the balls to come back and try again, and so I sit on the stairs and wait. I'm like Lois, all those months back, when Kirk had just dumped her. Except I'm not so patient. Two hours and a few failed calls later, I head back down to the parking lot, and just as I'm about to get back in my car, I spot her.

"Lois!"

She nearly trips when she hears me, and I stride over, taking in big gulps of air as I go.

"Can we get a coffee?"

She blinks a few times, raising her eyebrows, parting her lips to speak.

"I've been thinking, and I—"

"Nope."

Sharp, decisive. One little word cuts the breath out of me. She didn't even have to think twice.

"N-no?" I stammer.

"Nope."

She turns on her heel and walks away. I was expecting a whole other situation, and I suddenly realize just how bad I've hurt her.

I rush back home and fling open my laptop as soon as I step

through the front door. The thing. That thing I couldn't quite grasp, the idea hovering somewhere beyond my reach—now I get it. Now I know what it is. It's the part where I fucked everything up. I rewrite the moment, piecing it back together. In this version, there's no yelling, no red mist—just me calmly telling her everything that room means to me. Getting it all down on paper is freeing, but as I move on to the next scene, the blank page stares back at me. How do I write the part where she reacts, now that Lois is gone for good?

30

LOIS

Ever since Adam screwed me more than three weeks ago, ever since Lane asked me to grab a coffee, I've been dedicating all my brain space to studying. The way he came up to me like that—the exact same way Kirk did—is a stark reminder of how badly they both hurt me. The wound that had started to scar is raw and tender all over again, but I'm proud I stood my ground. Let him drive himself crazy, while I carry on stepping into my best self—no matter how much it stings.

Hope and Prudence have taken it upon themselves to spend every Tuesday night building me back up over a post–water aerobics bottle of wine. I was expecting them to bombard me with questions about how down I am and what happened with Lane; I thought they would be engineering some kind of sweet revenge plan for me to execute. Instead, they while away the hours with stories of the wild lives they've led, each anecdote more gripping than the last. It's unreal how strong these two ladies are—they've got more than sixty years on me, but I've never met such a pair of total badasses. Slowly but surely, they're rubbing off on me, and the Lois I hope to become is gradually taking shape in my mind. Was this their plan all along? I have no idea. All I know is that I'm so glad we met.

This morning, Adam got back in touch out of the blue. I was

hoping he'd forget how I promised to help decorate the house they rented for their party, but nope: I got a text telling me he'd swing by to pick me up from campus, and though I drafted a hundred different ways to back out of it, I ended up just sending an "OK."

Sliding into the passenger seat, I give him a long, hard stare. I'm through with playing games.

"Is Lane going to be there?"

"No—he's coming by with the booze around five, so you can just head out then."

Adam seems kind of upset by the whole thing. This guy is such a sweetheart—I kind of wish my heart had picked him instead.

Fifteen minutes later, we pull up outside the most unreal house, and I feel a pinch as I remember I won't be coming to the party.

"So now you know how to get here," Adam says as he unbuckles his seat belt.

"You know I'm not coming, right?"

"You know I'm not going to stop pushing, right?"

He shoots me a grin, and I smile back at him.

Adam always makes me feel so welcomed. Two hours drift by, and before I know it, I'm hanging decorations from the ceiling, singing my heart out and swaying from side to side, only realizing too late that the stepladder has started to shake, and as I feel the rung give way beneath my feet, I cry out.

"Shit!"

My arms windmill as I go flying through the air. I hear Adam lunge for me, and it's a good job he's so quick on his feet and big enough to take the hit. Muscly, too. And he smells just as good as Lane.

"Nice catch, Laney!"

I recognize Donovan's voice somewhere in the distance, and I freeze. Strong arms are wrapped tight around me. Arms I know all too well. My eyes are shut, and I don't want to open them just yet. *Put me down already.*

I mutter a quick "Thank you," my breath catching in my chest.

The smell of him is all over me, stirring memories that are still too painful to handle. Lane's green eyes scan my face, and I shift uncomfortably in his arms. A strange expression flits over his features when, finally, he lets me go.

Don slings an arm around my shoulders. "Good work, guys!"

"Adam runs a tight ship." I shrug. "I just followed instructions!"

Lane is still staring at me. I keep my eyes fixed on the fairy lights I just strung up—they better be worth the near-death experience.

"Need a hand, dude?" Don whips the piñata out of a plastic bag.

"Yeah . . . Let's keep Lois as far as humanly possible from the stepladder. Lane, just leave the bottles by the bar."

I watch Lane drift out of the room and decide to make a move before he gets back.

"I'm going to leave you guys to it."

"Thanks for helping out!" Adam pulls me in for a hug. "See you tomorrow?"

I mumble my goodbyes and practically sprint to the sidewalk, fishing my phone out of my pocket as I run. One missed call from Kirk. *Shit! I need to hurry—I'm gonna be late.* It's time for that coffee he mentioned. I ended up saying yes, and I have no idea what to expect. I felt like a nobody without him, and it's only now I'm realizing that I clung to Lane like a life raft, desperate for some kind of substance. *Emotional dependency*, as Carrie had called it, before diving back into another one of her books. I'm finally starting to lean in to the new, bad-bitch me, but there's still a weight wedged in my heart, and it feels like I'm standing at a crossroads with no way through.

I start to walk, turning my thoughts over in my mind, when something catches my eye. I glance over at the road. Lane's car. *Is he leaving already?* He's creeping along the sidewalk, driving as slow as he can to stay level with me.

He leans across to the passenger window. "Let me give you a ride."

The offer catches me off guard. I stop in my tracks, muffling the urge to say yes, mentally bitch-slapping myself back to reality.

"No, thanks. I'm okay to walk."

I can't handle letting him into my space again—not yet. I'm trying so hard to heal, I can't undo all my hard work.

"Get in the car."

I choose to ignore him, lengthening my stride. Last time, he just let me go—and it's hard, because my heart is pounding in my chest, all those memories I pushed back bubbling up to the surface. I glance over my shoulder. Car horns are blaring out in a chorus, a long line piled up behind Lane. Still he carries on crawling alongside me, refusing to let me go.

"You know you've started a traffic jam?"

"I'm not moving until you get in the fucking car."

What is going *on* with this guy?

"Lois!" he snaps.

No matter how edgy he sounds, the way he says my name sends butterflies skittering through me. I've missed him. And I hate how weak I am.

Stay strong, Lois. Go your own way. The problem is my own way is currently one long stretch of road, and there's nowhere for me to turn off. I could dip into a store—but I'm pretty sure he'll just stay parked there in the middle of the street. I'd forgotten how stubborn he can be.

A guy in a monster truck leans out the window. "You gonna move the fuck along, buddy?"

"I'm waiting for her to get in the car," Lane yells back. "Sorry!"

"Hey, you!" The same guy is waving at me now. "What's the holdup?"

I throw up my hands. "I don't know this guy!"

"Not my problem, lady!"

He hammers down on his horn, and some other woman jumps in, yelling in my general direction.

"What is *wrong* with you people?" I holler. "He's the one blocking up the road, and you're coming for *me?!*"

"Lois!" Lane calls out at me for the tenth time.

The man in the truck holds down his horn, and as a torrent of insults is launched my way, I make a split decision.

"You are *so* fucking annoying!"

I fling open the car door and slam it shut behind me as hard as I can, almost ripping the seat belt out as I clip myself in. I can feel Lane's eyes on me, but I refuse to meet them.

"Drive!" I fold my arms over my chest. "This is unreal. How come people always take shit out on me?"

Nice little sideswipe there, Lois.

"Drop me at the mall."

He hits the gas, and as the miles fly by, my throat tightens. He's so unbearably sexy when he drives—one hand loose on the wheel, jaw set—and it makes me ache with the shameful truth: I'm still as obsessed with him as ever.

I watch helplessly as he turns off down a random side street.

"You're going the wrong way," I warn.

He pulls over and unfastens his seat belt as I glance out the window. I've never been to this part of town before.

"What's the deal?" I snort. "This how I die?"

"I think we're past that, don't you?"

"We're past a lot of things."

He swallows hard, narrowing his lips.

"What do you want from me?" I sigh.

It's taking everything I have to keep my tone in check.

"Come back home."

For a split second, I forget to breathe. I wasn't expecting this—and from the way he's shifting in his seat, I don't think he was, either.

For the briefest of moments, happiness swells in the pit of my stomach, but the feeling is fleeting as I remember that Lane is the same old Lane he ever was. If there's one thing I've learned, it's this: nothing he ever says means what I think it does.

"No, thanks," I say primly. "I love sharing a room with Carrie."

"Listen, I know I messed up. I should've—"

"Don't wor—"

"Let me talk! I'm trying to say sorry, here!"

He grips the steering wheel harder, his knuckles blanching.

"Well, you could start by actually looking at me," I snap.

My voice cracks. This is what I'd been scared of. My instinct is to reach for the handle and shove open the door, so I start unbuckling my seat belt but Lane is quicker off the mark. He locks the doors before leaning over and jamming my buckle back in place.

"I'm sorry!" he yells. "Okay?"

For a moment, I freeze. And then I burst out laughing.

"You must be the only guy in the world to actually scream an apology."

I shake my head, suddenly exhausted. I've been waiting for this moment since the day I left, but I'm still hurting. I'm so sad he broke what we had between us. *Whatever I thought we had.*

"Come home with me, Lois."

"Nope."

"I said I'm sorry for the way I spoke to you."

"And that's great. I appreciate it, I really do. But the answer's still no."

I deserve more than a shitty couch.

He makes to reply, but I'm on a roll.

"It's better this way—and you know it. It went on for way longer than we planned, and now you want me back because you feel guilty, or lonely, or something, and that's just not going to work for me anymore." I take a deep breath in. "I don't want to be some girl crashing on your couch. What worked for me all those months ago is over. You helped me out, and I'm so thankful for that. But I don't need you anymore."

It's so painful to hear, and worse still, it's not true—my hands are shaking, my heart is pounding, but deep down I know I'm doing the right thing. I've just delivered a sucker punch, I can see it on his face. I keep my lips pinched tight, willing myself to stick to my word.

"You don't need me, either," I add.

He lets out a long sigh. And then he starts the car and pulls out in silence. We drive, and drive, and drive. I can tell his mind is racing, and I want to yell at him to speak, to say something—*anything*—but as per usual, he doesn't say a word. What did I expect? This is the mysterious Lane O'Neill in all his splendor, ladies and gentlemen! And I don't have the energy to try to figure him out anymore.

When we near the mall, I tell him he can drop me anywhere.

I'm late, and though my enthusiasm for getting coffee with Kirk has faded even more than before, Lane clearly has nothing left to say to me—we're done here. The guy sure knows how to rub salt in the wound. For the briefest of moments, I had thought . . . I shrug the idea away. It doesn't matter what I thought. All I know is I need to get out of this car ASAP. He pulls up outside the entrance, and I unclip myself, mumbling a rushed "Thank you" and swinging open the door. Just as I'm about to step out, he reaches for my arm.

"You're wrong. I—"

"It's too late. You said sorry, and I get that, but—"

"Are you meeting up with Kirk?" Lane leans back, his eyes drifting somewhere behind me.

I follow his gaze and swallow hard as I spot my ex just a few feet away from us. *Amazing timing.*

"Of course you are." His voice has chilled. "Now that Kirk's in the game again, who needs stupid old Lane, right?"

In another time, another place maybe, I would have leveled with him—told him I'm meeting Kirk for the hell of it, because I have no idea what I really want anymore. I would have told him a whole bunch of things. I would have laid my soul bare. But he lost that right a few weeks ago. Lane doesn't get to hear my innermost thoughts anymore.

"Are you kidding me? You're the one who—"

"You know what? Get out. I think I get the idea," he snarls. "You're right, I did feel guilty—but I'm feeling a whole lot better now.

You should be thanking me. Mission accomplished, huh? Kirky finally saw the light." Lane scoffs.

There's a pressure mounting in my chest. "Don't do this."

"Feel free to come crash on the couch next time you need to get laid—it was cool."

I thought our showdown in the apartment was the worst pain I'd ever feel. I was wrong. I should just leave him here with all his bullshit, but he needs to know he crossed a line.

"Who the hell do you think you are?" I spit. "I never signed up to be your hookup! After everything we had, this is how you talk to me?" I shake my head. "Don't get me wrong—I knew you were an asshole. I guess I just didn't realize you were this bad. I thought we were friends. You know, I actually thought I meant something to you, and that . . ."

I pause to catch my breath.

"I know this is stupid and I should just be the bigger person here, but you know what, Lane? Let me tell you something." I lean into him. "I was hoping so hard you would ask me to stay that night. Because I felt good, living there. With you. I actually felt like myself again, like there was someone who finally got me. So yeah, okay—I misunderstood your offer. I really thought you were saying I should take that room—"

"I never—"

"I know!" I yell. "I fucking *get* it, okay? Of course that room was never for me! Of *course* I didn't deserve an actual room for myself! Stupid, desperate me!"

"That's not it."

"You thought I wasn't worthy, or something—just say it!" I'm screaming at the top of my lungs. "Just fucking *say* it!"

"It was my brother's room!" he yells so loud, my heart skips a beat.

Silence falls across the car. I blink.

"You have a brother?"

"He's dead, okay?" He shoots me a dirty look, as if I killed the guy with my own bare hands.

His words land like gunshots. I don't know what to do with them. I glance at Lane. He looks pained and relieved in equal measures.

"I lost my shit when I saw you in there, because it's his room. It always has been. So stop thinking it's something you fucking *did*, okay?"

"You want *me* to stop? Listen, buddy, you're the one who 'lost your shit' with me, like I majorly fucked up."

I feel sick, my chest so tight I keep tugging on the collar of my sweater, desperate for air. This is even worse than I imagined. My anger has evaporated, as if Lane just hit the off switch, leaving me alone in the pitch black.

"I just couldn't tell you." He keeps his eyes locked on the gearshift. "I should never have spoken to you like that, but when I saw you in that room, I just . . . Anyway. I'm sorry."

"'Anyway'?" I say flatly. "You have no idea, do you? You just told me your brother died, Lane. In the middle of a fight—like that explains everything. We've known each other for six months now, and we spent almost that whole time living together; I invited you home to meet my family; I told you stuff nobody else knows . . ."

Hot tears are trickling down my cheeks. I brush them away with my sleeve.

"I trusted you—and you never thought to tell me?"

"Do you have any idea how hard it is?"

"I get that, I do. But this is us we're talking about. I thought we . . ."

I force myself to breathe, trying to make sense of the thoughts racing through my head. Lane has just told me he lost his brother, and I can't brush that off.

"What happened?"

"A bike accident. Three years ago. November twelfth."

A bike accident? I think back to how mad he got with Ethan, and it suddenly makes sense.

"November twelfth?" I whisper. "So that evening, when you forgot I was making us dinner . . . It was the anniversary of his death?"

He nods. My brain is scrambled.

"So now you know. Now you get why . . ."

It almost sounds like a question. But the truth is—I don't.

"You had so many chances to tell me," I say. Everything is slowly slotting into place. "*So* many. But you said nothing. Why couldn't you just *tell* me?"

Part of me wants to scoop him up in my arms and hug him tight, tell him I'm sorry, tell him I have brothers, too, tell him I can only imagine how painful it all must be . . . But there's another part burning even brighter inside me. I feel empty. Hollow. Lane helped me when I was down—true. But ultimately, all he's given me is a big, fat black hole of nothingness. It had hurt, thinking that we had slept together and it didn't mean anything to him. But this feels somehow worse. The truth is that I never mattered to him at all.

I'm shaking. He rests a hand on my wrist, and when I look into his eyes, I can't read him.

"Come back—"

I whip my hand away so fast, it slams against the window.

"So what's the plan? You think telling me some sob story is going to make it all better?"

He frowns. "No, but—"

"But nothing! Knowing the truth makes it even worse." I shake my head sadly. "I thought you were mad at me because you couldn't stand me being on your couch anymore. So yeah—it's kind of a relief that the *real* problem was the room, not me. And hearing about your brother breaks my heart, it really does. But you know what hurts even more?" I look at him. "That I didn't count enough for you to tell me the truth. Even when you knew how cruel you were being. You didn't care enough to tell me about him."

Before he can answer, I slip out of the car, but I barely have time to take a couple of steps when I feel his hand on my arm again.

"I just told you my brother died."

"And I'm so sorry for that," I say. "Genuinely. If I lost one of my brothers, there's no way I'd be able to get over it. Or maybe I could—if I had friends who mattered to me, people I could share my pain with."

"That's not me." He loosens his grip on my arm. "It took a lot for me to tell you just now. But it feels good. I'm glad you know."

I know I'm going to regret what I say next, but I can't keep it in.

"It's a shame it's all a little too late."

He lets go of my wrist, his face crumpling, and I look away, turning on my heel as I make my way toward the mall. Just as Lane's engine starts up, Kirk calls out from the entrance. *Shit. I totally forgot all about Kirk.*

While I wait for the lights to change, I stare across the road at him waiting for me. What the hell am I doing? Do I really want to hang out with my ex right now? I feel like I'm playacting my way through my own life. I should just leave and head back to campus—I'm not in the right headspace for Kirk.

I watch as he darts through the traffic, ambling up the sidewalk to join me.

"Hey!" He pulls me in for a hug, and I shudder. "Everything okay?" His eyes search mine, his hands still resting on my shoulders. "I saw you with Lane. What did he want?"

"Nothing."

"What did he say?"

I clench my jaw, suppressing the urge to shove him back. Kirk is standing too close, and the last thing I want is to discuss Lane with him. I'm still reeling from what just happened.

"Lois?"

His fingers brush my chin as he tilts my head up to look at him.

"Forget it."

"I don't want that guy sniffing around you anymore."

I blink. The anger layered under my pain is slowly sparking again. He can see the tear tracks running down my face, and yet the only thing he cares about is Lane.

"What?"

"I don't want some guy hanging around my girlfriend—"

"Your *girlfriend*?" I bristle. "Last I checked, you dumped me."

He leans into me, his lips pursed.

"What the hell, Kirk?!" I take a step back.

"Things change."

His confidence is unbearable. I'm tempted to slap him, I'm tempted to kiss him, too: just to see whether it erases the hurt of the past six months. I should try, at least. I should want to try. This is the moment I've spent so long daydreaming about after all, but as I scour the face I used to love, something in me is pushing back. Kirk takes my silence for consent, and doubles down.

When I feel his breath against my lips, I slam my hands into his stomach and shove him back.

"Stop."

"Why? I know you still have feelings for me."

I'm so tired of people using me.

"Not like that," I say, shaking my head. "Not anymore."

"I'm sorry, okay?" He shrugs. "I was an ass. I should've sat down and had an actual conversation instead of just throwing it all away. I really regret it, Lois."

"You dumped me two days before classes started. You told me I was too much—too 'me.' Oh, and too fat. Remember that?"

"I was confused, and yeah—I messed up. It was a dumb move." So slick. So smooth. "I get that now," he adds.

"Same here. It took me a while, but there's loads of stuff I'm starting to get. I never thought I'd hear myself say this, but—I don't want to get back together with you. I'm done here."

As I say the words, I wait for a rush of feeling. Nothing comes.

"This is because of Lane, am I right?"

It is, in a way. But not the way Kirk thinks.

I stare him straight in the eye. "It's to do with *you*, actually."

"I said sorry!"

I start to slow-clap. "Well done, you. Better late than never, huh?"

"We were together for four years."

Like I didn't know that already.

"Wow," I say. "You only just remembered? I would've given you everything. Anything you asked for." I laugh. "Who am I kidding? I *did* give you everything. And you just threw me out like trash. You went straight out to date other girls, you ignored me, you treated me like a piece of shit—"

"And you're telling me this because you're hurting and you want me back—"

"I'm telling you because it's the truth! You know, Kirk, when I really think about it, I'm not even mad at you anymore. You helped me grow. You made me realize I don't like the old Lois. I don't want to be that girl anymore."

And Lane helped me realize that, too. He gave me that much, at least.

"I was so obsessed with you," I continue. "With our relationship. I was so busy trying to be the perfect girlfriend, I forgot who I was."

"So now you know who you are, why can't we just get back together?"

"Because I don't love you anymore," I say simply.

And just like that, the veil lifts.

31

LANE

I'm lying on the floor when I hear a key turn in the lock. I should get up, but the truth is all my dignity and drive have deserted me. There's only one person who could get me jumping to my feet right now, and I know it won't be her. It won't be Lois, because Lois left her keys on the table the day she checked out. It won't be Lois, because I just screwed up my one last shot at fixing it all.

I used Mike's death as an excuse. I usually hate people acting all sad when they find out about him, but when it came to Lois, I really needed her to get it. I needed her to understand that every time I think of my brother, it's like a knife twist to the gut. I needed her to know it's a feeling I can't control, and one that messed things up between us.

My apology got off on the wrong foot, and then as soon as I caught sight of Kirk, I flipped. I was so fucking jealous, and I hurled every hurtful thing I could her way. *And now it's too late.* I saw them kiss. All I want is to curl up and die.

Why didn't I just take a leap of faith—tell her how I really feel? I've been such a fucking coward. All this time, I downplayed how she made me feel, hoping that would be enough to protect me from the pain. I was so scared, and I was so dumb to think that denying your own feelings could be that easy. When I think of how I spoke to her, I want to punch myself in the face. Now that I've accepted how I feel, it's all crystal clear to me. All those low-key moments were so much more than they seemed. All that time we spent together was proof that I needed her close to me all along. I want her in my life, even if she doesn't like me that way—even if I have to sit by and watch her with that asshole boyfriend of hers. *Fuck. All that time I had her to myself, and I royally fucked everything up.*

"Well, well, well—will you look at that?" Lewis's voice rings out somewhere above my head.

"He dead?" Adam asks.

"I hope not. That's one ugly-ass T-shirt. Nobody deserves to die looking this bad," Donovan says.

Great. The whole Brady Bunch is in town.

I hold up my middle finger.

"It lives!" Lewis yells.

Slowly, I open my eyes. My friends are standing in a circle around me, staring down at me. I feel like I'm some kind of human sacrifice.

"Is your couch grounded?" Lewis asks. "Why's it pushed up against the wall like that?"

Because I can't look at it without wanting to puke.

Donovan pipes up. "Forget the couch. Why are you lying on the floor, dude?"

Carter crouches down to me, and I know what he's thinking—he knows exactly why I'm curled up on my living room floor, and I'm guessing the other three know, too. Turns out everyone else knew how I felt, long before I did.

"He misses Lois," Cart says in a stage whisper.

"How long's the emo phase gonna last?" Don drawls. "Your clients think you're ghosting them. I mean, I'm drowning in your leftovers, which is awesome. But still . . ."

"I've been busy with the script," I say.

"Really? Which one?" Carter snickers.

"Cut him some slack, guys," Adam says, holding out a hand.

I scramble to my feet.

"You look like shit, man. Lois still freezing you out?"

"Who?" I raise my eyebrows.

"You're such a pain in the ass." Lewis glares at me. "You know since you guys had your fight, she's been ghosting us? I don't even think she'll come to the party tomorrow!"

"What do you want me to say?"

"Not me you should be asking."

I stalk over to the fridge, doing my best to ignore their stares.

"Why don't you just talk to her, Lane?"

"I did!" I gulp down a glass of water. "It didn't help—it made things worse. And now she's back with Kirk, so—"

"Fuck!" Lewis lowers himself onto the coffee table. "So what are you gonna do?"

"Nothing."

"Seriously?" Don whistles. "You're just gonna let that asshole win? Dude, you need to show him who's boss."

"How did he 'win'? She got what she wanted all along." I scowl.

"Oh, quit the whining and grow some balls!"

"I told her I was sorry, and it didn't change a thing," I snap. "I told her how my brother died—I thought she'd get it. But she said it was too late."

Don glances at Lewis, clearing his throat.

"Well, did you tell her that on top of being a total moron, you're also in love with her?"

The water goes down the wrong way, and I splutter.

"And did you tell her that you massively overreacted because you're scared of your big, huge, scary feelings?" he adds in a baby voice.

"What the—"

"Oh, Lane." Lewis bats his eyelashes at me. "Poor, sweet, clueless Lane. We've been friends for three years. I know how you roll when it comes to girls, and trust me—this is different."

Donovan pipes up. "Why do you think we came up with that whole Dexter Drake story? We knew you were in love with her, right from the very first day."

"What? Bullshit! We couldn't stand each other."

"Lois Lane, dude. It was written in the stars." Adam winks.

Carter smiles at me. "You're in love with her, buddy. You might be the last person on earth to realize it, but I'm pretty sure you fell for her when you saw her sitting on the stairs. Why else would you let some random girl crash on your couch for months?"

"A couch, for fuck's sake." Lewis shakes his head. "Absolute disgrace, dude."

"Did you guys forget the part where I said no at first? She was the one who just fell asleep here. Twice! And what—you think I set fire to her fucking motel, just so she'd have to stay at my place?"

"Who cares about when exactly it happened?"

I start to pace the living room, and Carter gives my shoulder a squeeze.

"This is so fucked up," I say, raking my hands through my hair.

"Why?"

"Because Kirk? Because she hates my guts? Because I'm such a fucking dumbass—"

"She likes you, too, Laney. I'm pretty sure she realized before you did."

"You think so?"

"Trust me on that one. Why else would she be so hurt when you lashed out at her?"

"Great, like I needed a reminder . . ."

"You need to get your ass moving, man. Kirk is one step ahead of you, but you've still got a shot. You need to man up and tell her exactly how you feel."

"Yeah. Let your heart lead the way." Lewis simpers.

"Fuck me. Look what I've been reduced to." I glance around at them. "You guys are literally the worst people to ask for relationship advice. I can't believe I'm actually listening to you idiots on how to confess I'm in love with a girl."

A wave of anxiety ripples over me just saying the L-word.

"This is all so moving. We're so proud," Don says, wiping away an imaginary tear.

"Are you implying we're just a bunch of fuckboys?" Lewis asks in a mock-offended tone.

"That is *exactly* what I'm implying."

"Fine by me!" He grins proudly. "Right, Don?"

"Oh, absolutely! I'll leave the girlfriends to Carter and Lane."

I bite my tongue. They're so naive—in a way, it's kind of touching.

Adam turns to me. "So—what's the plan?"

Do I even have a chance? Lois never gave me the slightest hint she had feelings for me—or maybe I was just too blind and stubborn to see it. I don't know, but I definitely don't want to live with regrets.

"I have an idea."

32

LOIS

I walk for a while, wandering aimlessly to help clear my head, and by the time I slip back into my room, it's been hours since I left Kirk standing there outside the mall.

I toss my bag on the bed and kick off my shoes, suddenly realizing just how drained I am. This has been way too much to handle for one day. I said everything I needed to say, to everyone who needed to hear it, and now all I want is sleep. On some level, I feel at peace. But there's another side of me that's rawer than ever, Lane's words echoing through my mind on loop. I fall back on the bed and roll onto my front, feeling a hard lump underneath my pillow. I prop myself up for a closer look: a large, blank brown envelope. Sitting up, I peel it open and shuffle out the thick bundle, and when I see what's written on the cover page, my eyes widen.

"What the..."

I run a finger over the bound sheets and shudder, my fingers trembling as they trace out the title page.

FAST LANE

Leaning against the back wall, I pull my knees up under my chin and start to read. It doesn't take me long to realize I'm looking at a screenplay—and while I know this must be Lane's work, it doesn't read anything like the movies he usually makes. Did he drive all the way over here to drop it off? And if he did—why? He had plenty of opportunity to say what he needed to say in the car.

I turn the page, despite myself. I don't get it. It's the story of how we met, starting with me sitting on those stairs, all the way to ... Who knows what. I flip the pages shut. I'm not sure I'm ready to read this—not while my head is such a mess. Why did he write all this down?

There were moments with him that felt amazing, and a part of me wants to read on, desperate for a chance to revisit the good times. It's a bittersweet story with a really shitty ending, though. I still can't believe I got it all so wrong. Disappointment pools in my throat. Today was a big deal—telling Kirk off finally felt like I was spreading my wings, but the memory of Lane floats back into my mind, and before I know it, I'm right back where I started. I refuse to put myself through this all over again. I will not make the same mistake twice. I rejected Lane earlier, sure—but somewhere deep inside me, I still care. He apologized—clumsily—but that doesn't make me feel any better. I can't hate him for not feeling the way I do. Still, it hurts that he didn't trust me as a friend. That would have been enough for me.

I toss the script on the floor and roll over onto my side. I don't need to read any more—there's nothing in those pages I don't already know, and I don't want to relive those painful few months. I'm going to need some time to move on, and I hope Adam and Lewis will understand my not showing up to their party. I can't go. I just can't. I'm about to start a fresh chapter in a whole new story—*my own* story. And I'm starting to realize that's all that really matters.

33

LANE

Pulling up outside the mansion the guys rented for their birthday, my nerves are fizzing. Adam and Lewis fling open the front door before I even have a chance to ring, and I slap a smile on my face.

"Happy birthday, assholes!"

Just a few more hours until the party kicks off. I'm not in the mood for fun, but these are my best friends—there's no way I'm ruining their big night. I've messed up enough lately, and I'm doing a shit job of making things right. My screenplay didn't work—there's been no word from Lois. And considering what my movie is about, that tells me everything I need to know.

"Thank you, Laney!" Lewis shrieks.

The pair of them step aside, and as I walk into the house, I see Adam looking at me expectantly. I shake my head in response.

"I tried calling Lois to see if she plans on coming, but it went straight to voicemail," he tells me.

"It's okay, dude."

It's not okay, but I'm an optimist—still clinging on to the faint hope she might just turn up and forgive me.

Adam beckons me over. "Before you drink yourself stupid, I need you over here."

I help Don hang up his fugly birthday banner. I fold napkins. I blow up balloons, like if we were getting ready for a kid's party. *Be nice, Lane.*

The dining room is huge. I stand there tapping my foot, staring out the bay window, craning for a better view as the guests start trickling in, hoping to catch sight of her. The crowds are pouring in thick and fast—looks like Lewis invited the entire basketball team and half the campus, at least.

I do my best to be useful, ferrying stuff around, laying dishes out on tables. When everything is done, I turn back to where my friends are standing in a huddle, whispering.

"What's up?"

Don nods toward the entrance hall. "Lois just got here."

I breathe out, rubbing my palms together. *Okay, so she came. That's got to be a good sign, right?*

Before I turn around, I take a moment to gather my thoughts and plan how I'm going to do this.

Just when I've taken a deep breath in and am readying myself to go find her, Carter puts a hand on my chest, frowning.

"She's with Kirk."

The sentence cuts me to the quick. I follow my friend's gaze, and there's a knife twisting in my heart. I want to grab the table and flip it over, but I bite down on my anger. This is all my own fault—losing my shit won't change that.

I had no idea this would hurt so bad, and I suddenly understand how Lois must have felt, back when I found her on the stairs, nursing a broken heart. I stroll over to the bar and pour myself a beer from the keg. I almost feel like crouching down and drinking straight from the tap, but out the corner of my eye I see movement to my left, and my fingers tighten around my cup. I know it's Lois without looking. I can feel her presence like the sun. My pulse quickens. I need a little more liquid courage before I can go speak to her. I drift over to a group of basketball players, listening to Lewis and Don debate their chances of winning the championship, batting back niceties, fending off a gaggle of wasted girls.

Time ticks by, and I still can't find the exact right moment to go and talk to the only person I can think about. I swirl my beer around my cup, until somebody staggers into me, and half my drink goes spilling over my feet. I look up. When I see who just trashed my best sneakers, anger hits me square in the third eye.

"You gotta be fucking kidding me."

Kirk glares at me without so much as a "sorry."

"Not my fault you're always in my way, man."

"Asshole," I growl, all my pent-up rage rushing out of me in two easy syllables.

The more I stare at him, the more I want to smash his face in—and he knows exactly how I feel, because he takes a few steps back. Before I know it, I'm striding toward him.

"Easy, Laney." Don muscles his way between us. "Beating up Lois's boyfriend is definitely not the game plan."

My friend has a point. I know that. But now that I've got Kirk right here in front of me, I know exactly how I feel. There's no way I can stand by and be secretly in love with Lois. I've already lost her. From where I'm sitting, I have nothing left to lose.

"I'll be gentle with him!" I protest.

"He's on the team." Don frowns, weighing up his options. "And I'm the captain." He glances over at Lewis. "It's your birthday, man—what do you say?"

Lewis pretends to think. "Go easy on him. We need him fresh for the games." He winks at me. "Just make sure he can still run."

Placing his hands on my shoulders, Don leans into me and gives the performance of a lifetime.

"Lane! Don't do this!"

I smile.

And a second later, my fist lands square in Kirk's face.

His hands shoot to his nose. "Are you outta your fucking mind?"

"You have no idea how long I've wanted to do that," I say calmly. "It's almost as good as I imagined."

He clenches a fist, ready to swipe back.

"Come on, Kirky-Poo," I taunt, bouncing from foot to foot. "Just do it already."

"Lane O-Fucking-Neill!"

I whip around to find Lois standing there, quivering with rage. Kirk seizes his chance to land a blow to my cheek, and I rip off my sweater and lunge for him, my whole body powered by pure, unbridled anger. Before I can make contact, I feel arms snaking around me.

"We said one shot, dude."

Don and Lewis drag me over to the bay window and lock me outside, and while the fresh air does nothing to cool my temper, at least it's helping to settle my mind. I may have gone a little too far. There's a commotion stirring inside the house, and so I make a beeline for the garden couch, sitting myself down to listen to the trickling fountain, when suddenly there's another sound.

Clap, clap, clap.

I glance up and my stomach flip-flops. Lois is striding toward me, slowly clapping as she goes.

"You're quite the showman, aren't you? Knowing Adam and Lewis, I was expecting a stripper."

"Did I break his nose?" I ask.

"No idea. Kirk's nose was always kind of weird."

Didn't stop you from loving him, though.

She stops in her tracks, and stands there staring at me.

"Nice T-shirt, by the way." She smirks.

I glance down at the supersize "S." That afternoon, when I realized I had pulled on the Superman top she gave me for Christmas, it felt right to keep it on. Now that she's seen it, I'm hoping to get some kind of reaction, but instead she just blinks, her eyes drifting back to mine.

"Did it feel good?" She arches an eyebrow. "Hitting him, I mean."

"Yeah." I smile. "I needed that."

Her eyes are boring into mine, and I would pay good money to know what's going through her head right now. I just punched her boyfriend, after all.

"You're so . . ."

She shuts her eyes and wraps her arms around herself. Her lips part, then close again. Is this the right time to tell her I'm dying to kiss her?

I'm doing my best to keep it on the down-low, but the truth is I'm drinking her in. She looks incredible in that dress—the same one she wore for Thanksgiving. Even back then, I thought she looked amazing that night. It's a shame it took me so long to figure out what it all meant.

I pat the cushion next to me. "Want to join me?"

"I'm considering it. I don't know whether I want to slap you or ghost you."

"Surprise me."

She rolls her eyes, a flicker of a smile playing on her lips, and it suddenly feels like we're back on my couch, eating pizza and passing the time.

"Why did you punch him?"

I rub my fist. "He makes my skin crawl."

"And?"

I feel like she's reaching out—throwing me a lifeline. The problem is I don't know what she wants from me.

"I don't like the guy."

"And?" she says again, taking a step toward me.

"When did you guys get back together, anyway?"

"Who said we're together?" she asks, her eyes widening.

"I saw you kiss at the mall."

"Okay, Detective . . ."

"So when did you hook up?"

"As soon as I realized I'm still crazy about him."

Wow. That hurt. It's a slap in the face, but I don't flinch.

"Which never happened, you total moron!" She glares at me. "Talking to him helped me get my head straight. When he tried to kiss me—outside a *mall*, of all places—I turned him down. It was the best day of my life. I know bitterness is never a good look, but it just felt so good. I felt iconic," she adds.

I get to my feet, my thoughts churning.

"But I saw you guys."

"He *tried* to kiss me. I pushed him away."

"You came to the party together tonight," I snap back.

"We came through the door at the same time, yeah. But we didn't actually come *together*."

"But—"

"I got here the same time as three other guys, too. FYI, Lane, I don't do poly." She appraises me. "This is a classic you move, isn't it? You whirled yourself up without even talking to me first."

"I thought you said you never wanted to talk to me again?"

"Put yourself in my shoes, Lane! You acted just like Kirk. You saw how bad he hurt me, and then you went and did the exact same thing. You treated me like shit for no good reason—"

"You were okay with bending over backward to get him back," I frown. "But you won't do the same for me."

"That's because back then, I was a total pushover. It was time for me to grow up and start living my life for myself, instead of clinging to people. In a weird way, everything that happened these past few months was actually good for me. I've learned so much." She shrugs. "I'm never going to make the same mistakes again. I'm never going to bend myself out of shape to fit around some guy. I'm never going to be 'just a girlfriend'—ever again."

She sounds confident, in control. She's changed, somehow. She suddenly seems more mature, and I swell with pride and sadness, all at once. First Kirk, now me: she's going on a man strike, cutting us out of her life so she can get on with living it. Just my luck. She's become the woman I was encouraging her to be, back when I scooped her up off the floor. I'm happy for her—even if it's tearing me apart inside.

"Now that I know what I want from life, we need to talk about *this*."

She pulls a stack of rolled-up papers from behind her back, and I rip them out of her hand, my heart pounding in my head as I glance through my screenplay. I put so much of us in this story... This is the moment of truth. I need to speak up. I have nothing left to lose. Just as I open my mouth, Lois cuts me off.

"Lane, seriously. I'm sorry, but..."

I stare at her, scared to move.

"That stuff you said on page seventeen? That never happened."

"What?"

She grabs the script from me and starts flicking through, the pages flying by in a blur of scribbles, dozens of comments scrawled in the margins, between the lines.

"Same thing here!" She jabs a finger at a page. "I *never* said that!"

She continues working through my script, pointing out mistakes along the way, and when she tries to hit me on the shoulder with the bundle, I reach out a hand.

"What are you doing, Lois?"

I try to hold her gaze, but now that I've accepted I'm in love with her, it hurts too much—having her so close, yet so far. She lets out a long sigh, and looks out across the garden, drumming her fingers on her thigh before leaning into me. Fuck. She's even more beautiful than I remembered.

"I don't get it. Your usual vibe is so..." She waves her hand in the air. "And this? This is just..."

She looks up at the sky, like I'm supposed to just read her mind. *None of this is making sense. What the fuck is going on?*

"Oh, and the playlist? It's boring as hell. You know the part where you act like some stupid guy who can't see how crazy he is about me? Well..."

I watch as she hugs the pages to her chest. I get the sense she's about to up and leave, and so my fingers close around the fabric of her dress as I pull her into me, so close our legs are grazing.

"You're the most confusing guy I've ever met," she whispers.

"What's the problem with the playlist?"

"I was thinking some Rihanna could up the tension. Like what about 'Hate That I Love You'?"

"And?" I can't stop staring at her mouth.

"That last part? That definitely never happened. You changed the whole fight scene and then made up the rest. You didn't explain a *thing* that day—you yelled at me, and then you left. The end."

She has a point. The whole screenplay is true to life, except for the part where I find her in Mike's room. I wrote my epic fuckup out of that scene—my way of trying to tell her just how much I regret it. And then I wrapped it all up with the happy ending I'm still hoping we can work out.

"What do you think about the new ending?"

"Honestly?" She snorts. "I think it's way too cheesy. What happened to all the sex scenes?"

I nearly choke on my own spit. "What? You always said I needed to add more romance!"

"Okay, sure. But we need *some* sex, too, damn it! All this tension and no release? I feel cheated." She exaggerates a sigh. "Absolute disgrace, dude."

I shake my head. I'm so confused right now.

"You . . . Okay, so back up: first of all, you need to quit hanging out with Lewis. And second of all—*I'm* confusing?"

She smiles. "Keep going. I love hearing you give me orders I definitely don't plan on following."

I slap a hand over her mouth. I need a second to get this out. Is she saying she forgives me? Or is she brushing me off? I can feel her lips moving under my palm, and before I know it, she's sticking her tongue out, licking my hand.

"What do you want from me?" I ask.

She raises an eyebrow in response, shoving my hand away.

"I want you to start using your words, you dumbass." She looks me straight in the eye. "And by the way, Lane—this is the perfect moment."

Perfect for what? Does she want me to say something—or kiss her? *Fuck, O'Neill!* My heart is hammering hard, and though I can't think straight, I know I don't have a second to waste. I bring my hand to the nape of her neck, covering her lips with mine, kissing her like it's the first time, because in a weird kind of way, this is our first real kiss. Not some confusing fumble. Not some bullshit "mission." This right here—it's everything I ever wanted.

"I was hoping you'd, like, open up or something." She pulls back. "Not stick your tongue down my throat."

"It felt open-ended . . ."

I run my hands down to her hips and pull her in as close as I can in a near-frantic motion. And when she doesn't push me away, I hold her tighter, breathing her in and diving in for more. I'm pretty sure I could tell her everything I need to with my tongue in her mouth. She lets out a soft giggle, clasping my face in her hands, slowing us both down as I kiss her over and over, deeper and harder. Though I'm not too sure what it all means, it feels fucking amazing. The minutes blur, and I lose myself in her until I pull back, just to keep from tasting more than her mouth.

"Don't think you're getting away with it that easily," she says, gasping for air. "I'm not that lovesick little Lois curled up on your couch anymore. I'm going to need a little more than a screenplay and a kiss."

My legs are like Jell-O, and so I pull her over to the garden seat, lifting her up to straddle my lap. There's so much I want to tell her, but I don't want this moment to ever end. I wrap my arms around her waist, and lean my forehead against hers.

"You're a real pain in the ass, Lane O'Neill. You know that?"

I nod, tightening my arms around her. I don't want to ever let her go again.

"You really screwed up."

"I know."

"I had to read that script three times to make sure it was you—to make sure I understood the twisted way your brain works. You're an all-or-nothing kind of guy, aren't you?"

"I guess. But I can work on myself," I add.

She rubs my nose with hers, pressing a thumb over my lips to stop me from kissing her.

"You know, I would've understood . . ."

I know exactly what she's talking about. I take a sharp breath in, lacing my fingers behind her back.

"Mike and his room, I mean." She gazes at me. "I would've understood, if only you'd told me. I'm so sorry, Lane."

"I'm sorry it took me so long to tell you." I plant butterfly kisses at the corners of her lips. "And I'm sorry I told you the way I did. I wasn't expecting you to be what I needed. To be *who* I needed, I mean."

Her eyes are shining.

"You know what? Let's talk more tomorrow. You can tell me about Mike—I want to know everything about him." She smiles at me. "I bet he was way nicer than you."

Laughter is bubbling up inside me. When she mentions my brother, there's none of that bitterness I would normally feel.

"You're right—let's save it for tomorrow. So what's the plan for tonight?"

She winks at me. "Why don't we work out those scenes I mentioned?"

I throw my head back and burst out laughing.

"Who the hell are you, and what have you done with Heartbreak?" I grin. "That chick was practically a nun. You're more like a—"

"If you say 'porn star,' consider yourself a dead man."

"You know, Hardbait would make a pretty good stage name," I say, tilting my head.

She arches an eyebrow. "Wow. You're just so clever."

I smile again, my hands sliding up her cheeks as I draw her in toward me.

"I missed you so fucking much."

I kiss her again, slow and hard. Hearing her moan against my lips makes it hard for me to think straight.

"So am I forgiven?" I ask.

"I'm giving you one last chance—but you're going to need to up your game."

"Got any workarounds for my super boring ending?"

Without giving her time to answer, I claw at her tights and hike her dress up just enough to wedge myself deeper between her thighs.

"How about something like that?" I breathe, rocking her back and forth, watching intently as she grinds on top of me.

"Lots of things like that, yeah."

Our rhythm gets rougher, messier. She grinds down harder, and with every one of her movements, I can feel myself getting closer to the edge. Just as I'm about to completely lose it, I grab her ass, palms full, and surge up, lifting her with me in one motion.

As our eyes meet, she raises an eyebrow.

"Not here," I rasp, breathless. "Not on a couch. Not this time."

I capture her smiling lips and make a beeline for one of the bedrooms, cutting through the fastest possible route.

"Hurry up," she pants, her breath hot against my ear.

I've spent so long fantasizing about this, obsessing over all the things we could do, so scared that I let everything we had slip away. It feels like I've waited a lifetime for this moment—long enough to make my kisses hungry and my touches rushed. But even as my mouth craves hers and my body aches for her touch, something deeper is uncoiling inside me. A rush of feeling spreading through my chest.

Something that finally matches the feelings I've been too scared to name. It's wild how I wasted so much time pretending I wasn't already hers. How the hell did I wait this long to admit how much I love her?

Her breath is coming hot and ragged against my tongue. I clasp her to my chest, kneeling on the bed as I lower us down onto the mattress. Despite the layers of clothes between us, the way I need her right now has my head spinning. When she pushes me back into the pillow, I have no idea where I am anymore.

I look up at her.

"Strip. Now."

Like I need any encouragement. Tossing my T-shirt on the floor, I realize Lois is still wearing her dress. I prop myself up on my elbows. Her eyes trail the length of my body.

"It's the first time I've seen you completely naked," she whispers, her eyes coming to rest between my legs.

"And?"

"You should've just shown up like this. I would've forgiven you straight off the bat."

"Damn. If I'd known all it'd take is a glimpse of my super body for you to fall in love with me..."

Did I really just say that? I'm about to take it all back, when Lois jumps in.

"I was in love with you *way* before that, Captain Super Oblivious. That's why it hurt so bad."

I've been so damn blind. In that moment, I make myself a promise: I'm going to make it up to her—starting today, and every day after.

Her eyes meet mine.

"So? You going to help me with these tights, or what?"

Before she has time to finish, I'm lunging for her, slipping two fingers under her waistband, pulling her closer.

"Listen carefully, Lois. Since sex is all you seem to have in mind tonight, I'll give you that ending you want," I whisper, pressing my mouth to her ear. "I'm going to make you come exactly three times. You're going to scream my name every damn time. And once you've earned it like the good girl you are"—I pause just long enough to let the words sink in—"maybe then we'll go back to the cheesy one-liners."

She bites her lip, pupils dilated. "That three times a week—or just tonight?"

"Why don't you find out?" I smirk. "Let's see how long you last before you're moaning that you're mine."

I yank her tights down to her ankles, then trail my hands up her back, fingers hunting for the zipper of her dress.

"You're real quiet," I say, pausing. "This still too romantic for you?"

"Oh, shut up!" She shimmies off her dress and jumps back on me, grabbing a fistful of my hair to pull me down into the bed with her. She kisses me deep and slow—easily the best damn kiss of my life—before suddenly pulling back.

She gestures between us. "I need to know—is this for real?"

"You read the screenplay." I frown. "Do you really need to ask?"

"No. But I really want to hear you say it."

I take a deep breath in. "Welcome to life in the fast lane, Lois—I'm crazy about you."

She smiles. "Great. Then we can wrap things up."

I gaze down at her. "I feel like I'm a bad influence on you."

"Is that a problem?"

"Fuck, no!"

WHEN WE FINALLY MAKE IT back to the party—about a thousand years later—Lois beelines for the buffet, and I crack up watching her glare at the guy blocking her path to the pizzas. I'm still watching her when I suddenly feel myself surrounded by my best friends.

"That T-shirt? Definitely not giving," Lewis says, shaking his head. "An absolute freaking disgrace, dude."

I smile. I still can't take my eyes off Lois.

"Oh God," he sighs. "It's official—Lane has unlocked obsessed-boyfriend mode."

"Relax. He's literally just checking out her ass," Carter clarifies.

"Maybe he's just really into piñatas?" suggests Don.

Lewis screeches. "Do *not* bring that up! I'm so triggered right now."

"I think it's a pretty good piñata," Adam says, dodging a kick.

"Looks like your screenplay did the trick." Carter smiles. "You switching to rom-coms now?"

"Don't worry." I smile. "There won't be a sequel."

Across the room, Lois waves a slice of pizza at me and takes a bite.

"I'm pretty sure that's a wrap."

EPILOGUE

LANE

I've literally just parked along the sidewalk, when Lois throws herself against the car window, cheeks flushed.

"You're late! I've been standing in the burning sun for fifteen minutes now! My Cardinals shirt is drenched." She points at her head. "And my hair's all wet and gross!"

"You should've just stayed home—you wouldn't have had to wait."

"You were late on purpose, I'm sure of it!"

"Nuh-uh." I shake my head, beckoning her in. "Anyway, let's get this party started."

She narrows her eyes at me and runs around to the other side, slipping into the passenger seat, muttering to herself as she goes. Just when she's about to buckle her seat belt, I cover her hand with mine.

"I meant this party here," I say, pointing at my lap.

"Okay, so first of all—I'm dying of heat here, so thanks, but no thanks, Lane. And second—we're on campus! Imagine what the dean would do if one of his spies caught us making out in a car."

"Do not disobey me, woman!"

She pauses, her gaze sweeping over me, then suddenly she's kissing me, hard. I grip her face and deepen the kiss, my tongue curling hungrily around hers.

"You think Don will be mad if we miss the first half? Because I really fucking need you—like, right now."

"It's the last game of the season." Lois shakes her head. "He'll kill us if we miss even the first minute."

I sigh. "The Cardinals are already champions—what's the point in playing a friendly when it won't change the rankings?"

"Do not disobey me, boy!"

She gives me a quick peck on the lips, and settles back into her seat. It's a glorious afternoon, and as we drive, she chatters about this and that, telling me about her exams, giving me the latest gossip on Hope and Prudence.

Pulling up outside the sports complex, I try again.

"Come on, just a quick—"

"Not until after the game!"

She darts out of the car, slamming the door shut as she goes.

"Meanie Lois!"

I jump out and sling an arm around her shoulders, and we walk side by side in the sunshine up to the entrance.

Just as we're settling into our seats, the two teams spill out onto the court.

Don spots us immediately, nudging Lewis, who lets out a high-pitched "Loooiis!" I watch as Kirk jerks his head from side to side, surveying the crowd until we lock eyes. I really want to flip him the finger, but I decide to go for a smoother, deadlier blow instead: propping an elbow on the back of Lois's seat, I tuck a lock of brown hair behind her ear and plant soft kisses along her neck.

"Does it feel weird to be at a basketball game?"

She shakes her head. "It's all good, and I promised Don I'd scream his name, anyway."

"What?!" I widen my eyes. "That's *so* not fair. I've been waiting weeks for you to scream mine!"

I run my fingers through her hair and kiss her, slow and deep, ramping up my moves for a sharper dig at Kirk.

She pulls back, laughing. "Okay, drama king. It was actually two nights ago."

"Lois, that's a whole fucking lifetime ago," I sigh. "You're torturing me. You need to come back home," I try for the hundredth time.

She scrunches up her nose. *Why is she so damn annoying!* We've been official for nearly four months now, but she's as stubborn as ever. She still won't move back in. She wants us to just take our time, "take it slow." In the meantime, she's still living with Carrie, in Becca's room.

"I said I'd stay in the dorms until summer break, and I meant it. You're not gonna change my mind—trust me. It's way too soon for us to live together."

"Lois, we've been living together since September!"

"But we weren't together-together then."

"We were kinda together, though . . ."

"We really weren't, though!"

The whistle sounds, the game starts, and as my best friends spring into action, I turn back to Lois.

"This is payback, isn't it?"

"Not at all, you stubborn ass!" She shakes her head, laughing. "I just want time to become a strong, independent woman."

"That's bullshit, and you know it. You're already a strong, independent woman—that's exactly why I love you."

"There's only three weeks left until school's out—just enough time for you to get used to the idea of me giving your place a makeover. I saw some supercute footstools that would totally slay with your couch, by the way."

"We could start by making over Mike's room . . ."

"Are you sure you're ready for that?"

I pause. I still don't really know. What I *do* know is that with Lois by my side and a little time, I feel ready to start making some changes—and even just *thinking* about it is a huge step in the right direction.

"No. But I'm pretty sure I will be once you move back in."

I beam at her, and watch as her eyes widen.

"Oh, that's low, Lane. Even for you." She shakes her head. "Using your brother's room to guilt-trip me? *Seriously?* Absolute disgrace!"

"Oh my God! If I hear that line one more time—"

"I think it's called coercive control. I'm telling my dad on you." She raises an eyebrow. "Maybe he can finally show you that shotgun in August."

"We're going to Fort Myers?"

"Yeah, did I forget to mention?" She smirks at me. "We're spending a month there. You'll be back in Grandpa's room—the hospital bed is ready and waiting. I told Mom you slept like a baby in there."

"Your brothers are on my side, though. Sure you want to play this game?"

"Please, Lane." She holds up a hand, deflecting. "I'm trying to focus on the game, here."

It's official: This girl owns my heart, and she's going to be the fucking death of me. I sidle up closer to her, feeling the heat of her body against mine, planting a kiss on her forehead before turning back to the game.

It's almost halftime, when suddenly a commotion on the Cardinals' bench catches my eye. Don got us some of the best seats, and as I peer down, it doesn't take me long to spot why the crowd has started spinning out of control. I glance back at the court, where Donovan is taking aim, too focused on his shot to notice the energy shifting across the room. Beside me, Lois lets out a sharp cry, echoed by the crowd. I'm on my feet before I even register moving, cold sweat soaking through my T-shirt. I vault down three rows of bleachers at a time, shoving past gawking spectators, and burst onto the court.

"Don!"

Lewis yells his name at the exact same time I do. When our friend finally turns to look, his face crumples as he realizes what's about to happen. And time skips a beat, as the whole world stands still.

ACKNOWLEDGMENTS

THANK YOU TO EVERY READER who jumped into this wild ride with the Campus Drivers. You're the fuel behind each chapter, each twist, each questionable decision Lane makes. I'm endlessly grateful for your enthusiasm and your love for this messy, chaotic crew.

A special shout-out to Ghjulia; thank you for joining me on this journey and for bringing so much heart into it. I'm truly grateful to be sharing this adventure with you.

To my friends and family, who pretended not to notice when I disappeared into my writing cave for questionable numbers of hours—thank you for the snacks, the patience, and the unconditional support.

And finally . . . to the Campus Drivers themselves—Lane, Donovan, Lewis, and Adam—thank you for being impossible, loud, dramatic, and absolutely irresistible. I had the time of my life creating you. You managed to blow up my fictional universe in the best way possible.

ABOUT THE AUTHOR

© Flora Baudet

C. S. Quill is one of France's top-selling romance authors, with more than one million copies of her Campus Drivers series sold and translations into more than ten countries. Known for her banter-fueled style, Quill crafts addictive love stories where bad boys confront their deepest vulnerabilities—and fall hard for the strong-willed women who change them for the better.

Don't miss the rest of the
Campus Drivers series!

Available now in e-book.
Coming soon in paperback